41

THE
MASSACRE
AT
FALL CREEK

Jessamyn West

THE MASSACRE AT FALL CREEK

G.K.HALL & CO.

 Boston, Massachusetts

1975

Library of Congress Cataloging in Publication Data

West, Jessamyn.
  The massacre at Fall Creek.

  "Published in large print."
  1. Sight-saving books.   I.   Title.
[PZ3.W51903Mas3]   [PS3545.E8315]   813'.5'4   75-19106
ISBN 0-8161-6324-3

Published in Large Print by arrangement with Harcourt Brace Jovanovich

Set in Photon 18 pt Crown

For Julian

with love

Book One   THE CRIME

1

Jud Clasby, hidden in the yet unleafed sassafras clump, watched the work going on in the camp. The three squaws and four children were as pretty a sight as he had ever seen. Pretty as does with their fawns, he thought. He did not actually think — he spoke silently to his listening self. He was a long hunter, alone for months at a time harvesting pelts, and though he never said a word aloud, he continuously commented to himself. Because of this habit, he never knew the loneliness other long hunters spoke of. He talked all day long to the silent self who accompanied him.

The three women were busy, as squaws always were about camp. If Indian men had been half as industrious as their women, the whole country would have been cleared, planted, and built up long ago. And where would he be then? Jud had no more farmer or storekeeping blood in him than an Indian. He was a hunter and trapper. Something knotted pleasurably inside him at the prospect of outwitting — that was the word; animals had wits — and killing an animal. If the government had tried to tie him to a hoe or latch him to a plow the way it had Indians, the government would be in a hard row for stumps. He would move on west ahead of the government. Just what the Indians were doing, too, he supposed.

This was a Seneca camp — though one of the squaws was half white, and old Tall Tree was at least half Miami. The Senecas had been pushed from New York to Pennsylvania and on, until now here they were halfway across Indiana. And Indian men still weren't "planting in the springtime, reaping in the fall," the way the song said. They were still hunting; as he was.

The hunters of this party had not had as much luck as the women trappers so far; but the season was early, and spring late. Now, in mid-February of 1824, the raccoons were just beginning to leave their holes in the trees to hunt the frogs who were pushing their way up from the muddy bottoms of the thawing streams. The two bucks, Tall Tree and Red Cloud, had complained to him that whites were springing the traps their squaws set. Jud didn't doubt this was true. There were only ten or twelve white families living around the creek, and if they had all trapped and hunted twelve hours a day seven days a week they wouldn't have skimmed the cream off the game. The amount of game taken wasn't what bothered the settlers: it was the Indians themselves, moving down from the north to the sugar camp as if they had a right, as in the old days, to go where they pleased and hunt what they wanted to hunt.

These particular men and their families had been meek as Moses, not even going into Pendleton, where other Indians were trading pelts and baskets for calico and beads and whiskey. But who knew what went on in an Indian's mind? Whiskey-drinking, bead-buying Indians let you

3

know where their minds were. But these men? Hunting was no better here than around their lodges farther north. Worse, to judge by the number of skins and pelts to show for their month's hunting and trapping.

Red Cloud's squaw, in her thirties or forties (age was hard to judge in a squaw except for a certain thickening in the body), was rubbing deer brains into a green hide to cure it. Tall Tree's squaw, no longer young or comely, sure-footed as an old she-bear, was chewing a tanned hide to supple it. The young breed was tending a pot of boiling maple sap. Busy as beavers, the lot of them, and the breed pretty. Yank that calico dressing sacque over her head and he'd find skin as white as his own.

Which didn't make her white. There were two ways of being an Indian. The first way was to be born one. The second was to be raised one. This girl was fifty per cent the first and a hundred percent the other. That made her a hundred and fifty per cent Indian. He had laid with many a squaw. He hunted Indians; and he didn't scruple to couple with what he hunted. Does were pretty, possums tasty, bears feisty; squaws willing. He agreed with the French: woods pussy was as flavorsome as town.

The wind that had been blowing across the Indian camp and into his face was shifting. He had been able to smell the Indians and he supposed they would soon be able to smell him. Smell was as important for a hunter as sound. Only once in his life had he missed Indian smell, and that failure had almost cost him his life.

He had been hunting and trapping far west of the White River Valley when a half-dozen Sioux began to close in on him, planning to get his hair and his packload of pelts at one swoop. He outmaneuvered them, abandoned his horses, and hid in a canebrake beside some unnamed western river. He was quiet as a coiled snake who had lost his rattle. There was no sound from the Indians either, which was to be expected. But if they were near, he would have smelled them. There was no smell but of river mud and the ferny odor of the reeds and of the water itself. He had had a hard run; he stood to lose two good horses and a season's harvest of pelts and skins. But he would save his hair, and under the circumstances he wasn't asking for more. Then, between one long breath and another, they were upon him. They hadn't killed him at once because their plan for him was something more entertaining: torture the next day with the whole tribe as audience.

He hadn't been prepared for Indians he couldn't smell; torture he had been prepared for since he had left home in York state at the age of fifteen. He believed he could make as good a showing when the fire and the slicing started as any brave: spit in their faces as long as he had a tongue in his mouth and the fires hadn't dried up his spit. So he, knowing what was going to happen, and the Sioux, anticipating what they were going to do, had traveled south together in comradely fashion.

''Why didn't I smell you? Jud asked.

They told him why, and it was an advantage they had counted on. They had

all been fasting and had ended their
religious rite with a long session in the
steam hut. They were as empty and
cleaned out as a wasp nest in winter.

"A man smells of what he eats," he was
told.

It was a truth he knew.

"I should have eaten Indian before I
started this hunt," he told them, and they
laughed, as he had known they would.
Their humor was as rough and ready as
his own.

"Tomorrow," they said, "we eat you
and smell white."

That was no joke. If he was brave, he
would be eaten. They ate enemy braves of
their own kind who showed courage under
torture. A man became what he took into
his body: the deer made him fleet; the
bear, fierce; the buffalo, strong. The
courageous enemy, brave.

Clasby didn't hold the prospect of being
eaten against them. Every hunter ate
what he hunted. He had eaten Indian.
Perhaps that accounted for the fact that
he had been able to escape his captors
that night. He didn't smell white and he

wasn't as noisy as a white. His hands were tied, but he was able on an ember of the still smoldering fire to burn the thong that bound him. Burned his wrists doing it, and he still bore the scars; but that had been a small price to pay for freedom. He silenced with a knife the one Indian who had been roused; cut his throat too deep for any outcry. He had slipped into the waters of the river more soundless than an otter, without a gun; but he had yet to see the man or animal who could best Jud Clasby armed with a knife.

The squaws smelled him now. He could tell by the looks they exchanged. He had no wish to make them suspicious. His intention from the first had been to walk in, talk casually, and have a careful look around. But he was a still hunter. He had the habit of watching and sizing up animals before he faced them. Were they hungry? Were they mothers with young? Was the weather making them nervous? He approached a camp or a lodge as carefully as he approached a herd. He wanted to look in a window, stand at the

8

corner of a lean-to, before he entered. Why walk blindfolded into a snare?

Before he was out of his sassafras clump, the two hunters, Tall Tree and Red Cloud, with Black Antler, the Seneca Faithkeeper, returned to the camp. Tall Tree was heavy-set in the middle-aged Seneca way, fleshy but without jowls or a potbelly. Red Cloud was an Indian in his prime, hair still long and Indian eyes the shape of arrow points.

Black Antler was the shape of Clasby's own father, all beak and Adam's apple. Black Antler was a follower of Handsome Lake, the Seneca prophet. He preached the Old Long House religion, the old faith of the Senecas. The Senecas had no writing for their scriptures. Handsome Lake's teaching had to be memorized, word for word. Folded Leaf, Red Cloud's son, eleven or twelve, a magpie for picking up words, was being taught the scriptures and trained to be a Faithkeeper.

The men knew at once that Clasby was near. His smell and the women's eyes told them. They all spoke Delaware, and anybody who had been around Indians as much as Clasby understood Delaware. They knew where he was and knew he would either disappear or come into camp.

The men had returned for their one cooked meal of the day. There was no set time for this, though it was usually eaten in midmorning, and the meal was usually what it was now: something between a soup and a stew of meat and dried or fresh vegetables. There was no table. Tall Tree's squaw handed the bowls around, and when Clasby stepped into the camp, he, too, was given a bowl. It would have been the same had the others not been eating. Indians had butchered a good many whites, but not those they fed who visited them in peace.

Black Antler refused food. "I will eat after I have taught the boy."

"Where is Folded Leaf?" Red Cloud asked the women.

"Down by the creek," Clasby told him, using their own language. "I saw him as I came to you."

"How long ago?"

"Time it took me to come here. He was playing duck-on-rock with his brother and sisters."

Red Cloud faced the river, put two fingers in his mouth, and gave a blast that Clasby felt inside his nose like a gust of red pepper.

The soup was good. He had tasted and made many a pot like it.

"How's the hunting?" Clasby asked.

"Bad. They spring our traps."

"Who?"

"The whites."

"Why?"

"You know why. They want to drive us out."

"You've moved in pretty close to them."

"Close to *them*. We were here before they were born."

Clasby didn't want to waste breath on this old argument. Besides, who was first cut no ice. What cut ice was who would be here last. Why couldn't the Indians see this? They could die in their tracks saying, "We were here first." Did they expect white men who had never owned an acre or been allowed to run a deer or even hunt a rabbit to go back hangdog to an English squire and say, "We've come home. Somebody else was there first"? No siree, Bob. They couldn't push the squire around, but they'd found that they could push the Indian. And if he wouldn't push, why, shoot him.

Black Antler, when the children returned, took Folded Leaf to one side without giving the boy a chance to eat. Clasby didn't think this had anything to do with the fact that what was being memorized was religious. Even the Indians hadn't hit upon anything as outlandish as the French: fast before drinking the blood and eating the flesh of their God. Eating your enemies made a lot more sense than that. Clasby's old backwoods Baptist father had figured that out before Clasby left home.

While the three men ate, Black Antler had Folded Leaf recite what he had memorized the day before. Next the boy repeated passages after Black Antler. The boy was small for his age, round and brown as a beaver pup, with the pup's

12

eyes, round and animal-curious, not yet gone Indian-sharp and hard. He was a wonder for remembering Black Antler's words — and he'd need to be. The rigmarole Handsome Lake had preached took four full mornings to repeat. Clasby had never had the patience to sit through one whole morning, let alone four, but he had heard enough to know that what he heard was nine-tenths Indian, one-tenth Christian.

"You call this the 'Old Long House religion'?" he asked Red Cloud. "There wasn't any preaching in the old days against liquor, was there?"

"We have always preached against what was bad. You have taught us new badness."

"Maybe." But listening to Folded Leaf made Clasby as uncomfortable as watching a trained bear dance, or hearing a starling with a split tongue cry, "Amen, brother." Let the wild stay wild; don't put pantaloons on bears or teach starlings to talk like hard-shell deacons. Let the Indian fight and wander, scalp and fornicate. He had no stomach for the sight

13

of a young savage mouthing what they called scriptures and growing up to be a Faithkeeper. Nevertheless, he could be at least as polite as an Indian when it suited his purpose. He said "Thank you" for the food he had eaten and left.

Once Clasby was out of earshot, Talking Crow, Tall Tree's old ungainly wife, said, "Watch that one."

Red Cloud answered, "I have known him a long time."

"Watch him."

"It is the other way around. He watches us."

"Like the game he hunts."

Tall Tree asked his wife, "How would you stop him?"

"In the old days, you would not ask that question."

"The old days are gone," Red Cloud said. "We are lucky to hunt here without trouble."

Talking Crow made a sound of distaste. It started deep in her broad chest and was a long time reaching her mouth. It was like the leveling wind you hear far off in the forest before any of the leaves about you begin to stir.

"In the old days no one called it luck when we hunted on our own land. Hunted what the Great Spirit had given us for food."

Tall Tree said, "A man's luck changes."

"I do not talk about a man's luck. I talk about the rights of a nation. We were the Seneca nation, the keepers of the Western Gate. We keep no gates now. We run. We call ourselves lucky to set a few traps and hunt a little meat for winter. Is that luck? Shame is a better word."

Red Cloud spoke up. Tall Tree had a wife with a sharp tongue, while Tall Tree himself was a quiet, easygoing man. Every word Talking Crow said was true, but there were truths there was no use raking over and over. He tried to turn Talking Crow's mind to something pleasanter. He gestured toward Black Antler and Folded Leaf.

"Some of the old ways we keep."

"We keep words," Talking Crow said.

"The Old Way was to say those words. We spoke to the earth, our mother. To the

Great Spirit. To the animals who fed us. Folded Leaf speaks the old words. Wherever he goes the words of the Old Way will go with him."

But Talking Crow would not take pleasure in the sight of the young boy, or in the words he memorized so quickly and spoke so well.

"The words will go to his grave with him."

"With all of us, I hope."

"We have lived our lives. We have seen bad times, but we ran and lived. It will be worse for the boy."

The old woman turned and went into the open-faced lean-to.

The boy for whom she was prophesying an early grave was Red Cloud's son. Red Cloud would unsay Talking Crow's words if he could, blow them away on a wind so strong that not even an echo remained. He would wash out Talking Crow's mouth with brine so strong that the taste and the shape of her words would be gone forever. In the day when the Senecas believed in the power of witches, words like hers, if any mishap followed, could send the speaker into the fire. Talking Crow was no witch, but he wished she had not spoken those words.

The boy was a born Faithkeeper. The words went into his head after one saying by Black Antler, then flowed out smooth and natural as sap from the tree. Though small for his age, he was strongly knit. He could outrun and outswim boys twice his size. If the good days had passed for the Seneca, if they must still move on, no longer keepers of the Western Gate, but defeated men using that gate for their own escape, Folded Leaf would carry the words of the Old Way of the Long House with them.

Red Cloud caught his son's eye and he knew that his father's pride showed; but the boy was too deep into the meaning of the Old Way to be distracted. While Red Cloud looked and listened, Talking Crow came to him again. She was an old woman, and in her day the affairs of the Senecas had been, except for the strategy of battle, in the hands of the women. Talking Crow did not know that times had changed. Red Cloud listened to her patiently.

"How many whites here?"

"I have never counted."

"How many houses?"

"Ten."

"Fifty, sixty people, then. How many of our people?"

"At the Falls?"

"I do not ask foolish questions. A day, two days' march from here? How many?"

"Many. More than the stalks in our cornfields."

Talking Crow's eyes were Indian, arrow-shaped. Red Cloud felt the wound of her looking. "You let them spring our traps. You let them stand in the bushes and spy on us like a man watching animals. You let them laugh at the sacred words your son speaks."

"Clasby did not laugh."

"Not for you to see."

"You saw?"

"I saw. Folded Leaf was like a chipmunk to Clasby. Inside, he laughed to hear a chipmunk speak."

"There is no law against laughing."

"In the old days a Seneca would not permit his son to be laughed at."

"Do you want me to tomahawk Clasby? Have all the men here from the Falls with long guns one sun later?"

"No. We have our great many to their little few. Rouse our tribesmen and friends. The river was ours. The Falls were ours. Make them ours again."

"Kill all who live there?"

"All. They stole our land. Give them their own punishment for thievery."

"You do not understand, Talking Crow. This is a time of peace. We have signed treaties."

Out of Talking Crow's throat, from deep inside her, as deep as her heart, as deep as her bowels, came the rumble of disgust, this time like the sound the earth makes when it moves, rather than the sound of a rising wind among trees.

"You will die signing treaties." She turned away from him. Red Cloud watched her re-enter the lean-to. He listened to the words of Folded Leaf, the words of the old Faithkeeper; they did have some overlay of the doctrines

Handsome Lake had learned from the Friends who were his neighbors. There was truth in what Talking Crow said. The white men have made us believe that they loved us and that we are brothers. They did preach forgiveness. But they did not keep their treaties.

Twenty-two years ago, Handsome Lake, the prophet, whose words Folded Leaf now memorized, spoke to Jefferson, the "Great White Chief of our white brothers," asking him for a "Writing on Paper" so that "we can hold fast our land against the seizure of our white brothers." If the Great Chief would do so, "we will be good friends here and when we meet with the Great Being above we shall have bright and happier days."

The Great Chief had sent the "Writing on Paper." "I said to you last winter that the land you then held would remain yours and should never go from you except when you should be disposed to sell."

The Great Chief perhaps did not know the methods that would be used to make them want to sell. "You are our brothers of the same land; we wish you prosperity as brethren should do," the Great Chief had said.

Wishes were not enough. The Seneca had accepted that paper, and their property had vanished. They were now catching possums and rabbits along a little river hundreds of miles from the Western Gate, which once they had defended.

What if he did as Talking Crow urged? Red Cloud was born a warrior and hunter. He had become a squirrel killer; men who had paid him nothing occupied the land the Great Spirit made for his people. He could feel the heft of a weighted tomahawk in his hand and the tension of a pulled bowstring in his forearms. Talking Crow need not think that it was lack of manhood that kept him from going to the Falls and bringing home the dripping scalps of those who were their enemies.

It was manhood that caused him to keep his word. He had agreed to the paper of the Great Chief. He had given his word. He could kill an enemy and rejoice. But he would rather die than not keep his word.

And Talking Crow was wrong about

Clasby. Clasby owned no land — of theirs or anyone else's. He was a wanderer and hunter, the enemy only of animals whose pelts and skins he needed.

Even so, keeping his word, listening to the quick sure voice of his son, his stomach full of the rich soup, a sadness as at the death of a kinsman filled Red Cloud. What had died? His eyes could find no change in the world he had always known. The trees were as thick, the sky as blue; the meat was drying in the old way, the hides stretched as taut as ever.

Old women like Talking Crow always longed for past times. Did the words of one grandmother, the eyes of one white man have this much power over him?

The heft of the tomahawk, the tension of the pulled bow was again in his arms as he heard Folded Leaf repeat after Black Antler, "The Creator has not privileged men to punish each other. The Great Spirit has given us a mother: the earth. Our mother we must love. The Great Spirit has given us brothers. To them we must be brotherly. The White Man has Jesus. We have Handsome Lake. If the

White Man follows Jesus and the Red Man Handsome Lake, the brothers will dwell in peace."

He was pledged to the way of Handsome Lake, not of Talking Crow.

2

When Jud Clasby showed up at the Cape house an hour after he left the Indian camp, Hannah Cape lit out to call on the Woods. Actually, she was going to court John Wood, Jr. She hoped that the others did not know what she was doing. Her mother knew, of course, but her mother approved. Since boys didn't come to court Hannah, the next best thing was to have Hannah court a boy. This was no place, here in the fringes of the forest, wolves still at large and more Indians to the square mile than whites, for a woman without a man. John Jr. wasn't the man Hannah's mother would have picked for her daughter. He was seventeen, just Hannah's age, and she had seen mullein stocks with more pith to them than John

Jr. had. But Hannah, more than likely, wasn't Mrs. Wood's idea of a perfect daughter-in-law either. Mrs. Wood probably thought Hannah would wear the pants in her son's family.

It wouldn't be true. Hannah's husband would wear the pants, if Hannah had to sew them onto him. Hannah wouldn't marry a man she didn't worship. The girl acted as if her brother, Ben, fourteen, were a god. She treated her father as if he were her Creator, with a capital C.

Just because Hannah was five foot ten, with a great swag of red hair, people thought she might be feisty. Oh, she wasn't. She'd fetch and carry for the man of her choice, the way she did for her father and Ben. She might be a little highhanded; but people who were high-minded had to be. Otherwise they'd soon be down at the trough fighting with the others for the swill.

Her size and her hair color counted against Hannah — but she had plenty to count for her. Hannah didn't freckle as much as most redheads. Her face was almost as creamy as her bosom; and her bosom was prominent enough to offset anybody's idea that, because she could use a bucksaw and axe as well as a man, she wasn't womanly.

She was womanly, even motherly. Hannah acted like an old hen, with Ben her one chick. Ben was as big for a boy of fourteen as Hannah was for a girl of seventeen. To look at Ben, you wouldn't think he needed *one* mother, let alone two. But what a person needed and what a person looked like he needed were stories with different endings. Hannah had toted Ben around since she was four and he was one. Ben, for all of his size, had a soft streak; perhaps he needed two mothers, after all.

Her mother wondered why Hannah wasn't courted. Hannah didn't. She knew. The minute a man sashayed up to her, he undermined her faith in his judgment. She wanted a man who dreamed of something better than Hannah Cape, a backwoods girl with a bucksaw. A man who wanted her didn't have his sights set high enough to suit her.

She decided to leave when Jud Clasby

arrived at the house. He didn't try to hide where *his* sights were. His staring made her uncomfortable; and his talk, not bragging, but matter-of-fact, like a farmer talking crops, of how many animals and how many Indians he had killed, made her queasy. You had to kill animals for meat; the Indians had to be kept from running settlers off their farms. But talk about scalp-lifting and the killing of does who wouldn't leave their fawns wasn't talk she cared to hear.

"I'm going over to the Woods'," she told her mother.

"You got your cap set for that milksop boy?" Clasby asked.

"Milksop" made Hannah mad. John Jr. wouldn't wring a chicken's neck — and that was a fact — but he read books, which was more, she bet, than Jud Clasby did.

"No," she said. "It's the old man I've taken a shine to."

This was pert of Hannah, and her mother was sorry to hear her speak that way. It was what people expected of a redhead. If it was pert, Clasby enjoyed pertness. He leaned his chair farther back, stretched his legs farther out, and laughed.

"You going to lose either way with the Woods. The boy don't want a wife and the old man's got one wife too many already."

Old Mr. Wood was a widower recently remarried to Reba Reese, a widow young enough to be his daughter.

"He's only got the one wife."

"I didn't say different, did I?"

He hadn't, and Hannah was ashamed at being so slow to catch his meaning.

"I'll tell Mr. Wood what you said," she flared, "and ask him if it's the truth."

"Hannah," her mother warned, "mind your tongue."

"Let her alone," Clasby said. "I'm used to catamounts. She don't daunt me in the least. Hannah, if you want to know the truth, you ask Reba Wood. She's the one who'll tell you."

Hannah was in over her head and knew it. Bandying words with Jud Clasby would be like trying to outgrunt a pig. In the first place, he knew more than she did; and in the second, he didn't care what he said.

"Good-bye, Mama," she said. "I'll be back before suppertime."

"You better be," her mother warned her, "or I'll send Ben after you."

"I'll bring her home myself," Clasby said. "I got an errand at the Woods'."

Hannah gave Clasby her bullet stare, but he was too tough for anything but true lead.

Hannah was bold, but not a bold wooer. She couldn't go to the Woods' without an excuse of some kind. When Reba Wood opened the door for her, Hannah held out a willow Indian basket, its contents neatly covered with a fringed napkin.

"Molasses cookies," she said. "Mama sent them."

It wasn't a bald-faced lie. Mama hadn't actually sent them, but Reba knew why Hannah was bringing them and for whom she had baked them.

"Johnny's favorites," Reba said. "How did you ever guess?"

"Everybody likes molasses cookies," Hannah answered coolly, and Reba couldn't argue with that.

Mr. Wood was stretched out for a rest or a snooze on the bed that filled one corner of the room. The Woods had more furniture than most of the people at Fall Creek because their cabin contained the belongings of two families. The Woods and the Reeses had headed west together after both had been suckered by land agents in York state.

The land agents had bought land from the Indians, then sold it sight unseen to would-be farmers who hadn't been able to resist the giveaway prices. The giveaway prices were possible because the land agents, before they suckered the would-be farmers, had suckered the Indians even worse: paid them for square miles of land with a bucket of beads, fifty yards of calico, and a jug of watered rum.

Smart farmers, when they saw what they were stuck with, mountainsides going straight up, swamps oozing water, and land with boulders the size of pumpkins, moved right on, with no more than an overnight stop to cuss the agents and themselves.

On the way west, Hosmer Reese had drowned in the White River, right on the edge of the Promised Land. A month earlier, John Wood's wife, Abbie, about ten years younger than he, had died of a bloody flux. It was the most natural thing in the world for the widow and widower, after they had reached Fall Creek, to combine forces, get married, and put all their furniture in one cabin.

Hannah didn't think that love-making could have been in Reba Reese's mind when she married John Wood. He looked to be all bone and gristle, his skin as gray as his long beard and hair. His mouth was as thin as the cutting edge of an axe and it turned down at the corners in the same way. Getting in bed with Mr. Wood would be as uncomfortable as getting in bed with an armload of kindling. Hannah had been taught that handsome is as handsome does; but even by these standards Mr. Wood wasn't pretty. He and Reba didn't get along and made no bones about it even before company.

Reba would be hard for anybody to get along with, Hannah thought. She was afraid for herself when she looked at Reba. Would she look that way when she was forty? Reba's hair was the red of maple leaves after heavy frost had smirched their color. Her cheeks were cobwebbed with veins. She had a plump little mouth like a buttonhole worked with a heavy satin stitch. She was sharp and mean to a man old enough to be her father; sharp and mean to the boy she had inherited from Abbie Wood. Was that what happened to pert and saucy girls when they got to be middle-aged?

"I reckon you want to see Johnny?"

"I thought we might read some more together."

The best gift Johnny got from his stepmother was the tin box of books that had belonged to Hosmer Reese. When Hosmer drowned, his tin box of books came through unharmed. There were books Hannah and Johnny didn't look into, spellers and arithmetics and principles of rhetoric — Hosmer had been a schoolteacher before the westward fever struck him down — but there were a half-dozen storybooks, and these Johnny read aloud to her. Hannah could read all right, faster and with just as much expression as Johnny, but he liked to read, and Hannah loved to listen to him. It was a good thing that they had the books. Johnny wasn't much of a talker, and sitting in silence would have been embarrassing.

"Do you want to go up and get him?" Reba asked.

The loft was Johnny's bedroom, and Hannah was too well brought up to go alone to a boy's sleeping room.

"No," Hannah said. "Maybe he's resting up."

"Resting?" Reba exploded. "What's he got to rest up from? The boy's been spoiled. He was John and Abbie's one and only, and he came after they'd give up hope. He's been carried around on a chip since he was born, and that poor old man there does the milking, carries in the wood, slops the hogs — all the chores a boy ought to do."

"You can't blame Johnny for being brought up wrong."

"I don't blame him. But it oughtn't to take bringing up to teach a youngun to help a poor old man he can see with his own eyes hobbling and panting.''

Reba went to the ladder that led to the loft. "Johnny," she shouted, "you've got company. Get downstairs.''

Everything about Johnny Wood made Hannah's heart ache. Born to old folks, now half an orphan, a stepmother who hated him, his father soured on life because of the loss of the land he'd bought in York state. Hannah wanted to be both a mother and a father to him — and something else besides, because he was so beautiful. Not in any golden-haired dimpled, pretty-boy way. Her mother said Johnny Wood might've been the devil's own son, he was so handsome; but he was a sight less energetic, she added, which was a blessing.

Johnny came down the ladder from the loft like a man walking onto a stage — though Hannah was his only audience. Reba was stirring up corn pone for supper; the old man still had his eyes closed. Though Johnny was seventeen, he might have been twenty-five. Born of old parents, he had maybe come aged from the womb. Hannah loved her brother, but Ben was a red-faced baby compared with Johnny. Johnny was a statue that breathed; all cream-ivory, with black carved curls and red lips firmer than flesh and a narrow, long-limbed body. Was he bashful? Was his mind so occupied with deep thoughts he had no time to talk with her? Didn't he like any girl? He liked to read to her anyway, and she didn't ask for anything more. Once in a while as they sat together, Johnny reading, his shirt sleeve would brush her arm as he turned a page. How could a piece of cloth make a feeling she couldn't name run like hot lightning from her arm clear down to her thighs?

Before they began their reading, Reba said, "Johnny, fetch me another armload of wood."

Hannah was on her feet before Johnny. She would do anything for him, and carrying stovewood was something anyone could see Johnny Wood wasn't cut out for.

Reba said, "He'd let you do it, too."

Hannah sat down fast, ashamed to have it appear that she, like Reba, thought

Johnny was a do-nothing. Johnny handed her the book to hold while he went out, and Hannah, when Reba wasn't looking, put it to her cheek. It was warm from his hands.

"You start toting things for a man," Reba said, "the first thing you know he'll be toting you to your grave."

"Yes, ma'am," said Hannah, with a tight hold on her pert tongue.

It was too early for candlelighting, and though the fireplace gave off light, Hannah didn't want to be that close to Reba while they read. Reba would scoff at every word she heard. Yet it was too chilly to sit outside. February had a little of spring in it, but more of winter. A brown thrush sang from a clump of hazel bushes, but the wind still carried the wet, cold smack of snow and the cut of the frozen lakes to the north. Hannah pulled the bench close to the Dutch door and opened the top door enough of a crack to let in some light, but small enough to keep most of the wind out.

They settled down there after Johnny had filled the woodbox. Reba was the kind of woman who liked to let people know she was working by making a lot of noise. Her clattering jarred on Hannah so she couldn't follow the story, but finally the story took over, and Reba might have been back in York state.

They were reading *Ivanhoe*. Had people a long time ago really lived like that? Worn such rich clothes, lived in castles, fought and died for such noble causes? Was the world going downhill? No shining armor now; nothing but linsey-woolsey, a crack of light through a half-opened door to read by, and an unfelled forest stretching for untold miles across — nobody knew what.

One thing hadn't changed: love. Johnny wasn't anything like Ivanhoe; perhaps he was more like the man who wrote the book, somebody who sat at the table with a pen in his hand, silent because his head was full of words he wanted to put on paper. Whether this was true or not, Hannah didn't know. But like Ivanhoe, or the man who wrote about him, she loved Johnny. He never touched her, but his voice went into her ears and through all her veins, and his black hair and red lips went into her eyes, and his touch would likely have been more than one could bear — so that she would faint dead away in the last place she'd want to faint: at Reba Wood's feet.

Jud Clasby saved her from such a fate. He came in at twilight as quiet as Reba was noisy. His very quietness roused up old Mr. Wood. Reba pulled her spider of corn pone away from the fire. Mr. Wood shook himself awake and sat on the bench across the table from Clasby.

"I've come to fetch Hannah home."

"There was no need," Hannah said.

"I promised your mama."

"We're just coming to the end of a chapter."

"Read on. It's John and Reba I want to talk to, anyway."

Johnny read on, but Hannah couldn't listen. Old Mr. Wood was deaf and couldn't hear how loud he spoke when he talked. Reba was naturally loud — maybe that was the reason John Wood married her, because he could hear her. Clasby was used to talking out-of-doors. He didn't know how to tone himself down for inside talking. Johnny read, but Hannah, who would have believed that she could hear Johnny through a thunderstorm, heard more of the talk of Clasby and the Woods than she did of Ivanhoe. This was in part because Clasby talked first of all about her own family.

"Cale Cape thinks because the redskins been hunting in these parts for the past four or five years there's no point getting stirred up about their moving in here now."

"Cale Cape is so kindhearted he'd share his wife with a grizzly," agreed Reba.

Hannah had to bite her tongue at that. Her father was a peaceable God-fearing man, but he knew right from wrong.

"The reds are treacherous. They'd wait five years to lull our suspicions."

Old Mr. Wood was an Indian hater. It was his religion. He didn't hate the land agents who had suckered him out of his money, but the Indians who had made the deal possible by letting themselves be cheated out of their land. Except for the Indians, he would never have had to move on west, and Abbie would still be alive. The Indians had as good as killed her. Except for the Indians, he would never have got teamed up with a woman like Reba. Except for the Indians, he would be sitting snug in York state with Abbie and their pretty boy.

"Run 'em out," he bellowed. "The sooner the better."

"Hush up about Indians," Reba ordered her husband. "You'd be the first one under the bed if a redskin doing no more than peddling baskets and berries showed up at the door."

Hannah hated to hear Reba talk like that to a man old enough to be her father. But old Mr. Wood wasn't cowed.

"You give me a gun and I'll tangle with them savages as fast as the next one."

"You got a gun," Reba said. "You've just forgot how to pull the trigger, that's your trouble."

"Give me the right target and I can pull the trigger fast enough."

Reba turned away from her husband to Clasby. "He's all wind and no weather. If you want somebody who means business, go talk to my brother, George Benson. He knows what's good for an Indian. Don't waste your time here. The old man's lost his sap and the boy never had any."

Johnny stopped his reading and quickly stood. Hannah thought he was trying to take a kink out of his back. He had been bent over with his nose close to the book, trying to catch what little light there was. Instead of stretching, he went directly to his stepmother and, with his open book pressed under her chin, pinned her to the wall.

"Have I got any sap?" he asked, giving the book a forward shove that brought Reba's popeyes farther out of their sockets.

"Answer me," he said.

Reba's red tongue waggled in her opened mouth but the sounds she made were not speech.

Hannah was dumbstruck. If the old man disapproved, he didn't say so. Before she could do so, Clasby rescued Reba. He wrenched Johnny away and threw the book onto the table. "You want to kill your stepmother?"

Johnny paid no attention to Clasby, who continued to hold him. "Answer me," he shouted, as if miles separated him from his stepmother. "Have I got sap?"

"Junior, if you want a woman to talk to you, don't half choke her to death first," Clasby said. He helped Reba to a bench at the table and got her a dipperful of water.

Johnny, as soon as Clasby went for the water, grabbed his book and ran up the stairs to the loft.

Restored by water, Reba said, "Goes up like a monkey, don't he?"

"Best not tease monkeys," Clasby advised.

"That wasn't teasing, Jud; it was God's truth."

"Best be quiet about some truths in front of a courting boy."

"Courting? He ain't got the sap to court. The girl's the one doing the courting."

Hannah felt her cheeks flame up like red-hot stove lids. "I visit Johnny," she said. "Is that courting?"

"You want to visit him now?" Reba asked. "Want to run up the ladder and smooth down his feathers? Tell him he's full of sap and his mother deserves choking?"

"Stepmother," corrected old Mr. Wood, sitting up on the bed he'd gone back to. "Only mother he's got."

Something had happened Hannah didn't understand. How could Johnny, book reader, kind to animals, turn on his stepmother that way? "He's never said a cross word to me."

"Did he ever say a word? 'Cept what he read? Well, you got a good look tonight at what he can do."

Clasby said, "We'd better be on our way, Hannah. I've got some other visits to make tonight."

Hannah didn't blame him for wanting to leave. Who wants to listen to fussing?

"Stop and see George Benson," Reba insisted. "What's on your mind is on his."

John Wood got to his feet. "They'd ought to be run out. I got banged up on the trip here, but I can still shoot. I killed one and winged another east of the Whitewater. I ain't got my quota this side yet. I'd like . . ."

Reba interrupted her husband as if his

words were nothing but a brag. "You go and see George, Jud."

Hannah was pulled in more directions at once than were comfortable. She wanted to tell Johnny, "I don't understand what you did, but whatever you do, I'll love you."

She wanted to say to Clasby and Mr. and Mrs. Wood, "The Indians have been peaceful. They haven't done a thing against us."

She'd already been called a courting girl that evening. She didn't want the men to shame her for advising them what to do about the Indians, saying, "Yes, General, whatever you order."

Old Mr. Wood made it easy for her to leave. "It was good-hearted of you, Hannah, to bring the cookies. They're my favorites."

Kindness in the midst of all she'd heard and seen that night was more than she could bear. She ran outside to hide her tears. Jud Clasby followed with her shawl.

When February came, you thought winter's back was broken. But February was like a snake with a broken back. It could still bite. The star Hannah had glimpsed earlier in the winter at sundown was tangled up tonight with the new moon. The little creek, running downhill to Fall Creek, *sounded* like summer. The frogs had got all the winter phlegm out of their throats and were singing as clear as whippoorwills. To look and listen, winter was past. But winter had another string to its bow, besides the two you see and hear. Winter wasn't a harp or a picture. It was a fire you couldn't see or hear, but which could burn you. Winter, like fire, was what you felt. Winter could drop down out of a clear sky, sharp as an icicle, and, without a sound, pierce your heart.

"You aiming to shake yourself to death?" Jud Clasby asked.

"No," Hannah said. "I wasn't even aiming to shake. I didn't know I was. It smells like spring, don't it?"

"You put this on," Clasby said. "No sense not being warm while you smell spring."

He draped the shawl over her shoulders. Then, as he adjusted the far corner across one shoulder, his hand brushed lightly across her breast. Hannah shuddered away from him, started to say something, but shut her mouth. Just because her breast tingled like nettles, that was no sign Clasby even knew he had touched her. Or that part of her, anyway. He was likely twice her age, old enough to be her father. Maybe when he looked at her the way he did he was thinking of a daughter he had lost. Any good man would be concerned about a girl's catching a chill. Praise God she hadn't screamed "Keep your hands off me." Where was her mind, anyway? First in love with a boy who didn't love her; now thinking that every man who adjusted a shawl for her had other ideas than her comfort in mind. Were other ideas what she wanted him to have?

"Thank you," she said.

"I thought for a minute you were going to bolt like a skittish colt at the first touch of the saddle."

"Oh, I've worn shawls before," Hannah

assured him.

"Of course you have. What am I thinking of?"

With her breast humming like a spun top, the idea crossed Hannah's mind that they both might be thinking of the same thing. Still, she was glad she hadn't yelled out, in case she was mistaken.

"I had it in mind to stop at George Benson's and the Bemises' on the way to your place. If you don't like the idea, I'll take you home first."

"I don't need to be took. I go this way alone all the time."

"Not tonight. I promised your ma I'd see you home, and I will. I can come back to the Bensons' and the Bemises'. It's about suppertime. We might get asked to put our knees under a table."

"Ora Bemis's my best friend," Hannah said, leaving George Benson out of it. She'd as lief visit a bull buffalo as George; but sitting in the presence of George and Sarah Benson for half an hour would do her no harm.

Luther Bemis lived half a mile up the creek from the Woods. They had a good fire blazing on the hearth of their one-room cabin when Jud and Hannah arrived, but supper was over.

"You didn't miss much," Ora said. "Nothing but mush and milk."

Ora was a couple of years older than Hannah and she was expecting a baby. Even so, it would take two or three of her to make one Hannah, and several bleachings to get her as light-complexioned. She'd been born with a harelip, and somebody unhandy with a needle had sewed it together. Her lip was in one piece now, but the stitch marks showed like a tattoo.

Some people were surprised when a wandering dandy like Luther Bemis had taken to a girl as swarthy and marred as Ora. Some weren't. They said that a man who'd spent ten years trapping and hunting far from all whites must've had an Indian wife or two, and that Ora's color and decorations made him feel right at home.

However Ora made Lute feel, he'd been a changed man since he married her. Hannah knew that Lute had grown up in

Ohio in the same town as her own folks. He had been saved at fifteen, but three years of walking a chalk line in the town of Blue Glass had been all his system could stand. At eighteen he broke loose in all directions at once: took up drinking, fighting, hunting; gave up farming and churchgoing as if he had been born a redskin. After he half scalped his stepbrother in a drunken fight, he lit out west for good. For the good of everybody in Blue Glass, Hannah's father said.

In the ten years before he reached Fall Creek, he had calmed down considerably. He still looked like a rakehell instead of a Baptist elder, which he'd become since marrying Ora, but pious living, given time, might cure that. He'd given up drink entirely, farmed as hard as if he'd never been a forest roamer, and hunted only for meat for the table. Whatever he might have felt about Indian girls before he was married, he now had eyes only for Ora.

He'd have been crazy, Hannah thought, otherwise. Ora was as sleek and pretty and little as a dove. Hannah had no desire to pet other women, but Ora was so plump and lustrous she hardly seemed human — more like a kitten or a gray squirrel. Whatever her looks, her acts were those of a Christian woman. Hannah's father said that Ora lived in the Light, and Hannah believed him. Married to her, any man would be willing to change his ways for the better.

The two girls sat together on the deacon's bench beside the fire. The two men faced each other across the table. Lute brought out a jug of cider and poured a mug for each.

Clasby looked around for a place to spit at the first mouthful, but he was too far from the door or the fireplace for a carrying shot. He swallowed and looked as surprised as if he'd had a helping of quinine.

"Sweet cider? I'd rather have teakettle tea. Ain't you got anything in the house better'n this, Lute?"

"Spring water."

"What's hit you?"

"Common sense's likely the name."

"When I think of the jugs you and me's emptied!"

"We're back in civilization now."

"I don't call any place I can't get a drink civilized."

"You're free to light out for civilization."

"Don't get your dander up, Lute. You didn't used to be so touchy."

"I've changed."

"That don't take saying. Well, there's nothing so strong as a pretty woman's apron strings to tie a man down."

Clasby smiled at Ora when he said it, but it was a jibe nevertheless. As if before Lute had got tangled up with her, he'd been more of a man, free-roaming, free-drinking, and free-whatever else — he wasn't likely to say before two females.

Lute didn't turn a hair at the mention of apron strings.

"It's a fact. Tied the strings myself and don't plan to ever unloosen them of my own free will."

Hannah, tied by something stronger than strings, by touch, to Jud Clasby, couldn't keep her mind on Ora's talk of baby clothes and names for the baby. She heard Ora's words and could reply to them, but inside her head she paid more attention to what the men were saying.

"We're way off the matter I came here to talk about," Clasby said.

"Nobody's holding you back."

"What I came here for was to ask your help in tracking a lost horse of mine. You've fallen off in some ways, but I reckon you can still track."

Lute paid no attention to the soft soap. "What d'you mean, lost? Strayed?"

"Stolen's likely the name for it."

"Got any idea who?"

"The Indians down at Rocky Point."

"You seen any of them with him?"

"They're smarter than that. But I seen his tracks in that neighborhood."

"What's your plan?"

"Track him. See if they've got him staked out someplace."

"I'm through fighting Indians."

"Who's talking about fighting Indians? You through helping your friends?"

"I ain't reformed that far yet. When did you think about looking?"

The sooner the better. Tomorrow. I'm on my way out of here and I need that horse. If you're willing to give me a hand, meet me at my lean-to tomorrow noon."

A quarter of a mile from the Bemises', Hannah found that once again she had left her shawl behind her. She wouldn't hear of Clasby's going back after it. It would look too much like she was asking for another shawl-fixing like the last one.

"I left it myself and I'll get it myself. I'll enjoy the run. I'll be back by the time you've counted twenty stars."

She enjoyed the run and enjoyed letting Jud Clasby know that she wasn't asking to be touched again.

Ora and Lute had banked the fire for the night and were saying their evening prayers when she got back to their place. They were on their knees, elbows on a bench and their faces in their hands. Lute was praying out loud, and the question in Hannah's mind was which would be worse: interrupting a prayer or eavesdropping on a man talking to God?

Hannah decided on interrupting.

"I forgot my shawl," she said in a loud voice.

Ora and Lute looked up, but neither rose.

"We were just to the blessings," Ora told her. "Join us."

Hannah's father was the nearest to a preacher the settlement had, and praying was as natural to Hannah as breathing. It won't hurt Jud Clasby to count to a hundred stars, she thought.

Before Lute had finished asking God's blessing on all living souls in Indiana, not forgetting his yet unborn baby, Clasby had maybe run out of stars. Hannah couldn't leave while the praying was going on, but the minute it was over she draped the shawl closely about her shoulders and said good night.

"We'll see you at church Sunday," Ora said.

"Look out for that Jud Clasby," Lute warned her. "He's a lady killer."

"Jud's the one better look out if he tries anything out of the way with Hannah," Ora told her husband.

As soon as Hannah was down the log steps, Clasby stepped out of the shadows at the side of the house.

"Were you eavesdropping?" Hannah demanded.

"I didn't think it would be polite to bust in on a prayer meeting."

"You could've come in and prayed."

"I don't pray."

"Don't you believe in God?"

"I leave that to Christians and Indians."

"Indians!"

"They believe in a Great Spirit. I don't see much difference."

"You're worse than an Indian then."

"You know many Indians?"

"No."

"Judge not that ye be not judged."

"That's the Bible."

"So I was told, back in Ohio."

Hannah shut her mouth tight.

"I notice you got your shawl back on nice and snug now, so you won't need any more help from me."

Hannah shut her mouth still tighter. This was no subject to get pert about. She wouldn't have gone on to the Bensons' with Clasby except that the Bensons lived on the way to her own home. And whatever she thought of George Benson,

Sarah Benson and her six children were good neighbors.

At the Bensons', supper was late, and they were asked to join the family meal. Four of the children were sent to sit on the floor, where they used the raised hearth as a table. The fare was good: stewed squirrel, johnnycake, and hot sweet sassafras tea.

George Benson's hair and beard were black, but with some of his sister's red in them. When the candlelight hit hair and beard, they looked as if a fire might be smoldering deep down in those dark thickets. Benson was a big-shouldered, heavy-handed man. When he clapped a hand down on the table, the crockery jumped and the cutlery rattled.

"I heard you were here, Jud. Where you been keeping yourself? You're just the man I want to see. I could do the job singlehanded, but two hands are always better than one — especially if one of the hands has had the practice you've had."

"You mean Rocky Point and the sugar camp?"

"You been thinking about it, too?"

"I been sounding out folks. I've about got it lined up, I think."

"Wasn't you going to ask me?"

"What do you think I'm here for?"

"Sparking Hannah, maybe. She needs a full-grown man, not that weedy Wood youngun."

"George," Sarah Benson warned her husband. "Hannah's company, and her folks are the best neighbors we ever had."

Benson gave Hannah's broad shoulder a hearty slap. "Hannah knows I'm teasing her. Why, if I hadn't met you first, Sarah, I'd be courting her myself."

"She's man-shy," Clasby said. "I've found that out."

"What man's she known? Father's nine-tenths a preacher, and John Junior's nine-tenths a girl."

Hannah wanted to sail into George Benson, talking that way about her father and Johnny. But she wanted even more to get the talk turned away from herself.

"What are you planning to do at the sugar camp?"

"Break up the camp."

"Break it up? How?"

"Quickest way would be to use a little lead."

"What harm have they done?"

"Harm?" Benson stepped over the bench he was sitting on so that he could shake his fists without upsetting the dishes. "If a man asked me that question, I'd flatten him. What harm? They killed my grandfather. They thought I was dead or they would've killed me. They're animals. They're worse than animals. Animals don't torture each other. They bite off an enemy's fingers — red men's fingers. They cook a prisoner alive all night and eat his heart in the morning when he dies. We kill wolves, and wolves do us less harm. Nothing's safe as long as they lurk around. There's land and to spare west of here. What're they doing squatting right here on our doorstep? This is our home, not their hunting ground. Who knows what they've got in mind? They ought to be given their walking papers. And the only walking papers they understand is lead."

"What harm have *these* Indians done?" Hannah persisted.

"They're Indians. That's the harm they've done. They're the same blood as those who killed and murdered our kin. If you're so Indian-crazy, go live with them. Be a squaw. You don't belong here."

Hannah slid off the bench. "I'm going home. Don't come with me, Mr. Clasby. It's no more than a step. Good night, Sarah.

Sarah said, "Hannah, he went through all that when he was young. He don't know what he's saying. You heard him say he'd be courting you if he was a widower."

"I heard him."

"Don't hold what he said against him. He's out of his senses on that one subject."

"He told me, 'You don't belong here.' And I don't. Good night, Sarah."

"I'll see you across the crick," Clasby said. "That footbridge is slippery after dewfall. Now don't get your dander up, Hannah. You can have your own way. Go home alone. I want another helping of that stewed squirrel. And George and me's got more talking to do."

In the middle of the footbridge, Clasby

said, "If you make a wish over running water, you'll get it."

"I wish I was home," Hannah said.

At the other side of the bridge Clasby said, "Now just use them long legs of yours and you'll have your wish in five minutes."

Hannah, half crying because of what George Benson had said, was in disarray: her shawl on one side hung almost to her knees. Clasby pulled the shawl even, crossed the ends neatly; then with one hand on each breast made a firm circling movement, ending with a soft easy touch on the upraised nipples. Hannah's first inclination was to throw herself crying into his arms. But she'd been called a courting girl once already that night. And was she going to ask this man, who had said nothing of love or kisses, to handle her again in his free and easy way? She would not ask that. He could not make her ask that. But she had to do *something*. She hit him, half-shove, half-hit, with the heel of her hand. He was on a slope, no more expecting to receive a blow than she was to give one. It was either slide into the creek or sit down. He sat. Yet Hannah, whose sole desire had been to get home, didn't go there.

"Did I hurt you?"

"No, you didn't hurt me, you damn little wildcat. But the next time you want to rassle with me, give me some warning, and we'll have a real tussle."

"I'm not little."

"You damn *big* cat. Let me know when and I'll rassle you to a fare-thee-well."

Then Hannah turned and ran.

The fire was banked and her father and mother were in bed when she got home. She felt her way up the ladder to the loft without lighting a candle. Ben slept at one end of the loft, she at the other. There was a window at her end, a nicety given to her instead of Ben because she was a girl and glass was too scarce and precious for everybody to have his own window. The window was closed. The cabin was well chinked, but enough air seeped past the chinking to keep the loft well ventilated on a raw February evening. Nevertheless, Hannah wanted more air. She opened the window and leaned out as far as she could. She threw aside the shawl, which she had been holding as tight as a bandage about her. Her breasts throbbed, a sore aching hurt that maybe the cold air would ease.

She was looking north, across the creek. There was a glimmer of light from the Bensons' cabin. There George Benson was likely still stamping up and down the floor, or maybe laughing at Jud Clasby's story of the wildcat he'd met.

Hannah tried to put the evening's happenings out of her mind and let the peace of the cool night in, the sky bright with a winter glitter and the great forests turned black now the new moon had set. She wanted to think how small she was under the distant stars and in the midst of trees stretching north and west farther than any man knew, inhabited by red men who had lived there before any white man had dreamed of them. The earth was turning round and round, and as it spun it was making a still bigger circle round the sun. She knew that. What were the circles of her two breasts, and the fire Jud Clasby had stirred up in them, compared with all the blazing circles she looked out on? Nothing, nothing. God Himself could not care about them. What was the hurt of Reba's calling her a courting girl and George Benson's calling her a squaw compared with what they had gone through? Nothing, nothing. Stand in somebody else's shoes instead of your own for a while, she told herself. Love Johnny, forgive Reba, forgive Benson, forget Clasby.

There was a rustling from Ben's cornhusk bed. "Shut that window, Hannah. You want to freeze us to death?"

She would shut it, of course. Whatever Ben wanted her to do, she did. But she would wait one more minute. In that minute an owl hooted his hollow sound of water falling from high eaves into an empty rain barrel. Off in the forest, like an echo, came a softer answering cry. Indians signaled each other like that, she knew. Sounds that had meaning for them, but to a white man's ears were nothing more than the cries of night birds and prowling animals.

She pulled the window shut and went to

Ben's bed. "Did you hear that? What was it?"

"An owl."

"It could be an Indian."

Ben grunted. "Listen," he said.

"All I can hear is the wind round the corners of the house."

"Could be an Indian, breathing hard," Ben said.

"Could you shoot an Indian, Ben?"

"If he was going to shoot me."

"But not in cold blood."

"No."

"They're our enemies."

"Who said so?"

"George Benson. Everybody says so, except Papa."

"You go shoot 'em if you want to. I'm going to leave them alone and set them a good example."

Hannah wanted to sit down on her brother's bed. She wanted to tell him everything that had happened since she had left the house. But Jud Clasby's touch had changed her baby brother; it had made Ben a man. She thought twice now before throwing her arms about Ben's neck, pressing her cheek to his and telling him all her troubles. They weren't troubles she was proud of.

"Good night, Ben."

"Good night, Sis."

She undressed, put on her heavy nightgown, and knelt by the side of her bed, but she could not go through her usual prayer of thanks and blessings. All she could say, over and over, was "Help me, God. Help me, God."

She turned her irritation at her own laxness toward Ben. "Did you say your prayer, Ben?"

"I don't remember," Ben mumbled.

"If you don't remember, you didn't."

"Tomorrow," said Ben.

"Tomorrow may be too late, Ben."

Ben was sound asleep.

3

The next day was Saturday. Hannah's mother, Lizzie, with Hannah's help, spent the day cooking. Since there was no church in the settlement, settlers who were churchgoers met at the Cape cabin, where Caleb Cape (everyone except his wife called him Cale Cape) did the preaching. It wasn't necessary to belong to any church or to have any intention of being tied down by the Ten Commandments in order to enjoy churchgoing. It was the one chance of the week to see a face that didn't belong to your own family, and to hear, in addition to whatever news might be making the rounds, one of Caleb Cape's hair-raising sermons. It wasn't that Caleb was any hell-and-brimstone preacher (though he didn't let you forget that either). What Caleb had that made people willing to ride ten miles, fording streams and picking their way around fallen trees and through tangles of fox grapes and sumac, was a God-blessed gift of gab. He could lay his tongue to the world and its furniture, to its inhabitants and their possibilities, and, listening to him, people thanked God that they were alive and living in such a paradise. It was usually a comedown after the preaching to ride home to a lean-to or shanty, what furniture there was full of splinters and knotholes, and all the younger inhabitants bawling their heads off for supper.

Each Sunday, after the house was clear of his listeners, Caleb promised his wife that *next* Sunday he would not ask everybody to stay and have a bite with them. But the next Sunday, elevated by his own preaching, praying, and singing, and in love with all God's creatures, he did ask them. Lizzie wished Caleb would remember that she, also, was one of God's creatures. Or she wondered if he believed that God's grace would descend upon him to the extent that he could feed the multitude with a couple of johnnycakes and a half-dozen squirrels without her spending Saturday cooking. The neighbors, in any case, had taken to bringing in some food of their own, since they knew that they were going to be asked to stay — and that they would accept.

Caleb himself, who had been doing two jobs at once outside, chopping stovewood and boiling down a kettle of maple sap, brought her some syrup in a saucer.

"How's this strike you?" he asked.

"Depends on what you're aiming for. Syrup or sugar?"

"Sugar," said Caleb.

"It needs a couple of hours more at the least."

Caleb drank what was in the saucer, then licked off what was left.

Lizzie was thirty-four, Caleb thirty-six. They thought of themselves, and so did everybody else, as middle-aged. If Hannah hadn't been so standoffish with the boys, they'd have been grandparents by now. Lizzie had no trouble seeing herself as a grandmother. Caleb as a grandfather gave her imagination quite a stretch. She thanked God her husband had turned to Him.

He was as pretty as a May apple, too pretty for a man, but so big and slab-sided you forgave him his long eyewinkers, his glossy locks and red lips. If Caleb hadn't known that in the sight of God he was a naked soul, he might have been carried away by the sight of the face that looked back at him from the looking glass. If a man wasn't headed toward God and His glory, a face like that could get him into a lot of earthly trouble.

Caleb Cape wanted everything. Except for God, he would have been like Adam in the garden: conceited enough to name all the animals and foolish enough to taste all the fruit. He made no bones about wanting everything, but said to all that God was the only One who asked for all a man had and more. Once accustomed to the upward pull of God stretching your earthly frame skyward, a man who lost it slumped down to the size of a cowpat.

He was a jackanapes, a cutup, a clown. There was nothing he liked better than making people laugh. Lizzie endured and Hannah winced when Caleb, drunk with high spirits, started playing the fool. He knew he had this weakness, and held himself on a tight rein, though he didn't think that man, made in God's image, glorified his Maker by going around looking like he'd just bit into a green persimmon. Nor were folks who were holding their sides from laughing in any proper mood for a bath in the Blood of the Lamb. He knew that.

Sunday began to boil up in Caleb as soon as Saturday dinner was over. By midafternoon Saturday, where they were now, the love of God was beginning to fizz up in him, too high for safe corking.

Since the only congregation he had at hand was Lizzie and Hannah, they got the full force of his pre-Sabbath jubilation. Hannah was taking something in the nature of a pudding from the oven — dried pumpkin, sweetened with maple sugar thinned down with milk and thickened up with four precious eggs.

"Never seen a prettier dish," Caleb said.

He tasted from the pot of cornmeal stirred into venison broth and enriched with venison chunks that Lizzie was cooking.

"That's not scrapple," he said, "but it leans in that direction."

"February in the wilderness," he said, "and it smells like back home in Pennsylvania at Thanksgiving time."

He picked up Lizzie, squeezed her tight, kissed her on the mouth; then, as if finding the taste too good to forgo, kissed her again.

Lizzie squirmed in his arms like a hooked eel. "Hannah," she reminded him.

Caleb kissed her again before putting her down. "High time that girl learned that there are worse things in this world than hugging and kissing."

Hannah ran outdoors as if shot between the shoulder blades with an arrow.

Caleb was proud of his strapping daughter but he didn't take any nonsense from her.

"You get back in here," he called. Hannah came in. "The day you get too fine-haired to see your father kiss your mother, you better change your religion and go live with the Romish Sisters."

Caleb was far from being all soft soap. There was a plentiful streak of pure lye in his make-up. When he came up against what he thought was wrong or just simple-minded, he let people have the rough side of his tongue. He was no namby-pamby preacher too delicate for the world the Lord had put him in. He knew Lizzie liked to be kissed; and he hadn't married his wife to suit his daughter. He was not coarse-grained. It had crossed his mind to say, "Hannah, if I hadn't liked to kiss your mother, you wouldn't be here." But there was no point in making the girl feel beholden to him for what he had done without her in mind. He wished there were men Hannah's equal nearby. Between one slack-kneed boy and a number of loose-living hunters who'd as soon mount a girl as spring a trap, she didn't have a suitable supply to choose from.

He put Lizzie down, didn't say anything further to embarrass Hannah, and went outside. Ben, that softhearted young giant, puffed up from some business of his own back in the woods and said, "Pa, can I go hunting with Johnny Wood?"

Caleb's folks hadn't hailed in the beginning from Massachusetts for nothing. He didn't think you could slide into holiness at sunup Sunday morning without some preparation the night before.

"You've had all week to hunt, Ben. I don't like the sound of guns popping off on Sabbath eve."

71

"Can I go if I don't do any shooting?"

"If you want to go for a run through the woods, I got no objection. Only see you run back in time for supper."

"I'll be back before dark."

He kept his word. It was early twilight and they had just settled down to their supper of milk gravy and corn bread when Ben came in the door. One look at him stopped all forks in mid-air.

"What happened to you, Ben?" his father asked. "You meet a bear?"

"Maybe he met an Injun," Hannah teased.

Ben, who had been about to pull out his stool, jumped like he was bee-stung and ran for the door. He went down the path toward the privy, but didn't get there. He ran behind the woodpile, and all forks at the table were put down at the sound of his dry retching.

"Nothing more to come up," Caleb said.

"I hope he didn't try sampling something poisonous out in the woods," said Lizzie.

"He's got too much sense for that.

Besides, Ben can swallow two gallons of anything and keep it down. Hannah, take him a dipperful of water," Caleb said as the retching went on. "He'll be puking up his socks next. Water'll give him something to bring up even if it don't stop the puking.'

Hannah carried the water to Ben. He was on his knees, his head resting against a rick of wood. He had stopped puking but his sides were going in and out like a horse's with the heaves.

"Ben," Hannah said.

Ben didn't reply. She put her hand on his back, gently and he shuddered. "Rinse your mouth out," she said. "You'll feel better."

Ben's eyes were red and deep in their sockets; he looked like a person just out of bed after a long sickness. He took the dipper and rinsed out his mouth.

"Drink a little," Hannah said. "It'll maybe settle your stomach."

Ben drank down the dipperful. The last swallow going down met the first coming back up.

"Ben, is it something you ate?"

Ben shook his head.

"Come on in. You can't stay out here all night. It's getting cold."

Ben, who had been kneeling, sank lower, burrowing deeper into a jag in the stacked wood. "Let me alone," he whispered.

Hannah ran inside. "He's sick, Mama, and he won't get up or move."

Lizzie half rose, but Caleb said, "If he don't want to move, there's no way to make him. Best leave him alone for a while, Lizzie."

No one had much appetite for supper with Ben sitting out in the dark with nothing but the woodpile to keep the cold off. Caleb didn't even try to bring him in for Bible-reading and prayers.

"If his heart ain't in it, he'd as well stay out there in the woodpile."

"Maybe he's praying out there, alone," Hannah defended her brother.

"Maybe," her father agreed.

But when bedtime came and Ben hadn't stirred, Caleb said, "The boy'll have to come in, if I have to lug him. Whatever ails him, a bout of lung fever's not going to help.''

Lizzie and Hannah half expected some struggle from Ben. Though softhearted, he was stubborn. He wouldn't raise his hand against anyone else, and he expected the same treatment from others. There was no struggle. After a few minutes, Ben walked into the house a step or two ahead of his father.

''It's bedtime, Ben,'' Caleb said, as if talking to a two-year-old who'll fall asleep before he gets to bed.

Ben did not look at anyone.

Caleb filled the big washbasin and put it down in front of his son. ''Take your shoes off, Ben.''

Ben took off his shoes and put his feet in the water. That seemed to use up all the strength he had.

Caleb dropped to his knees and rinsed his son's feet. Hannah expected Ben to either push his father aside or run upstairs to the loft. *She* wouldn't let her father humble himself that way. Ben let his feet be washed and dried by his father; he let him throw the wash water out. He was sitting just as he had been when Caleb returned.

"What's the trouble, son?"

"I'm sick."

Is it anything you ate?"

Ben shook his head.

Caleb put his hand on his son's forehead. "You don't feel hot. Touch of the ague, like as not. Now you get up to bed. A night's sleep's the best medicine there is. By morning you'll be yourself again."

Ben climbed the ladder to the loft without a word.

In the middle of the night Hannah came down the stairs to her father's and mother's bed.

"Mama," she said.

Lizzie roused up, fully awake at the sound of her name.

"What's the trouble, Hannah?"

"It's Ben."

"Is he being sick again?"

"No. He's crying. Then he goes to sleep. Then he grinds his teeth, wakes up, and cries some more."

"No more puking?"

"No."

"It's something on his mind. Maybe he and Johnny had a falling-out. He's always looked up to him so. Talk to him. Try to comfort him."

"He won't talk to me, or even let me get near him."

"He'll just have to suffer through it then, I reckon. You get back in your own bed before you catch a chill."

4

Caleb had always contended that he didn't need to see a calendar with dates or to hear church bells ringing to know it was Sunday. The minute he woke up Sunday morning, there was a fullness in his heart that told him what day it was. He remembered the Sabbath day. He did as little work as possible. He cared for stock, of course; did what emptying of slops and carrying in of wood and water he could to help Lizzie. He was clean from the night before's bath, and his clothes were his best. Caleb was not only a Christian, but also a Sabbatarian. He relished the existence of a whole day in which to praise his Creator. He loved life and liked to give thanks for it. His greatest deprivation in a Godless universe would be the absence of a Creator to whom he could direct his praise and offer his thanks.

Caleb was not unaware that the morning following Ben's sickness was Sunday. Ben still lay in his bed refusing to move, speak, or eat.

"Let him alone," he told Lizzie. "Nature will force him up soon. He's not going to lay up there and wet his drawers."

"He cried so much last night," Hannah said, "he's wrung dry of water. He might not have to get up for a couple of days."

"Piss is one thing and tears another," her father said. "One's from the heart, the other's from the bladder. I guarantee you, he won't lay there 'til his bladder pops."

It was near to meeting time, and Ben's bladder was still holding out. Caleb walked up and down the clearing round their cabin. It wasn't just Ben's sickness, if sickness it was, that took the Sunday feeling out of his heart. The day, after a chilly night, had faired off; too warm for February, more like late May. May, like as not, would right the balance by producing a blackberry winter of snow, nipping budding trees with frost. He liked nature to hold steady, not upset the balance by making you sweat in February. Such weather brought deaths in March when the too trustful, taking the false summer for the real thing, threw off their winter underwear. For these reasons he did not thank God for the day's balminess. The weather had a mind of its own, but God had given His creatures the sense to outwit it.

His uneasiness about Ben's state and his dislike of the unseasonable weather caused Caleb to start the morning services off in a quieter manner than customary. Usually, when about half of those expected to attend the service were in their places, he led them in singing without waiting for the stragglers to come in. This morning he hadn't the heart for singing. The Woods were there, the Bensons, the Pryces, who were the farthest away of any. Luther Bemis, faithful churchgoer, hadn't yet arrived. Jud Clasby, no churchman, but who had come to the meeting (for the home cooking, likely) the last two Sundays, was absent.

Four or five families who lived in the opposite direction from those already present — settlers from down near the north fork of Fall Creek, and on most Sundays among the first to arrive — were not yet in their places.

Caleb said, "We'll put off our singing until we're all together." When the North Fork worshippers arrived, Phoebe Hall could lead the singing if he still had a heavy heart. "Meanwhile, I will read to you the Twenty-third Psalm." He was reading for his own sake, hoping the comforting words would limber up his throat and raise his spirits.

" 'The Lord is my shepherd; I shall not want. He maketh me to lie down in green pastures: he leadeth me beside the still waters. He restoreth my soul: he leadeth me in the paths of righteousness for his name's sake. Yea, though I walk through the valley of the shadow of death, I will fear no evil . . .' "

Caleb had his eyes shut. He knew the psalm by heart and was praying it rather than reading it. His heavyheartedness was easing up. He had forgotten that he had listeners; he was speaking directly to God. A shout brought him back.

"Get her out of here!"

In the open door of the cabin, carried on a quilt held at the corners by four men and in the middle by two women, lay a blood-soaked squaw.

"Get that squaw out of here. Don't you know this is a church meeting?" Benson shouted again.

The North Fork people hesitated for a second before Caleb, with a voice more carrying than Benson's bellow, said, "Bring the woman in. She's been hurt. Put her on the bed."

Caleb, who had been standing on the hearth, his back to the fireplace, went to help the men place the woman he knew to be Talking Crow on his and Lizzie's bed.

He was sorry for the bloodstains that would be left on Lizzie's best coverlet, but there was no help for that. He didn't value a coverlet more than a human being. The squaw had a wound near the base of her throat — a gaping bullet hole, by its looks.

Caleb need not have worried about the coverlet. The squaw would not stay down, and no one wanted to use force on a woman whose throat bubbled bloody air as she breathed. Talking Crow first sat, then rose slowly to her feet. She was gray from loss of blood; the terrible bloody bubbles became larger with her effort.

"You kill me," she said in English. "I not die on your bed."

She faced George Benson. She spat at him, a bloody froth that ran down his face. "Woman killer. Child killer," she said hoarsely.

Benson rose, reaching for the wooden ladle laid out on the table for serving the hominy-and-meat stew.

Caleb wrestled him down to the bench he had risen from. "George, this is a church meeting."

"Not when the savages come in."

The disturbance — women had screamed at the sight of Talking Crow, Caleb and Benson in their tussle had overturned a bench — brought Ben halfway down the ladder from the loft. Even without a bloody, pulsating neck wound, he looked fully as sick as Talking Crow.

"What's going on?" he asked blankly.

"Nothing you had backbone for, you puking youngun," Benson said.

Talking Crow looked at Ben steadily. Finally, as if her sight had cleared, she said, "You no help Folded Leaf."

Ben did not appear to hear her. He came on down the ladder as if sleepwalking. At the bottom he either missed the final step or fainted. Or perhaps both. He fell with a sodden thump of flesh onto the floor and lay there, face down.

Talking Crow watched him fall. "You kill me," she told the others. "I not die in your house."

Caleb, at her side, said, "We will help you. I promise you."

Talking Crow took her hand from the

table on which she had been supporting herself and stood erect. "Help!" Her voice, filled with scorn, came bubbling up through the blood that was choking her. Benson held up an arm as if expecting another spray of bloody spittle. Talking Crow had no more blood to waste on George Benson.

"You help us die!"

She passed her hand over the flowing wound on her throat, then pointed a finger dripping blood at Benson. "When you die, you remember."

Slowly but without wavering, she went out the door and down the two log steps. On the bottom step she gave a last cry, muffled, blood-soaked, the cry of a brave at death. Then she fell face forward and lay unmoving.

Some started toward Talking Crow; but Caleb barred the way. "I'll tend to her — if she's alive." He bent over and studied her. "Her troubles are over." When the settlers started to crowd round, he said, "Don't make her put up with what she was trying to get away from."

"What's that?" Luke Steffens, a North

Forker, asked.

"Us," Caleb answered.

Hannah, while the others were watching Talking Crow, went to Ben. He was pale, clammy, limp as a dead snake. But he was surely alive. She put her ear to his chest; his heart was beating as steady as a pump bolt. She sat on the floor beside him, waiting.

Everyone in the room was talking at once. Hannah tried to sort out the words so that they made sense. The North Fork folks were trying to tell where they had found Talking Crow. How they had found her. Each one wanted to tell exactly what he had done, said, felt. How upsetting it was that Indians as peaceful as those at the sugar camp had been killed. Nobody doubted that settlers had done it. The Indians were crowding in too close. If it was to be a white man's country and people were to be free to move westward without huddling like prisoners behind stockades, the Indians had to be taught to keep their distance. Indiana was a state now, a part of the Union. She wasn't a frontier settlement any more and had as much right as Massachusetts or Old Virginia to cast out the red men. Somebody had done this killing — how or when, who knew? But why was plain enough to all.

Caleb put an end to the hubbub. "This is not the Tower of Babel," he said. "We need to know what you saw, and one at a time is all we can hear. Ebon Hall, you tell us."

Eb Hall was the right man to call on. He wasn't tongue-tied. Nor was he inclined to make an account of human hapchance sound like God's report of the Creation. He was a long-nosed, lank-haired, dark-visaged man who looked down in the mouth at the best of times. He didn't look much different this morning.

"All of us from up North Fork way was on our way to church, except for the Bushnells, who're always late. The weather was so good everybody walked. We come along — well, you all know the trace we follow — a hundred yards or so from Stony Point and the sugar camp there. There was no one around. I didn't think anything of it. Indians don't follow any rule I know about in their comings and goings.

"About a couple of hundred yards — well, you all know where the Talbot Jessups first settled. Dug a well because they were afraid they'd get milk fever from the spring stream. Then filled in the well when they pulled out. It was right there the Bushnells caught up with us, and right there that Maggie Bushnell said, 'I hear something.'

"Well, you can always hear something in the woods, but we stopped, listened. It was a human voice. Sick or hurt. We followed the sound to the Jessup well. The stuff the Jessups had put in it had sunk. Now it's more of a sinkhole than a well. Kind of a deep saucer. The voice was coming from there. From down under a lot of dead bodies we saw when we got there."

"How many?" Titus Andrews asked.

"I'm coming to that. We pulled out the bodies one by one. Two girls. Two boys. Three women. The woman we brought here was at the bottom of the heap. I don't know how she breathed there. Let alone lived with that hole in her neck."

"Where are the two bucks?" Cyrus Shannon asked.

"I don't know where they are. All I know is what I've told you. Three women, four children dead in the sinkhole of the old Jessup well."

"One woman was alive, you said."

"Half alive. You seen her."

"How'd they been killed?"

"Shot. Beaten."

"What'd Talking Crow say when you pulled her out?"

"She didn't say a word. Except for the groaning, I'd of thought she was dead. She didn't really come to 'til we carried her in here."

George Benson got to his feet. "Why did you bring her here? Why didn't you leave her where she belongs? With her own kind."

Ebon Hall's wife, Phoebe, answered for her husband. "She's an old woman. When I'm an old woman I don't want to be left to die like that."

Benson had an answer to that.

"She's an old woman for sure. She's the

mother and grandmother of men that killed my folks. She's likely hacked white prisoners to death with her own hands. I killed her, or tried to. Those redskins been asking for what they got. We warned them not to move in here so close. They take the best of the skins and game. None of us would be here except our fathers fought off the Indians. We going to let them push us back? Leave our children to fight battles we ought to fight? Where's our backbone? They been warned year after year at Rocky Point. They got from here to Texas to hunt. Don't tell me they don't have a scheme to get their foot in the door, open it, and let the whole pack of redskins north of us come pushing in like wolves. I shot the old squaw. The time'll come when you'll thank me for it. Next year you'll see that the redskins keep their distance. And you'll all breathe easier."

The minute George Benson sat down, his sister, Reba Wood, jumped up. "Every word George says is true. But one thing he left out. He didn't do it all singlehanded."

Benson called across the room, "I

wasn't meaning to hog all the credit, Reba. But in this sort of thing, every man's got the right to speak for himself."

"Well, my husband's one to hang back when it comes to claiming credit. I'll take some of the blame for that. John's older than me, as I guess you all know, and I've kind of got in the way of speaking up for him. Well, I want you to know he was right there at Stony Point, and he done every bit as good as brother George. Young John did his part, too. And if any of you been wondering if that boy was ever going to grow up, stop wondering. He growed up yesterday. Fought like a man. If he was here, he'd blush to hear me say so, but it's the point-blank truth. My two men gave every bit as good account of themselves as brother George. Can't praise them higher than that, can I, George?"

Hannah, who had been huddled over Ben, half hearing, did hear Reba's last sentence. She lifted her head and called out, "What did you say about Johnny?"

Reba replied, "I said Johnny fought like

a man. Killed Indians with the best of them."

Hannah, not believing, asked, "Johnny did that?"

"You been doing your best to make a man of him, ain't you, Hannah? Well, what you couldn't do, the Indians done. He's a man now. He's been blooded."

"I wasn't trying to get him to kill anybody."

"A man finds his manhood the best way he can. Some one way. Some another."

Ben, hearing the argument, if that was what it was, pulled himself, unnoticed, back up the ladder to the loft.

Ebon Hall said, "I ain't concerned about John Junior's manhood. He wears pants, so I reckon he's got some. What I worry about is what Colonel Johnston, the Indian agent's going to do about this when he hears about it."

"How's he going to hear about it?" Benson asked.

"Don't you think for a second Indian runners won't have the word to Johnston by sunup tomorrow."

"Who's in charge of this country?"

Benson shouted. "Indians and their softhearted agents or us? Move in with the redskins if you're so sweet on them, Eb Hall. You'll never be missed."

"We'll all be missed if the tribes to the north take it into their heads they got a little revenge coming."

Benson erupted violently, like a wounded bear.

"I never thought I'd live to see the day when men of my own country and color would take the side of Indians against me!"

"Come on, George," Reba said. "I know when I'm not wanted. Let's clear out of here. These folks want to have a powwow, not a church meeting."

"You're right, Reba. The place has got an Indian stink."

George and Sarah Benson, their six children, and the two Woods left the meeting — before any prayer had been said, any song sung.

"Judge not that ye be not judged, Ebon Hall," Benson called back through the open door.

A hot gush of feeling ran along Hannah's

veins. Her father, his church, and God Himself were being discredited. She sprang to her feet and called out, "This has stopped being a church. But it's still Sunday, and if we pray, maybe God will forgive us."

Caleb and Lizzie urged upon their neighbors the food they had brought, but the neighbors left their food behind, as if it, too, had been sullied by what had been said and done. "We'll pick up the pans later."

The Capes weren't hungry either. Ben lay on his bed, refusing to move or to talk. Lizzie had gone up to reason with him. They had some idea now of what ailed the boy.

Caleb and Hannah carried Talking Crow to the bed of the wagon. There they put the bloody quilt over her and fastened it down at each corner with a rock.

"We can't leave her here," Hannah said.

"For a while we can," Caleb answered. Hannah asked no more.

Caleb was too upset to stay home. "I'm

going to talk over to Stony Point," he told Hannah. "I want to see for myself what happened there."

"Can I go with you?"

"What you'll see won't be very pretty."

"I know that."

It was a three-mile walk, with no cabins except the Mungers', up on a knoll a quarter of a mile off the trace. Nothing but the woods, there like they'd always been. They didn't have to fight through underbrush. Fires over centuries had burned leaves, saplings, brush, leaving only the great trees: oak, walnut, hickory. The sycamores towered over all. Sugar maples were plentiful. That was the reason the Indians had returned each year to Stony Point. There were poplars, from which the Capes' own house had been built. But all the building and clearing that had been done around Fall Creek made no more than a nick in the forest that covered the ground thick as grass in a water meadow, westward and westward clear to the sunset.

The trees weren't leafed-out yet, so they walked through bars of sunshine. It was

94

the kind of weather, as well as the day of the week, to rejoice in. Caleb's feeling for Sunday made him reflect. He said, "It should've happened on another day." Then he took it back. "The day won't matter. The deed makes the day, not the other way round."

Hannah said, "Reba drove Johnny to help George Benson."

"How do you know that?"

"I heard her. She told Johnny he was a weakling. She shamed him into doing it."

"There are other ways of proving your strength."

"That's the way that come up first."

There was no arguing with Hannah about Johnny Wood's reasons for doing what he did. If he did anything. They had nothing but Reba's word for that.

Caleb missed the praying and singing of that morning's Lord's Day service the way another man would miss a meal or a night's sleep. His mind felt dry and his body tired. Instead of worshipping, neighbors had quarreled; his own son had been struck down in a fit of remorse of some kind; the blood of a dying woman was on his floor; her body lay in his farm wagon. Before the afternoon was over he'd likely see more bodies; not bodies killed on a battlefield, but squaws and children struck down in a sugar camp.

His mind was split three ways, divided among what had been, was, and would be. He remembered the dying woman, her look and words. While he remembered that he also saw a raccoon peer out at him from the hollow of a tulip tree. A pair of eagles sat motionless at the top of a lightning-blasted sycamore. Squirrel chatter was louder than bird song. But more vivid than either the present he walked through or the morning just past was the imagined scene toward which he advanced.

The afternoon was warm to sweating. He was still in his winter underwear, and would be, if he had sense, for a couple of months to come. Cased in by wool, his sweat was not summer's thin and cooling wetness but the thick bad-smelling dampness of exertion and dread. Why was he plodding toward what he dreaded to see? The dead wouldn't be helped by his presence. The sight he was searching for wouldn't purify him.

Near the sugar camp they saw four buzzards soaring in the sky.

"I don't like the look of those birds," Hannah said.

"They don't have anything to do with what we're going to see. They're a quarter of a mile or so away."

Before they reached the camp, at the half-cleared place where the Jessups had lived before they pulled up stakes and went home to Ohio, Caleb sighted what he'd come to see: the bodies pulled out of the sinkhole of the well and sprawled where they'd been laid in the haste to get at the woman who still lived.

For a minute Caleb couldn't continue. "Well, George didn't lie about what had been done," he said.

Hannah faced away from the bodies. She stared at an old beech tree as if her life depended upon memorizing the shape of its scars and the number of its limbs.

"You go first, Papa."

"There's no call for you to come at all."

She listened to her father's retreating footsteps, then ran after him. "I don't want to be left alone."

Hannah had never seen death before. She couldn't remember the little brother who had died when she was young. At first sight these dead were as lifeless as boulders or stumps. They were forest litter, dead branches to be stepped over. As she came closer they became human beings asleep in awkward positions. They'd wake up numb, their legs full of pins and needles.

All except Folded Leaf. He was not asleep. He was not forest litter. He was a boy she'd seen playing in the creek, sleek and brown as an otter, but a boy. He wasn't a boy any more. Where his face had been there was a clot of offal like she'd seen at butchering time when the job had been botched: torn flesh, splintered bones, blood, and what she supposed must be brains. They were tidier with hogs.

A pain sharp and sickening, of the same kind she'd felt when Ben had split his toe open with an axe, went through her. It started under her heart and ended someplace in the region of her crotch. It was sickening, sour-sweet; nothing short of fainting or puking would relieve it.

"Look the other way, Hannah."

She wished she'd never left the beech tree.

"Ben saw this?"

"Saw it done, maybe."

"Johnny?"

"We don't know. Nothing's for sure yet."

"But Reba said . . ."

"That woman'd say anything to get attention."

"Where were their men? Hunting?"

"Indian men don't hunt in the afternoon. No man with sense does."

"Why didn't they help?"

"How do I know?" Caleb was exasperated with his daughter. This was no time for chitchat.

The old Jessup place was melancholy enough without dead bodies. Somebody had tried here and given up. Headed west with hope, then backtracked east, defeated. They had dug a well to save their girls from the fever a spring creek was said to give. And the girls had died from drinking well water. The Jessups had filled in the well to keep livestock from breaking a leg; now the filling had sunk down far enough to provide a hidden nest for dead bodies.

Newcomers had helped themselves to the logs of the Jessup house. The stone chimney still stood, a bare backbone; the pole-fenced cowyard had not been disturbed. It was a place most people stayed away from. It put them in mind of what might be in store for them: death and defeat.

The old Jessup well had been the perfect place in which to hide the dead Indians. It was a short haul from the sugar camp and a place to which nobody came. The grave markers for the two Jessup girls were up at the top of the rise, facing southeast toward Ohio, where they'd been born.

Caleb was sorry for snapping at Hannah. Her wonderment about the Indian men had been natural. He could figure it out in only one way.

"The men were ambushed," he told her. "I'm going to take a look around. You don't need to come with me."

She needed to. She couldn't stay there alone with the dead bodies. But the dead bodies went with her. Her father was tracking, reading the message of footprints and trodden leaves and broken twigs. She couldn't fasten her mind on what was underfoot. It was filled with the images of the dead who had been flung out of the well in order to get to the one who still lived.

She could see the young woman, the breed, her calico blouse torn open to the waist, her skin white, each breast bullet-punctured. Somebody's gun had said, "Don't be white, don't have breasts like those." With her own blood that gun had made her a redskin.

The older Indian woman's calm had not been disturbed by death or by being thrown into a well and then hauled out again. She lay on her back, her eyes closed. She took no heed of what the whites had done.

A little girl had her arm wrapped

around her stomach. Hannah knew what the words were she could not hear. "It hurts, it hurts."

Her father spoke, ridding her mind of those pictures of the dead they had just left. "There he is."

She followed her father's pointing finger. There he was, up the trace ahead of them, kneeling, forehead to the ground, a man in prayer. But he was a dead man, his shirt black with dried blood. The sight of him did not fill her with the sickening splinter of pain she had felt when she saw the others. She could not see this man's face. He appeared to have knelt down, tired of being. He had had enough of life, had drawn his last breath and put his forehead to the earth.

"Shot in the back," said her father. "Tolled away from camp on some trumped-up excuse so they'd be free to finish off the women and children."

"There were two men," Hannah reminded him.

"The other is probably nearby. Hannah, I know you got the strength for it. Have you got the stomach for it?"

"I can do what has to be done," Hannah answered.

"I'm not going to leave these people laying around here like scraps thrown out for the dogs to chew on. I'm going to put them back in the well for tonight. Tomorrow I'll bury them and Talking Crow. You'll have to help me carry Tall Tree. A lighter man I could manage by myself, but I can't lift a man his size. Dragging him would tear him to pieces. And me, too."

Caleb took the bulk of the load. Even so, Tall Tree's legs angled downward in Hannah's grasp. A moccasin dropped from his foot.

"Papa," Hannah called, then shut her mouth. What did Tall Tree care now whether he had two moccasins or one? He wouldn't be walking again. Hannah staggered under his weight. The effort kept her mind off the burden she carried. A dead man. A few drops of blood oozed from the wound in his back onto the hem of her dress. She saw them strike, and spread, but went grimly on.

Red Cloud was where her father had

thought he might be — in the opposite direction and about the same distance from the camp. Shot in the back like Tall Tree, but face down, a man taking his rest. He was lighter than Tall Tree and easier to carry.

They lowered the children into the sinkhole first, then the women, and finally the two men. Caleb figured that was the way the men would want it.

"That covering of branches won't fool any animal hungry for fresh meat. The men weren't much help at the sugar camp. They'd want to take the brunt of it now, if the worst comes to the worst."

It was full dark when they got home, bloodstained and bone-tired. Lizzie didn't pester them with questions until they'd washed and changed. They sat down to the good food that hadn't been eaten at midday, and that they hadn't the heart to eat now.

"What did you find?" Lizzie asked when she saw there was going to be no eating.

"Just what George said we would. Dead Indians."

"All dead?"

"Every one."

"Women and children?"

"Women and children."

"There was a fight?"

"No signs of that."

"Shot down in cold blood?"

"Worse than cold. Planned. I'm going back in the morning to bury them."

"That'll be quite an undertaking, Caleb."

"Ben can help."

"Ben's still sick."

"I can help you," said Hannah, "if Ben's still sick."

"You done more than a girl's share already."

"I know who'd help, Papa. Luther Bemis. I was at the Bemises' when Jud Clasby talked about the Indians moving too close. He wanted Lute to help drive them out. But Lute said not to count on any help from him. He was through killing Indians. He'd be just the one to help you now."

5

Caleb took Hannah's advice. After the supper he couldn't eat, he walked the half mile to the Bemis cabin. It was a cold clear night after the warm clear day. There was a quarter moon for light. Owls hooted, their voices ricocheting among trees so that it was impossible to say whether the hooter was behind you or ahead of you, or one or a dozen. Indians knew this, and whites, fooled by their imitations, moved on unsuspecting to be slaughtered.

The Bemises had no candles lighted, no fire burning. The light through the one curtained window was dim. Caleb thought twice about rousing them up if they'd already gone to bed.

While he was thinking it over, Ora called out sharply, "Who's there?"

"Cale Cape," Caleb answered. "If you've gone to bed, I can come see Lute in the morning."

Ora herself unbolted the door. "Come

in. We're not in bed. Lute's feeling poorly, but I'm up and wide awake."

Ora put a couple of sticks on the fire and seated herself in the rocker, hunched up in her wrapper like a bird in cold weather. Caleb stood, his back to the fire, facing the corner bed, where Lute lay face to the wall, knees drawn up, a big bundle of bedclothes.

"Nothing serious, I hope."

"He's been resting and dozing all day. He can't hold anything on his stomach. But he's got no fever. By morning he'll be good as new, I hope."

"I missed you both at church."

"We missed coming. But Lute was in no shape, puking and shaking, to put in an appearance. And he didn't want me to make the walk by myself."

"It's just as well you didn't try — in your shape. What happened wouldn't have been good for the baby."

"What could hurt a baby at church?"

"We didn't have any church. The folks from North Fork brought in a half-dead squaw from the sugar camp. She said a few words and died. Benson and old Wood, or at least Reba Wood, admitted they'd done it. Boasted about it's nearer the truth. And whoever done it, it was done. They're all dead, men, women, and children. A couple of dogs, even. Hannah and me went up there.''

Ora said nothing.

Caleb went on. ''I reckon you'd 'bout as well've come to church as hear it all spelled out like this.''

Ora said, ''No. Words are easier to take. You saw it?''

''Hannah and me together.''

''Hannah's got a lot of grit for a girl.''

''No more per inch, I reckon, than you.''

''Did she tell you about being here with Clasby?''

''That's why I'm here.''

''Clasby was here with Hannah night before last. Lute's known him from away back. Jud talked then of wiping out that camp — he was trying to recruit Lute for the job. He didn't say so in so many words, but Lute and I both knew what he was up to. Lute told him he was leading a new kind of life, and shooting down peaceful Indians had no part in it.''

"That's what Hannah told me. That's why I'm here. I'm going to give those folks a resting place underground, not leave them out for wolf bait. I'll need some help in the digging. I come, knowing from Hannah how Lute felt, to get his help."

"He's so poorly," Ora began, but Lute himself interrupted her.

"I'll be at your place tomorrow at sunup, Cale. I ain't too poorly to know my duty. I'm throwing this off gradually. I'm better now than I was this morning."

'If you don't feel like it . . . there's been enough dying around here without you catching lung fever."

"I'll feel up to it. Did anybody at church mention Clasby?"

"Nobody. Reba was so anxious to claim all the glory for her men, nobody else could get an oar in once she'd started."

"The squaw?"

"She died before she'd had her full say."

Lute, with an unexpected movement, threw all the bedclothes aside and stood tall and white in his long underwear.

"Pray for me, Cale. I missed church today. I ain't so steady in the Light as I'd like to be. I need help."

Caleb said, "There was no church to miss today — as things turned out."

"Where two or three are gathered together in His name," Ora reminded them, "that's church."

So the three had a little church of their own then and there, and Caleb walked home easier in his heart than he'd been since morning.

Caleb and Lizzie were at the breakfast table next morning when Ora arrived. She wouldn't eat, said she was too dauncy of a morning nowadays to hold down solid food.

"I come to tell you Lute's had a setback. He's feverish now and got the shakes. I set my foot down against his coming. I'm in no shape to be a widow." She was the only one who laughed at her own joke.

She wouldn't eat, she wouldn't linger. She wouldn't hear to anyone walking home with her.

"The walk'll do me good."

There was a cold drizzle of rain, but Ora had a shawl, she said, that turned away water. "The baby's snug," she assured them, "and Lute needs me. Outsiders upset him when he's sick. He was out of his head for a while last night after you left. All that talk of killing was too much for him."

She had her own way. There was no means short of rassling her into taking somebody's arm, or of tracking along behind her like a man running down a deer, to see her home.

"That rain'll be sleet in another hour," Caleb said, as he watched her leave.

"Don't fret yourself about Ora," Lizzie said after she had left. "She won't do anything to harm that baby."

"Sounds like Lute and Ben both been hit by the same complaint," Caleb said.

"Don't say that," Lizzie urged. She'd lost one son with a fever. The first thawing days of spring were the most dangerous of the year. More deaths then than from lung fever in the depths of winter, or from the bloody flux in a torrid summer.

Caleb put his hand on Lizzie's. "I don't think it's a killing sickness Ben's got. He's going with me this morning."

"Did you have to threaten him?"

"I told him he had to go, if that's a threat."

"Ben being what he is and you what you are, I reckon it was."

"Oh, he's willing to go. Now that Lute's under the weather, I'll take Hannah, too. She can dig circles around Ben any day."

"You oughtn't to say that so's Ben can hear."

"I ain't saying it so he can hear."

"Ben needs back-patting. With Hannah for a sister, always running faster and digging deeper, he's had a hard row to hoe."

"Hannah's carried Ben around on a chip since he was born."

"That's part of the trouble. He needs to do something on his own."

"He'll have his chance today. This rain'll freeze before it lets up. I don't mind digging wet ground, but frozen ground's something else."

"You sure this has to be done, Caleb?"

Caleb rose from the table. "Sometimes I think women spend so much of their store of tenderheartedness on their families they ain't got a smidgen left for the outside world. Yes, I'm sure it's got to be done if I'm to sleep nights."

Caleb went to the loft ladder. "Ben, Hannah, get down here. We're leaving in fifteen minutes."

Brother and sister came down at once, Hannah first, then Ben. Nobody, unless it was Hannah, had had a good look at Ben outside the gloom of the loft for two days. A day and a half had gone by without his eating. Missing three or four meals didn't show up on a boy whose bones were as well covered as Ben's. But something showed up on him. He was tallow-colored, as pale as a man with the ague when the fever dies down. His hair hung down lifeless as a sick cat's. It was combed, though, his shirt buttoned, his back ramrod straight. He looked like a man ready to walk to his own grave. When the corn dodgers and syrup were put in front of him he shook his head.

"My stomach's still unsettled."

"You can't work on an empty stomach, son."

"It'd be empty, anyway, the next minute after I swallowed something."

"You ain't in a family way, are you, Ben?"

"Caleb," Lizzie protested, "that's no joking matter."

"With Ben, I figured it was," Caleb said. "Ben, you got some reason you're not telling us for not wanting to help me this morning?"

"I want to help you. I'm going to. I never said not."

"If you can work without eating, we been wasting a lot of good food on you these past few years. Hannah, I'm going to need you after all. Luther Bemis's sick."

Ben said, "Maybe he drank too much."

"Now, none of that kind of talk."

Caleb sat on the floor of the wagon to keep the body of Talking Crow from rolling about; and the grave-digging tools from clattering. This was, in a sense, a hearse, and the squaw had suffered enough already without going to her burial with the rattlety-bang of a shivaree celebration.

Caleb had told Ben to drive; some small job might keep his mind off whatever was eating at him. Hannah, her arms folded tight inside her deerskin cape, held her chin down, trying to take the force of the rain, which had turned, as Caleb had prophesied, into a nasty sleet, on her cap and forehead. The sleet, before it melted and ran off, stuck to their faces like a kind of cold slimy gravy. Skim-ice was already forming on the roadside puddles.

No wheels had turned into the old Jessup place for a long time; but the ruts made by earlier Jessup comings and goings were still plain to be seen.

"Up there by the old well," Caleb directed Ben."

Before they were there, he saw that the branches he and Hannah had put in place so carefully lay scattered about. Caleb was out of the wagon before Ben could pull up the horses. He did not find what he had expected: that animals had been at the bodies of Tall Tree and Red Cloud. This was not the work of animals. Indians had been here. All the bodies were gone. There were tracks of moccasins and unshod horses about the sinkhole. The hair on the back of Caleb's neck rose as his skin tightened. Decent burial for a dead Indian was one thing. The presence of live Indians was a different matter.

"Get down in the wagon bed," he yelled to his children.

He peered into the trees. He scanned the gaunt fireplace. Was there any movement behind it? He was here on a mission of mercy: to give decent burial to a woman he'd had no hand in killing. Those were facts, but no Indian would care about any fact but the color of his skin. He was white, and white men had killed red men. Let white men die, they'd argue.

He thought better of the command he had given Ben and Hannah before the words were cool in his mouth. If redskins were still about, revengeful as redskins were, better be out in the open than crouched behind the foot-high sideboards of a wagon.

"Hannah, Ben. Come here."

Hannah, there first, exclaimed, "The bodies are gone!"

"I'm glad they're gone," Ben said.

"They didn't just go, Ben. Somebody took them."

"How did they know where they were?" Hannah asked.

"These woods are full of Indians. They keep a pretty good track of each other."

"Will they be back?"

"What would you do, Ben, if you came home and found your mother and me and Hannah scalped?"

"*You* haven't been doing anything wrong."

"What's wrong with a half-dozen Indians making maple sugar?"

"They were doing more than that. They were trapping the streams empty. Deer were twice as hard to find."

Ben was coming out of his shell, and Caleb didn't want by any word of his to drive him back into it.

"That's what Mr. Wood said," Ben added defiantly.

"They've trapped here and bored trees here before we ever set foot in America, let alone Indiana."

"That's Indian talk, Mr. Benson said."

"If you want to stay alive, you better try to figure out the meaning of Indian talk."

"I didn't do anything."

"Nobody said you did. But try telling an Indian with a tomahawk, 'I was there and didn't do anything,' and see how long he listens to you."

"You got a gun with you, Papa?" Ben asked.

"You know I have. I never leave the house without one. But this is a burying party, not a shooting party. Only there's no point burying now. The Indians'll be back for Talking Crow. Save them and us both trouble just to put her back in the well and cover her up."

"Do they know where she is now?" Hannah asked.

"My guess would be they do. Ben, you gather up the branches. I'll carry Talking Crow to the well."

Hannah, while Ben and her father put Talking Crow back where she'd been found, walked up toward the sugar camp. The sleet had slacked off, and the air was colder. The sky had not cleared. If those black clouds held more water, it would be hail by the time it reached earth. She wasn't frightened by her father's words about Indians. Since Friday evening she had felt that the course of her life had gone out of her hands. Nothing she had planned had happened — unless there was some planning so deep in her it was hidden from her knowledge.

She counted the days: two whole days, Saturday and Sunday; the evening of Friday and the morning of Monday. Few hours, yet in that time either she was a changed girl or she was only becoming acquainted with the girl she really was. On Friday she had gone to Johnny Wood's home her heart engraved on every cookie she gave him. Two hours later she was willing to let Jud Clasby walk off with her breasts in his hands.

On Sunday morning, she had seen a dying squaw spitting blood on churchgoers, and she watched without falling down in a swoon. In the afternoon she had dragged dead men to their graves, then gone home and washed as calmly as if she'd come in from milking. Now she'd been told Indians might fall upon them at any minute. She still felt calm. If it was to happen, it would.

She stumbled, without noticing where she was walking, onto what she took at first to be a boulder. It was boulder-colored, all right, a big deerskin bag stuffed tight and the top held close by a rawhide drawstring. Burned in the skin were the initials J. C. — Jud Clasby. Instinctively Hannah put her hand to the initials, then drew it slowly across the soft suede bulge of the bag. It was his. He had carried it. It was filled with what belonged to him. She lifted it to her face, but the smell was only of leather and hides. The bag was almost as heavy as a man. She carried it slowly back to her father.

Caleb and Ben had once again carefully covered the sinkhole with boughs.

Her father, who never swore, said when

he saw her, "In God's name, Hannah, don't go wandering off that way without letting us know. Things have changed. You could've been scalped by this time. Don't you know that?"

"You told me so," Hannah reminded her father.

"Well, when it happens," Caleb said, "I don't want to be the last to know. What've you picked up?"

Hannah pointed to the initials. "J. C. Jud Clasby's belongings, I reckon."

"Where were they?"

"Up toward the sugar camp."

"Ben, was Clasby there?"

Ben looked at the ground.

Caleb stared at his son. "I can't thrash you into talking. You know that. But the sooner you tell me what you know, the better it'll be for everyone. You included."

Caleb untied the drawstring of Clasby's bag. What spilled out was none of Clasby's belongings, but the best peltries of the Indians' trapping. Caleb took them out slowly, one by one. Between skins there had been packed a few knives, beaded decorations, and small bowls. Clasby had skinned the camp of its valuables. When the bag was empty, Caleb gave the mound a small kick. "Thievery," he said.

Killing Indians was one thing. Robbery was another. Killing Indians, like it or not, was the only way they had survived. Picking off redskins hadn't endangered anyone but the redskins who got picked off. But stealing endangered them all. Benson could boast and expect approval when he said he had rid the countryside of a few more red men, but "I stole" was a confession nobody was likely to make.

Caleb didn't have to tell his children this. He left the bag and its contents where it had fallen.

"Won't the Indians find it?" Ben said.

"Let them," said Caleb. "It belongs to them. Alongside the bodies they've already found, this won't cut much ice."

"They'll know who did it," Hannah said.

"They already know. They were likely chasing Clasby when he dropped his bag."

"It could just've slipped off, couldn't it?" Hannah asked.

"It could've. Clasby no doubt was in kind of a hurry."

The three of them sat wedged together on the wagon seat going home. It was hailing now, little stinging pellets not much larger than grains of sand. The horses, Acorn and Oak, so named by Caleb because one was the father of the other, one little, one big, walked with lowered heads and at a good pace, barn-eager. No one spoke.

The grave-digging tools, shovel, pickaxe, spade, rattled around on the floor of the wagon. Hannah sat between her father and brother trying to draw herself up into a knot of unfeeling flesh — not against the hail, but against memory. On a single day she had been ready to clasp two different men: one a murderer and the other a thief and murderer. That's the way my nature turns, she thought.

She was riding with her eyes shut and would not have known that they had turned into their own lane except for her father's wild shout and the sudden jerk of the wagon as it was stopped by horses being pulled back on their haunches.

She opened her eyes to see her father already halfway to the door of their cabin.

"Ben! Ben! What's the matter with Papa?"

Ben pointed. An arrow was planted in the door, not lightly, but sent with force and standing almost straight out.

"Lizzie, Lizzie," Caleb was calling.

Hannah, jumping clear across Ben's knees, ran after her father screaming, "Mama, Mama!"

Lizzie herself opened the door, alarmed by all the commotion. "Caleb, what's happened? What's the trouble? Is somebody hurt?"

Caleb grabbed his wife in his arms. Hannah circled round, patting both. She had something she could cry for now without having to explain, so she sobbed, "Mama, Mama."

"Oh, thank God, praise God," Caleb said.

"For what, for what?" Lizzie asked. Lazarus raised from the tomb had caused less of a fuss, she thought.

"You're sure you're all right?"

"I may have a cracked rib soon," Lizzie said, "if you don't let up your hugging. But I was pretty sound 'til you got home."

Caleb loosened her arms. "You didn't see or hear anything?"

"I heard the sleet and the hail. I was up in the loft changing the bedclothes. After Ben's staying in bed twenty-four hours a day, things needed freshening. What was there to see or hear?"

Caleb pulled his wife out of the doorway and closed the door. Lizzie, when she saw the arrow, didn't sway or scream, but all the color went out of her face.

"You didn't hear or see anyone?" Caleb asked.

"Not a soul. The hail on the roof's noisy. I wasn't looking out the window. What's the meaning of it, Caleb?"

"I thought the meaning was I'd find you scalped."

"That's why you took on so?"

"Well, I *was* relieved," Caleb said, "when I saw you with your hair." Caleb's tendency, when stirred up, was as strong to joke as Hannah's was to cry.

Ben, who had got the team into the shed

out of the weather, asked, "Did somebody shoot that to tell us they'd be back?"

"No. Indians don't fight that way. They don't warn you, 'Get ready, we're coming.' When they're ready, they come and are gone, and the first you know about it is your hair's missing. Other parts, too, sometimes."

"Would a white man do that?" Lizzie asked. "Just to scare us? Someone who didn't like the idea of your going to bury the Indians?"

"Well, there's no call not to like us for that. We didn't bury them."

"Why not?"

"They weren't there."

"Indians?"

"There couldn't be anyone else."

Lizzie looked at the arrow again. "Is there any need for us to be standing out here in the hail?"

"No," said Caleb, "there ain't." It took a hard tug to get the arrow out of the double oak door. It had been sent with enough force to go through a man's ribs to the heart, or through belly muscles to the guts. It was an arrow of the old days, feathered with red hawk tail and tipped with chipped quartz.

Caleb turned it over in his hands. He could not help admiring its beauty. It was the nearest to a bird a man had ever made; but man, when *he* made a bird, made a bird of death. It flew to kill. Its song was a scream. It hatched blood and the blood gave birth to worms. Caleb handled it gingerly: dead snakes still had poison on their teeth.

When they were all inside, Lizzie, who now was as upset as she had been calm, bolted the door. Caleb stood in front of the fireplace turning the arrow in his hands.

"Burn it," Lizzie begged. "Burn it. Break it in two and throw it in the fire."

"No, I ain't going to do that, Lizzie. I'm going to keep it. In the first place, nothing but the wood and the feathers would burn. The killing part will last after all of us and this house, too, have gone to dust. In the second place, it was sent to us by a friend."

"It was sent to us by an Indian, wasn't it?"

"I judge so. But he sent it as a warning."

"What makes you think that?"

"There's no other way to think. Indians never been ones to sit back and watch their women and children shot down. If ever there was an eye-for-an-eye people, they're the ones. And they don't warn you before they take their revenge. Somewhere there's a friend saying, 'Look out.' "

"Who, Papa?" Hannah asked.

"I don't know, Hannay." Caleb put the arrow on the mantelpiece with the pewter candlesticks, the daguerreotypes of Lizzie's father and mother, and the picture little Caleb had drawn the week before he died. Lizzie would as soon have a stuffed copperhead coiled there, no longer dangerous but too remindful of past threats to be pretty.

"I just don't know who, Hannay," Caleb repeated. "I just don't know. I know somebody thinks we're in danger and has warned us. Considering what's been done, that's more than we've got any right to expect."

"We didn't do anything."

"We're part and parcel, as far as Indians are concerned, of the murders at the sugar camp."

"Murders," Hannah repeated, shocked. "Is killing an Indian murder?"

"If all he's doing is boiling a pot of maple sap, I don't know what other word fits."

Lizzie knew where this kind of talk would take Caleb with their neighbors. They'd forgive Caleb a lot because he was a preacher and had, because of his calling, to swallow whole such commands as "Thou shalt not kill" and "All men are brothers." They expected that kind of talk from their preacher on Sundays; but after Sunday was over they wouldn't cotton to his calling them murderers because they had sent a few redskins to their happy hunting ground. They'd call him Indian lover, and worse. Say he was on the side of men who had scalped and burned his own kind — and ought to grow a scalp lock and start eating roast dog. But Caleb knew this as well as she did — and she wasn't a woman to try to put words in her husband's mouth.

It was still storming after they'd had an hour's rest and a bowl of hot bean-and-venison soup: snow, sleet, rain, hail, everything that can come down from heaven but tadpoles and spiders. Nothing violent, but constant, cold, and wet.

"It's not going to let up," Caleb said. "Now's as good a time as any to go."

"Go where, Caleb?" Lizzie asked. She thought the burying trip was expedition enough for one day.

"Tell the neighbors. Let them know the bodies were taken. Let them know somebody warned us there'd be trouble. I can't do less for them than that fellow did for us."

Caleb picked up the arrow and turned it over and over in his hands like a letter he'd read once, but whose meaning required a second scanning.

"Put that down, Caleb," Lizzie said sharply. She'd as lief see him fondle a scalp.

Caleb did so. "Ben, you take Acorn and let everyone on the east side of the creek know what's happened. I'll go up the west side."

"What am I supposed to say?"

"Not a thing but that the bodies are gone. And that someone put an arrow in our door."

"Then what?"

"Then, nothing. Get home. If the weather turns worse, if a blizzard blows up or it starts snowing hard, stay wherever you are."

"When'll you be back, Caleb?"

"When everyone is told. Before nightfall."

"Is there danger?"

"I wouldn't be leaving you if I thought there was. Not now, anyway. Once the news gets north, there may be all hell to pay."

"And you won't blame the neighbors?"

"I never said that."

"Saying it to the neighbors won't help anyone."

"Lizzie, if I'd never said anything except what'd please the neighbors, I'd be tongued-tied by now."

"One day's trying won't strike you dumb," Lizzie said, but knew the advice was useless.

Ben was home an hour before his father. He'd followed orders, delivered the news, then sent Acorn home through a clattering spring thunderstorm at a pace that the old stud didn't know he still possessed.

Caleb, though later than Ben, kept his word. He was home before candlelighting time. After an early supper, Caleb shooed the children up to their beds in the loft.

"I want to talk to your mother," he told them. "You've both had a big day. Now, scat."

He didn't himself go to bed that night. Oh, he took off his outer clothes and stretched out now and then beside Lizzie, who had her nightdress on and was under the covers. But for the most part he stood in front of the fire, which he kept burning with a daytime brightness, and rehearsed what had happened and what he thought he should do. After he knew what he thought, he was accustomed to weigh his conclusions against Lizzie's convictions.

Lizzie was no "As my husband says" woman. He listened to her, knowing that.

So when Lizzie disagreed with him, her convictions had to be strong. So far she had listened with only a question or two about what he had said.

"The Brewsters," he told her, "are already packing to move into Pendleton until this blows over."

"There's no blockhouse there."

"No, but Pendleton's twenty miles southeast, and that much nearer other settlements. And there're two hundred people there instead of twenty. Of course, the Bensons and the Woods say that arrow wasn't a warning of any kind. Just somebody trying to throw a scare into us."

"Why us instead of them?"

"That didn't come up. I reckon they think we scare easier'n them."

The wind rose and there was a letup in the sleet. No wind could shake a house built of logs, but it could find breaks in the chinking. Fingers of iciness reached into the room. The wind whine got louder. Caleb put two more logs on the fire.

"Didn't winter ever enter our head when we come north?" Caleb asked.

Lizzie couldn't be turned aside by questions like that. "Don't it enter their heads that what they did may stir up the tribes to the north?"

"If it does, they don't let it be known. To hear them talk, they think what they done was just the warning needed to persuade the redskins to keep their distance."

"Weren't they grateful to you and Ben for riding out in this storm to tell them the bodies had been taken?"

"Nobody's grateful for bad news."

"Even if the news might save their lives?"

"Nobody except the Brewsters think it could come to that. Or've got sense enough to understand what Indians on the warpath can do. They're all so used to these peaceful sugar-camp, calico-buying folks. They think a handful of trinkets and a jugful of rum would settle things."

The word "trinket" reminded Lizzie of something. "Hannah told me about Clasby. Did Benson do anything like that?"

"Steal, you mean?"

Lizzie nodded.

"I saw a few things at their place I never seen there before."

"Did you say anything?"

"By the grace of God, I kept my mouth shut."

Caleb, in his sock feet, walked noiselessly back and forth in front of the fire. The wind died down and the room was filled with the soft owl-feather swish of falling snow. Lizzie dozed off. Caleb stretched out beside her for a while.

Lizzie woke somewhere near her usual time — before daylight. Caleb was up, dressed, and had a kettle boiling and cold sliced mush frying in the three-legged spider.

Lizzie, wondering how she could oversleep at a time like this, threw off the covers and pulled on her wrapper. "What time is it, Caleb?"

"Four."

"No need to be up so early on a day like this. What can you do?"

"I've thought about it all night, Lizzie. I'm going to Piqua."

"Piqua? That's two hundred miles."

"That's where the Indian agent is."

"Colonel Johnston? What can he do?"

"I don't know. But if Brewster's right, Johnston's likely the only man who can head the Indians off if they're thinking of making a sweep down here."

"Why don't you wait 'til you can get the advice of the neighbors?"

"I know what their advice would be. 'Stay home.' I intend to go. It may be a fool's errand. The Indians up north may not have any notion of coming down here for the sake of a passel of Senecas and Miamis they never laid their eyes on. In that case I'll have made my ride for nothing. On the other hand, they may be painting their faces this very hour. They may limber up their tomahawks on Johnston's skull first of all if he tries to stop them. But if they've got thoughts of coming down here, Johnston's the one man who has a chance of talking them out of it. I can't sit home here and gamble that ain't the case."

"Wait 'til the weather moderates," Lizzie urged.

"That's the one thing I can't do. It'll

take some time for the Indians to get a band together for an attack. If that's what they plan, they'll wait for better weather. And I won't."

" 'Bout as well stay home and be scalped as go out and die in a snowbank."

Caleb laughed and didn't know why. "No, I'd choose the snowbank any day — and take you with me, if I thought that was the choice. But I'll tell you something, Lizzie. I ain't got no choice about making this ride. And I'm not intended for snowbanks, nor you for scalping. We're going to have to tough it out along more everyday lines."

The fried mush was overfried and the sassafras tea had steeped too long. Lizzie couldn't swallow a bite, and Caleb didn't want to. He filled himself full anyway. He wasn't going to fizzle out for lack of fuel.

When he had finished he said, "I'm going up and have a few words with Hannah."

Hannah, at the sound of her name, was awake. Caleb sat down on the edge of her bed and kept his voice low. No use rousing up Ben.

"Hannah, I'm going to ride to Piqua to tell the Indian agent there what happened. I don't know just how long I'll be away. I wouldn't go if I thought there'd be trouble here."

"Trouble?" Hannah whispered.

"Indians. If there is, if you get enough warning, get your mother and Ben into Pendleton. If there's no warning, give up. Don't fight. You wouldn't stand a chance anyway.

"I'd rather die fighting than just die."

"You and Ben are young enough, if you don't fight, they'll likely adopt you."

"Make a squaw out of me?"

"Yes."

"Marry me to some Indian?"

"There's been more than one child adopted by the Indians who wouldn't go back to their families when they had a chance. Indian ways wouldn't come too hard for you."

"Maybe not," Hannah said. "Maybe I'm already part savage."

"Stop that kind of talk. You're a Christian girl. The Indians already worship a Great Spirit. Maybe it's God's plan for you to teach them who that Great Spirit is."

"If we don't fight, what's to become of Mama?"

Caleb didn't answer.

Hannah said, "They'll kill her, won't they?"

"They'll kill all of you if you try fighting. Burn you alive in this house. None of this is likely to happen, Hannah. I wouldn't be leaving if I thought it would. I told you because I trust your good sense."

"I don't know's I've got much, Papa."

"You've got enough to know that what I've told you's true, don't you?"

"Yes."

Hannah followed her father down the ladder. There, with Lizzie, they knelt before the fire, and Caleb prayed. "May the Lord watch between me and thee while we are absent one from the other," he ended the prayer. Then he folded Lizzie in his arms, kissed her, and talked to her in a voice so low Hannah couldn't hear what he said.

He kissed Hannah, called her "Hannay," as he did on special occasions, and gave her a hearty handshake. "Ben's too young and your mother's too ladylike for the job, so I appoint you man of the house while I'm gone."

Hannah wanted to cry, but the appointment she'd just received made that out of the question. She and her mother stood tearless in the doorway as Caleb rode south, gray in the first gray light, his chin low on his chest against the heavy sleet.

About ten o'clock there was a heavy rapping on the door. Hannah's first instinct was to grab the gun her father had left for Ben's use and start shooting. She felt ashamed of the way she had kept her father's trust when she heard George Benson's unmistakable shout. "You home, Mrs. Cape?"

"We're home," Hannah answered. "Mama's coming." She opened the door herself, thankful she hadn't riddled a neighbor with squirrel shot.

Jess Abernathy, a tall man, part Indian himself, people said, who lived a mile or so beyond the Bensons, was with

George. He was farther away from the settlement than anyone else; for this reason, or maybe because he wasn't a believer, he and his family never came to church.

Lizzie, who had felt dauncy all morning after the wakeful night and Caleb's early departure, was back in the corner half hidden by the bed curtains, finally getting into her day clothes. She didn't come out 'til firmly buttoned and neatly combed. The men, wet from the icy drizzle, stood steaming in front of the fire, turning first backside, then frontside to the heat.

"Mrs. Cape," Benson said, his voice cracking a little, "where's Cale?"

"I don't know."

"Do you know where he's headed?"

"Yes."

"To Piqua?"

"Yes."

Benson turned to Abernathy. "You were right. Why would he tell you and not me?"

"He knew you'd raise a ruckus."

"You're not backing him, are you?"

"I'm here, ain't I?"

"My husband is going to Piqua at the

141

risk of his own life to see if the agent there will quiet the Indians. He told you what happened, didn't he?'' Lizzie asked.

For so big a man, Benson was very light on his feet. He pranced. He gave the table a slap Lizzie knew he would rather have given her husband.

''The agent! The agent! Whose side is Cale Cape on? All any of them agents been doing lately has been babying the Indians. But that man Johnston in Piqua outdoes them all. He carries them around on a hand-carved chip. We got to pay for our land. Not the Indians. They get it free. While we're clearing the land and putting in crops, they hunt and fish. We get what's left over. All they got to do is whine, 'Oh, Great White Father, help us.' And the Great White Father takes money out of the till we put there and says, 'Oh, noble red brother, thank you for asking.'

''What do we get free from the government? Not a cent. They're all minted special for red brother. I tell you, you got to be the right color nowadays if you want to be heard.

''And now Cale runs off to this Indian

142

lover to get help. What this Johnston will do is to get us forbidden to drop a hook in Fall Creek or trap a muskrat on its banks. You wait and see."

"Caleb's risking his own life in this weather to try to save your life," Lizzie said sternly.

Benson snorted. "There was no call for Cale to be so allfired unselfish. Preachers would be better off to stay home and pray. Not ride off, mixing in what they don't understand and stirring up more trouble. Cale wasn't satisfied to leave matters in the Lord's hands. Oh, no. Cale wants a finger in everybody's pie himself, the Lord's included."

Hannah grabbed the heavy twig broom and swung it in a semicircle that caught Benson across the side of the head.

"What's going on here?" he shouted. "You lost your senses?"

"You get out of here, that's what, or I'll knock *you* senseless."

Benson made a move toward Hannah, but Abernathy took his arm. "You can't fight a girl, " he said. "The preacher's girl."

"She's no girl; she's a hellion. She's been prayed over too much and thrashed too little."

Hannah, using the broom as a battering ram, shoved Benson toward the door.

"You get out of my father's house before you say another word against him."

"I'll get out with pleasure. But I'm going to ride after your father and I'll bring him back before he ever lays eyes on Piqua and that Indian lover over there."

Hannah closed the door with a bang, then set the broom in its place by the hearth.

"He can't catch Oak. He knows that. He's just talking big," she reassured her mother.

6

Hannah was right. Abernathy talked Benson out of even trying to follow Caleb. "He'll never make it in this weather anyway."

Caleb made it; but not in the three or four days he had planned. Far later than his imagination might have stretched his delay, a matter of many weeks, Caleb entered Johnston's office in Piqua. Johnston wasn't in. Caleb knew the agent by the color of his hair. The official behind Johnston's desk was a dark-haired, sallow-faced young fellow who looked as if he'd never been out from behind that desk. He was the man, Caleb supposed, who looked after the papers while Johnston was out along the rivers and in the forests looking after the Indians. That was what Caleb hoped. This clerk would never be able to hold his own in any Indian powwow.

There were only three chairs in the room — a chair with arms behind the desk and two straightbackers against the wall opposite it. Indians preferred the floor to chairs. The young clerk leaped to push a chair toward Caleb, thinking maybe that a tattered woodsie like Caleb might never have seen such a contraption before.

"Have a seat, sir. You look pretty peaked."

"I been sick," Caleb said. "I still feel like I been pulled through a knothole."

"Got the shakes?"

"I shook some. What I had, though, was the grippe. I set out in a storm from the Fall Creek settlement."

"How near's that to Pendleton?"

"Twenty miles north. More or less."

"That's where the trouble is."

"What trouble?"

"Haven't you heard?"

"I haven't. I left home in a snowstorm to see Johnston. I came down with what I thought was the grippe but what turned out to be lung fever. I'd of died except for a family outside Winchester who took me in and dosed me and nursed me. I was in and out of my head. I thought I was there two weeks. They said three. Might've been four weeks, they were so set on making out I hadn't been a burden to them."

"Wasn't a mite less than four weeks," the clerk said. "Maybe more. There's been more than Indians killed now."

"Where?" Caleb whispered. "Where? Not at Fall Creek?"

146

"No, no, Fifty, sixty miles north of there. You from the Fall Creek settlement?"

"I told you so. Anyway I thought I did. I started on this trip to tell Johnston that nine Indians had been killed at a sugar camp there."

"We got that news right after it happened."

"How could you do that?"

"Indian friend of Johnston's, Black Antler, sent a runner."

"What did Black Antler want?"

"Same as you, I reckon. Get Johnston to smooth down the Indians up north."

"Can he do it?"

"If he's there, he can. But the news of the killings beat him there. The tribes up north, when they heard what happened, burned a couple of homesteads and killed everybody in and around them."

"That's what I want to stop. That's what I came here for."

"You couldn't have done any more good than Black Antler. And Johnston himself didn't have power to quiet the tribes 'til the government promised that the men who murdered the Indians would be tried and punished exactly the same as if they'd murdered white men."

"Murdered," Caleb repeated. "Murdered." He remembered Hannah's shock when he had labeled the killings murder.

"What else is there to call it?"

"I never heard folks call it that before. A white man's killing an Indian."

"What you heard — or didn't hear — don't change facts, do they?"

"No. What I heard or didn't don't have any bearing on the facts. But it's got bearing on the way I feel hearing it now."

"You'll likely hear it more often from now on."

"Who is making this promise that there'll be a trial? Governor Ray?"

"You folks up there in the woods don't really know our governor very good, do you?"

"We helped elect him."

"Well, the governor knows that, all right. He's figured that out without help. You woodsies vote. The Indians don't vote. Governor Ray is not about to call voters 'murderers,' or take any risk of losing a voter at the end of a rope. No siree, Bob. Our governor knows which side his votes are buttered on.''

Caleb was beginning to think this clerk might not be such a bad man at a powwow after all. He had a tongue limber as any Indian's — and maybe an Indian's staying power.

''If it's not the governor who's making the Indians these promises, then who is?''

''Say, how long did you say you'd been sick? The United States government, that's who. Calhoun, the Secretary of War. Calhoun ain't a man to dally.''

''Washington's a thousand miles away.''

''An Indian runner can make a hundred miles a day. And the Bureau of Indian Affairs is in touch with Indians who got a personal interest in seeing those killers tried. The promise that there'll be a hanging if the men who killed their women and children are found guilty put wings on their feet.''

''The Indians have heard a lot of promises.''

''They'll believe Johnston. He's never

149

broke his word to them yet. When he says these men are going to be tried, they'll believe him."

"They may believe him — but how's Johnston going to do it? He can't go down to Fall Creek singlehanded and set up court and start trying people."

"Don't you think Calhoun knows this? He's already sent word out to track down the murderers. The burnings and killings up north wasn't wasted on the folks where you come from. Better a few men in jail for what was done than the whole settlement wiped out by a bunch of whooping painted savages. Captain Berry didn't have the least trouble getting the accused to jail."

"Jail! We ain't got a jail."

"You got one now. Or Pendleton has. They built one on purpose."

"Who's in it?"

"Their names? I don't know. But it's occupied, and the accused are awaiting trial as soon as the circuit court meets there."

"Those men don't have money to hire lawyers."

"Calhoun knows that. The Indian Bureau knows it. Seven thousand dollars have been set aside for this. Three of the best lawyers from Ohio state are on their way to Pendleton right now. The regular state prosecutors will handle the case against the murderers."

"They ain't murderers 'til they've been proved murderers."

"What'd you make this trip here for?"

"To report some killings."

"Well, we're now acting on the report you were going to make."

The contents of Caleb's stomach started roiling about. It was a sunny day, but cold, and the stove that kept the end of the room by the desk warm didn't do much for the spot where Caleb was. He was sweating as much as though hoeing corn in July. He could feel the drops run down his sides and stop where his britches belt caught them. He'd soon be in a puddle from the waist up. He hadn't come here to get his neighbors thrown into jail and accused of murder. He'd come to save bloodshed, not cause it.

"You feeling all right, mister?"

151

"No," Caleb said. "I think I've had a setback of some kind. I feel dauncy." He sat down heavily. "I was aiming to start home this afternoon. I think I'd better plan to lay over a day or two. Is there a good boarding place in town?"

"Mrs. Holland's the best. You might have to share a bed."

"My cough'll scare off bedmates."

He leaned forward with his head in his hands, trying to strangle the fit of coughing he felt coming on.

"Has any white man ever been convicted of murder for killing an Indian?" he asked finally.

"Not to my knowledge."

"But that's what Johnston's up there telling the Indians? White men will be tried for murder?"

"Yes."

"And if guilty?"

"You're sick, Mr. Cape. You know what happens when a court finds a man guilty of murder."

"These Ohio state lawyers? The defense?"

"I told you. The best. Calhoun's no Ray,

vote-hungry. But he don't want it said that these whites were found guilty as a sop to the Indians."

Caleb stood, but there were no floor boards beneath his feet. He was standing on air. He sat down quickly. The chair was made of air, too. He couldn't feel it. He was floating above the chair, about to float right off in a heap onto the floor that had melted away.

The clerk's hard hands, thumbs like real thumbscrews, bored into his shoulders. The chair firmed up under him.

Caleb looked up at the man supporting him.

"Do I know your name?"

"Hardesty, Jacob Hardesty."

"Thank you, Mr. Hardesty. I was weaker than I thought."

"Mr. Johnston keeps some Kentucky corn here. A glass might do you good."

Caleb nodded. "I need something."

Hardesty brought him a brimming shot glass. "You ain't joining me?" Caleb asked.

"I don't drink. My body is the temple of the Lord."

"Mine, too," Caleb said, "but the Lord wouldn't care for a temple as shaky as mine. It needs building up."

The drink did its work. He could feel the floor under his feet and the chair under his bottom again.

"I don't drink, Hardesty," he said, "except for medicine. I'm a preacher. I don't want to set you a bad example."

"Nothing sets me a better example than a drunk. You all right, now?"

"I think I can walk. I don't know what to think about what I just heard. I rode down here to get Johnston to stop the Indians from raiding the settlement. What I've done is to get my neighbors thrown in jail for murder."

"You didn't do that. Black Antler and Mr. Calhoun did that."

"Who got here first ain't going to cut much ice with men in prison accused of murder."

"A preacher's got to take a stand for the right. Ain't he?"

"He ought to," Caleb agreed.

He ought to, he surely ought to, he thought. The man who killed a man ought to be hanged. He had never doubted that. But wispy old John Wood, henpecked in life and hung up by his chicken neck to die? The Wood boy, who had no notion of right or wrong outside a book? Benson, big ox of a fellow who needed somebody saying gee-haw and whoa to him if he was to be kept on any straight path? Hang them? Praying churchgoers? And he the one, no matter who got there first, who went to Piqua to carry the news to Johnston. What was he? Some kind of a Judas?

He asked Hardesty, who seemed to have an answer to everything, the answer to that.

"What would you do if you was in my shoes?"

Hardesty didn't have to think twice about that. "Move my family back to Cincinnati."

"We're only a hundred miles away from there now. What's a hundred miles?"

"Going some directions, nothing. Going your direction, north and west, a hundred miles is a long time. We went through all you're going through years ago."

"A man's got a right to push on. To live where he wants to."

"You go home and tell your neighbors that, then."

Caleb took his first good look at Hardesty. He had a face as smooth as a pebble at the bottom of the falls on the creek. Fifty years ago was a story long past to him. Why anybody would ever want to live *that* story over again was something Hardesty would never understand.

Book Two   THE TRIAL

7

Hardesty was not exaggerating when he told Caleb that the federal government was supplying the accused men with superior counsel. Up from Ohio to Pendleton came Patrick Conroy, Noah Beazley, Isaac Vickers, and Charles Fort. All were accomplished and experienced: able, eloquent, and capable of taking a jury's mind off the facts of the Indian killings under consideration by powerful reminders of past Indian atrocities. They were lawyers, and lawyers with every intention of winning a decision for their clients. They were also men of a city called "Queen of the River," a substantial community that had earned its stability, they believed, by conquering the Indian population. This little settlement of Pendleton, lost in the forests, hanging on by its teeth amidst bands of roving red men, would never be safe until it had done the same. If they could help it, no white man was going to be hanged for trying to protect Pendleton in the same way their own forebears had protected Cincinnati.

These men had on their tongues' tip accounts of massacres of whites by Indians that would make this little sugar-camp fracas look like what it was, no more than a backwoods frolic. Before any jury decided the fate of these patriots, they would have to listen to a little history.

Before the Ohio lawyers were through with them, the jury would hear the story of Daniel Boone and Simon Kenton. They would be told of the battle of Blue Licks and Bryant's Station; they would hear about the blood shed there by white men, scalped, mutilated, mangled, by reds. They would be asked to remember the defeats of Braddock, St. Clair, and Hamar.

The federal government had one paramount purpose: it had no intention of giving the Indians who would attend the trial the impression that this was a powwow called to belittle the red man. The defense lawyers were well known. They had to be. But the prosecution lawyers were famous.

Heading *them* was General James Noble, former soldier and Indian fighter and now a United States senator. The Secretary of War had given him permission, and money, to fee an assistant. Noble had chosen his own son-in-law, Abel Trask, a young lawyer with the reputation of being able to charm the rings off a raccoon's tail.

Jonathan Armitage, the state's attorney, had also been given an assistant, Oscar Achilles Dilk, a black-haired, bullet-headed young man with a mind like a bear trap and a jaw the shape of a Shawnee's battle-axe. Dilk was obviously headed for the Senate. And barring slip-ups, the Presidency itself might be just around the corner.

The Indian agent, Colonel Johnston, would be present during the entire trial. He would see that witnesses showed up when needed and that their fees were paid. He had also been instructed to have

Indian chiefs and lesser chiefs, the Mingos, present when possible to observe the trial and send the news back to the tribes: "White men are being tried for murder for killing Indians. It is a fair trial. If found guilty, they'll be hanged."

Charlie Fort, the youngest of the defense lawyers, twenty-four on the twenty-fourth of December (he thought this signified something) of 1823, had drawn the best lodging in town. Drawn, he knew, was not the right word. There was no lottery, no choosing by means of long and short straws. He had been offered, by the widow Culligan, the loft room in her Pendleton home. She had ignored the general; ignored Patrick Conroy, originally, like herself, from the old sod; given Noah Beazley, the very picture of a dark and handsome city lawyer, the go-by. She had offered the room to Charlie because, she told him, "You look like my late son."

Charlie was accustomed to having lonesome widows tell him that he reminded them of their late husbands.

Reminding a widow of her late son was more to his liking. He moved into the widow's loft room at once, without wasting time or pity on his fellow lawyers. They, the general among them, were piled two in a bed in less commodious lodgings. The feathers of the ticking and comforters he slept between smelled sweet and fresh. Some heat spilled into the room from the fireplace chimney that took up one end of the loft. He had that frontier luxury a looking glass — spotted, to be sure, like a pond with lily pads — but between the spots he could see his own face.

He doubted he looked like the late son. "Charles Fort," he had been told, "you're an oddity." Not a mud-fence, ugly oddity. Kisses had told him that. But no one else's spit and image, for sure.

He was dish-faced, with a head of fine black hair that a brisk wind parted to show a blue-white scalp. His eyes, big, round, and set shallow in his head, were the color of water in a rain barrel, neither blue nor gray. His nose didn't have much of a bridge, but it made up for the lack at the top by flaring out into race-horse nostrils at the bottom. He bared his teeth to the glass. Nothing lacking there. He could bite with a beaver. He was longheaded and a trifle lantern-jawed, but his long head was set on a stud-horse neck, a neck broad as his face at the cheekbones. The looking glass didn't show him below the Adam's apple, but he knew what was there: a body wide-shouldered, spare in the short ribs and waist, and supported by thighs heavy and meaty, like his neck.

"I'm no Adonis," Charlie admitted to himself. But who needed looks when he had luck? He got good horses at livery stables, helpings from the first serving at boardinghouses, and whiskey from the bottle hidden behind the front row of bottles at taverns.

The Secretary of War himself, or at least the general, had asked that he come to Pendleton on this historic case. The widow offered him her spare room because he, with a face like no one else's, looked like her son. When his family had been killed by Indians as they were moving from Kentucky to Ohio, he, the sole survivor, age two, had been found, carried into Cincinnati, and adopted there by the man he thought of as father, Enoch Leverett. Leverett had sent him east to Harvard, where the bright Yankee boys went, planning for him to take over the Leverett newspaper, the *Western Spy,* when he graduated. In spite of himself, Charlie turned out to be a lawyer. A newspaper writer has to tone things down; Charlie had watched Leverett do this for years. A lawyer could tear the rag off the bush, could tell the jury facts that would lose an editor every subscriber he had. Charlie's mouth wasn't gentled enough for newspaper work. Leverett recognized that and so made use of what Charlie *could* do: send him facts that he could cut, dress up, water down, add to, until they were fit for print.

Beneath the spotted looking glass, when Charlie had moved into the room, was a deal table holding washbowl, pitcher, soap dish, and drinking glass. The room had no washstand. The chamberpot was under the bed. Charlie took all this paraphernalia from the table, moved the table under the loft's one window, and had himself a desk. He brought a rush-bottomed chair upstairs, put his paper, newly sharpened quill, and newly mixed ink on the table, and sat down to write Enoch Leverett what he had promised, a report of this outlandish place and of this outrageous trial.

He knew the *Western Spy* wasn't interested in how Charlie Fort was making out amongst the woodies and redskins. He didn't begin his writing with "Dear Pa." That would lead him into a request for new shaving soap and an account of a red-headed girl he had seen who made him want to follow her into the green gloom of the unending stands of trees the way men run after fox fire in a swamp.

He wrote in what he considered a newspaper style, but for a newspaper whose sole reader was Enoch Leverett. He said Pendleton had a population of two hundred souls, not people. That was newspaper lingo. But he couldn't bring himself to substitute "we" for "I." "We saw." What other pair of eyes saw what he saw? No, he wasn't much of a reporter.

Extracts from a letter by Charles Fort to Enoch Leverett:

Pendleton is a town of two hundred souls. I made the mistake when I first arrived here of calling Pendleton a settlement. The Pendletonians wasted no time setting me right on that score.

A settlement is a place like Fall Creek, twenty miles upriver — no stores, streets, or taverns there. Pendleton is a town. My idea of a town naturally is Cincinnati. Two theaters, three thousand books in our library, board walks, street lights. I doubt if half a dozen books could be scared up in this entire settlement. Excuse me, I mean town. Excluding, of course, the Good Book. They own that, even if they don't always follow it — as the recent murders prove.

On my first day here I was told that I was expected at midday to take dinner with Judge Giddings. Three judges sit here: a presiding judge appointed by the state legislature, and two elected associate judges who are local. The presiding judge is Amos McGowan. Giddings, a man much respected here, is one of the associate judges, as is Omer Oursley, the town blacksmith. Oursley ironed the prisoners after they all climbed over the walls of the prison stockade on the first night of their incarceration. Nobody here, including the prisoners, takes this trial very seriously. They look at it as a kind of play-party tableau to impress the Indians. Wait until that Indian agent Johnston gets through with them. He intends another kind of party. Oursley appears to be a good man with hammer and tongs, but he can't read or write.

Ezra Fenton, the clerk of the court, can, they say, write his own name. He is a justice of the peace and won his election to this post by declaring, "I have been sued on every section of the statute and know all about the law, while the man running against me has never been sued for anything whatsoever and knows nothing about the statute." This made sense to the citizens of this town and they elected him. Knowledge is knowledge no matter how you come by it, they figure.

Samuel Brady, the sheriff, in buckskins, moccasins, and with a side knife the size of a pigsticker, is a sight to scare wrongdoers without ever hearing the sound of his voice; a sound they say can be heard as far north as the Lakes and as far south as the falls of the Ohio.

Brady, being bigger than most men, would be an awesome sight in his underdrawers without the knife. He is actually no different from the rest of the men here in what he wears, in the size of his side knife or his lack of shoes. Every man, woman, and child here is in moccasins. I have yet to see my first pair of shoes. They look at me as I go clip-clopping along in my brogans as if I was half horse, and had been shod by Oursley himself.

I am here, however, to report the trial to you, not to take up your time describing a way of life we outgrew some years ago. But the truth is, I don't feel much different here on Fall Creek than I would on the banks of the Congo. As Pendleton now is, we once were. But as a grown man forgets the time he crawled and hung to his mother's skirts, so we in the civilized city of Cincinnati forget how we lived when the town was first settled. Infancy, judging by Pendleton, is a state to outgrow as fast as possible.

Judge Giddings invited me to dinner; it was not an invitation to be turned down lightly. It wasn't issued out of any concern for my comfort, but because it is felt to be a duty of visiting lawyers and the like — if there is a like — to provide some entertainment for a populace starved for something lighter than murder, Indian abduction, ague, and death by snakebite.

Play party or not, trials here are attended by as many as three hundred people. Lately, I am told, a lawyer from out of state asked permission of the presiding judge in a polite but somewhat lengthy way to "plead his case."

"Plead, plead," the judge ordered him testily. "For what other reason do you think three hundred people have gathered here except to hear you lawyers orate? Get on with it." The rebuked lawyer did, for three hours, and the woodsies listened to him spiel the way we would have listened to Patrick Henry declaim.

I was glad to find that I wasn't going to have to carry the burden of entertaining Judge Giddings alone. Also present for dinner were Jonathan Armitage, the circuit prosecutor, and a friend of his, Dan McGowan, brother of the presiding judge. Giddings, after Armitage had declined, asked the blessing. A very large nicely browned goose was then placed on the table; it was well stuffed, as we discovered, with a dressing of tasty bread and onions.

Dan McGowan, after *his* first bite, said by way of compliment, "Judge, this is a damned fine goose."

Giddings, to my astonishment, replied, "Yes, it is a fine goose and you are fined a dollar for swearing."

It seems that in the town of Pendleton there is a statute imposing a fine of one dollar on any person who should "profanely curse, swear, or damn." My God, I'm glad I didn't open my mouth about that goose, which *was* damned fine.

After McGowan's profanity and Giddings's fine, not another word was said during the entire meal. Armitage and his friend McGowan could scarcely swallow for rage. The judge and I chomped away without interruption.

When we finally pushed back our chairs, the judge said, "Squire McGowan, pay me a dollar."

I was beginning to get some idea of the kind of man I was going to have to plead my case before. Invite a man to dinner and fine him a dollar for complimenting your goose!

Squire McGowan, from Indianapolis, no mean town itself, to hear him tell it, said, "I haven't a cent with me, Judge."

"Perhaps your friend Armitage will loan it to you," Giddings said, accepting no excuse.

Armitage said, "I have barely enough to pay my tavern bill, Judge."

I had the money but I thought, It isn't my goose that's being cooked. Let these Hoosier friends and lawyers fight it out among themselves.

Judge Giddings asked, "What's to be done?"

"Loan him the money, Judge, and take his note. Or bind him over to court," suggested Armitage.

"If I bind him over, will you go his security?"

"The law forbids lawyers going security for anyone, Judge. But you can go security yourself," Armitage reminded Giddings. "Just draw the recognizance saying Daniel McGowan and Henry Giddings appeared before Henry Giddings, Associate Judge of the Madison Circuit Court, and acknowleged themselves indebted to the state in the penalty of twenty-five dollars each, for the appearance of Daniel McGowan at the next term of court, to answer."

Now *I'll* be damned, fine me or not, if this preposterous idea wasn't accepted. the paper was drawn up and signed. Thus ended my first dinner party in the town of Pendleton. I left thanking Judge Giddings for his goose, which I was careful to call "tasty"; though in truth, as McGowan had said earlier, it was damned fine.

After the dinner I went over to talk with my clients, whom I hadn't yet seen. This town had had no jail and no courthouse until what they have been calling "the massacre" took place. The citizens here are accustomed to throwing up buildings on short order out of necessity. They arrive, bag and baggage, with no roof over their heads until they raise one. They have learned to get one up fast if not fancy.

This jail, though more substantial, is about on the order of what a Buckeye would call a farrowing pen. It is square, built of heavy beech and sugar-tree logs notched down carefully and fitting tight above, below, and on the sides. The place has one door and no window. Until the escape of all the prisoners soon after they were brought over from the settlement, there was no stockade. Now a stockade manned by guards day and night surrounds the prison. The guards are paid by the Indian Bureau and have a daily ration of meal for corn pone and liquid corn for drinking.

I was let into the stockade and through

172

it into the jail room itself. It is, as I said, no better than a shed for animals. No furniture, straw on the floor; a bucket in a corner for an outhouse. The men themselves, though heavily ironed and in such disagreeable surroundings, were in good spirits. Old Wood, sitting on the floor, was reading his Bible. Young Wood was reading a novel, obtained God knows where. The guards let them crack the door enough to get a sliver of light for reading. No one, ironed as these men were, was going anyplace if the door was wide open. But the nonreaders objected to an opening wide enough to let the wind whistle in.

I introduced myself as one of the lawyers come to defend them. They were not at all happy to see me. They were not much fazed by being accused of murder. Mad, yes, that their neighbors, gone chickenhearted about the possibility of Indian revenge, had helped round them up and bring them to jail. But not fazed. They were more taken aback because the very Indian Bureau they all hated took these charges seriously enough to provide them with defenders like myself. Anybody can be accused of anything. But to have the Indian Bureau take these accusations seriously enough to provide defense lawyers galled them inordinately.

Benson, clanking like a gristmill, strode about bellowing at me. "Get me out of here," he demanded. "What's this country come to? Lock a man up for shooting a redskin? Where would we all be if our fathers and grandfathers had been too thin-skinned to do that? Bones, is what. Skulls without hair. Or driven back into the sea. There wouldn't be a white man alive in the U.S.A. today if we hadn't fought them red devils. My father and your father was praised for what I done. And now you lock me up. Iron me like a mad bull."

I tried to calm him down, or at least to quiet him down. "Mr. Benson, I didn't lock you up. I'm not disagreeing with a word you say. I'm here to get you out of here just as soon as possible. There'll likely have to be a trial. Colonel Johnston and Secretary Calhoun have promised the Indians that if they hold off from attacking the settlers, the men who were responsible for the massacre — that's what they're calling it — will be tried just as if they'd killed white men."

"If I'd killed a white man, I'd expect to be more than tried — I'd expect to be strung up."

"There have been white men killed — justifiably. That's one reason I'm here. Undoubtedly there was some reason, some reason a jury will understand, for your shooting those Indians."

"The jury will understand why I did it. Just one word from you."

"And that word?"

"Indians. And the Indian Bureau didn't need to go all the way to Ohio to find a man to say it."

"Those tribes up north aren't going to swallow setting you free for a reason like that. They're all Indians, too, and they're clean against shooting a man because he's an Indian. Now if there was some act of aggression . . ."

"What d'you mean, 'act of aggression'?"

"If they shot at you first — or made you

think they were going to. If they stole your horse. Or made a run at you. Or taunted you. Or threatened you. Did anything like this precipitate the shooting?"

"Hell, no. They were a bunch of squaws and their brats. How could they threaten? Except breeding the way they do."

"So there was no reason for the shooting?"

Benson, in spite of the load of metal he was wearing, jumped a foot in the air and came down in the straw, raising a cloud of dust.

"There was reason. How many times do I have to tell you? Are you deaf? They were Indians. They were fishing in our streams; trapping everything with fur. Killing off the deer. Bleeding the maple trees. Pushing in right next to our homes. Asking our women for handouts. How'd those Indians up north like it if we started doing that? These are facts. And every man you can set on a jury knows it. The Indian Bureau taxes us, then wastes our money hiring men like you to come up to Madison County and tell us what we already know.''

George Benson was about like a boy who's picked windfalls in his neighbor's orchard all his life. . . . No, that's a bad example. He was like a man who's shot wolves all his life in the belief that he's protecting himself and his neighbors and who's suddenly told *wolves* must be protected — young and old, male and female — unless by chance the wolf has got his fangs at your throat. That's the way he'd been brought up and lived; and that's the way his father and grandfather had lived. And nothing Calhoun or Colonel Johnston could say was going to change him. Not overnight, anyway.

I decided there was no use wasting more breath at this point on Benson. Wood Sr. was deep in a nest of straw, as comfortable as a setting hen. He wasn't shaped anything like a hen, thin and brittle as a cornstalk after the first frost; but he was the gray and white of an old Plymouth Rock. He closed his Bible on his finger when I approached and said, ''Sorry I can't ask you to pull up a chair.''

He was the opposite of Benson: calm,

understanding, and seemingly not too put out to be sitting in a straw nest in a jailhouse. "We'll spend a week or two here 'til the whole thing blows over. After the burnings up north, I guess our neighbors didn't have much choice. In their shoes I'd of done the same thing, likely. Better for us to have a little spell of setting here than for them heathen to sweep down on our women and children."

"There's going to be a trial," I told him. "That's why I'm here."

"I never been in a trial, but I've seen more'n one and I'll know how to handle myself. You're the one appointed to get us off, ain't you? You just let me know what to say and you'll find me an apt pupil. I ain't as young as I was, but I've got all my wits about me still."

The boy reading the novel said something like, "Hrrumph."

"That's my son," the old man said. "John Wood, Jr. He thinks I lost my wits marrying again."

"Nothing wrong with marrying. It's who you marry," said the son.

"Reba's my problem, not yours."

"Well, there's one thing she can't say about me any more."

"That's a fact, and she knows it. Benson here says he couldn't have done better himself at the camp. And he told her so."

I wasn't interested in the home affairs of the Wood family.

"I heard down at the tavern that others besides you three ought to be here," I told Wood.

"Clasby, you mean? He's clear to Texas by now," said Wood.

"Was he the leader in this?"

"What d'you mean, 'leader'?" Benson, who had clanked over, asked.

"Did he put you up to it?"

"What do you mean, 'put us up to it'? We been fighting Indians all of our lives. We wouldn't be alive today if we hadn't. We're grown men, Counselor, we don't need anybody to put us up to anything."

Benson gave me strong thoughts about applying for a job with the prosecutor. If I hadn't already been feed to save his neck, the sight of Benson twitching at the end of a rope wouldn't give me too much pain.

I ignored Benson. "Mr. Wood, I heard down at the tavern that besides Clasby there was another man at the shooting. Is that right?"

Wood Sr. didn't get a chance to answer.

"If anybody else was there, let Calhoun and Johnston ferret them out," Benson said. "You got three of us here chained up like wild animals. Ain't that enough to satisfy the redskins and their guardian angels, the Indian Bureau?"

"I am hired by the Indian Bureau to defend you. I didn't ferret you out or chain you."

"I ain't done anything to be defended for."

"There was one other there," old Mr. Wood said. "A boy. And he didn't have a gun or take any part in it."

"He sure as hell didn't. For all the help he gave us, he could've been a redskin himself," Benson declared.

"Who was this boy?"

"Ben Cape. The preacher's son," Benson replied. "Nothing but a soft pile of guts. Never saw a preacher's son who wasn't either a hellion or a soft pile of guts. Don't know why, but a preacher's son . . ."

Wood Jr. said, "Shh," and Benson, who wouldn't bat an eye at old split-foot himself, said, "Well, speak of the devil!" Not the most courteous way to address your pastor, but Cale Cape, as Benson called him, had lived too long among these rough Indian killers to take offense.

"Well, George," said he, "your body may be in chains but your spirit, I see, is still free and soaring."

Caleb Cape had left Piqua before I passed through there, but I had heard about his ride to bring the news of the killings to Colonel Johnston. He must have known this wouldn't endear him to the killers — but there were more people to think about at the settlement than the killers. And in case of a raid from the north, none of the braves from up there was going to inquire as to who had done the bloody work at the sugar camp in order to spare them. If anything, Benson and the two Woods would be spared for special attention after the quick work was over. So they didn't have any reason to be mad at Cape. Besides, the Indian Black Antler had been the one to get the news to Colonel Johnston while Cape was laid up someplace with the grippe. Cape doesn't look much like our Ohio preachers, plumped up on chicken and dumplings and with a paunch to put a pretty curve on a watch chain. Cape is a tall, lean man. I can see some God-searching in his eyes, but there's a sardonic turn to his mouth that looks more like punning than praying to me.

Be that as it may, he said, "Mr. Fort, I understand. These men are members of my church. This is the Sabbath and they've been denied religious service. I've come over to read the Gospel and pray with them. You're welcome to stay if you've missed divine worship today yourself. Welcome, in any case."

I thanked him and said he'd likely prefer to be alone with his parishioners. What he preferred, I didn't care, but if I'd sized up Benson right, *I'd* prefer to be absent when *he* started praying and testifying.

"My daughter's waiting outside. The

guards didn't think the jail a place for a young girl. You might keep her company for a while."

He was right. The jail *wasn't* any place for her. Cape's daughter was the girl I had caught sight of earlier, the fox-fire girl. The place for her was out in the open, with plenty of cooling air for all. I said who I was and she said who she was. "Hannah Cape." What a name for a girl who flares up like a pine-knot torch on a dark night. Hannah Cape! Some slipshod backwoods slattern, from the name; and here she was fresh from Parnassus, neither backwoods nor frontwoods, but from that peak where gods and goddesses live. I just stared, and she wasn't abashed by staring. No stubbing her toe or chewing her sunbonnet strings. She stared back. Girl, I thought, you're hungry for kisses, and I'm the man who can supply you.

Pa, it has perhaps become apparent to you that you're not going to be able to print everything I write you. It has certainly become apparent to me that I can't write only what I think subscribers to the *Western Spy* crave in the way of reading matter. I've got to write what I feel as well as what I see and hear. Once I pick up my pen I can't resist putting myself and my feelings in the story. Now I know that I'm not important to the story. (If I succeed in winning the case, I may be.) The subscribers to the *Western Spy* don't give a tinker's dam whether Charlie Fort has or has not fallen in love. And as a matter of fact, Charlie Fort doesn't know himself.

So this is what you'll have to do: edit me. You're an editor, so you know how to do this. Every word I send you will be a fact. You don't have to worry on that score. No hearsay except when I label it so. No making the prosecution out to be blackguards and the defense angels of mercy. No failure to give the Indians their due. Also, I'll try, insofar as my poor pen is able, to give you a picture of this bleak (at this time of the year), outlandish, still tree-covered backwoods.

So with that warning: this girl, Hannah Cape. A lot of these backwoods girls are so bashful they throw their aprons over their faces when a strange man puts in an appearance. Not Hannah. She stood there ready to give me as good as she got. If I wanted to stare, she would stare back. It was a raw March day, darker and gloomier down here because of the woods. The sun comes up later and goes down earlier here. Hannah, with her red hair flamed like Midsummer Day. I know red hair, because so many ne'er-do-well drunken Irish are redheaded, isn't well thought of in Cincinnati. Well, see it here in the gloom and on the head of a milky-white six-foot girl with eyes put in with a sooty thumb, as they say. Hannah's hair is as bright as a sugar maple after it's turned in the fall.

I don't know how long the staring match went on. There wasn't a winner. I know that. No one gave up. The lawyer wasn't the first to find his tongue, either. I know that.

Hannah said, "Which side are you on?"

The correct answer to that would have been "I'm on the side of justice." And I am. But to Hannah that would sound pompous. With her, I wanted everything to be bedrock simple. "I'm one of the defense lawyers,'' I said.

''You're going to get these men off?''

''I'm going to try.''

She didn't say anything to that.

''Do you want them to be hanged?''

''No.''

''I don't think they should be, either.''

''The boy in there shouldn't be.''

''He your sweetheart?''

''He never kissed me or anything like that. He was just trying to be a man at the sugar camp.''

''That was a poor way.''

''His stepmother hounded him. Called him a weakling.''

''I had a stepmother.'' If she pitied boys with stepmothers, she had as well spread some of her tenderheartedness around.

''It didn't hurt *you* any, did it?''

''No.''

''I wish you'd talk to my brother.''

''He was there, too, wasn't he?''

''I know that.''

''Benson?''

I nodded yes.

''My brother's sick from not telling someone.''

"But he's told you?"

"Yes. He saw it all."

"He'll have to tell someone. They'll subpoena him, and he'll have to."

"What's subpoena?"

"Come to court and tell what you know or go to jail for refusing."

"There's something he's ashamed of."

"Everybody has something. Haven't you?"

I shouldn't have asked that. She dropped her head.

"I have, anyway. Most of us have. We're safe, though. We won't be subpoenaed."

I took her hand. I didn't want her to be ashamed of anything. She didn't jerk her hand away but let me fold it up in mine like a young kitten.

Kisses would have been next in order if her father hadn't come back at that minute.

"We're going to have a singing service now and we need your voice, Hannah. The guards say you can come in for that. Mr. Fort, won't you join us?"

My singing, as you know, sounds about

like a strangled bull-frog's; and my inclination at that moment was to put my best foot forward before Hannah. So I said I had other business — which was to get over here, write this, and think about Hannah.

End of extracts from a letter by Charles Fort to Enoch Leverett.

8

Lizzie Cape, having cleaned up after the turmoil of Sabbath worship and eating, sat in front of the fire with her tired feet on a footstool. The service for worship hadn't been very worshipful. If God had listened to that morning's praying, His head must be spinning. He had been asked to release the imprisoned; to restrain the Indian Bureau, punish the redskins for their killing and burning up north; to send Clasby back to make a full confession that the guilt was his alone; to bless Colonel Johnston in his efforts to appease the heathen; to protect them from attack; to have Colonel Johnston scalped; and the praying was divided about half and half to have Caleb Cape himself either blessed or shut up, once and for all.

A trial for killing an Indian was an unheard-of thing, even if this was just a mock trial to settle down the northern tribes. But, mock or not, George Benson was down there in jail, while Sarah Benson was left alone with her six children. That wasn't play-acting for her. Reba Wood probably could make out as well without her two men as with them. But that didn't make living in a straw-floored prison pen any easier for an old man like Wood Sr. Junior likely had a book and didn't know where he was. But apart from discomfort for the men and Sarah Benson's real misery, separated from her husband, there was something more terrible: loss of face. How could white men ever hold up their heads again, after being clapped into jail for killing an Indian? Instead of quieting the Indians down, wouldn't this embolden them?

Lizzie didn't know. She hadn't Caleb's faith. Or his high spirits, which made him feel, she believed, that even if God didn't help him he would be able to make out on his own. He and Hannah were over there praying and singing with the men in the Pendleton jail now. Caleb was a true Christian. He could do that after being berated by his own churchgoers this morning for making the ride to Piqua to tell Johnston what had happened.

Ben was out of his doldrums enough to do the evening chores. Lizzie was glad that she knew where everyone was, all passably well and content. She was glad to be alone in the house. The jailed come to no worse pass than sitting on straw; Caleb and Hannah praying and singing; Ben out of his bed and finished with his speechlessness; the Indians at least biding their time. The dead Indians quiet in their graves far from Fall Creek, where they had died.

Caleb had made her a rocker, much less smooth than the walnut chair she had left behind in York state. This one had as much bump as rock to it. But the movement was soothing; fire purring; March wind with now and then a spring whisper; food enough left from the midday feasting for supper.

In the letdown after the day's work and the past weeks' worry, she dozed off, a light doze so that she knew where she was, but near enough sleep so that the fire and the faint squeak of her rocker seemed a part of her dream. She dreamed she heard a voice calling "Lizzie, Lizzie." This did not awaken her, but her own voice answering "Who is it?" did.

"It's Lute, Lizzie. Luther Bemis. I hope I didn't scare you. Ben said to come on in."

"No. I was only dozing. Come in and shut the door. Warm yourself," she said. Bemis was rubbing his hands, and he had his jacket collar turned up like a man bone-cold.

"The wind's raw."

"I reckon you're not still suffering from your sickness."

"The only sickness I had, Lizzie, was heartsickness."

"We all get that at times, Lute. I've been laid low with it more than once."

"Not like mine."

"I didn't say that."

Bemis pulled his bench right up to the edge of the ashes and used the fire's warmth like water to lave his hands, turning them over and over like a hired man at the washbasin after the dinner bell's rung.

She and Lute were at home with each other. It was strange that it should be so. He, a long hunter, a wanderer, had had more than one Indian wife, it was said, and a knife that had spilled much blood, human as well as animal. They were about of an age, and she couldn't tell herself she felt motherly toward Lute. Or sisterly, either. She felt like a woman in the presence of a pleasing man. Perhaps most women felt that way with Luther Bemis. She was easy in her feeling about him because the bond with Caleb was so strong. Caleb was her husband the way her mother was her mother, a flesh-and-blood tie nothing could change. But just as there were women she could never imagine being a mother of hers, so there were men she could never imagine as a husband. Lute wasn't one of these. They were one flesh the way the Bible said.

Nothing she felt about Lute would change or would need to be hidden if Caleb came in. Caleb had converted Luther Bemis, made a Christian out of a hard-drinking, loose-living wanderer; seen him settled and married, felling trees and planting corn; expecting now a young one born of a Christian marriage. She was no minister of the gospel, but she was Caleb's right hand in his work — he himself said so — and in this way they were both Luther Bemis's spiritual parents.

"I came looking for Cale. He around someplace?"

"I hope so. But he's not around here. He and Hannah rode over to Pendleton to see the men in jail there."

"They're still holding them?"

"There's going to be a trial. You surely know that."

"I thought they might've come to their senses."

"They?"

"The government."

"It makes sense to the government to try the men who did the killing, if that'll stave off an Indian uprising. Don't it to you?"

"They're our own folks, Lizzie."

"The ones the Indians'd scalp would be our own folks. Us, maybe."

"Sometime last week the world went round a bend, Lizzie. What was is past and out of sight. What's to come's too far ahead to see."

"Went round a bend? What happened last week?"

"Lizzie, women are the most matter-of-fact beings in creation. Nothing happened last week except that we suddenly caught sight of what's around a corner we'd never turned before."

"What was that sight?"

"A world where an Indian is a human being who can't be killed like a bear or a wolf."

"What's that mean for us?"

"I don't know. There's darkness ahead."

It was full dark when Lizzie heard the horses come into the yard. Ben went out to unsaddle and feed. Both Caleb and

Hannah were wet with the drizzle that had started up after Bemis left. Lizzie could feel the tiredness in Caleb as she helped him out of his coat. Hannah was as lit up as if she'd made the whole trip on wings under angel-kindled starlight. She was even less wet than Caleb. Lizzie let Hannah take care of herself. She pulled her own rocker to the fire for Caleb and brought him a cup of hot sassafras tea and a slice of sweet cake. She didn't intend to lay the burden of Luther Bemis's need on his shoulders until he was, if not rested, at least dry and fed.

"How are they?" she asked. She didn't need to say who.

"They're dry," Caleb said. "That's more than I can say for myself."

"How're they taking it?"

"The Woods might as well be there as any place. Both reading. Benson may tear the place down."

"Ain't he ironed?"

"I've seen a bull with a ring in his nose bust through a fence even though he lost a part of his nose in the process. Benson's bull-mad."

"They're not in any danger, are they?"

"They don't think they are."

"What do you think?"

"I think the government means business."

"Business?"

"Try them. And if guilty, hang them."

"Treat Indians like whites?"

"They ought to, I reckon. At long last. But I wouldn't stake my life on its happening. Lizzie, could I have a little hot milk with some rum in it?"

"I'll fix it for you, Papa," Hannah said.

She swooped to put milk in a saucepan, saucepan next the coals, rum in the milk.

"The ride don't seem to have tired Hannah."

"She don't know she rode. There was a young defense lawyer over there too busy making eyes at her to pay much heed to his clients."

"Better the lawyer than that poor accused boy."

"Nothing's been proved yet about him. All's hearsay so far."

"I didn't say guilty."

"Lizzie, you'd make a fine lawyer."

After Caleb drank his hot milk and rum, Lizzie told him about Bemis's visit.

"I told Lute you'd be played out."

"I am. But I'll have to go. Ora needs someone to talk to."

"You know what's the trouble?"

"I've got an inkling."

Charlie Fort was always able to start his Ohio letters with real news of the impending and unheard-of trial: whites being tried for killing Indians. His concluding paragraphs were about himself and Hannah. He tried, in the real-news part of his letters, not to editorialize, to hide his amazement that so much back-country ignorance could exist so near a center of learning like Cincinnati. He did permit a little of his amazement to show. Otherwise his fellow citizens of the Queen City would find his reports unbelievable.

Extracts from letter by Charles Fort to Enoch Leverett:

The town of Pendleton (I've learned finally not to call it a settlement) had first of all to build itself a jail to hold the only prisoners it has ever impounded. It has now also built itself a courthouse in which to try these prisoners. It is, I *suppose,* a courthouse; but there is nothing to distinguish it from a livery stable or a low-class tavern in our parts. It is a log building with two rooms, one for the court, one for the grand jury. The courtroom is about twenty by thirty feet long with a heavy puncheon floor and a platform about three feet high at one end enclosed by a heavy railing. Inside this railing is a bench for the judges; a deal table and chair for the clerk, the aforementioned Fenton, who got himself elected justice of the peace by his claim that he knew all about the law, having been "sued on every section of the statute."

In front of the platform is a long bench for counsel. Here I will sit.

Near this bench is a little pen for the prisoners I'll be defending. There is a side bench for witnesses just behind counsel.

A long strong pole, substantially supported and attached to the floor, serves as a railing which it is hoped will separate the court and bar from the crowd that will be attending this trial.

Feeling, as I need not say, is running very high here. Half the populace is so fearful of retaliatory vengeance by the tribes, and especially by the always warlike Seneca, that they would, I verily believe, roast every prisoner alive to calm down the Indians and save their own hides.

The other half of the populace are friends and relatives of the prisoners and those who believe that trying whites for killing Indians will be taken by the red men as a sign of weakness on our part and will bring down upon us the worst massacres we have yet experienced at their hands. Persons of these convictions would like to free the prisoners, and, though outnumbered, are prepared to fight off any reprisals, shot for shot.

But the government is standing firm in its determination to hold this trial. Colonel Johnston will be back with Indian chiefs and Mingos to let the people of Madison County understand what will surely happen if there is not a legal trial with due justice to follow. Johnston has been empowered to fee witnesses and to require their presence at the trial. And the very employment of General James Noble, a United States senator, to prosecute the men accused of the killing will convince the Indians that the Great White Father is on their side. We defense lawyers will have our work cut out for us, as I am fully aware.

There are some few, a handful at most, who regard this trial in the light of any other trial, and disregard color. Men have killed men. Let the law of the land, if guilt is proved, prevail. Caleb Cape is no doubt one of these. Black Antler, the Seneca Indian prophet, goes even further. But I don't expect him to have a hearing. He doesn't want *any* executions.

At the time of my first visit to my clients, recounted earlier, I met Caleb Cape, the preacher at the settlement where the prisoners live. Cape is not a preacher by virtue of any ordination, nor does he profess to be of any particular denomination. He is a preacher by virtue of the fact that he preaches. He does preach with power, and the settlement couldn't hold him in higher regard if he had arrived anointed by archbishops, wearing robes, and bearing certificates and seals.

At the time I met Cape (since he isn't ordained I won't call him Reverend), I also met his daughter, Hannah; and I heard from my clients, Benson and the two Woods, that her brother, age fourteen, had been at the sugar camp at the time of the fracas; though all said he had taken no part in it.

I met Caleb Cape on Sunday at the jail. Three days later, on Wednesday, I rode over to his place. I didn't expect too much trouble defending my clients; they were white men protecting themselves against the nuisance, if not the menace, of having Indians move in on them, fish their streams, kill their game, and scare their women. But if the Cape boy could report some threatening word or gesture, my case would be further strengthened.

Seeing Hannah again didn't go against my grain, either; that low voice that could be mistaken for a boy's if you hadn't seen the throat and bosom from whence it rose, that hair strong as sunlight. Though to tell the truth, so overwhelming was my feeling for this girl seen for an hour at the most that I had been blinded to remembrance of her features. I could remember her voice clearly enough. And no one could forget that bonfire of hair she carried. But eyes, lips, nose, brow? Feeling had covered my eyes like a film. Here I was brooding about a girl I wasn't sure I'd recognize in a crowd if she had her hair covered. I was homesick for her. But how can a man be homesick for a land he can't remember? So I wanted to go over and find out what I was homesick for. Perhaps be lucky and lose my homesickness, for, as it was, I was not much use to myself or to my case with my heart in a knot of ignorance and aching for knowledge.

In any case, Hannah or no Hannah, it was my duty to see and talk to Ben Cape, so I had no trouble persuading myself to saddle Bay Boy at sunup Wednesday morning. My little pacer, eager as I was to cover ground, stepped off the near to twenty miles in something less than three hours.

It is now full spring. Not that this far north there won't be sleet, snow, and even a blizzard or two before May Day blooms. And even in May there is always the chance of a blackberry winter, white snowflakes bigger than the white blossoms of the vines they settle on. But April was just around the corner. I smelled it all the way riding to Hannah; smelled the dogwood, redbud, and elder blossoms in the season ahead of me. All came floating rich and fragrant on a tide of warm wind and of water freshened with the melting of winter's snow.

In this back country, anyone who steps out of his house is visible — unless he's gone behind a tree to dodge arrows or to relieve himself. There are no hedges, fences, not even a little low picket fence; no rows of trees, no lilac or snowball bushes. There's not even the clutter of rigs and farm implements that sometimes fills our farmyards at home. If you were of a mind to keep track of it, you could cast up an account of the number of trips made by a family to the outhouse each day. This would mean keeping an eye on the women (men here in the back country think privies sissified, and take to the bushes themselves). Keeping an eye on women on such errands wouldn't set well with them or their menfolks, and I don't intend to attempt it. The point is, except for the trees, it's a wide-open country, and what isn't done inside four walls or behind a tree can be seen as far as your eyes are good for.

These woodsies have houses or cabins, but these cabins are not suited for a lot of the work that has to be done. You can't butcher inside, or tan a hide, or boil down maple sap, or pluck a goose, or smoke a ham, or make soap inside where you're sleeping or eating.

I mention soap because that was what I saw Hannah making that spring day on Wednesday. The winter's ashes had been leached out, and she was mixing the lye in a big twenty-gallon iron pot with the grease — hog, bear, chicken (grease is grease) — to make soft soap. I'd as soon try to find a girl Hannah's age in Cincinnati who could raise a barn as make a bar of usable soap nowadays. Time was when every girl in Cincinnati had the art of soapmaking mastered. Who knows that art now, younger than mothers and grandmothers?

Pause in extracts from letter by Charles Fort to Enoch Leverett.

At this point Charlie knew that he wasn't going to send the rest of his letter home for publication in the *Western Spy*. Not the part he felt he had to write about Hannah, anyway. But he couldn't stop talking about her. He was man of words — every lawyer is — but at the minute he was less a lawyer than a would-be lover. If I were a poet, he thought, I'd write a poem. Hannah would be a damned awkward word to work into a poem, and the words men used in poems to describe their loves — doves and evening stars and timid violets — were far from suiting Hannah. "Hannah, my dove." What nonsense. He had fallen in love with something more feral.

He had no closer friend than the man who had adopted him, and his father would listen if he wanted to write pages praising Hannah. But he wasn't presumptuous enough to try to pass off passion as news for the readers of the *Western Spy*.

He had come to a fresh sheet of paper and was prepared to write on it for the pleasure it gave him, as if he were talking to his father. His father would laugh at him, say. "This is a story I seem to have heard from you before, Charlie, but the heroine is new, so spiel on."

Well, she was not only new, she was final, if he could trust his present feelings.

He continued to write, though his feeling was of talking. To his father? Maybe. Maybe to Hannah herself.

Continuation of extracts from a letter by Charles Fort to Enoch Leverett:

I had ridden twenty miles, more or less, to see this girl, to rid myself of the torment of trying to paint her face each night under my closed eyes. Now the minute I saw her a couple of hundred yards away, my heart gave such a jump I was half of a mind to turn Bay Boy in his tracks and head back for Pendleton. What if all my heart-throbbing had been over a girl with a face like an Irish potato? And would I be any better off if I saw under that hair and above that bosom the face that launched the thousand ships? How was I going to live through that? Hannah Cape wasn't the first girl I had looked at and clasped. College boys back in Cambridge are judged something of a treat by town girls there. But Hannah Cape compared with those girls was like an eel among flounders. And eel or flounder, I had my work cut out for me in Pendleton. I hadn't been chosen for nothing by Johnson and Calhoun. And choice apart, for my own future and for the sake of those poor fellows set up as sacrificial scapegoats, I intended a defense that wouldn't soon be forgotten. I intended to remind that jury of every Indian raid and torture from 1700 to 1824, omitting not one faggot of the burnings or knife of the slicings.

Potato face would be the best for me.

But she looked up at me from over her soft-soap mixture and I saw the launching face. Some remnants of Presbyterian upbringing and sense of duty to my clients prevented me from pulling her up onto Bay Boy and riding off with her. I think she would have gone without undue fuss.

She had the launching face. She also had some boyish straightforwardness that made me jump down and greet her like a teammate, handshake and all. At this point I don't know whether what I wanted most was to bed her or wrestle her for a fall. So I talked. It's our great human protection and cover-up. Nice mess of soap, if I ever saw one, said I. Fine open weather for this early in the year. Sorry for the uproar the trial is bringing to your folks. Was her brother home? I knew he was. I'd seen him cut for the house as I came into the clearing.

She couldn't lie. "He's at home."

"I've come over to talk to him." She told me truths and I told her half-truths.

"He doesn't want to talk to any lawyers."

"Sooner or later he'll have to."

"How will he have to?"

"The court has the power to bring witnesses into court and to make them answer questions."

"Any questions?"

"Any pertaining to the case being tried."

"What if they won't?"

"They'll go to jail 'til they change their minds."

"How can they send a boy to jail for not talking?"

"If the court orders a witness to talk and he won't, he shows contempt for the court. That's punishable under the law."

"How do you know Ben was a witness?"

"My clients say so."

"Benson and the Wood men?"

"Yes."

"Ben will never talk."

"Nobody accuses him of having a hand in what happened."

"Why do you want him to talk? Do you think he can tell you something that will make things easier for Benson and Johnny and his father?"

"I hoped he might."

"He can't. I know all he knows. You're better off never to say a word to him."

"How do you know all he knows? You weren't there, were you?"

"Of course not. But he's told me."

"You could tell me. Just the parts you think he wouldn't mind my hearing."

"I won't tell you anything. I don't even like to stand here where he can see us talking about him."

"Let's walk down to the branch. Can you leave your soap?"

"You don't know anything about soapmaking, do you?"

"I use a lot."

She didn't laugh. But she did start to walk downhill toward the branch that circles the knoll the Cape house is built on. We walked in step, not touching. Arm in arm with some girls, you can't keep step. They mince, prance, lurch, and, willing as you are to match mince, prance, and lurch, there's no match possible. You're as mismatched as a pacer hitched to a trotter. Hannah and I advanced step for step, right foot with right foot, left with left, not touching, except hip or shoulder occasionally, lightly, as if we weren't both big-boned and well fleshed, but some species of winged insect.

When we got to the branch we naturally stopped. Wading wasn't on the program. Soap was a finished subject. She refused to get started on brother Ben. What country people call frog spit was shimmering along on the surface of the branch, green as emeralds in the clear noon light. It was dazzling. I've never seen an emerald, but the glitter was like jewels. There was nothing to say.

I didn't ask. She didn't offer. When we kissed we were up off the ground for a while. I was, anyway. We rose to that meeting like creatures of air.

End of extracts from letter by Charles Fort to Enoch Leverett.

Remembering the kiss, Charlie stopped writing and for some minutes lived again in that feeling, relived it and floated once again in that sustaining air. Then he shook himself, poured water into the bowl, doused his head, and splashed his face.

Wake up, Charlie, he told himself. Wake up. Come to. Kissing's not the job you came to Pendleton to do. Defend the accused. Send Pa the news. Try to keep your hands off the preacher's daughter. That's the line of action for you to take.

He looked back over what he had written.

What Ben had said *was* news — up to the point where Hannah confided in him that she knew all the boy knew. That was between him and Hannah and no business of readers of the *Western Spy*. He dried his face and hands and sat down to rewrite his report.

Ora Bemis arrived at the Cape house soon after Charlie left on his return trip to Pendleton. She was on foot, bedraggled, downcast, bigger each day with child. Afternoon had passed and evening had not yet arrived. It was the nameless part of the day; dayshine past and sundown colors not yet arrived. The Cape cabin door stood open. The house needed all the freshening sunshine it could get after absorbing a winter of wood smoke and the smell of boiling beans and drying moccasins.

Ora, at the open door, called, "Lizzie, it's Ora."

Lizzie, polishing case knives with brick dust, wiped her hands on her apron.

"Ora, you think you should be traipsing around the countryside, as far along as you are?"

"My mind's too uneasy to let me sit still. I came over slow and careful as I could."

"Well, come in and rest now. I'll make you a cup of tea."

"It's Cale I came to see."

Lizzie had been a preacher's wife too long to be surprised at the number of women who needed to have a talk with her husband. She sometimes wondered if their need would be as great if the man of God were a woman of God. Ora wasn't one of the women she wondered about. Ora had her own man.

"Caleb's out milking, Ora. He ought to be in any minute now."

"What I've got to say is private, Lizzie. I'll go on out to the cowshed now. That'd

213

be all right, won't it?''

"Caleb'd be glad for company.''

Caleb was down to stripping the cow when Ora came into the shed.

"Sit down, Ora,'' he said, motioning to the last of winter's mounded hay. "I've got to finish here. If I don't take all Daisy's got, she'll get the idea she can let up on making milk. I can't let her get any idea like that.''

When tugging and squeezing produced no more, Caleb hung the bucket on a peg and went over to stand above Ora.

"Should you have walked over here?''

"I rested a good many times.''

"How's Lute?''

"Like he was when you saw him. Cale, have you told anyone? What he told you?''

"Not a living soul.''

"Not even Lizzie?''

"She's a living soul.''

Ora couldn't smile, but her face showed that inside she recognized that a smile would not be out of order.

"You think Lute has to go through with it?''

"I still think Lute's got to do what he

214

thinks right. You know that. He's a converted man. He's God's man. You and me can't tell him what to do."

"I can pray, can't I?"

"You can pray. But don't ask God to upset His own laws."

"What law has God got about this?"

"About half the Ten Commandments. 'Don't bear false witness,' for one. And a few not there. 'Render unto Caesar the things that are Caesar's.'"

"Who's our Caesar? Colonel Johnston?"

"And Secretary Calhoun and the federal government. And Governor Ray."

"They can't stop me from praying."

"No. But there're some prayers God can't answer. You ask God to strike me and Daisy both dead, and I misdoubt your prayer'll be answered."

Ora, who had been half crying, began half laughing. "You know I'm not going to ask God to kill your cow, Cale."

"How about me?"

"You said yourself God wouldn't do it. What'd be the use?"

"Ora, why don't you pray God that Lute does what he thinks is right? And ask God to give you the strength to stand by him?''

''Lute's going to do it anyway, ain't he, Cale?''

''I hope so. And if he don't, the court'll make him.''

''He'd feel better doing it on his own?''

''Don't you think so?''

''Yes. Pray for me, Cale.''

Caleb got down on his knees at Ora's feet. He didn't know a thing he could ask the Lord but to strengthen Lute in his resolve to do right, and to comfort Ora in what likely lay ahead. He ended his prayer, ''Bless this babe-to-be, here in the straw, as Thou blessed another Babe born in the straw. All this we ask in the name of the Father, the Son, and the Holy Ghost.''

Before he could pronounce ''Amen,'' Ora was out of the straw, imploring, ''Don't make a prayer like that for my baby. I don't want my baby killed. Like that other One.''

''He brought blessings, didn't He?''

''I don't want any blessings that come from killing.''

''Jesus didn't kill.''

"He was killed. I don't like that, either. Why do men put killing and dying and blessing so close together?"

"What would you have, Ora?"

"No killing, no killing. Then blessings wouldn't matter. We wouldn't feel the need."

"We need God's blessing."

"No, we don't. All we need is to love each other. Cale Cape, you got Lute into this. He was a happy man until you got him saved and started him to worrying about his soul and what was right and what was wrong."

"He's a better man now."

"I don't care about better. I care about happy. Why did you have to go and save him?"

"I didn't save him. God did."

"Will God take care of him now?"

"Yes."

"You mean, take him to Heaven when he dies?"

"I hope so."

"I mean now, now." Ora scrambled across the slippery hay. "Will He take care of him *now*?"

"The hairs of our head are numbered in His sight."

Ora, who had been standing straight as a pike stick, a foot lower than Caleb, but staring him straight in the eye, wilted.

"You don't know and you won't say. Stay away from my husband, Cale Cape. I will pray that Lute forgets he ever laid eyes on you."

Ora ran out of the shed, and Caleb didn't try to stop her. She was of a mind to tussle if anyone laid a hand on her, and Caleb knew it. Jacob had wrestled with an angel, but Caleb was no angel and Jacob wasn't in a family way. He stepped out of the shed and watched Ora until she had safely crossed the branch. The day of sweet warmth was ending in a red glare. The water had a blood sheen. Tomorrow would be even warmer.

He went into the house slowly, head lowered.

"What's the matter, Caleb?"

He was heartsick and couldn't use his best remedy for that disease: tell Lizzie all about it.

"Couldn't you help Ora any?"

"No. She wouldn't have anything to do with the only kind of help I had to offer."

"She's backslid?"

"I told her I wouldn't talk to anyone about her trouble."

"I put the kettle on for tea for Ora. I'll make you a cup."

While he was drinking, Hannah came in with the bucket of milk. She was rosy and glowing, a strapping milkmaid, if ever he saw one.

"Pa, you're getting forgetful. Milk the cow and leave the milk outside."

"Thank you, Hannah, The forgetful old man thanks you."

He thanked God he didn't have a notionate flyaway girl like Ora Bemis.

9

Next Sunday morning, Caleb and Lizzie were still in bed, though planning every minute to get up. It was a couple of hours before sunup, but by the feel of the air that seeped into the room, down the chimney and through the chinks, they knew the day would be balmy for April.

"Praise God for that," said Lizzie. Her head was on Caleb's shoulder, the last rest and comfort she would have that day — and the way things were going, perhaps forever. The fit of man and woman always surprised her. It was a detail you might have thought God wouldn't have had the time or foresight to arrange. The heavy bone of a man's big shoulder left a hollow before it reached the bulge of the muscle in his upper arm that just fitted a woman's head. Her hair was as springy as a down pillow there, though not really necessary. The socket of fleshed shoulder and big muscle, soft when not in use, formed a bowl just skull-sized. *My* skull, Lizzie thought comfortably.

"When was the last time we had a real Sunday, Lizzie? Got to sleep a little late and could look forward to the peace and fellowship of a church service to follow?" Caleb asked.

"Before the killings," Lizzie said, then wished she hadn't used those words. Now they'd have to face the day that was ahead of them.

"Church has about lost its meaning here."

"We could have a regular service before they arrive. Just the two of us."

"It'll have to be right here and now, then, otherwise they'll start riding in before you've put a comb to your hair."

"What about you?"

"I'm a short horse and soon curried."

"You'll have to shave today."

"I will for a fact. Can't be outshined by the redskins."

"The meeting's not set 'til eleven."

"The time set ain't going to carry a pennyworth of weight with folks who want to see this day's meeting. There'll be people here who've been traveling all night, or I miss my guess. They're fording cricks and trying to follow traces from as far away as Indianapolis this very minute."

"Indians and whites have set down together before."

"Not for any powwow like this. Indians being told white men'll be hung if found guilty of killing them."

"They been told a lot of things before

this that never turned out."

"Not by Johnston."

"Why is Johnston having the people here at all? Why don't he take them straight to Pendleton?"

"Here's where it happened, Lizzie. Here's the sore spot — and the hotheads. If anybody's liable to fly off the handle about the killings up north, or the trial in Pendleton, it's the people here. Johnston will go on to Pendleton with his Indians. But here's where oil has got to be poured on the water. And if I don't miss my guess, the Indians Johnston will bring in here will make everybody think twice before they decide to tangle with them."

"What kind of a man is the colonel?"

"He's nothing special to look at. Not at first glance. Second glance tells you here's a man that don't back up. He's hewn out of the old rock. You could pull every toenail out of him and he wouldn't change expression. The Indians know this. They don't fool with him. They ain't got no cause to. So far. He's worked for them."

"Is he a good man?"

"In the sight of God I reckon he is. In the sight of most whites he's a traitor."

"Couldn't a fight break out here today? So many men hating the Indians."

"It'll be a fist fight if it does. Nobody's bringing a knife or a gun beyond the lane into our place. Johnston's seen to that."

"Can he just give orders?"

"He can. And he's got militia down at the foot of the lane to see his orders are carried out."

"Right now?"

"They slept the night there."

"You didn't tell me."

"No use your getting worked up."

"They're going to protect us. Ain't they, Caleb?"

"Yes. But if I'd told you, you might have got to thinking who they're going to protect us *from.*"

A cock crowed, one of their own, likely. They were too far from the Bemises' to hear crowing unless the wind was carrying from that direction.

"Did someone turn in our place?" Lizzie asked.

"Like as not. But you listen to me,

Lizzie. Don't start asking people in. The house won't hold them, in the first place. In the second place, once they got in, you'd feel you had to feed them — and there ain't enough supplies in the settlement to feed the crowd'll be here today. In the third place, the Indians don't want to come inside. They ain't used to chairs, and much as they trust Johnston, they don't trust us. They'd think what we had in mind was to get them inside and set the place on fire — the way we did at . . ."

Lizzie stopped him before he could finish his sentence. "We? There's not a person here would think of doing a thing like that."

"Whites thought of it once. That's what Indians remember."

"Well, I don't want any Indians in my house anyway. A lot of them are light-fingered."

"You've never seen any Indians like the ones you'll see today. There's nothing in our house they ain't got better. Look what Clasby tried to steal from them. You only know those poor town reds down around

Pendleton — drunks and beggars, and thieves if you give them a chance. They weren't that way 'til we came along. Johnston will bring Indians here today we ain't touched yet. Chiefs and braves in furs and skins and war bonnets 'til we'll all stand chopfallen before them in our calicoes and linsey-woolsies."

"We're all equal in the sight of God," Lizzie said.

Caleb laughed 'til the bed shook. "God save me from arguing with women. Men ain't women's equal when it comes to that."

Lizzie was offended. "I wasn't arguing. I was repeating what I've heard you say a million times."

"I said it the other end to."

"Listen. There's more horses," Lizzie said.

"If there's going to be any church here today, it'll have to be here and now," Caleb told her.

"I can't pray in bed," Lizzie said.

"I can. That's where I said most of my prayers when I was a youngun."

"Well, I ain't a youngun any more.

Could you sing a hymn in bed, Caleb?''

Caleb demonstrated. ''Hush up, Caleb. You'll bring the children downstairs.''

''Nothing wrong with singing hymns on Sunday. And the better the place, the better the deed, I always heard.''

When Caleb was in a bantering mood there were only two things to do: ignore him or give him his head. Lizzie ignored him. She knelt by her side of the bed, her face deep in the covers. Caleb joined her. Not touching her. He'd told her long ago never to lay a hand on him when he was praying. ''God's got His hand out to me. I know that. But I'm an earth-bound man by nature and the bond could be broken very easy.''

The creak of wheels up at the end of their lane disturbed them both. They lifted their heads, then rose.

Ben, who had tried to hide himself from himself, felt at home with the crowd of strangers who filled the yard. To them he wasn't the Cape boy, who had been at the sugar camp at the time of the killing; to them he could be an onlooker from far down in White River country, or perhaps a Buckeye up from Ohio, or a Keystone state man from distant Pennsylvania. He didn't look a whit different from these strangers, and no one paid him the least heed, not even Hannah, who usually kept an eye on him. She was a hen and he was her only chick; that's what he'd heard said. That time was now long past. Hannah didn't know he lived or breathed today. She was so busy talking to one of the trial lawyers, she wouldn't have noticed if he'd dropped dead in his tracks. He was accustomed to having her answer the questions that left him dumb-struck. No one was asking him questions today. He watched his father and mother; they were shaking hands and talking, no different from the way he'd seen them at a protracted meeting.

He knew the Cape yard better than any out-of-state man and had chosen a better place to watch than most: the angle where barnyard fence met the barn. He had a wall to lean against, a squared-off rail to sit on, and a good round sapling to brace his feet against. In case of any trouble, he could be up and into the barn at the first click of a trigger — or war whoop.

No Indians had arrived yet, but a space was kept clear for them. That's what the people were here for: to hear the Indians say they'd be willing to let the white men take the punishment of the white killers into their own hands. If the Indians didn't believe white men were going to do that, they'd swoop down five hundred or a thousand strong. That's what Johnston, the Indian agent, said. And that would be the end of the Fall Creek settlement, of the town of Pendleton, and of every human being living between.

Ben was so interested in the crowd, he scarcely noticed that he had been joined on the top rail. Squirming around to find out who had crowded in, he saw a man who, except for his clothes, looked like a blacksmith — big, dark, and somehow sooty-looking because of the stub ends of the dark beard under his skin. His hands were as big as a blacksmith's, but Ben could see on second glance they had never handled horseshoes or hammers. His shoulders were up on a level with Ben's, and his butt, though big, was firm. It didn't give an inch when Ben shoved into it to keep from being pushed through the barn wall.

"You feeling pinched?" the man asked, kindly.

Ben was, but hesitated to say so. Some soft fiber in him (he was ashamed of it as being unmanly) made him hesitate to tell people that they were in the wrong. They would be ashamed to learn it, he thought. He was ashamed when he was in the wrong, and he had had too little experience of the world to understand that the world wasn't made up of duplicates of Ben Cape.

"I'm O. A. Dilk," the man next him said. "I shoved in here on purpose. You're Ben Cape, aren't you?"

Ben didn't see any way of avoiding a yes to that, though he preferred remaining a stranger with other strangers.

O. A. Dilk didn't make any remarks about the sugar camp. He did say. "I'm a lawyer for the state."

Ben wasn't positive what a lawyer for

the state did, but he was pleased that he had been right in guessing the man wasn't a blacksmith.

"Who's the beauty over there talking to silver-tongued Charlie Fort?"

Ben didn't see any beauties, but when Dilk pointed, he had to admit, "That's my sister, Hannah."

Dilk scanned him as if searching for some family resemblance. Ben knew it wasn't there.

"You'll likely see plenty of lawyers the next couple of months," said Dilk, dropping the sister subject.

Ben kept his mouth shut.

"All of them shining up to your sister?" said Dilk.

This was a new idea to Ben. He wasn't in the dark about Hannah's feeling for Johnny Wood, but Johnny, as far as he could tell, would choose a book any day over Hannah. Maybe lawyers were more hot-blooded than other people.

"You know all the people here, Ben?" Dilk asked.

"I know our neighbors."

"You know the families of the prisoners?"

"I seen Mrs. Wood here."

"Point her out to me."

Ben pointed.

"I thought she'd be older."

"She *is* old," Ben said, for whom old age began at about thirty-five. After that everyone was old. He was surprised that O. A. Dilk, a state lawyer, was not very much older than Johnny Wood. He *was* twice as big, with not a gray hair in his head and a big cleft in his chin. Ben would never have thought the state would choose a lawyer with a dimple in his chin. He wouldn't. It looked childish.

"Mrs. Benson not here?"

Ben pointed.

"The one with all the younguns?"

Ben nodded.

"I'd think they'd all stay home."

"They want to see the Indians."

"Their pa didn't have any love of Indians."

"Who told you?"

"Why do you think he's in jail?"

"Lots of people get in jail by mistake."

"You're a smart boy. And lots that ought to be there are passed over by mistake.''

Ben looked at O. A. Dilk. If I was in trouble, I'd like him on my side, not against me, he thought. He kept his mouth shut.

''Clasby ought to be in jail,'' Dilk said.

Ben was silent.

''Your sister, Hannah, found Clasby's saddlebags with stuff he had stolen from the sugar camp. Thieving as well as killing.''

''How do you know that?''

''That's what I'm here for, to find out facts like that. Then to prosecute the guilty.''

''Prosecute?''

''See that they are punished.''

''Hung?''

''If guilty. That's the law. Who's that big fellow?''

''The one with . . .'' Ben was too delicate-minded to say, ''The woman who's going to have a baby.'' Dilk said it for him.

''Mr. and Mrs. Bemis are their names.''

''Poor lady,'' said Dilk. ''Poor lady.''

Ben knew having a baby was no treat

for a woman, but he'd never heard them pitied before because of it.

He was hungry. He had had nothing since breakfast, and his father had told him not to be seen with food until the last person had left the place. "We can't feed them all, and there's no use tantalizing them with the sight of food. Now you can stay out of the house and if your pangs get so you can't stand them, sneak into the barn and have a couple of mouthfuls of chicken food. That'll keep you going 'til nightfall."

He was thinking about doing that when all the people in the yard turned as if by a single lever to face outward and every one, as if all their throats had become one big throat, half yelled, half whispered, "Here they come."

It was the Indian chiefs who were coming.

They moved into the lane where the other visitors had been forbidden to come.

"They're not supposed to ride in," said Ben. "Other people couldn't."

"*They* can," Dilk told him. "Johnston arranged with your pa. If you were a dozen Indians would you walk into a crowd of half a hundred whites after some of them had just finished killing your women and children?''

Ben didn't say anything.

''Not if you had good sense, you wouldn't,'' Dilk answered for him.

Ben kept his mouth shut. He wasn't sure what sound would come out if he opened it. Maybe he'd yell a warning like any boy seeing Indians crouched behind the farm's snake fence before making a run for the safety of the house. Maybe the sound would be a whoop for joy, the way it was when geese went over in a shifting V half as big as the sky, crying their own messages back and forth. Maybe he'd turn his face to the barn, hide it in his arms, and cry for Folded Leaf, who'd never grow up now to ride a horse like this.

He made some sound.

''You never seen the like, did you?''

He never had. He didn't know the like existed. Fifteen men, not on half-starved Indian nags, but on big arch-necked stud horses, all colors, but all high-stepping, came up the lane.

"They don't look like Indian horses."

"Most of them likely stolen."

"Ain't you here to defend the Indians?"

"I'm here to prosecute men who kill Indians."

At the head of the line, which was coming at a walk, giving everyone time to take them in, regalia and mounts, were three white men.

"They squaw men?" Ben asked.

Dilk snorted, deep as an old man's snort, thick and phlegmy.

"There's Indians coming here who have powwowed with the President of the United States himself. You call President Monroe a squaw man? He's talked with Indians."

"He never come riding into our place with a bunch of them."

"Back here in the woods you think anybody who says howdy to an Indian is a squaw man. The first horseman in that line is General James Noble, United States senator. You want to call him a squaw man?"

Ben didn't.

General Noble was thin and straight as

a musket. He rode his horse solid as a heavier man. He was no woman's man, Ben thought, squaw or white. He'd like to see the woman who'd yell to the general, "Bring me in an armful of wood while you're about it." The general belonged to the general.

"Who's that coming next?"

"Colonel Johnston."

"The agent?"

Dilk nodded.

Johnston was as big and heavy as Dilk himself, but colored yellow and white like a miller, instead of dark like a smith. He was burly enough to hoist sacks; his face sharp and his eyes going everywhere. He would keep tab on whose corn meal was whose, and no arguing about it later.

"Connor, owner of the inn at Connorsville, is riding with Johnston."

Connor was in looks, the soldier of the outfit, more like a general than even Noble. Maybe sitting in the Senate day after day had robbed the general of his fierceness. Connor was the equal of any Indian in the saddle and on a better horse. A lot of blood would flow before anybody scalped him. Maybe that was why the Indians were his friends.

Behind the three white men came the Indians, a line of them, who, because of their headdresses, looked as much like birds or beasts as men. Nothing had prepared Ben for the sight, no pictures, nobody's accounts.

"I never seen Indians like them before."

"Not many people have."

A band of angels would have been less startling. Ben knew how they would look; like himself, only with wings and long gold hair.

This wasn't a war party. There was no war paint. But there was enough finery to start a war. If Clasby, who had looted the sugar camp for the few pelts there, could see the skins and furs and feathers and jewelry now riding up the lane, he'd start a war of his own just to get them. No, it wasn't a war party, and the Indians were outnumbered ten to one. Ben wasn't afraid. Why, then, did his scalp tighten up so? Why were his ears pulled up so high they ached, and why had the back of his neck turned ice-cold?

If he wasn't afraid, what was he? Eagle feathers coming up the lane made into a cap and the cap finished off with a beak and glaring eyes. Hawk feathers held in place with a silver band. Owl feathers shaped like a pinwheel. Earrings, shoulder-long, swinging. Doeskin white as chalk. Tanned skins the color of sassafras bark. Black wolf fur, shiny as chokecherries. Spotted lynx. Snow rabbit. Ermine paws. The nearest he'd seen to anything like this was a line of maple and beech and hickory trees after the first hard frost had hit them. The nearest he'd felt to anything like this — well, he'd have to think about that.

"They're not all dressed the same," he said.

Dilk harrumphed again. Ben wished he'd cough and spit. "Indian fighters aren't like our soldiers. They don't all dress alike. Rich Indians have better clothes than poor ones. Young warriors don't dress like great chiefs."

They're like women, Ben thought. Not in dresses, like women, but in putting on their best and wearing beads and feathers and bright colors.

Not a sound was made except by the horses, the clop of their feet and a stud's occasional whistling snort. The Indians were still, no movement except as they were moved by their horses' swing, which they held down to a running walk. The onlookers were as quiet as the oncomers. Once in a while a man in the waiting crowd made a horselike wheezing sound himself, as if words that had come up as far as his teeth had been choked off there. Babies cried, but babies cried no matter what.

"Are they all one tribe?"

"They're a mixture. Mostly Senecas or related to Senecas. It was Senecas got killed. But Senecas have killed so many Indians themselves they ain't overflowing with friends. There's a Miami there. A Winnebago maybe, though the Senecas tore them to pieces a while back. Oneidas. They're a part of the Five Nations, along with the Senecas. There's a breed or two there. One of the women killed at the sugar camp was mostly white."

Ben made a sound softer and more broken than that of the horses being reined in.

"You choke on something?" Dilk asked.

He had choked on his tears. Better to keep Dilk talking. "Have you lived with Indians?"

"I was brought up in New Jersey."

"How do you know so much about Indians?"

"I'm here to prosecute men for killing Indians. I've got to know something about the men they killed."

The line of horsemen was all in the yard in the space that had been kept clear. Ben was able now to see the faces under the feathered headdresses: beaks stronger than eagle beaks and eyes harder than owls'. Except for Folded Leaf, who had first come to the camp three or four years ago, Ben didn't know any Indians. He was ashamed to look at the Indians in Pendleton; dirty and drunk, staggering and begging. He wouldn't want anyone to look at him if he was in their case. He tried to do as he would be done by. In Pendleton, he lowered his eyes. These

240

Indians asked to be looked at. They were
Folded Leaf grown tall. They were Black
Antler grown rich and a chief of his
people. He wanted to say something about
these horsemen, these braves bedecked
with beads and feathers.

"They make us look like a bunch of sick
muskrats," he said.

"Nonsense," said Dilk. "They're
savages. These men you see have eaten
dogs. Worse than that, the hearts and
livers of their enemies. They'll keep a
man alive for twenty-four hours just so
they can roast him longer. They've run
red-hot pokers up the asses of white men.
They . . ."

Ben wouldn't let him finish. "If I was an
Indian, I wouldn't have you for my
lawyer."

"I'm not *their* lawyer. I'm the state's
lawyer, prosecuting white men for
breaking the law. It's against the law to
murder human beings. The law don't say
that if the human being ate dogs or men's
livers, he can be murdered. The law's got
to be respected. I don't care what the
savage did, the law don't give a man the

right to kill him.''

"Folded Leaf wasn't a savage. He never ate dogs. He never ate anybody's liver.''

Ben was crying.

"How do you know?''

"He was my friend.''

"Wasn't ten pretty young for the best friend of a boy of fourteen?''

"How do you know how old he was?''

"That's what I'm here for. To find out things like that.''

"He wasn't ten. He was twelve, but little.''

"Big enough to swing a tomahawk. Or fire a gun, I reckon.''

"He didn't have a gun or a tomahawk. And Black Antler taught him not to kill.''

"Who's Black Antler?''

"His teacher. I studied with Folded Leaf. I learned what he learned.''

"How to scalp?''

"No. I learned by heart verses like Bible verses, only Indian.''

"All forgotten now?''

"No. 'I dreamed that the sun in the firmament spoke to me. He told me that the Great Spirit is very angry with

Indians for their wicked ways. Tell them they must repent their wicked ways and forsake them or the judgments of the Great Spirit will come upon them. If they do not repent . . .' "

"Who said all this?" Dilk asked. "This Black Antler?"

"No. Handsome Lake. The brother of Corn Planter. Black Antler taught what Handsome Lake preached. That's what Folded Leaf was going to do."

"Well, Folded Leaf made a mistake when he fought the whites, didn't he?"

"He didn't fight the whites. Nobody had any chance to fight the whites. You said you came here to find out what happened. Why don't you ask people who really know?"

"I am," Dilk said. "I'm asking you."

Ben took one look at Dilk, saw that he meant what he said, then jumped down from the top rail and pushed his way through the crowd into the barn. He wasn't hungry any more but he chomped on corn to ease his feelings. Chomped on corn 'til his gums bled.

O. A. Dilk spread out a little more

comfortably after Ben's departure. Any other way of getting at him would have made the boy dry up. He wasn't a man who liked to hurt others, but every single thing had to be weighed against every other thing. Better the boy suffer some now, and because of it decide to tell what should be told, than clamp his teeth shut and keep the truth from being known.

The Indians and the three white men didn't dismount. There was going to be a palaver, and Johnston intended that he and the chiefs be heard. Down on the ground some shoving might start; and shoving led to blows, and blows to blood, and finally what happened at the sugar camp might seem a frolic compared with this.

Dilk was glad to be working with Johnston. The man was an anvil. Hit him and the sparks flew, but he didn't budge. The Fall Creek folks didn't give Johnston credit for it, but what he had done and was doing had saved and was saving them from being wiped out — houses burned, hair lifted, stock slaughtered or stolen.

There were no Indians so proud and vengeful as the Seneca. They believed that the spirits of their slain tribesmen would never rest until those responsible for their killing were themselves slain. It was a duty the Seneca accepted with enthusiasm.

Dilk had no idea how Johnston had been able to persuade these masters of revenge and retaliation into letting the white man take care of the punishing. It was possible that to the Indians the nasty business of white men pinioning the arms of other whites, then letting them dangle at the end of a rope, fighting in mid-air for breath, was a revenge sweeter than any they could devise. "They are killing their own." That would be a sight they might like to see.

Johnston was likely the only man whose word they would accept in such matters. He had never lied to them. And if he lied this time, there would be nothing to prevent their carrying out their first plan: burn, scalp, slaughter. Johnston was counting on the settlers to remember this. Dilk was, too.

The agent had brought the right men in the right dress and on the right horses. Where he had got the horses, Dilk didn't know. Woods Indians could ride, though they did most of their traveling on foot or in canoes. But they had no such numbers of good mounts as these: Johnston had had no need to outfit them so far as clothes went. An Indian told who he was in two ways that the white did not; by his body, naked or next to it; and by the display on his body of a rich covering, which told where he had been and what he had done and who in his tribe he was. The very sight of these big men, reared up proud as birds of prey, pennants of animal scuts and feathers flying from their upheld lances, shrunk the settlers down to rail-chopper size. Dilk, a big man seated on the top rail, felt himself dwindle before their display of strength.

Johnston, for all that he was riding with a general who had become a senator and Connor, a rich innkeeper, was the best mounted there: a fifteen-hand blood bay with a long black switch tail. He sat in front of the band he had got together and he spoke first. He had a deep, tumbling voice, sometimes hard to understand. Johnston appeared to know this. He spoke slowly, a word at a time. Every person with two ears and a brain between them could hear and understand what he was saying.

"White people can read and write. Or most of us can. Because of this we have long records on paper which we can read and reread. And all these records tell us how much we have suffered at the hands of the Indians.

"The Indians don't have any way of keeping track of what they have suffered at our hands, no records that we can read. And if they did have, we probably wouldn't read them anyway. But *I* have been keeping records and *I* can tell you they have suffered.

"Many of these happenings you know about already and I don't intend to keep you standing out here for the time it would take to recount one-tenth of them. What's just taken place here you all know about. It's not my place to determine who were the killers; or why they killed. A court of law will decide that. The Indians know who the dead are. They know that kin of theirs were killed by men of this neighborhood. They know that the dead were not warriors or horse thieves. Nine people died. Seven of the dead were women and children. They know that.

"They know — you do, too — what happened to some Wyandots over in Hancock County a few years back. A Wyandot chief with his wife was on a hunting expedition. Three white men came to his camp and asked to spend the night. The Wyandots were Christians. They shared their camp with those they supposed to be their Christian brothers. They fed them. They knelt and said their prayers with them. Then they went to bed. As soon as they were asleep, these white men rose up on them with axes, killed them, robbed their camp, and stole their horses.

"These murderers and thieves were caught and put in prison. But very soon after, while the officials were looking the other way, they broke jail and escaped. And that was all the punishment they ever had: the inconvenience of a few days in prison.

"I have told the chiefs with me that this will not happen here. That we will try, then punish, those found guilty of murdering Indians in exactly the same way we try and punish those who murder white men. I have told them that we will not have a mock trial. That there will be no jail breaks after the sentencing. If the accused are found guilty and condemned to hang, they will hang, and the hanging will be public.

"Only because they believe me have these chiefs been able to keep their young men from descending upon you. It is not Indian nature to suffer in this way without reprisal. Some have become Christians, but turning the other cheek comes less natural to an Indian than to any other people I know.

"Two of the chiefs will speak to you now. The first is a Seneca. His English name is Sun Fish. Two hundred braves look to him for command. He will speak in his own language; what he says will be interpreted for you. You should listen well.''

Johnston should have been a lawyer, Dilk thought. His witnesses were well chosen. Sun Fish was a young chief, his face full of violence and his eyes aglitter with hatred and pride. He didn't need to say a word to convince those looking up at him astride his roan that, except for Johnston's promises, he would, with or without the help of his two hundred braves, attempt to avenge the deaths of his kinsmen.

His speech was short, clanged out in a rush of brassy sounds. He spoke as a man who scorned words, who had other and better means of defense. He didn't pause between words as Johnston had done, but threw what he had to say at them, in one hard blow.

The Indians had minds trained to retain words. They were without books. What had happened, what they believed, what their wise men had said, had no place of storage other than their heads.

The translator spoke as if the speech were his own. Even his voice had the clang of Sun Fish's.

"There is a treaty between your people and mine. We are not at war. This was not a fight between warriors. There was a time when we called each other brothers. I do not call you brothers today. Brothers do not kill each other's women and children. We have been promised that the murderers will be punished. We have promised that we will wait and see. We are waiting."

The Seneca wheeled his horse and rode slowly down the lane away from the crowd. He had had his say. Dilk scanned the faces of the listeners. From these men and others like them would come a jury he must convince. What these men had just heard would make his task easier.

The departure of Sun Fish had likely not been part of Johnston's plan. He let him go without a look. The impression he wanted to make on the settlers was one of Indian unity.

"One of the men killed is represented here by his uncle. He is Mingo, son of the great Mingo."

Mingo was a man of forty or more. The grooves from his nose to his mouth were like runnels in clay land after a hard rain. No Indian was more richly dressed and ornamented than he. Unlike Sun Fish, he spoke slowly and quietly.

When he had finished, the translator, also speaking slowly and quietly, said, "I was born by the falls below here. This was all Indian country. There was food for all. No man, red or white, was ever turned away from the red man's lodge hungry. The land belonged to all. We killed only the animals we needed to eat. Then the white man came. He killed for pleasure and money. The land belonged to whatever man could seize it. The red man was made many promises. We signed many treaties, many times. 'Only this much land and no more.' Pushed back, pushed back. Driven from our own homes, from our own forests, from our own streams. While taking the sugar sap from our own trees, our women and children are killed.

"We had no jails, no judges. We had no thefts. And except in war or in the drunkenness you brought to us, no killing. You have these.

"If you do not punish the wrongdoers in your way, we will punish them in ours. The agent says you will do this. If he is right, only the guilty will die. If he is wrong, you must blame yourselves."

Mingo was as self-contained as Sun Fish was tempestuous. When he had finished speaking, he moved his horse quietly back into the group behind Colonel Johnston.

The colonel was silent for a time after those speeches — letting the words sink in. The words *had* sunk in. There was no outcry, no movement toward the Indians. Then Johnston spoke again.

"Indians are not great speechmakers."

This, Dilk knew, was less than the truth. When it came to speechmaking old Tom Jefferson himself had to back down. Dilk had read history and the settlers hadn't. What Johnston wanted to convey was that the Indians didn't fight with their mouths. They talked with their mouths, more eloquently than most white men could manage. They honored their speechmakers as white men didn't honor theirs. "All wind and no weather" tended to be the white man's judgment about a talker. The Indian was more all of a piece. A man good with words wasn't, in their opinion, handicapped in his use of a tomahawk or arrow.

So Johnston wanted the listeners to remember that these talkers were also fighters.

"Now we ride to Pendleton to say there what we have said here. The chiefs will then depart for their homes and the trial will begin."

The horsemen rode off the Cape place through a quiet crowd — quiet, insofar as words went. Dilk thought he could hear a sound like that of a hive of disturbed bees: a sound of breaths sucked in, of heart thumps, of groans, of belly rumbles.

But what could they do? The agent had asked nothing unreasonable. "You made these laws. Now keep them." He had the right. But had Indians the right? To stand up bald-faced and say, "When you kill us, you murder. Hanging is your way with murderers. Keep to your ways."

There was no doubt in Dilk's mind that many men in Cape's yard, if they thought they could do it, would mow down all Indians present — and their agent first of all. Mow them down and to hell with what came next. But other men were thinking twice; and some women were crying; and some, like Indians themselves, had squatted on the dry, sweet April ground and had put their arms on their knees and had buried their heads in their arms.

The trial would be a mortal tussle, and Dilk felt the power rise in him to win it.

He saw the Cape boy, his great lank of a redheaded sister, and Fort, the young Ohio defense lawyer, standing together over by the wellhead. Fort was not the chief defense lawyer, any more than he, Dilk, was the chief prosecutor, but they both came to the trial with reputations to defend — and to make. He had to see the Cape boy again; it would be good manners to have a word with Fort; and Hannah, apart from any trial maneuvers, struck him as being a manifestation of the mysterious ways in which God moved.

He had prayed for guidance when the chance came to take this appointment: lost in the backwoods, trying to persuade white men to do what they had never done before, to have one law for both the white man and the red man. It was not a job he had much stomach for. He needed to stay in the public eye if he was to run for public office, which he intended to do. He needed to win cases if he was to get elected. But after praying, he had decided that, in spite of all the drawbacks, it was his duty, even if out of the public eye, and in danger of losing the case, to take his stand for the law which he intended to serve. He had never expected to find as reward here in the backwoods a girl like Hannah Cape. She would grace, she would light up, any marble staircase, Indiana or Washington.

The Cape boy had a bloody mouth.

"You been in a fight, son?" Dilk asked.

Ben wiped the back of his hand across his mouth, then examined the stains. "I chewed down too hard on some cracked corn, I reckon."

Dilk had half expected Ben to run on sight, but he stood his ground and answered the question, which wasn't really Dilk's business. Ben didn't know,

256

however, that etiquette required him to introduce his sister and Mr. Fort to Dilk.

Dilk introduced himself.

"Miss Cape, may I make myself known? I'm O. A. Dilk, lawyer for the prosecution."

Hannah said, "I'm pleased to meet you, Mr. Dilk."

"Oscar, isn't it?" Fort said, not waiting for further formalities.

It was. But Dilk didn't fancy Oscar as the name for a rising young politician. George and Thomas and John were the names of presidents. Where did any Oscars come in? He tried to hide behind initials. He couldn't expect Fort to have any interest in such an undertaking. And he couldn't expect, and didn't want, Hannah to be calling him "Mr. Dilk." She certainly wasn't going to be Miss Cape to him any longer than he could help.

Fort, who was a smooth-tongued man, he had always heard, began to prove it.

"That bunch of Indian dandies didn't help my cause any."

"What do you consider your cause, Fort?"

"Save white men from being hanged for defending themselves against savages who have been molesting them for a hundred and fifty years. What's yours?"

"The law. But I'm sure that Miss Hannah doesn't want to have the trial argued here."

"I don't want to have it argued at all. Now or ever," Hannah said.

"You want to leave it to Indian justice?" Dilk asked. There was room for brain behind the girl's white brow — and plenty of space for heart, too, lower.

"I want it never to have happened."

Dilk smiled. She was a woman.

"We live from day to day in what *has* happened, and in what will happen, if we don't act."

"Hannah," said Fort, "we're going to have the trial argued here and now, like it or not."

Dilk wouldn't have that, have himself put in the light of being a sobersides while Fort and Hannah had better things to think about. This was no time to lock horns with Fort. Leave that for the trial, and let it be seen then who was the better man.

"Miss Hannah," he said, "Ben and I had our talk cut short by the speechmaking. If you'll excuse us, we'll go on with it."

10

Charlie Fort could charm a bird out of a tree. This wasn't his fault, but the ability made some people back off from him. The charm, they were convinced, wasn't the man himself but something he exuded like birdlime to catch the unwary. Such persons were proud of themselves for escaping. They had scorn for those who did not. The Charlie-resisters attached themselves to some blunt bumblehead, proud of their ability to discern qualities more than skin deep.

Mrs. Culligan, Charlie's landlady, wasn't unaware of Charlie's charm, but she was knowledgeable enough to know that the best wood takes the highest polish.

She was also too honest to fool herself into thinking that her feeling for Charlie was maternal. She *was* able to fool Charlie. She had enough sense to keep her hands off him, and to recognize that a young lawyer working on a murder case didnt have time to gab with a woman who appeared to him to be an elderly widow. In her heart, however, she was a girl in love. And though she called herself "elderly widow," she knew from the attention paid her by men of thirty that her forty-five years didn't show. Her cheeks were pink, her hair as bronze-gold as it had been at twenty, and, when she had a mind to do it, she could cinch in her waist so that the belts she had worn twenty years ago still spanned her waist. Nevertheless, she tried to bear herself in Charlie's presence like a good old aunt. This didn't prevent her from providing Charlie with comforts a landlady didn't usually give roomers.

He was eating at 8:00 P.M. on a mild April evening a dish of fresh tender-grained clabber dusted with brown sugar, which Mrs. Culligan had brought to his room with no more than "I thought this might help you through your evening's work.''

He had a long evening's work ahead of him, so he eased into it like an ox who sees the hill ahead of him becoming slowly steeper.

His father's letter made him laugh. Not that he didn't hit the nail on the head and hit it hard — but he used a funny hammer for the job.

''If you want to write a story called 'Hannah, the Hoosier Maiden,' I'll try to get it published for you. But readers of the *Spy* generally are not interested in the girls you spark, up there in the woods. And Hannah herself, or I miss my guess, wouldn't be very set up to see herself made reading matter by you for my subscribers.

''Now I know you didn't intend parts of your letter for printing: but I tell you, son, it doesn't even make proper reading for me. I appreciate your willingness — from the first day we met — to share your experiences with me. I hear plenty of parents complain they haven't heard two words in ten years from sons who don't live any farther away than you do. And I thank God I've got a son who's willing to talk to his father. So I'm not trying to stopper you up. Just telling you a fact: the words haven't been invented that'll tell one man what another man feels about a woman. And I reckon especially son to father. Or vice versa. Even more specially vice versa, no doubt.

"Did you ever think about trying your hand at poetry? Pearly teeth, bosom like the drifted snow, heart of ice? *Spy* readers understand words like that.

"Another kind of thing I can't print. Or won't. In the Springfield, Ohio, paper, an article by General Sampson Mason says, 'As I entered the Pendleton courtroom the judge was sitting on a block, paring his toenails; just then the sheriff entered out of breath, and informed the court that he had six jurors tied, and his deputies were now running down the others.'

"Now I'm not saying this wasn't the case, though I know the general can draw the longbow. What I am saying is that I'm not going to print stuff like that. I don't consider when or where the judge trims his toenails news. And even if it was news,

I'm not going to put the *Spy* in the position of a city newspaper looking down its nose at folks out on the frontier.

"I won't say I didn't get a chuckle myself out of that picture. What I suggest is that if there are happenings of that kind you put them on a sheet marked personal. Put Hannah there, too. If you have to write about her. If you do that, you'll save me the trouble of sorting through your reports to weed out what's not suitable for print.

"You may save your own self from embarrassment by doing this. If I'm down with the ague, I wouldn't put it past old Ames, who doesn't love either of us, to print the lot just for the fun of seeing your face red.

"Now I'm not trying to discourage your writing — or courting. I don't know anything else that's set this town on its ears like that trial in Pendleton. They can't hear enough about it. I may even be wrong about the judge's toenails and Hannah."

Charlie finished the letter, finished the clabber, and picked up his pen. Writing about Hannah was now out of the question. Pa was right. The words hadn't been invented that would tell one man what another felt about a woman. As to toenails, there was no way he could report this trial without reporting scenes nearly as outlandish.

Extracts from a letter by Charles Fort to Enoch Leverett:

On the day the trial began, Judge McGowan was unable to preside, due to some temporary sickness. One of the side judges, Omer Oursley, took his place. Oursley is the blacksmith who ironed the prisoners. As a first matter of business Isaac Vickers, defense attorney, rose and made a motion that the out-of-state defense lawyers be recognized. "Judge Oursley," he said, "I ask that these gentlemen be admitted as attorneys and counselors at this bar. They are regular practitioners but they have not brought their licenses with them."

Judge Oursley said, "Have these men come here to defend the prisoners?"

"They have," replied Vickers.

"Let them be sworn," Oursley said. "Nobody but a lawyer would defend a murderer."

Mr. Vickers was naturally taken aback at this kind of talk from a judge in a trial, the purpose of which was to decide if anyone had been murdered; and if so, who the murderers were.

He didn't let this deter him, once the attorneys were sworn, from getting on with the business of the defense.

"I now move the court," he said, "for a writ of habeas corpus to bring up the prisoners who are at present illegally confined in jail."

"You demand what?" Judge Oursley asked.

"A writ of habeas corpus."

"For what? What do you want to do with it?"

"To bring up the prisoners and have them discharged."

"Is there any law for that?" Oursley asked.

Vickers then read the statute regulating the writ of habeas corpus.

Judge Oursley, the blacksmith, then

said, "That act, Mr. Vickers, has been repealed long ago."

Vickers, an attorney of much experience, was not accustomed to being instructed about writs of habeas corpus by blacksmiths in frontier towns. He kept his temper in hand, but his manner was curt.

"Your honor is mistaken about that. It is constitutional writ, as old as Magna Carta, and has never been repealed."

Judge Oursley was not in the least put out of face by Magna Carta.

"Mr. Vickers," he said, "to cut the matter short, it would do you no good at all to bring those prisoners out of jail. I ironed them myself, and you will never get them irons off until they have been tried, habeas corpus or no habeas corpus. Motion overruled."

Soon after this wrangling between Judge Oursley and Mr. Vickers went on, Judge McGowan himself had recovered sufficiently to assume his rightful position between the two side judges. Matters now went more smoothly.

Judge McGowan ordered the grand jury

to be called. All were present, answered to their names, and were sworn. The grand jury then brought into court an indictment for murder drawn by Mr. Armitage against each of the defendants.

Readers of the *Spy* may be informed, albeit taken aback, by the rough-and-ready methods of this court. Their procedures may differ from those of more settled communities but their goals are the same: justice.

This same grand jury, just before the present trial began, was presented with a case against a man for selling whiskey without a license. The jurors voted for a bill to be drawn. Armitage, the state's prosecuting attorney (then as now), drew the bill and presented it to the foreman and asked him to sign it.

The foreman refused. "I sell whiskey without a license and always have. I don't intend to indict others for what I do myself."

"If you don't sign it, I'll take you before Judge McGowan."

"What do I care for McGowan?" asked the foreman. "He don't know anything about selling whiskey — or making it, either."

Armitage is a man I will soon be confronting in the courtroom myself; and I recount this happening not only as a report on how legal matters are handled in this neck of the woods but also as a reminder to myself of the nature of my honorable opponent.

Armitage ordered the grand jury to follow him into court. In the courtroom he said, "Judge McGowan, the foreman of the grand jury refuses to sign his name to a bill of indictment against a man for selling whiskey without a license."

Judge McGowan asked, "Have a majority of the grand jury agreed to find the bill?"

"Yes, your honor."

"Foreman," asked Judge McGowan, "do you refuse to sign the bill?"

"I do."

"Well, Mr. Prosecutor", said McGowan, "I see no other way but to leave him to his conscience and his God. Take the grand jury back to their room."

Back in the grand jury room the

foreman said, "I told you, Armitage, that Judge McGowan knew nothing about whiskey cases."

Armitage answered, "What the judge doesn't know about such cases, I do. I will take the necessary legal steps to have the bill signed."

Armitage began to take off his coat. "The law now requires," he said, "that the last step be taken."

"What step is that? Can't you take it with your coat on?"

"No; with a foreman like you, I can't. The last legal step with such a foreman is to thrash him until he signs a bill the majority of the jury has agreed to."

The whiskey-selling foreman had sampled too much of his product for too many years to be in any shape to stand up to Armitage, who is built like a bear and, from all I have seen of him, is about as bad-tempered.

"I'm not a fighting man," the foreman said reasonably. "Hand me the bill. I'll sign it."

When he had signed, Armitage marched the grand jury back into the court.

"Has the foreman signed the bill?" Judge McGowan asked.

"He has," Armitage replied.

"I thought his conscience wouldn't let him rest until he had signed," the judge said — not indicating that he knew the means Armitage had taken to arouse the foreman's conscience.

This is a digression from my reporting of the Pendleton case. But if you don't understand the informal nature of the courts here in our great sister state, some of the happenings of this trial may seem unbelievable to you. I assure you that everything I report happened; and happened with just as much verisimilitude as my pen can command. My hands are too full with preparing a defense for these imprisoned men to leave me any time for concocting possibly entertaining but untrue stories.

To get back to this trial, the trial jury was chosen and seated without any of the "tying up of jurors" as reported by General Mason in the Springfield paper. The jurors are all hardy, heavy bearded fellows. Not one wears shoes — all wear moccasins, made by themselves or their women at home. And not one is without a side knife thrust in his belt. They are men who know the woods, who have fought their way west in spite of sickness and Indians. The first sight of them gave me considerable confidence. These are men, I thought, who know what it means to stand off the savages; men who have managed to bring Christianity and civilization westward with them in spite of constant peril from the red man.

The courtroom was crowded on the first day of the trial. Some people came for no other reason than to see "the monkey show," as they called it. Settlers from up Fall creek and in Pendleton, whose lives may hang on the decision reached by this jury, were there and gave earnest attention to the trial. Friends and families of the accused men, their faces drawn with anxiety, were there. These were people I had come to know. The families of men I will be defending, clustered together like sheep in a storm. They sat on the front benches with their minister, his wife, and two children with her. Next

271

to the minister sat Luther Bemis and his wife, Ora.

There's more to tell, Pa, much more, I'm too sleepy to continue now. I'm not overly satisfied with the part I played in what follows but will try, when I get around to it, to give you an honest report of the proceedings. Enough to say now that the defense received a great shock — and setback in the testimony heard by the court today.

End of extracts from a letter by Charles Fort to Enoch Leverett.

11

The courthouse was already crowded when Caleb Cape, with his family and the Luther Bemises, arrived. A bench up front had been saved for them. Jonathan Armitage had seen to that. Hannah, Ben, and Lizzie went in first. Then Ora and Lute. Caleb had the seat on the aisle.

The turnout for the trial turned Caleb's stomach. It always did. Let a churn be stolen or somebody's coon dog shot, and if the matter came to trial, settlers for twenty miles around traveled to hear the lawyers spiel. It was not to be expected that a trial like this, with generals and United States senators and city lawyers from Ohio pleading, would go unnoticed. Or that the first trial of its kind, white men tried for *murder* for killing Indians, and already ironed and in jail, would not bring out ten times as many onlookers as usual.

Caleb supposed that for settlers, lost off in hidden nooks and crannies of the woods, the mere sight of another human being was a treat — trial or no trial. The arguing of the lawyers was for woodsies what play-acting was for city folks; except that this wasn't play-acting. There wasn't any make-believe here. The tears shed would be real tear water flowing from the eyes of real people. The families that would be separated if the prisoners were convicted and given jail terms would be real — honest-to-God wives, real flesh-and blood sons and daughters.

Whatever the crowd's purpose in congregating, the lawyers' speechmaking would be in itself a seven-day wonder. All those long-tailed words strung together without pause for breath, three hours at a time on occasion! Why, it was more remarkable than watching dancing bears.

Then there were those Indians, splendid as play actors (though they weren't actors), upright as trees, at the back of the room. Their slit-stone-agate eyes saw every move that was made. Real playgoers never had to pay any heed to how the rest of the audience was reacting; never had to wonder if some of the onlookers were whetting their knives or eying nearby heads for handy scalp locks.

Caleb understood all this. Still, he didn't like the flushed, staring faces — not much different from faces he'd seen ogling a two-headed calf. Was anyone there praying? For the men in jail? For the Indian dead? For the jury that would have to search its heart about right and wrong? For the judge who would have to sentence? Gawking and gaping, that was about the size and whole of it.

He said so to Lizzie, and she whispered,

"Shhh," to him.

He whispered again. "Somebody ought to open the windows in here."

Lizzie again whispered, "Shhh."

It was a mild day, and the heat of all those bodies packed into a space too small for them had raised the room's temperature to that of humid midsummer. Only, the smell wasn't that of midsummer. It was the smell of nervousness and fear, of curiosity and cruelty, with a strong whiff added of winter underwear not shed since last November.

He reached over, put a hand on Luther Bemis's.

Lute knew what that meant. Armitage was about to call him to the stand, and Caleb was giving him comfort. Or would give him a shove with a hand, hard and splintery as a roof shake, if he saw any signs of faltering.

Lute wouldn't back down. He had committed himself ahead of time for fear of that very thing. He kept his eyes on Ora. He didn't know for how long he might be separated from her. He wasn't sure what she might do now. She had never denied that what he planned to do was right, or that he should be the judge of what was right for him. But she had never been two-faced enough to pretend (though she knew pleasing God had to come first with Lute) that she herself felt at one with God if that meant prison for her husband. What she wanted first of all was for Lute to want to please *her*. This was wicked but she preferred Lute wicked and with her, to separated and holy as Moses.

The cross-grained devil that had lived in Luther Bemis so long was not yet dead enough to permit him to love wholeheartedly any woman who could say, "Forget me and do your duty." Duty was *his* job. Loving him was hers. And Ora had always done that job so well, he half expected her to grab his coattails when Armitage called him and cry, "Stay, stay, you fool."

Did he half want her to? Did he half believe that a God who truly loved him would never ask him to go the whole way in this business of confessing his sins?

276

Armitage was speaking. He only half heard him but he knew what he was saying without hearing the words. Armitage was asking the court for permission to disregard for the time the indictment brought by the grand jury against John Wood, Sr. He wanted to bring another witness to the stand.

Judge McGowan protested. The grand jury must not be bypassed. Armitage argued him down. Why drag out a trial that already promised to run on for days, perhaps weeks, with unnecessary formalities?

"Bring on your witness," agreed Judge McGowan.

"Will Luther Bemis, commonly known as Lute Bemis, please take the stand," said Armitage.

Lute had lived through this scene in his imagination so many times that he moved through the actuality like a man through a dream remembered. Ora did not cling to him. Caleb did not have to shove him forward. He did not feel floor boards beneath his feet. He floated past faces of neighbors and strangers as featureless

277

now as bleached winter cabbages. Only, at the back of the room, the Indians were truly visible and themselves. What he had to say would be said to them. He would try to keep his eye on them as he talked.

Fenton, the clerk, asked him to tell the truth, the whole truth, and nothing but the truth. In God's name, did they think he had got up here to tell them some tall tale? He glared at Fenton, then remembered that Fenton did not know, as Armitage did, what was to come next.

Armitage started him from the beginning. Armitage was the state prosecutor. What Armitage cared about was getting a conviction. Lute knew that. He intended to tell the truth. If that convicted him, and it would, so be it.

"Mr. Bemis, where were you on the evening before the day of the alleged killings?"

"I was at home."

"Did you have any visitors that evening?"

"I did."

"Name them."

"Jud Clasby, accompanied by Hannah Cape."

"Why were they there?"

"Jud Clasby was seeing Hannah home from a visit she had made to the Woods. Our house is between the Wood home and the Capes'."

"So the call was just a social one?"

"For Hannah, it was."

"For Clasby?"

"He was sounding me out about the Indians at the sugar camp."

"What do you mean by 'sounding you out'?"

"He asked me if I didn't think the Indians at the sugar camp ought to be cleared out."

"What did he mean by 'cleared out'?"

"Killed."

"Did he say so in so many words?"

"I don't remember his exact words. That was his meaning."

"What was your answer?"

"My answer was that I was finished with that sort of thing."

What do you mean, 'that sort of thing'?"

"Killing Indians."

"You had killed Indians before?"

"Yes."

"Why?"

"To save my life."

"Always in self-defense?"

"Not always. Sometimes because they were Indians. We were pardners, Clasby and me, hunting and trapping out west. It don't make sense to wait for a dangerous animal to attack you."

"That's how you considered an Indian? A dangerous animal?"

"Out west when I was younger — yes. Since I came here, I've been converted. I've become a Christian. But even the Bible don't say that if somebody is going to die, you've got to choose yourself to be the victim. It does say, 'Don't kill.' I told Clasby I wasn't going to kill Indians for using a sugar camp and trapping a creek they'd trapped along for years before we ever showed up here."

"Did anyone hear this conversation?"

"My wife. And Hannah Cape."

"What happened next?"

"Clasby and Hannah left. My wife and I

went to bed."

"Did you see Jud Clasby again?"

"Mr. Armitage," Bemis replied, "it's my intention to answer every question you can think of to ask. It would maybe save time if I'd tell the court what I did and you ask questions only when you think I'm leaving out something."

"Proceed along those lines, Mr. Bemis. I'll stop you when it seems necessary. Now, when did you see Jud Clasby again?"

At this point, the chief defense counsel got to his feet.

"Judge McGowan," he said, in a voice accustomed to being harkened to, "may I address a question to the witness?"

Judge McGowan, a man who ruled in his own courtroom, nevertheless harkened.

"Address your question, Counselor."

"Luther Bemis, first of all, may I remind you that you are under oath to tell the truth, the whole truth, and nothing but the truty."

"You don't need to remind me of that," Bemis answered. "I ain't forgetting it for a single minute. What do you think I'm up here for?"

"That's exactly what I'm trying to get at. Did you talk over with Mr. Armitage what you have just said?"

"I did."

"And what you plan to testify to later?"

"I did."

"And did Mr. Armitage promise you that if you gave testimony helpful to the prosecution in this case, he would see to it that your sentence was light?"

Luther Bemis's hand instinctively went to his belt, where ordinarily he carried a knife. "That's a damn lie, and you know it."

Judge McGowan's gavel startled Bemis, and the courtroom, which was immediately in an uproar at this exchange, went into silence.

"Mr. Bemis," the Judge said, "may I remind you that you will be held in contempt of court if there is any more profanity. The defense counsel is trying to help you to recognize the fact and try to co-operate with him."

"Judge McGowan," Bemis said, "No man is trying to help me who stands in the way of my telling the truth." Still belligerent, he glared at his own counsel.

Caleb Cape rose. "Judge McGowan," he called out.

Caleb was well enough known to be permitted this interruption of a trial that was proceeding, except for the experience of men like McGowan, by guess and by gosh anyway.

"Pastor Cape."

"I am not an ordained minister."

"Mr. Cape."

"I have testimony that might be useful to the court if they care to hear it."

"Step down, Mr. Bemis. Mr. Fenton, call up the witness."

Duly sworn, Caleb said, "Before Luther Bemis ever saw Mr. Armitage, he came to me with the account he now wishes to give to the court. My advice to him was to seek out Mr. Armitage, the state prosecutor, and to tell him what he had told me. It was Mr. Bemis who sought out Mr. Armitage. Not the other way around. No deal for special treatment was made."

"Mr. Cape," asked McGowan, "why didn't you advise Mr. Bemis to make his report to the defense lawyers?''

"I didn't think the defense lawyers wanted to hear what Luther Bemis had to say. I thought Jonathan Armitage did. It was on my advice Bemis went to Armitage. For the sake of his own soul, I may add."

After this interruption, Judge McGowan ordered the questioning of Bemis by Armitage to continue.

"Mr. Bemis," Armitage asked, "may I now repeat my earlier question? When did you next see Jud Clasby?"

"After he visited our house with Hannah Cape?"

"That is right."

"Jud Clasby came to our house around nine or ten o'clock the next morning. He said that his horses were missing — strayed, stolen, no telling which. Would I come with him and any others he could roust out to look for them? Well, there was no question about my doing that. I told my wife good-bye and set out with Clasby. Told her I might not be home before nightfall."

"I reckon you took your gun with you?"

Armitage asked.

Fort was on his feet at once. "Judge McGowan, I object. The prosecutor is putting words into the witness's mouth. What Mr. Armitage 'reckons' and what Mr. Bemis did are two separate matters. Let Mr. Armitage 'reckon' all he wants. But let him put direct questions to the witness. Not make suggestions."

"Objection sustained," said McGowan. "Mr. Prosecutor, question the witness directly."

Armitage, with a great show of being obliging, rephrased his question. "Did you take a gun with you, Mr. Bemis?"

"I did," answered Bemis.

"Why?" asked Armitage.

Fort was again on his feet. "I object. By asking 'Why?' Mr. Armitage would like to lead the jury to believe that Mr. Bemis went with malice aforethought, armed for the purpose of killing Indians. Mr. Armitage may live in the capital of this great state of Indiana, but he knows as well as I do, and as every man on the jury does also, that no man up here and in his right senses goes five hundred feet from his house without a gun."

"Objection overruled," said McGowan.

Armitage repeated his question, "Why the gun, Mr. Bemis?"

"Habit, mostly," said Bemis. "And good sense."

"Where did you go after leaving the house?"

"We went toward the shack where Jud Clasby has been living since he came back here. On the way he showed me two small piles of corn. You don't usually find piles of corn out in the woods far from any barn lot. I wondered about them. Clasby said he figured they had been put there by the Indians to toll the horses away from his place."

"Did you see any tracks around the corn?"

"Yes, I did. Horse and moccasin tracks. At the time, I thought the horse tracks were Clasby's and the moccasin tracks Indians'. I think now I was tricked."

"Why? How?"

"I was tricked by somebody's putting that corn there and seeing that some horses come to it. The idea was to make my blood boil at Indian thievery — and it did boil. There's nothing lower than a horse thief — but my only thought then was to get the horses back to Clasby. Clasby said, 'Let's go to the sugar camp and see if the horses are there.' That was agreeable to me, the only reasonable thing to do.

"Before we started out, Clasby asked me into his shack. He got out a bottle and took a pull on it himself. Then he handed it to me. When I was converted, I gave up drink. I'm not myself when drinking. I do things and afterward I don't know why I done them. But Clasby and me were old friends and we've emptied many a bottle together. I thought maybe going without it for so long had settled me down so drink wouldn't work on me the way it had when I was younger. I was wrong. If anything, it worked on me harder. I was drunk. While we were still at the shack, Benson, the two Woods, and the Cape boy came along."

"Did these men have guns?"

"All but the Cape boy. He was just traipsing along because young Wood is his friend."

"Did they drink?"

"Benson and old Wood had a pull, but by that time the supply was about finished."

"What happened next?"

"We went to the sugar camp. It was agreed that the two Woods, Benson, and the Cape boy would stay in camp with the women and children, while me and Jud Clasby, with the help of the two Indian bucks, went to hunt for the horses."

"If you thought the Indians had stolen the horses, what made you think they'd lead you to them?"

"We didn't think that. If they stole them, they'd lead us as far away from them as possible. They'd lay down a cold track."

"What was the idea of taking them with you?"

"The plan was to kill them."

"Whose plan was this?"

"Clasby's. But I went along with it. I was took in by the corn and the tracks. And by the whiskey. I was thinking the way I did when I was Clasby's pardner out west and every redskin was our enemy. I was ready to kill then! I thought I'd be saving our own lives in the long run. That's what I thought."

"What happened when you got to the sugar camp?"

"First of all, the Indian squaws gave us food. They always do. It sobered me up some, but not enough to bring me to my senses. Clasby didn't mention to the Indians what he'd told me — horses stolen. What he said to them was 'horses *strayed.'* Would the two men help us look for them? Tall Tree didn't think much of this plan. He said, 'How do you know but maybe if I go, I shoot white man?'"

"Clasby joshed with Tall Tree, saying, 'White man has had more practice with guns than the red man.'

"Tall Tree didn't argue about this. 'More practice,' he agreed. 'But red man shoot faster.'

"Red Cloud, a leader among the Indians and a man very open and friendly to whites, said he'd be glad to help.

"Red Cloud went with me, Tall Tree with Clasby. Clasby had told me what he would do and what he wanted me to do.

When I heard the sound of his gun, it would be a signal that he had killed Tall Tree, and that I was to kill Red Cloud."

"Didn't you have any compunction about going ahead with this plan?"

"Compunction?"

"Second thoughts? Twinges of conscience?"

"I did, yes. But by now I was bound by an agreement. I'd told Clasby what I'd do, and I've never been a man to back down once I've given my word."

"So you thought it was better to kill a man than to break your word to a man who'd fooled you into murder."

"I didn't know I'd been fooled then. And I was drunk."

At this point Fort again interrupted. "Judge McGowan, may I put a question to the witness?"

"This is irregular," replied McGowan, "but with the prosecutor's permission, I'll grant you your request."

Mr. Armitage, a man who knew he had nothing to lose, granted the permission.

"Mr. Bemis," said Fort, "you keep telling us you were drunk. But you also keep remembering like a man cold sober. You remember what Clasby said. You remember what the squaws fed you. My belief, Mr. Bemis, is that a man as drunk as you say you were could not remember such small happenings. My belief, however, is that you were indeed as drunk as you say you were. I know something about your past life. I know what a little corn liquor can do for you. I believe that you were just as drunk as you claim. But that what you are now passing off as what you remembered are items you've let Mr. Armitage, for reasons best known to you and Armitage, persuade you to present as 'remembered.' Isn't that true, Mr. Bemis? Mr. Armitage's not your lawyer, Mr. Bemis. Don't you know that? Are you still drunk? Don't you know what Mr. Armitage has in mind for you?''

"I know what Mr. Armitage has in mind for me," Bemis answered, steady as a rock. "That's his business. My business is to tell the truth. Armitage didn't tell me a thing to say. He listened to me. That's all he did. It may be I've made out I was drunker than I was just to ease my conscience. I wouldn't say that'd be past me. Even now."

Armitage, with the generosity of a winner, said, "Are there any more questions you'd like to ask the witness, Mr. Fort?"

Fort bowed out of the exchange with all of the poise he could muster. "Thank you, Mr. Prosecutor. For the time being, that is all."

Armitage then continued from the point where he'd been interrupted by Fort.

"My question was, Mr. Bemis, did you think it better to kill than to break your word to a man who had fooled you into murder? And your answer was that you didn't know then that you had been fooled. And that you were also drunk. Is that still your answer?"

"It is."

"You still say that at that time you believed a man's life was of less account than your word to a murderer?"

"Nobody up to then had ever called Clasby a murderer. And he *was* my pardner. And just how drunk I was, I don't know, but I *was* drunk, and keeping my word to Clasby seemed the right thing to do. So that's what I done."

"How did you persuade this Indian, who had no reason to trust a white man, to go off with you on a trumped-up search for horses that weren't lost?"

"I told you Red Cloud was goodhearted and friendly to whites. I didn't have to do any persuading. He went along just as helpful as if he'd been looking for his own horse."

"You know who's in this courtroom listening to your words?"

"I'm looking straight at them. I'm confessing to them as much as to anybody. More to them than anybody except God. I confess to them both the wrong I did."

"An honest confession may set you right with God. But the Indians want more than that. You understand that, do you, Mr. Bemis?"

"I understand that."

Judge McGowan decided to get Armitage and Bemis back on the track of the trial proper, which was: Who killed Red Cloud?

"Honest confession," he agreed, "is good for the soul, be it to man or God. But this trial will last from July to eternity if it's opened up to all the confessions that might be, and maybe ought to be, made here. But this is, however, a circuit court, and I got dates elsewhere and soon. Mr. Armitage, let's get on with what the witness did after he left the camp with Red Cloud."

Armitage then said, "Mr. Bemis, you have heard Judge McGowan."

"Well, after we left the camp, I let Red Cloud range on up ahead of me, making excuses myself for little side trips so I'd always keep him in front of me. He was about thirty steps ahead of me when I heard a shot from the direction Clasby and Tall Tree had gone.

"A shot from Clasby was the signal for me to finish off Red Cloud. Red Cloud turned at the sound of the shot toward me, and I bungled my shot. I hit him in the belly. The shot went clear through him, and blood spurted out front and back. I wish to God I could forget Red Cloud's look. He couldn't believe I'd done it. He was helping me and I shot him. He said, 'You kill me?' ''

''Well, what did you say to that, Mr. Bemis?''

''I didn't say a word. What could I say? I'm saying it now. I hope Red Cloud can hear me.''

Bemis, who up to this point had spoken without much emotion, buried his face in his hands. What he had to say from behind his hands was too muffled to be clearly heard.

Judge McGowan said, ''Take your hands down, Mr. Bemis. We can't hear you.''

Lawyer Armitage hadn't become state prosecutor by being a man who didn't press an advantage when it was given him.

''I can't vouch for what Red Cloud can hear, Mr. Bemis, but *I* can't hear you either, and I am listening very carefully.''

''Mr. Bemis,'' McGowan said, ''you asked for this chance to speak. It's out of order for you to do so, and we have interrupted the usual order of things to let you do so. Now you'll have to take your hands down so that we can hear what you are saying. Otherwise you can step down.''

Bemis straightened up at once. His eyes were dry as sandstones. His supply of tears had long since been used up.

''I ask the court's pardon,'' he said. ''What came next ain't easy to tell. I walked toward Red Cloud, who was still standing. I don't know how. Blood was leaving his body by the bucketful. As I came near him, Red Cloud said, 'If you shoot me again, shoot me through the head.' By the time I reached him, he had sunk to the ground, but was sitting upright, not sprawled out. He didn't speak or beg, but he was making a sound. A sound anyway was coming from him. It wasn't a moan or a scream. It seemed more like something inside him broken and running down. You know the whirr a grindstone makes when you stop pumping? Red Cloud just sat there, bolt upright, making that sound. And dying like an Indian. I've seen them die before. Many's the time. They don't whimper. They don't beg for mercy. Red Cloud opened his mouth just enough to let two words out. 'Finish me.' I took my knife from my belt, and Red Cloud nodded. His eyes were wide open and he was asking me to do what I done. There was no wrong in that. It was the first shot that was wrong."

"What was it you did?" Armitage asked.

"I cut his throat."

"And he thanked you for it?"

"He did. He thanked me with his eyes 'til they closed. That's one reason I'm here. I want to say Red Cloud done no wrong. That I killed him while drunk, and that he died like a brave man."

"Why have you made this confession?" McGowan asked. "Were you coerced by the prosecution?'"

"I made it to get some peace with God and my soul."

There hadn't been a sound in the courtroom during Bemis's confession. The listeners held their breaths as much as if they'd been out there in the woods watching the whole affair — the tracking, the gunshot, the blood, the knife at the throat, more blood, the closing eyes.

Armitage asked Judge McGowan if, in view of Bemis's full confession and of his expressed desire to share the jail with those already accused and indicted, the formality of a grand jury indictment for him might be overlooked.

Before Judge McGowan could agree or disagree, Charlie Fort was on his feet.

"May I cross-examine the witness?"

Judge McGowan, surprised, said, "Yes."

Fort planted himself in front of Bemis, but turned aside enough so that the courtroom could see Bemis's face.

"Mr. Bemis," he said, "have you any witness who can substantiate the truth of what you've just said?"

Bemis, who had sunk back into a kind of torpor after the ordeal of the confession, appeared not to take in the import of what he'd been asked.

Fort reworded his question. "Did anyone see you do what you claim to have done?"

This question struck those in the courtroom as ridiculous. Did a man who confessed killing have to produce witnesses before his word would be taken?

Fort didn't give the rustle of what was the beginning of a nervous titter a chance to break out into a laugh.

"There have been numerous cases of confessions of crimes by men who never committed them. In Clinton County, Ohio, two years ago, a man confessed to the murder of his wife who had disappeared. By virtue of that confession, the man was tried and had been sentenced to hang when his wife turned up alive."

Armitage interrupted Charlie without a by-your-leave from the judge. "Counselor Fort, if Red Cloud turns up alive, I'll gladly accept your argument that Mr. Bemis did not kill him."

The onlookers did laugh at that. But Charlie Fort was too nimble-witted not to have foreseen such a rejoinder from Armitage.

"Mr. Prosecutor," he said, "I had addressed a question to the witness. Will you be so kind as to let him testify? You," he said to Armitage, "will be given ample time for your own comments later. Mr.

Bemis, were there any witnesses to this act?''

Bemis answered, ''Besides Red Cloudd, you mean?''

This answer appeared to astound even Fort. He answered very gently, as if to a sick man. ''Yes, I mean besides Red Cloud.''

Bemis shook his head. ''The two of us were alone. Just me and Red Cloud. First I shot him. Then I cut his throat. He asked me to do that.''

''If the court will have a little more patience with me, I would like to cite another Ohio case. This was in Bartholomew County, where a man testified to a killing he did not commit.''

Judge McGowan was getting impatient. ''We're not overly interested down here in miscarriages of justice in Ohio.''

''You're interested in justice, Judge. This case has bearing on that. A man in Ohio assumed the blame for a killing there because of a debt he felt he owed a friend. I submit to this court that Luther Bemis, admittedly drunk at the time of the shooting, does not know but that

Clasby killed Red Cloud. He admits that he did what Clasby told him to do. What proof is there that he is not now saying what Clasby told him to say?''

Before this unthought-of possibility had time to sink fully into the minds of those in the courtroom, Ora Bemis, pushing past the knees of the Cape family, ran toward her husband.

''Yes, yes. That's what happened. That's what happened, Mr. Fort. Lute told me. He said he had to tell it the way he has; Jud Clasby saved his life once out west. Now he wants to take the blame off Jud's shoulders for the killing of Red Cloud.''

Ora, unwieldy with the child she was carrying, went on to where her husband sat, dropped to her knees and looked up into his face. ''Tell them, Lute, you didn't do it. Tell them what you told me. You lied for Jud's sake.''

Luther Bemis didn't say a word. He bent forward, put his cheek against Ora's, and stroked her hair.

It was a hard scene to interrupt, but Armitage did so. He had not built his career as prosecutor on softheartedness.

"Judge McGowan, may I call the court's attention to the fact that Mr. Fort, by placing the blame for the death of Red Cloud on Mr. Clasby, has not lifted the charge of murder from Bemis. He is not suggesting, is he, that Clasby murdered both Red Cloud and Tall Tree? All he has done is to prey on the feelings of an overwrought wife, insult the intelligence of this jury, and harm the case of his client."

Fort, Caleb Cape, Bemis, who had also risen, began to speak together. Judge McGowan, an old hand at outbreaks in rural courtrooms, gaveled them all into silence. It was already well past the noon hour. Food was overdue and might settle tempers and restore a little reason.

"The court is adjourned for two hours for dinner," he said.

12

The day after Bemis's confession was Thursday. Judge McGowan was down again with another bout of his intermittent fever. At McGowan's request, and because they had no wish to stumble through this tangled legal forest without an experienced guide, both side judges moved to postpone the trial until the next morning. That Thursday had an unreal feeling to it; people were uncertain what the confession meant and how they felt about it. The postponement heightened this sense of bewilderment and, during the morning, a stunned silence lay over Pendleton. But by midafternoon some of the shock had worn off and the town began to chatter like a family facing a new, unexpected problem.

Charlie Fort had prevailed upon his landlady to provide a little supper for him and Hannah Cape that evening.

"Norry," he said (Mrs. Culligan's name was Norah, but Charlie had long since left "Mrs. Culligan" behind and called her by the name used by her neighbors), "I know you're not running a boardinghouse and that you only took me in out of the kindness of your heart. But I wonder if you could give me and Hannah Cape a little supper tonight?"

"As you said, Charlie, I'm not running a boardinghouse."

"It's this way, Norry. What with her family and that raft of cousins they're staying with here in town, to say nothing of the brother she carries around like a helpless papoose, she now has O. A. Dilk pawing around her like an ox. . . ."

"Like a bull," Norry corrected him.

That was a word Charlie, who had been brought up not to name male animals before ladies, would not repeat, though he recognized the greater accuracy of Norry's description.

" 'Pawing,' anyway," he agreed. "Well, with all this going on, about my only chance to talk to Hannah alone is here. Or take her out for a little walk in the woods."

"Plenty are traipsing off for just that purpose."

"Don't think I don't know that. That's why I thought it'd be a lot nicer here."

"It would be," Norry said.

For her, too, Norry thought. She was a woman of good sense as well as passion. Her good sense didn't deny the passion but provided ways, when it was possible, for bits of the passion to be expressed. Her preference would have been to cook a supper that she and Charlie could eat alone together. That being out of the question, why deny herself the pleasure of hearing Charlie laugh and talk, of seeing him throw back his long silky cowlick and stretch out his long strong-thighed legs. Say no to him about this supper and he would traipse off to the woods with that big redhead. Who would be the gainer by that? In her own day, when she was dark and sparkling, Charlie would never have given that big redhead a second glance.

Well, that day had passed. No one, to her knowledge, had learned how to turn back the clocks. Turn them ahead and make Charlie her age? That wasn't what she wanted, either. What she wanted was the girl she had been to be with the young

305

man Charlie was. That girl was alive inside her, a sleeping beauty now to others, but wide awake to herself. That girl didn't need any kiss to wake *her* up, but, alas, no kiss of hers would wake another.

"You courting this girl, Charlie?"

"I haven't asked her to marry me, if that's what you mean."

"That's what I mean."

"I've only known her two weeks and talked to her three times. I don't want to scare her to death."

"I guarantee you won't scare her. What would you like for supper?"

What they had for supper Charlie didn't know. The table was set pretty, not in the kitchen, where Norry ate, but in the sitting room in front of a nice little slow-burning fire of oakwood in the grate. The table was the one Norry used at night to play patience on and in the daytime for rolling out pastry and cutting up pieplant in the kitchen. It was covered with a tablecloth and decorated with a little jug filled with the first Johnny-jump-ups of spring.

There wasn't a restaurant in Cincinnati that could've provided them with a turnout any more stylish. And not half so comfortable.

Hannah made Charlie proud. She wasn't a preacher's daughter for nothing. She knew how to talk to strangers, was accustomed to putting them at their ease. She admired the table, smelled the flowers, helped Norry bring the food from the kitchen.

When the supper was on the table, Norry said, "Now there's more where this came from. You help yourselves. I've promised to go sit with old Sam Randall for a spell tonight. He's down with lung fever and his poor wife hasn't had any rest for a week. Now make yourselves at home. If I ain't back before you leave, Hannah, I'm pleased to have met you."

Norry shut two doors firmly between her and the young couple and went down the path toward the Randalls'. If she couldn't be happy with Charlie, she could at least be happy with herself. She had done the right thing. Cleared out. Done unto others as she would be done by. Die a Christian if not a sweetheart.

When the last of the two doors closed, Charlie and Hannah, moving slowly, as if carried by a wave or by the wind, went into each other's arms. They fit there. They felt an ache each had endured since the last clasping disappeared. They did not need to kiss, or want to. That was too special. It denied the all-overness of the pressure of cheeks and arms and thighs. They were not ready yet for anything so concentrated as a kiss. It was enough to have the feel of each other's names in their mouths.

"Charlie, Charlie."

"Hannah, Hannah."

Such beautiful sounds. They couldn't get their fill of those words. They delighted their mouths with them. After a time they remembered the table.

"What're we going to do with all this food, Hannah?"

Hannah, practical as well as lovesick, her stomach growling with hunger, said, "It would hurt Mrs. Culligan's feelings to leave it untouched."

They ate, or tried to eat, one-handed. They could not unclasp hands. Hannah's throat, though her stomach was hungry, felt swollen. Food went down painfully. She gave up trying to swallow and watched Charlie. He had been talking all day, going over the case with his fellow lawyers. He ate, but slowly, as if he, too, found it a task; he swallowed like a man taking a dose of medicine.

"Oh, Charlie," she said.

"Yes, Hannah?"

She wanted to say, "My darling love, you are so beautiful. I will never be separated from you all the days of my life." But he hadn't said, "I love you," yet. A woman who said that first could drive a man off with her forwardness. The game was hide-and-seek, and it was the woman's place to hide and the man's to seek. Otherwise, no game.

She said, "I thought what you said yesterday about Luther Bemis's maybe lying to spare Clasby was good."

"You were about the only one."

"Ora Bemis thought it was good."

"Do you think it's true?"

"No."

"Neither do I. But that jury needs to be given some doubts. Otherwise they'll decide to string up those fellows just to save their own necks."

"They wouldn't do that."

"What do you think that row of Indians is standing back there for?"

"To let them see we are keeping our word. Having a trial the way we said we would."

"There is another reason. Don't think Colonel Johnston doesn't want everyone to have a good look at the customers the Pendleton and Fall Creek folks might have to deal with if the murderers aren't hanged."

"Hanged? They wouldn't hang poor Johnny Wood, would they?"

"If he's found guilty, that's what Johnston expects. But I've got a trick or two up my sleeve yet. That jury ought never to have been seated 'til each man was asked if he'd vote 'guilty' just to stave off an Indian attack."

"Would anybody admit to that?"

"I don't know. But they ought to have

been asked. And the fact they weren't might be grounds for charging a mistrial."

"What's a mistrial?"

Charlie put down his fork, took both Hannah's hands in his, and groaned, "My God, I've lost my mind. Mistrial! Miss Cape is the only miss I care anything about. I've talked to lawyers for so many days I've forgotten there's anything but Indians and trials and murderers in the whole state of Indiana. I didn't ask you to have supper with me for any more talk like that."

"What kind of talk?" Hannah asked, so bold her eardrums pounded with blood.

Charlie closed his eyes and laughed. Then he opened them wide. "You want me to say it?"

"I think so."

"My darling Hannah Cape, I love you."

"I love you, Charlie Fort."

They leaned across the table, ready to kiss now. Charlie's cuff dragged in the gravy bowl.

"We've got to get rid of this damned table," Charlie said.

Hannah's startled look reminded Charlie that he was talking to a preacher's daughter. He wouldn't get fined for every damn and hell he said here, but his stock wouldn't go up any with her, either.

"I didn't mean the cuss word," he said. "I told you I was out of my mind. Let's get rid of the table and some of the food. We don't want Norry to think we ate so little after all the trouble she took. You help me carry the table to the kitchen and we'll give the leftovers to the dog."

When they came back from the kitchen, they stood in the center of the sitting room like actors waiting for a cue. They had said "love" and the dialogue from now on would be different. Charlie had some familiarity with the next lines, but Hannah was tongue-tied. She expected "Marry me" next, to which she would instantly say "Yes," go home and start plucking geese for feather beds and hemming linen for sheets.

Charlie said, "You are the most beautiful girl I have ever seen."

This wasn't a proposal, but it was

perhaps the kind of talk that should come before a proposal, like grace before a meal. It made Hannah even more tongue-tied and self-conscious. She hid her face against Charlie's shoulder — he was tall enough so she could do that. The minute she did so, she didn't care about proposals. Or anyone speaking, she or Charlie. Her body spoke, "Touch me, touch me, touch me," and Charlie's body heard and answered. They were strong enough for kissing now, and kissing was strong enough for a time. But what their lips felt, their blood carried to every other part of the body.

Norry Culligan came home at the decent hour of ten. First into the kitchen, then opening the door into the sitting room — which was also her bedroom. There in front of the fire, built up enough to shed some light as well as heat, naked as jaybirds, lay Hannah Cape and Charlie Fort, sound asleep and fondly entwined. Norry stared for a time, then quietly closed the door to the kitchen.

What did you expect, she wondered.

Then she went further: What did you want? She sat down at the table where the two had eaten, and cried. Tom, she thought, though in her thinking she was talking to Tom, the husband of her youth, not thinking of the Tom dead and in his grave, and she the old widow. It was you and me I saw there. Don't think me a silly old woman. I'll never do anything to shame you, Tom. I'm your true wife 'til they lay me in the grave beside you. But I feel. I haven't stopped feeling. If I was the one who had gone, and you the one who had stayed, you would've remarried long before this. But no one asked me, Tom. No one I'd have, after you. No old sack of bones like Mr. Wood. Charlie's the spit and image of you the first day I saw you. I won't shame you and I won't make a nuisance of myself to Charlie. You can count on me, but I can't help crying.

Norry put her head on the table and cried a big wet splotch of tears that quickly spread on the white linen tablecloth. Then she got up. Those two must put their clothes on and Charlie must get Hannah back to her home.

She took the poor cat out of its nighttime crib in the woodbox, and set him on the step. "Run for your life, Goldie," she said. Scooter could never catch the big tom, but he'd sit under the tree Goldie climbed and bark for an hour. If that didn't arouse the young people, she'd clatter around in the kitchen until she did it herself.

Goldie ran, Scooter after her, baying. Norry went behind the springhouse, out of sight from the house, and leaned there until she heard the house door close. She watched the young people, arms around each other, move off quickly under the light of a moon growing toward its full.

Inside the house she went to bed, leaving a night light burning on the stand table by the door that led to the attic room — as she always did when Charlie came in after her bedtime.

She went to sleep at once. The light was gone when sometime later she awakened and turned over.

Upstairs at his table, Charlie blessed old Scooter, still prowling around growling at cats, he imagined, and at real raccoons and polecats, likely. Except for that dog, he and Hannah would have been still lying on the floor when Norry came home — or, worse still, when Hannah's father came looking for her. That would have been a pretty howdy-do. Well, pretty, all right, depending on who looked at them; but a howdy-do for certain. With Scooter's help they were up, dressed, and out of the house with no one the wiser.

Charlie was of two states of mind at the same time, and each state was the absolute opposite of the other: so happy and keyed up, sleep might never again be necessary; so filled with lassitude and near to sleep, if he closed his eyes it might be a few days before he opened them again. Go to sleep and dream for two or three days; dream that that long naked body, pink and gold in the fire glow, never once left his side.

He went to the washstand, poured the bowl full of water and doused his head in it. He had his weekly letter to write for the *Spy* — and yesterday's happenings were real news, not storytelling about strange doings in the backwoods. Though a man led off to jail without any indictment by the grand jury, and without any witness to the truth of what he was saying, simply because he was determined to go to jail, was a far step from a jury trial as they knew it in Cincinnati. He recounted the factual happenings of the day before — not of this night — to his father. Then he could not resist a lapse into commentary.

Extracts from a letter by Charles Fort to Enoch Leverett:

If there are no further interruptions of the kind experienced yesterday, the trial of George Benson will at last begin tomorrow. Benson, before he had any idea that he would be brought to trial for killing an Indian, boasted at a public meeting of his part in the killings. The two Woods were with him at the time, but both the Wood men and Benson have, since the trial began, refused to speak of the part played by the others in the affair.

So we have the peculiar circumstances of three men in jail because they themselves boasted of what they considered a good deed, and of a fourth now there because he feels he has committed a crime. And thus far, unless the men start accusing each other, there are no witnesses to the killings they claim they committed. It is a trial based upon circumstantial evidence. No one saw the crimes committed, and the accused are jailed on say-so only, albeit their own. It is also constitutionally questionable whether the court can, after two hundred years of recognizing the necessity of killing Indians in order to survive, suddenly reverse itself and declare such killing to be a crime.

Another circumstance, having to do with the trial but not with its constitutionality, is the presence of Black Antler, the Indian teacher of the boy Folded Leaf, who was killed. Black Antler is what the Indians call a prophet, a follower of the famous Handsome Lake. Black Antler preaches and teaches Handsome Lake's doctrines. One of these was that no one should be put to death for any crime. Handsome Lake was a Seneca from Pennsylvania who was influenced by the Quakers there. What he preaches is four-fifths Indian and one-fifth Quaker. Either alone is hard to swallow, and the combination sticks in most throats. Particularly when Black Antler argues that Colonel Johnston is wrong when *he* says that the men who killed the Indians must, if found guilty, be hanged.

When Black Antler, a Seneca, which of all the tribes has been the most revengeful and bloody, argues against the hanging of men who killed his own people, the Fall Creek folks don't see anything in his argument but a plot: a plot to provide the northern tribes, if Johnston and Calhoun's promise for strict justice is ignored, an excuse to swoop down on the settlements here, ravage, burn, and kill.

Here is this old Indian arguing for mercy for the accused while even the families of the accused think he's likely scheming to provide an excuse for *his* kinsmen to kill them all. Black Antler preaching charity, while half or more here think Johnston, preaching hanging, is on the right track. Hang the four hotheads who did the killing, five, if they can catch Clasby, and save the lives of the hundred or more an Indian uprising would be sure to wipe out.

There are others who argue that the thing to do is to get a detachment of army regulars in here, march north with them, and put an end once and for all to the Indian menace in this area. It's going to have to be done sooner or later, they say; better do it now, before the red man strikes first.

With Calhoun heading up the Department of War and Johnston in charge of Indian Affairs for the Northwest Territory, it's unlikely the government will send soldiers to put down a rising of Indians — who haven't risen — Indians who, to boot, have as an excuse for doing so — the murder of their kinsmen.

This community is split down the middle in its opinion as to what should be done. Half think that Johnston was right in promising the Indians a trial of the killers and punishment under the law if found guilty. Half think that no promises should have been made and that the Indians should have been dealt with as they always have been before, with force.

It sometimes appears that there will never be any need for another Indian raid on Fall Creek. Neighbor will have fallen upon neighbor and by the time the redskins arrive their erstwhile settlement will be extinct as the result of civil war.

Two families, unable to face the prospect of watching friends condemned as murderers — or, if this isn't done, of being themselves killed — have already pulled out. And more are threatening to leave.

More guns are being carried here now and more prayers being said than at any time since Pendleton was founded. The combination may seem odd. But they represent the debate going on in men's minds: What is the right thing to do? What is the safe thing? Pendleton doesn't know the answer to these questions.

Pa, I wish I could talk over this trial with you. The job ahead of me isn't easy. As I see it, I must do three things — and the last may be impossible.

1. Recall to the minds of the jurors what settlers have suffered at the hands of the Indians.

2. Bear down hard on the fact that these men had been brought up to believe that killing an Indian served a better purpose than killing a deer.

3. Root out, if I can, somebody who will testify that these Indians by some word or act posed a real threat to the community.

I'm up against tough opposition. Armitage, the state prosecutor, is hard as nails and with a mind like a bear trap. O. A. Dilk, his assistant, is young, ambitious, and wily. I think he sees winning this trial as his first step toward the Presidency. The senator hides his experience and determination behind a mask of urbanity. But he didn't come out to this little backwoods town to lose, that's certain.

Well, you better pray for Charlie, Pa.

Also, you better prepare to meet a Hoosier daughter-in-law before too long. I'm following your advice and not talking about Hannah. But you didn't advise me to stop seeing her — and I'm following your

advice there, too.
End of extracts from a letter by Charles Fort to Enoch Leverett.

Charlie had outlasted his bout of sleepiness. What he would like to do now was get into bed with Hannah, sleep with his face tangled up in that mane of her long bright hair. But Hannah was over there at her cousins', the Baldwins, sleeping, no doubt, on a pallet in the loft with a half-dozen girl cousins tucked in around her. He undressed in front of the opened window. The moon had set and there was only one light to be seen — the light in the window of the old man Norry had been sitting with, perhaps dying at this very minute of his lung fever. Charlie could see the jail, merely a dark outline, of course. You didn't go to jail with any expectation of being able to stay up all night playing seven-up or reading. He wondered what Bemis thought of jail now that he had talked himself into it.

If I was ever so crazy as to kill a man, Charlie thought, I'd keep my mouth shut. But perhaps confession was a part of the craziness: kill and tell.

He didn't expect to sleep. Thinking about what had happened only made him crazy to have it happen again. He envied Norry, calmly sleeping, undisturbed by any thoughts of lovemaking. There were some advantages to being a woman, especially a woman of a grandmother's age.

He was asleep before the feather bed had completed its enfolding movements.

13

On Friday, Judge McGowan was still down with fever. Side Judge Giddings's wife was having a baby, their first after eleven years of marriage; he moved that the trial be postponed until Monday. Side Judge Oursley, the blacksmith, was more than willing for the postponement. Every horse in the township would be running barefoot if he didn't get in some licks soon. The defense lawyers were especially glad for the break. Bemis's confession hadn't made their job any easier.

Caleb Cape and his family, together with Ora Bemis, left Pendleton Friday morning when the news of the second postponement was announced. Ora wouldn't ride in the same buckboard with Caleb. Except for Caleb's meddling with Lute's life, Lute wouldn't be in jail now, and she alone.

Ben and Hannah drove Ora home in the rig the Bemises had driven over to Pendleton. They would spend the night with her, Ben doing the barn work that the Riggins boy, only twelve, had no doubt had to scamp; Hannah doing housework and keeping Ora company. Ora was within a month of her time, and what she had had to go through in the past few days might speed things up.

Ora didn't hold Caleb Cape's making a Christian out of her husband against his children. If Caleb's teachings had caused Lute to make a confession that would do no one any good, she didn't suppose Caleb's children were able to get off scot free in their life with their father, either.

Hannah was as strong as a man and a

lot handier and neater in kitchen and bedroom than any man Ora had ever known. First she got Ora undressed and into bed; a few minutes later she had a fire going, a kettle on the crane, corn dodgers mixed, and side meat frying.

After supper, Hannah sent Ben, who clamored for a game of jackstraws or checkers, up to bed.

"You've got a big day ahead of you, Ben, first with the work here, then over helping Pa. You stay up late tonight, and I won't be able to roust you out of bed 'til way after sunup."

After Ben had gone, Hannah pulled a stool to Ora's bedside.

"Is there anything more I can do, Ora?"

"Bring Lute home," Ora said.

"I don't think he'll be away long."

"What makes you think so?"

"I was talking to Mr. Fort, the defense lawyer."

"If there were ladies on the jury, I'd banter Mr. Fort could get this case dismissed out of hand if he wanted to."

"He is a very good lawyer."

"Maybe. That don't stop him from

being a ladies' man."

"You think he's a masher?"

"Maybe not. But when a man's as good looking as Charlie Fort, women can't keep their hands off him. And men being like they are, Charlie Fort can't help liking that."

"Don't it make any difference to them *who* the woman is?"

"Oh, sure, it makes some difference. Men think so, or they wouldn't settle down and marry one woman instead of another."

"Did Lute ever love anybody besides you?"

"Hannah, Lute left home when he was seventeen. I never laid eyes on him until he was twenty-six. He was out west, a lot of the time with Clasby."

"Is Clasby a masher?"

"He is. And he plans on staying that way. You won't catch him settling down with any one woman. He and Lute both had Indian wives. More than one."

"How could they have more than one?"

"They just called them wives. They weren't really married by any preacher."

"But they acted . . . like they were married?"

"They acted like it.' "

"Did they have babies?"

"Of course."

"Did Lute tell you?"

"Yes."

"Did you want him to?"

"I knew it anyway . . . from people's talk."

"Do you think he might go off and have another wife, after you?"

"No, I don't. What your pa did, converting Lute, makes him think it's wrong to have more than one wife. Besides, he's older now. He likes staying in one place now and having a home and a baby."

"How soon did your baby start to come . . . after you were married?"

"About a year."

"They don't come right away then?"

"There seems to be a rule. If you don't want one, it comes quick as a wink. If you do, you sometimes wait for years. Look at Judge Giddings and his wife. Took them eleven years."

"That's not the rule, though."

"There's no rules, in spite of what I said. It's all hapchance, and I think God Himself keeps pretty clear of such matters and lets men and women work such things out as best they can."

"Don't you think God cares whether men and women act like they're married, when they're not?"

"He may care. But I don't think He thinks He can do much about it."

"Aren't you a Christian, Ora?"

"Of course I'm a Christian. That don't mean I blame God for everything that goes on in the world. I blame your father, not God, for getting Lute into a state of mind where he thinks God wants him to confess every bad deed he's ever done." Ora sighed. "I never thought I'd be able to sleep on a night like this — Lute in prison laying on straw. But I'm dead beat. I could sleep on straw myself — and I wish I was — beside Lute. But I'll sleep anyway — if the baby'll consent to do the same. He's kicking like a bay steer now. Want to feel him?"

"No," Hannah said. "No, I don't."

"Bank the fire, then, and come to bed."

"I could sleep on a pallet on the floor and not bother you."

"You won't bother me. An empty bed's what'll bother me. This is the first night but one I've been separated from Lute since we were married. You know what it feels like sleeping alone when you ain't used to it? It feels like sleeping in your coffin. Cold and alone. Cold and alone forevermore. That's what I fear."

"Mr. Fort says Lute won't be gone long."

"You like to talk about Mr. Fort, don't you, Hannah? As much as I like to talk about Lute."

"He's trying to help Lute and Johnny Wood and the others. I have to admire him for that."

"Me, too," Ora said. "I admire him for that. Let's try to sleep now."

Ora did, sighing and moaning as she slept. Hannah couldn't. She got out of bed carefully and noiselessly walked in her bare feet up and down the room. She knelt and prayed. "God forgive me" was what she intended to pray. "God, I thank Thee" was the way the prayer came out.

O. A. Dilk arrived at the Bemis cabin at ten the next morning. The horse he was riding was warm but not lathered. Dilk started with a long day's riding ahead of him, Pendleton to Fall Creek and back, and he was a man who believed that haste makes waste.

Hannah answered his knock. He wanted to talk with Ben but he would be pleased to have the talk include Hannah also. For a young girl, Hannah looked stately, better turned out at ten on a weekday morning than many a cabin woman at four on Sunday afternoon. She knew, and he was glad to see it, that appearances counted in this world.

She immediately protected Ora Bemis, for which Dilk was glad. Mrs. Bemis could not be expected to look kindly on a lawyer who was trying to get her husband convicted of murder.

"Mrs. Bemis is feeling poorly," Hannah said. "She is in bed. She can't see visitors."

"I'm sorry to hear she is indisposed,"

Dilk said. "Yesterday must have been a very trying day for her."

Hannah thought, He talks like a lawyer no matter where he is. It seemed a good trait to her. Nothing two-faced about such a man.

"I didn't come to see Mrs. Bemis. I came to see Ben. And you, too, if you'll join us."

"Ben's down at the barn, cleaning out the stable."

"It's such a nice spring day. Isn't there some place out of doors where we could talk? I don't want to upset Mrs. Bemis any more than I have to."

"Has something more come up about Lute?"

"Nothing more about Lute. You can tell his wife that he said this morning that he'd had two of the best nights' rest since the shooting. He feels he's clear with God and ready to render unto Caesar what is Caesar's."

"I don't know's that's a message she'd like to hear. She spent the night mourning for him."

"You use your own judgment about

what you tell her. I'm going down to get Ben now. I'd like you to be with us when I talk to him. He puts a lot of store in what you say."

Hannah went back in the house to get her sunbonnet. The sun wasn't hot but it was bright and she freckled easily; and she was getting too old to enjoy being called "turkey egg."

Dilk fetched Ben from the barn, and they used the upended chunks, sawed but not yet split, at the woodpile for seats. The sun brought out the sweet wood smell of the freshly cut oak. Redbud and dogwood were beginning to froth out along the edge of the woods. Frogs down in the branch were tuning up for tadpole time. They could hear the gravelly riffle of the water as it broke clear of the bank at the bend. It was the weather and the place for a picnic, Hannah thought. The biggest stump of all should be covered with a fringed tablecloth; fried chicken, light bread, and a sour-cream sweet cake should be set out on it. It was not the time or weather or place to talk about killing.

There were no fireworks about Mr.

Dilk. He was steady and thoughtful. Pleasant as a basket of chips, her mother would say. Nor did he have that mortal sweetness that makes folks keep their distance for fear of a heart scald they'd never get over. He let the trial he'd come to talk about ride easy for a while.

"Mr. Dilk," Hannah began.

"Call me Oscar," Dilk interrupted her.

"I heard you didn't like that name."

"I don't like it. And when I come to run for Congress, it'll be a drawback. Some Thomas or Josiah will beat me out because people'll think those names sound more dependable. But it's my name and I'm not running for anything just now."

"But that's what you plan?" Hannah asked.

"To begin with, yes. Congress. But I'm not campaigning now. And neither of you can vote anyway. So let's be Hannah and Oscar and Ben now. When I get to Congress, I can be 'Mr. Congressman' to you if you want."

"What'll I be then?" Hannah asked, filled with an exciting boldness she had never known before.

"Well, I'll wager one thing," Dilk said. "Not Miss Hannah Cape, I'll vouch for that."

Am I flirting, Hannah wondered. How could that be? Be too imtiate with a man one day, and the next start flirting with another man. The answer to that was love. She loved and was loved. That made her happy and happiness made her loving toward everyone; not afraid to flirt, because nothing hinged on flirting now; it was a play-party game, fun but no more important than weevily-wheat or go-in-and-out-the-windows. What she and Charlie had done was wrong, and they would never do it again. But in the life ahead of her they would be married, and it wouldn't be wrong any longer. And even now it was very strange that an action so wicked could make her feel so full of grace; as if she had gone to a protracted meeting and been sanctified. She was just a moon reflecting Charlie's warmth onto this anvil-hard Congressman-to-be.

Ben seemed as much changed as a boy as she was as a girl, and with nothing more to help him than some sensible talk with O. A. Dilk. To Ben, Oscar must seem just as reliable as any Tom or Josiah. He was going to do whatever Oscar wanted. She could tell. Testify in court as to what he had seen, if Oscar thought that right.

"I'm not saying it'll be easy," Oscar told him. "I am saying it'll be simple. Just tell what you saw. It's your duty to do it and you'll feel better afterward. If they cross-examine you . . ."

"What's cross-examine?" Ben asked.

"It's what the defense lawyers may do. After you've told your story they may try to mix you up by asking a lot of questions."

"Why would they want to mix me up? Don't they want to know the truth?"

"Not if what happened makes their clients more likely to be convicted."

"Well, they can't mix me up," Ben said. "I know what I saw and heard. If they ask me questions, I'll tell it all over again just the same way. They'll get sick and tired of hearing me."

"They'll be sick, all right," Oscar said, "when they hear what you have to say."

"It's what I did makes *me* sick."

"Tell it," Oscar said, "and get it out of your system. It'll be like having a boil lanced. Get the pus out of your system, and you'll mend fast."

"I'm going to," Ben said resolutely. "I'm going to tell it all. My part, too."

14

Court resumed on Monday morning. Judge and side judges were in place. Benson was in the prisoners' pen. Ordinarily a florid, heavy-set man, he was noticeably thinner and paler. Sitting over there in the straw in the jail, cussing and sweating and fuming, had worn him down. He was still cussing and sweating and fuming, but there was noticeably less of Benson for the job.

The Indians, if they found the proceedings tedious, gave no sign of it. Unaccustomed to sitting on benches and chairs, unable to see what went on if they sat cross-legged on the floor, after their custom, they stood. The row of them, straight, motionless, seemingly untiring,

337

attracted about as much attention as the proceedings up front. No one forgot them. Or forgot why they were there. No one was able to attend continuously to the oratory of the lawyers or the testimony of witnesses without turning to see how the Indians were taking it. Had one crumpled, leaned against the wall, sat down? No, there they stood, a handful of red men, surrounded by their enemies, impassive, unafraid, waiting to see the justice they had been promised done.

The courtroom was even more crowded than it had been on Wednesday. Bemis's confession had whetted the appetites of all. Was there more to come? The shooting of two bucks in the open was not as compelling as the slaughter of women and children at the sugar camp. Who had done that? The two Wood men and Benson had boasted earlier in open meeting that they were responsible for the killing. This was before there was any hint of trial or jail. What they had expected was praise. Varmints wiped out. Thieves of the settlement's fish and game taught a lesson. The settlement owed them thanks.

There were some in the courtroom who still felt that way. Those who had lost relatives at the hands of Indians were shedding no tears over the deaths at the sugar camp. It would give them pleasure to hear exactly what had happened, and what had happened they hoped included suffering as well as death.

Even those to whom Indians had done no harm had a sneaking feeling, of which they weren't proud, of wanting to hear the worst. Their throats were dry. They couldn't look their children in the eye.

O. A. Dilk, as assistant to Armitage, wasted no time in asking Ben Cape, the preacher's son, to come to the witness stand. This caused a gasp in the courtroom. Caleb Cape had had a hand in getting Bemis to confess. Was the preacher going to get his comeuppance now? Hear a confession squeezed out of his own son by the prosecutor?

Dilk handled young Cape as tenderly as a china dish. He all but lifted and carried the big lunk of a boy to the witness stand. Moved his own lips in the swearing in as if to show the boy anybody could do it.

Once he got under way the boy didn't need any more help than a sledder going downhill on glazed ice. Dilk kept slowing him down so that there wouldn't be any cracks in his testimony into which the defense could later poke their prying noses.

"How did you happen to go to the sugar camp on the afternoon in question, Benjamin?" Dilk asked.

Did the fact that Dilk didn't like his own name give him a delicacy in his use of the names of others? So not "Ben," but the full dignity of the Biblical name?

"Johnny Wood came by our house with a gun. I thought he was going squirrel-hunting. He's my best friend. My sister —"

"We're not interested in your sister, Benjamin. Now go on. What happened next?"

"I asked Johnny if I could go with him and he said I could. But Pa wouldn't let me take a gun."

"Why not?"

"Saturday afternoon is getting close to Sunday, and Pa thinks that on Saturday afternoon you shouldn't go frolicking."

"Does he think squirrel-hunting 'frolicking'?"

"It's lots of fun," Ben said, as if agreeing with his father.

"But he let you go with Johnny Wood."

"Just to watch and pick up squirrels for him. Not to do any shooting."

"Did you pick up any squirrels?"

"No. Johnny didn't shoot any."

"Why?"

"He was in a hurry to meet his father and uncle."

"George Benson and Wood Sr.?"

"Yes, sir."

"Where?"

"At the Indian sugar camp."

"Were these men glad to have you with them?"

"No. Old Mr. Wood wanted to send me home. But Johnny's Uncle George said, 'Let him stay. It will do him good.'"

"Did he say what it was that would do you good?"

"No, sir."

"Who was at the sugar camp?"

"Besides the Woods and George Benson?"

"Yes."

"The Indians. Three women and four children. One was my friend Folded Leaf. I was learning Indian gospel with him from Black Antler, the preacher."

"How did your father feel about your memorizing Indian gospel, Benjamin?"

"He said that what Black Antler preached was about what he preached. Except the names was different."

"Can you remember any of the words you memorized?"

Ben said, "I know by heart lots that Black Antler preached."

"Just a few lines will do," Dilk told him.

"Black Antler said, 'Our land will decay if we do not think on the Great Spirit. We must renew our minds and think on the Great Being who made us all. Then when we put our seeds in the Earth, they will grow and increase like the leaves on our trees. If any man, whatever he may be, will look on the Great Being above us all and do his will on Earth, when his days are out and the spirits about find he is a good man they will grant him more days to live in the World, and if he lives a good man, doing no evil in those days, when those days are out, the Great Being will take him to himself. The like of this . . .' "

Charlie Fort, on his feet at once, his resonant tenor bugling his protest, addressed Judge McGowan. "Your honor, I protest. What is this, a court of law or a camp meeting to convert whites to the religion of the Senecas? My understanding was that we were here to try the case of George Benson, indicted by the grand jury for murder. Now if the Great Spirit had a hand in this, I will listen to *his* testimony. Is the prosecution prepared to produce the Great Spirit?"

There were hoots of laughter, the soft thumping of moccasined feet, the high jinx-shouts of play parties and cornhuskings.

Before Judge McGowan could say a word, or even gavel for silence, there was a carrying sound from the back of the room: the ominous hoot-owl call of one Indian signaling to another. This silenced the courtroom faster than any crack of wooden gavel on wooden table. Then, in the muffled drum roll of a voice that had never had to give a command twice, the words, "Let the boy speak."

All turned toward the speaker. Dilk, who had not expected support from this quarter, and wasn't sure he wanted it, said, "What was that?"

All, now looking to the back of the room, saw the largest, most richly dressed, likely the oldest of the Indians take one step forward. He repeated what he had said. Not more loudly, though perhaps more slowly, "Let the boy speak."

Fort, undaunted, ignored the Indian and said, "Your honor, the boy's testimony does not require any further recitation of the doctrine of Handsome Lake as preached by Black Antler. These doctrines have absolutely no bearing on the case we are considering. Further talk about them simply wastes the court's time. We have already been forced to listen . . ."

Judge McGowan did not permit Charlie Fort to finish his sentence. "Objection overruled," he said.

True, it was not customary to permit listeners, red or white, to dictate courtroom proceedings. But this case was not customary in any way. Better, McGowan believed, to permit jurymen and onlookers alike to believe that the chief's request was not unusual. Let the judge lead the jury, by some rebuke to the chief, to believe that the red men were out of order and those twelve jurymen, all with side knives, would be at the back of the room with such speed and fury as might make the sugar-camp massacre a Sunday-school picnic.

"Let the boy continue," McGowan said, as if the order had originated with him.

"Continue, Benjamin," Dilk said, as calmly as if the idea had been, from the beginning, *his*.

Ben, rattled by the interruptions, made a couple of false starts, reconsidered, and finally got under way again.

"Black Antler taught us, 'Never forget to be thankful to the Great Spirit above us all. We will be good friends here and when we meet the Great Being above we will have brighter and happier days.' "

Ben looked apologetically at his Indian listeners. "I know more, but right now I can't seem to remember. The way we always did it, Folded Leaf would say it with me. He knew it better'n me and I could follow him when I forgot something."

At the back of the room the chief who had spoken made the Indian sign "We are satisfied."

"Continue with the boy's testimony," McGowan ordered.

"Benjamin," Dilk said, "why did you think Benson and the Woods went to the Indian camp?"

"To visit them."

"This is something you have done before?"

"Yes."

"What happened to the squirrel hunt?"

"I thought we would hunt after we ate."

"They fed you?"

"Indians always do."

"Did everybody eat?"

"Yes."

"What happened next?"

"We just talked around for a while."

"How long?"

"I don't know . . . 'til we heard the shots."

"What shots? Where?"

"I don't know. I can't remember." Ben dropped his face into the cradle of his arms.

At the back of the room one of the younger Indians spoke. "You tell, boy."

Dilk turned his anvil face toward the Indians. "He is going to tell. You won't help him by yelling at him."

The Indian who had first spoken, the tall, richly beaded and feathered chief, made a sign of rebuke to the younger Indian. "The boy tells well. Let him take his own gait."

"Benjamin," Dilk said, "was the first shot from toward the river or away from it?"

Ben looked up, puzzlement on his face. "The first shot was toward the river."

"Then . . . ?"

"Then a single shot from the other direction."

"After that, Benjamin?"

"The killing began. It was then they started doing it."

"Doing what?"

"I told you. Killing. They all started killing the Indians. They started shooting. As soon as the other shooting stopped, they started shooting the women and children."

"Who did the killing?"

"They all did it."

"Did you see anybody in particular?"

"I saw two. First of all I saw what Johnny Wood did."

Charlie Fort was on his feet. "Judge McGowan, I protest. We are now considering the case of George Benson. If the boy has any testimony relevant to the actions of George Benson on the afternoon in question, let him continue. If not, let him step down."

"Your honor," Dilk spoke harshly, "this court will have to make up its mind whether it wants to hear the gentleman from Ohio spiel or whether it wants to hear from an eyewitness an account of what actually happened. I ask the court to remember that the witness is a young lad, and that the horrifying events of the afternoon . . ."

Charlie Fort was once again on his feet, his tenor voice high and carrying after Dilk's bass. "Your honor, I object. The prosecutor is prejudicing the minds of the jury by using words to characterize the acts of the men I defend; and no testimony has yet been produced to justify such language."

"Objection sustained," said Judge McGowan.

"I withdraw the word, your honor. But I do ask you to remember that the witness is young. He is unaccustomed to being questioned about a . . ." Dilk paused dramatically. "A disturbing event." He paused again, giving Fort his opportunity to argue that what happened at the sugar camp was not "disturbing." Fort remained silent. Dilk continued. "As I said, the boy is young and the events he witnessed did not happen in any order or sequence which Mr. Fort may feel most suited to the defense's case. They happened, and Benjamin remembers them as they happened. We will, I assure you, Mr. Fort, get to Mr. Benson. And when John Wood, Jr., is tried for the act for which he has already been indicted by the grand jury, my witness will then repeat for the jury what he saw, in the case the jury feels the need to hear that act described once more. But I beg of you, Judge McGowan, out of consideration for the feelings of the boy and out of a judicial concern for the most complete account possible of the events of that day that you permit the witness to tell the court of the happenings in the order that they happened."

"Permission granted, Mr. Dilk. Continue with your witness."

"Benjamin," Dilk said, "you have told us that after you heard the shots fired away from the camp, shooting then began at the camp. You also said that you can only say positively who was responsible for two deaths? Is that true?"

"Yes, sir."

"Which was the first of these deaths you witnessed and who was the killer?"

"When the shooting started, two squaws fell down right away. Everybody thought they were dead. But one of the squaws wasn't dead, because they brought her to church at our house the next day. She died then.''

''You said there were three Indian women.''

''Yes, sir.''

''Did you know the other one's name?''

''Yes, sir. Her name was Wide Eyes.''

''Wasn't she hit?''

''Not at first. George Benson told Johnny he was leaving her for him because she was younger than the other women.''

''Hadn't Johnny done any shooting?''

''No. He hadn't lifted his gun. When Mr. Benson said, 'What are you waiting for, Johnny?,' Wide Eyes said, 'I am a Christian. The Lord Jesus Christ is my savior. Don't shoot me. I love the Lord Jesus Christ.' Then Mr. Benson said, 'She's a redskin, Johnny. Let her have it.' Then Wide Eyes tore open the front of her dress so that all of her skin down to her waist showed. And she was as white as we are. And she said, 'Brothers, my skin is white as yours.' And it was. But Mr.

Benson said, 'She's a breed, Johnny. Her father forced a white woman. Whose side are you on, anyway?' Then Johnny raised his gun and fired. It hit one side of her chest — right in the center. But she just stood there, and not even any blood came out. Mr. Benson said, 'She's got one more, Johnny. You got one bull's-eye. One more will do it.' So Johnny shot her again — in the same place — on the other side. She went down to her knees like she was going to say her prayers and she said, 'I love the Lord Jesus Christ.' Then she fell on her face and then she died. When she died, Johnny raised up his gun and ran over to Mr. Benson.''

''To shoot him?''

''No. The gun wasn't loaded then. To hit him.''

''What did Mr. Benson do?''

''He took hold of the gun, and Johnny held on, and Mr. Benson threw Johnny to the ground.''

''Did he hurt him?''

''I don't know. Stuff came out of Johnny's mouth, but it was puke, not blood.''

Ben leaned over, his face in his hands again.

Dilk said quietly, "So all the Indians were then dead?"

There was no response from Ben.

Dilk repeated somewhat more loudly, "So all the Indians were then dead?"

Ben shook his head. "Not all."

"We can't hear you, Benjamin."

Judge McGowan said, "Mr. Dilk, your witness will have to speak up. This is not a private conversation between you and the boy. It is public testimony given to a jury trying men for their lives."

Ben sat up with a jerk. His eyes were red-rimmed and his round cheeks glazed with tears.

"Hang me," he said.

"Did you kill anyone, Benjamin?" asked Dilk.

"It would been better if I had."

"You did not kill anyone. Who did?"

Ben stood up and pointed at Benson. "He did."

"Sit down, Benjamin," Dilk said. "You have already told us that both Benson and Wood Sr. fired at the women and children and that with the exception of Wide Eyes, who was killed by Wood Jr., and of Talking Crow, who died next day at your house, everyone was dead when the firing ceased. Have I misunderstood you?''

"Everyone looked dead."

"But everyone wasn't?"

"No, sir."

"Who was alive?"

"Folded Leaf. He was alive."

Having said these words, Ben stood, repeated them again in a strangled voice. "He was alive. He was alive." Then he bolted from the witness stand and appeared to be headed for the door, the street, and the woods beyond. As he passed the bench where the Cape family sat, Caleb Cape shot out an arm and pulled his son down onto the seat Caleb had vacated.

The crowd murmured, but the disturbance was not loud enough to require Judge McGowan's gavel.

If Ben had been seated next to Hannah, he might have buried his face on her shoulder and cried. He was next to his father, and crying on his father's shoulder was an act he wasn't encouraged to perform in private, let alone public. So he leaned forward, head to his knees, and rocked soundlessly, tearlessly, backward and forward.

He heard Dilk say, "The court will understand and excuse the witness's very natural emotional upset. Give him a few minutes to recover and we will continue."

Ben felt his father's arm across his shoulders, supporting him, so that his rocking was easier.

"Ben," his father whispered, "this is a big test for you. The biggest and the hardest you've had yet. You got through this. Now you do what you ought to do here — tell the truth — and things will likely smooth out for you from here on. It don't matter what people think — or what you think they'll think — you just set your jaw and tell the truth. This ain't between you and them — the people out there. It's between you and Folded Leaf and God. And me. You're my son. I set some store in you — and what you got the backbone to do. Telling the truth, no matter how much you wish it could be different, will clean the slate. It'll make everybody who loves you proud.''

Caleb had murmured these words in a voice so low Ben hardly knew whether it was his father or his own mind speaking to him. Maybe it was Folded Leaf, forgiving him and whispering to him to tell what had happened. He didn't have to rock any more. The pain in his chest had let loose of him so that he could sit up straight and take notice of where he was.

Dilk said, "Is the witness ready to resume his testimony?"

Ben felt the weight of his father's arm lifted from his shoulders. He stood. He said, "I am ready." His voice had a strange cracked sound in his ears, so he repeated the words to make sure they carried. "I am ready." It still wasn't the voice he was accustomed to, but it carried.

Dilk said, "Please take your seat, and we'll resume where we left off."

Ben reseated himself.

"The witness has already been sworn," Dilk said. "The question, Benjamin, was that though everyone *looked* dead, everyone wasn't dead. Do you remember that?''

"Yes," said Ben. "I remember that."

"The next question was 'Who was alive?' "

"Folded Leaf. He was alive. He'd been shot in the leg and was stunned. But when Wide Eyes was shot, he sat up and tried to crawl to her. He couldn't because his leg was shot and the bone was sticking out. Bone is white like chalk, Mr. Dilk."

"That is a fact, Benjamin. Then what happened?"

"Mr. Benson yelled, 'The damned little bastard is alive!' "

"There are ladies present, Benjamin."

"Do you want me to tell what happened?"

"Everything that has bearing on the trial. Bad language has no . . ."

"I'm keeping back most of the bad language. There was lots more than I've told."

"Thank you, Benjamin. When Mr. Benson saw that Folded Leaf was still alive, what did he do?"

"After the cussing?"

"After the cussing."

"He shot at Folded Leaf but his gun misfired. Then he started toward Folded Leaf, and Folded Leaf called to me, 'Help me, Ben. Help me, Ben.' When he called I ran ahead of Mr. Benson toward Folded Leaf. But Mr. Benson caught me by the arm and said, 'Preacher's boy, if you don't want the same medicine I'm going to give that redskin' — he cussed some more — 'stay out of here.' "

"Did he hurt you?"

"He didn't hurt me bad. I could've stood it. He slung me down. But what he did was scare me. His eyes were popping out and spit ran out of his mouth.

"Then Folded Leaf called again. 'Help me, Ben.' But I didn't run to him."

"Why?" Dilk asked.

"I was afraid of Mr. Benson. When I got halfway up, he turned back toward me and lifted his foot like he was going to kick my teeth out or kick me somewhere."

George Benson, eyes once more bulging, spit at the corners of his mouth, got to his feet. He had been brought into the courtroom ironed, and the chains rattled as he stamped his feet. "That's a lie, that's a lie," he bellowed. "I was trying to save the boy. The redskin was crawling toward him. Ben, you know that's a lie. It was your safety I was thinking of. I pushed you to save you."

Judge McGowan saved Ben the need to reply. "Mr. Benson," he said, "sit down and be quiet or I will instruct the sheriff to remove you."

Benson sat down, but he kept talking. "The boy is lying, Judge. He never did like me. I run him off our place once."

"Sheriff," McGowan said, "will you remove the prisoner?"

Benson stopped speaking. "Mr. Benson," McGowan said, "you will be given all the time necessary to tell your story. But the court cannot give proper attention to two witnesses at once. Now, Mr. Dilk, if you will have your witness continue. I trust we'll have no more interruptions."

Dilk said, "Benjamin, will you tell us what happened next?"

"I didn't go to help Folded Leaf. I was

afraid to."

"What did Mr. Benson do?"

Ben put his head in his hands again.

Dilk took hold of Ben's shoulder. "Mr. Benson was right, wasn't he? Folded Leaf tried to kill you."

Ben jerked upright. "He didn't, he didn't. I told you, he couldn't move. His leg was shot in two. When Mr. Benson saw he had me buffaloed, he walked over to Folded Leaf. And Folded Leaf said once more, 'Help me, Ben.' But I didn't move. Then Mr. Benson picked Folded Leaf up by the heels and swung him around in a circle so that he fetched his head up at the end of the swing against the trunk of a big beech. Then he swung him the other direction and did the same thing."

"Did this kill the boy?"

"He didn't have any head left. Mr. Benson smashed his head like an egg. There was a body left, and running down the body was blood and stuff like pus and more little white bones. You couldn't tell if the body was a boy or a girl. Or if it was an animal, except for the clothes."

"What did Mr. Benson do then?"

"He threw what was left of Folded Leaf away. Like hog guts. Then he pulled up some grass and wiped his hands on it. Then he said, 'I reckon that finishes the job.'"

"What did you do then?"

"When he said that, I got up and run."

"Where did you run to?"

"I was heading home. But I was sick a lot of times and I couldn't go fast."

"Did you hear any more shots back at the sugar camp?"

"I couldn't hear anything for a long time but Folded Leaf's head breaking open against the beech tree. And I could hear him ask me to help him. I still can. And I remembered how quiet he was when Mr. Benson picked him up. He didn't beg Mr. Benson. Or ask me any more to help. He knew what was going to happen to him, but he didn't make a sound. But his head made a sound. His head made a sound like . . ."

Judge McGowan said, "We have heard that before. You don't need to repeat it."

"No, you haven't heard it, Judge McGowan. *You* didn't hear it. You don't

361

know what it sounds like. Not the head of somebody who asked you for help. Not the head of . . ."

"Ask your witness to step down, Counselor."

Dilk put his arm around Ben, said something only the boy could hear, then led him back to where his family sat.

The courtroom was silent. No one moved. Judge McGowan stared out at the crowd. They had come to see the monkey show. Well, they had seen it. He thought he could hear heartbeats; he certainly heard hard breathing. He certainly heard Ben Cape crying and George Benson muttering away low enough not to be told to stop, but loud enough to prove no judge could shut him up. Would the crowd sit there silent all day? Did they want to hear more of the same? He gaveled to wake them up.

"The court will adjourn for two hours for dinner."

There was one door. The prisoner, his wife and six children trooping behind him, was taken out first. The Cape boy's

362

account had taken some of the feistiness out of him, but he was far from broken. A white man in chains and Indian bucks parading like peacocks. Benson was rolling a mouthful of spit around like a cow with a cud of poison. There was no target within reach. He carried it as far as the door and loosed it like a hot cannonball on the new spring grass.

Judge McGowan watched him go. Benson would pass through the door someday hearing dreadful words he had spoken. God in heaven, God of mercy, why did he ever become a judge?

The jury followed. *They* would find guilty or not guilty: Sanders, Johns, Roberts, Gunn, Stephenson, Smith, Bentley, Wilson, Kilburn, Morley, Marsh, Fielding. They had listened to something they could not forget. What wrong had that Indian boy done besides being born red? Guilt or innocence was their responsibility. Life or death was his. He wanted to put his face as low in his hands as that boy had, hearing again a head break open with the sound of a pumpkin busted for cattle food, and cry. He wanted to, but he was a man, not a boy, and a judge, to boot; which is hardly a human being, he sometimes thought.

He sat upright, features as impassive, he hoped, as the Indians he faced.

The lawyers, talking, but quiet for lawyers, left together — except for Dilk, who went out with the Cape family. Mrs. Wood, enjoying herself, wife and mother of stars in the play, went out in a prance.

The onlookers left. The trial was many things to them. Most important, human beings instead of trees. Orators battling. A contest between lawyers, with words flying like bullets. The listeners all had real bullets, could make them or buy them. But none of them had a lawyer's store of words to fight with. Blood had been shed and more might flow. The onlookers filed out like fever patients from a hospital, their faces heated and their eyes bright. Judge McGowan had seen this happen time and time again. Considering the vein of cruelty that pulsed in all men, the love of violence, the fascination with death, it was a wonder so few heads were broken, so few breasts mangled with bullets.

He did not believe the Indians were any different in nature from the white men — in spite of Handsome Lake's prophecies and Black Antler's teaching. They, too, were brutal, but their training was different. Their faces were not open books. The Indian boy had not cried out. His kinsmen had not uttered a sound as they listened to the manner of the boy's death. They left the courtroom, their faces as sealed as old tree butts around the living sap that fed them.

Judge McGowan envied them.

When the side judges and Fenton, the clerk, had left the room and he was alone, he did what he had wanted to do before: he put his arms on the table in front of him and his head in his arms. He was not a young man, not old either — thirty-eight. There were strands of white in his brass-colored hair, like a dandelion getting ready to go to seed. He was not ambitious, like Fort and Dilk. He was judicious by nature. Judicious in practice, he had learned, was another kettle of fish. Judicious in practice required that one man, sitting on a bench, Amos McGowan, in his case, declare that in the name of justice one man should die, another serve ten years at hard labor, a third go free. There were hairlines here too fine for the human eye (which was all Judge Amos McGowan had) to see.

A hand on his shoulder roused him.

"Amos, I hope I didn't wake you up."

It was Johnston, the Indian agent. "I wasn't asleep."

"Will you come eat dinner with me?"

"Thank you, Colonel. I don't feel like eating. My stomach turns at the very thought."

"That wasn't a very pretty story."

"I've heard worse."

"I reckon you have."

"There are times I think I should never have been a judge."

"You've built up a fine reputation all over the state."

"Reputation don't chew like food. Happiness neither."

"This sort of thing makes us all bilious."

"There's nothing wrong with my liver.

I've got a troubled mind. No one man can hand out justice the way a judge is asked to."

"No one man is asked to, Amos. Behind you is a grand jury that indicts. A petit jury finds guilty or innocent. All a judge is asked to do is to sentence."

"It shapes up that easy to you?"

"Besides the juries, you've got a framework of law and of court practice almost a hundred years old to support you."

"Court practice for the past hundred years won't help me in this case. You know as well as I do no court has ever handed down a judgment against a white for killing an Indian."

"Don't you think it's about time? We've got enough treaties with the Senecas to roll up and make a corduroy road of paper from here to Washington, D.C. We're not at war with them. Don't you think it's about time the law recognized them as human beings, under the law?"

"Oh, it's time, all right, Colonel. God knows it's time. *We* know it's time. But did the men who did the killing know it was time? For two hundred years it was time to kill Indians. How was Benson and the Woods to know the time had come to stop?"

"Something told Bemis. It's a lesson the others can learn in this courtroom."

"All right, string 'em up. What use to a man with a broken neck will that lesson be?"

"Their sons will learn the lesson. The Indians will learn."

"What lesson will the Indians learn?"

"They'll learn there's justice for them, too. They'll learn they don't have to raid and scalp and burn to get it."

"You admit they've done those things?"

"For God's sake, Amos, where do you think I've been for the past fifty years?"

"There's those who wonder."

"There's no need to wonder. I been right here. Born here. Living in Ohio state. Watching the Indians get the dirty end of the stick for fifty years. It's time they got justice."

"Colonel, there's no such thing as justice. There's chance. It won't be justice that hangs these men. If they hang. It'll be chance. The chance that put an Indian agent like you in the Northwest Territory at the time of the killings. It won't be justice that saves them. It'll be the chance of a judge who wonders how settlers can know that time has had a turnabout; that justice, who has had her blinders off and her eyes wide open to see who was red and who was white, has put them back on again; that's what may set them free."

"Chance and justice could go together sometimes, couldn't they?"

"I pray they can, sometimes. In God's name, I pray it, Colonel."

"Leaving justice out of it, Amos, you know what this trial can mean in the matter of saving lives?"

"Oh, I know that, and don't you remind me of it. This court, while I preside, won't be run on the principle of providing victims to appease attackers. We're not savages. I'd rather we'd all be wiped out together than have any man who wasn't found guilty by the jury sentenced by the judge to appease the Indians and save our own necks."

Judge Amos McGowan slumped against the headrest of the tall fan-backed chair brought in from somebody's parlor for the trial. He looked up at the chunky Colonel. The *Colonel's* decision had been made from the minute he heard of the killings. Get the killers hanged. With this promise made to the tribes (time and chance and justice all bundled together for him), he had staved off an Indian uprising and had brought the chiefs to Pendleton to see with their own eyes that his promise was being kept. Behind the Colonel, backing him up, stood the Secretary of War, Calhoun. And behind Calhoun stood Monroe, the President. And both were providing money to transport Indians, fee lawyers, pay the expenses of witnesses.

What did *he* have? McGowan asked himself. The law and his conscience. And the terrible knowledge that all courts up to this time had ignored the law. And that Benson, the Woods, and Bemis had killed out of knowledge of this fact.

"Come on out and have some dinner with me," Johnston urged again. "It'll do you good."

McGowan shook his head. "I think I'll go out to the backhouse and have a good puke," he said. "That's the slant my stomach is taking right now."

15

Charlie Fort didn't feel like eating, either. He didn't know what anyone could have done about the Cape boy's testimony that morning. In the long run it didn't make much difference how a man died. He was dead — shot in the guts, a blow on the head. But a boy with his skull bashed open *sounded* worse to a jury. There wasn't any law providing clemency for tidy killers, but a jury, a judge, too, were inclined to find a savage killer guilty faster than one who hadn't bloodied up the landscape.

Charlie had a revelation or two of his own to make, and this afternoon, when he put Benson on the stand, if he could keep the big fire-eater from rattling his chains and threatening to brain someone, he might undo some of the harm of the morning's testimony.

It was June in April. No June flowers or leaves yet, of course, but June's breath, warm and sweet as a midsummer day. It happened thus sometimes, a few days stolen from summer before summer's time, as there were a few summer days hoarded to be used in October or November. Those later days made an Indian summer. A day like this one, less certain in coming, had no name. It was less heartbreaking, too, since it wasn't a farewell to what would be a long time absent, but a welcome to what was just around the corner.

Charlie had two hours before he had to be in court. He headed toward the woods; out of the village, past blacksmith, tavern, and the newly made jail, past the Baldwin house, where the Cape family was staying — all sitting outside on stumps and benches eating a cold picnic dinner. Dilk was with them there, acting cosy as a member of the family. And Ben, still solemn, was able to handle a drumstick. Hannah was there, handing out the victuals, her back to him. When she turned and saw him, he felt in his own veins the impulse he knew was in hers to do away with all distance between them. Jump stumps, turn over rocking chairs, send bowls of coleslaw and platters of fried chicken flying. Give the sanctimonious Dilk a clout on the head in the process. What was Dilk doing there, anyway? He had been sent to Pendleton to prosecute, not spark.

Yet Charlie was able to greet them all like a lawyer, not a lover. Congratulate Dilk. Tell Ben that he had done the right thing (he had, though Charlie wished he had kept his mouth shut). Not say Hannah's name at all until his mouth was clear of all the others.

"Have you eaten yet?" Caleb Cape asked. "We've got God's plenty here. Join us."

"I thought I'd walk out in the woods. There's a number of things I'd better think over before court this afternoon. The prosecution has put the defense on its mettle."

Lizzie Cape said, "Hannah, fix the poor man a piece of chicken and bread and butter. You can think while you eat, can't you, Mr. Fort?"

"Think better, maybe," Charlie said.

"The horse don't run without hay," said Caleb. "Nor the bird fly without seed."

Hannah brought him bread, chicken, and a square of sweet cake wrapped in a fringed red-and-white-checkered napkin.

"If you don't mind, Mrs. Cape," Charlie said, "I'll take Hannah with me to listen to me practice my afternoon plea."

Dilk said, "Pleading's not going to change facts, Charlie."

"The facts are maybe less one-sided than you think, Oscar."

Charlie was talking over his shoulder as he headed himself and Hannah toward the woods. When the trees shielded them from sight, he threw the contents of the napkin away. "Fly away, little chicken," he said. He put the napkin in his pocket and took Hannah in his arms.

"My God, my God, Hannah, where have you been?"

"You must not curse, Charlie."

"I'm praying, Hannah. I'm praying, 'Oh, God, don't let Hannah stay away so long again.' "

"Do you know how long I've been away? Only three days."

"Does it seem that short to you?"

"No," said Hannah. "It seems forever."

They moved two steps forward, deeper into the woods, then kissed; two more steps, then kissed again. Hannah was more breathless than after an uphill run. She was weak in the knees. In the midst of her tremors and gasping she was still able to look at Charlie and to think, Oh, Charlie, you're nothing but a sweet-looking love-making man. You're not an angel from Heaven but a lawyer from Cincinnati. Then it came to her that she wouldn't care to be in the woods with an angel from Heaven. She would feel out of face with an angel; with Charlie she was more at home than at home. Hugging Ben was sweet. Waiting on her father and mother gave her heart-ease. But Charlie, outlining her eyebrow with one finger, gave her more bliss than her heart could contain. Her heart ached. It was a pain: but a pain that only more pain could cure.

They said that of some diseases: she'd have to feel worse before she could feel better.

The roots of a giant sycamore, spread out like the fingers of a hand, offered them hammocklike depressions.

"Let's sit down and rest," said Charlie.

Rest was the last thing she needed. Climb the tree, maybe. Chop it down. But not sink down into one of those root spaces, more a pallet than a chair.

She had already decided how it would be possible to see and talk to Charlie without encountering the danger of what had already happened once: always stand up.

She was no ignorant backwoods girl who thought that babies were delivered by storks. She knew where they came from and how. Her talks with Ora had taught her even more. She had no intention of having a wood's colt, or of being pitied because of a watermelon under her apron. There was no way she could stop loving Charlie, no way she could stop daydreaming about him, or of living over and over again what had happened at Mrs. Culligan's. There was no harm in that.

Babies weren't daydreamed into happening. Babies came from lying on your back and letting a man plant his baby-seed in you. When she and Charlie were married, as they surely would be, and when Charlie was finished with the trial, they could spend whole nights, and days, too, if they wanted, in bed and never worry about babies. The more babies the better.

Now, no matter how she felt, she would always, when with Charlie, stay on her feet. Always. Hug, kiss, fondle, taste, smell. Hands didn't get babies, nor did lips, or eyes, or noses. They were made in another way and came from another place.

Touch, as long as she stood on her feet, as much as she wanted to. Feel the silky hair; the sharpness of whiskers; the small fleshy ears, the Adam's apple outthrust but not bony; the flat strong back; the curve of the back before it lifted into the muscled bottom; the inside of the mouth clean and sweet; the outward curve of the inside of his thighs, firm as plow handles.

Loving of this kind, touching of this

kind, was not wrong, because as soon as the trial was over they would be married. They hadn't talked of this yet, but they would as soon as Charlie had time to think of something else besides the defense of his clients. And it was all right because she would always stand on her feet, upright, firm as a soldier who knows his duty. Lying down was when the trouble began.

"My God, Hannah," Charlie said, "what are you doing?"

"I am loving you."

"Now I am going to love you, Hannah," Charlie said.

He didn't ask her. He told her. He put his knee into the back crook of her knees and she folded up like a jackknife. She went down and Charlie with her, between the sycamore's outspread fingers into a nest of leaves left over from fall.

She remembered, "Always stand up." But they were nothing but words now, and words had no power to get her up onto her feet.

She *could* say, "No, no, no," but very faintly. Charlie was no fool. He knew, and

Hannah knew, that anyone who really meant "no, no, no" could get up and run. He hadn't hit her on the head with a stone or put an armlock on her. All he did was do what he'd done before: plant that watermelon seed, breed that wood's colt. That was all he did. And she lay there as happy as if planting and breeding were the world's whole purpose, and nowhere forbidden, not by Bible or preachers or parents.

Because he was tired, because he had the notes from which he had spoken, Charlie decided to make his own defense of Benson the subject of his piece to the *Western Spy*. He had some reservations about doing this. Readers might think that vanity had prompted him to embellish the written report with eloquence and wisdom he had not displayed in the courtroom. The conclusion might be natural. The fact was that he could not remember all that he had been able, in the heat of the courtroom conflict, to say in George Benson's defense.

Most readers of the *Spy* knew that he

was the adopted son of the editor. They would for this reason be more interested in his report of his own actions than in the report of another journalist. And they would know also that the editor of the *Spy* would expect his son to lean over backward in avoiding any representation of himself as shrewd or eloquent beyond the facts. Up to the facts he was prepared to go.

Mrs. Culligan, when he came in after the late-afternoon adjournment of the court, had seen that he was tired.

"My poor boy," she said, "you look tuckered out. Let me fix you some supper. It'll save you a trip to the tavern."

Feeding Mr. Fort was no part of her obligations as his landlady, but she assumed it with pleasure.

"You go on upstairs and catch a few winks while I dish up. I've got an A-1 stew. I'm adding dumplings. As soon as they're done, I'll bring you up a tray. Then you can write with one hand and eat with the other."

He couldn't quite do that; but he did sleep, and the stew with dumplings steadied the pen in his hand and the brains in his head.

He wrote of himself in the third person. It made the task of writing more objective, he believed; and it would certainly read more impersonally. "I did this" and "I did that" might all be true as a die. But the reader, hit in the face with all those I's, would likely conclude, "He believes in giving credit where credit is due, doesn't he?" So he wrote of Charlie Fort as lawyer observed, not reporting.

Extracts from a letter by Charles Fort to Enoch Leverett:

On Monday morning, the trial in Pendleton of the four men accused of murder in what is being called the "Fall Creek Massacre" resumed, with Judge Amos McGowan on the bench.

The morning session was given over to the testimony of a fourteen-year-old boy, produced by the prosecution as a witness to the part played by George Benson in the so-called massacre. Benson was being tried for the death of one of the squaws, but Judge McGowan permitted the prosecution to interrogate the Cape boy about the death of one of the Indian children.

In the afternoon, when court resumed, the original order of business was restored: Benson was then tried for the first crime for which he had been indicted. Before putting Benson on the stand, Charles Fort, for the defense, reminded the jury of facts they must not forget: i.e., that the trial of a white man for killing an Indian could not and must not be separated from the history of the two-hundred-year relationship of these two races. "What happened at the sugar camp cannot be judged except as history," he said.

Fort quoted Benjamin Franklin, who said, "Our frontier people have been continually butchered by the Indians. We shall never have a firm peace with the Indians until we have drubbed them."

He quoted the Reverend Joseph Doddridge, who said, "The Indian kills indiscriminately. His object is the total extermination of his enemies. Children are the victims of his vengeance because, if males, they become warriors, or, if females, they become mothers. Even the state of the unborn is criminal in the redman's view. It is not enough that the unborn should perish with the mother. It is torn from the womb and elevated on a stick or a pike. If an Indian takes prisoners, he spares their lives only in order to torture them."

"These, gentlemen of the jury," said Fort, "are the opinions of, first, one of the America's greatest statesmen and, second, of one of her greatest clergymen."

Fort's speech was interrupted at this point by Senator James Noble for the prosecution.

"Judge McGowan," said he, "I object. I ask that these words, prejudicial to impartial justice, be stricken from the record. We are not here for the purpose of reviewing the statesmanship of Ben Franklin or the spirituality of Joe Doddridge. As to Indian methods of warfare, we are here for the sole purpose this afternoon of determining the guilt or innocence of George Benson in the murder of an Indian woman. We need cool heads for this. We do not need to have our temperatures raised and our time wasted by silver-tongued lawyers attempting through recitals of past conflicts to keep our minds off the one issue here at stake: Did or did not George Benson without provocation kill the Indian woman known as Bright Water.''

Judge McGowan overruled the objection.

''In this case I do not believe that it is inappropriate for us to be reminded of the happenings of the past two hundred years. This reminder should not influence the jury in any way in its verdict of guilty or not guilty. George Benson did or did not kill this Indian woman. History may have played its part in his killing her. History won't bring her back to life. George Benson did or did not kill her. That is all that you, gentlemen of the jury, must decide. The judge in sentencing must consider the circumstances. *Must* consider them. Continue with your plea, Counselor.''

Counselor Fort thanked the judge and

continued, "Before I put Mr. Benson on the stand, I would like to recount for the jury a happening not two hundred years old, not one hundred years old, not fifty years old. What I am about to tell you happened within the lifetime of many of you in the state of Ohio, from which Mr. Benson and I hail. The report I bring you is firsthand, and in my own words — not as eloquent perhaps as Mr. Ben Franklin's or the Reverend Doddridge's, but equally authentic. I was given an account of these events by the mother and daughter whose dreadful fate it had been to experience them.

"A family by the name of Ferguson, of Scotch descent, lived on a farm some forty miles west and south of Cincinnati in what is now the state of Kentucky. The father of the family, Adam Ferguson, and his fourteen-year-old son were ambushed and slaughtered by Indians while trying to harvest his corn crop.

"Mrs. Ferguson, with a babe at the breast, and three older children were captured, tied to horses, and made to travel furiously to escape pursuers.

During the first night, the babe began to sob. The Indians, fearing that its cries would alert followers, snatched it from its mother's arms and brained it with a tomahawk.

"When the lodges of the Indians were reached, the mother and her two daughters, age fourteen and sixteen were bestowed as spoils of war on leading chiefs. They were passed from chief to chief. I will not dwell on their experiences. At one time the mother was traded by one chief to another for two horses. Mr. Ferguson's scalp was taken by whatever Indian had possession of his wife and was hung at his tepee opening to remind her of what could also happen to her. The youngest girl died in captivity. The seven-year-old boy was taken farther west and never heard from again. Mother and daughter, after three years, escaped. What I have told you I heard from the lips of Rachel Ferguson herself. When I was a boy it was still common for mothers to warn their children against straying too far from the house by saying, 'Remember what happened to the Fergusons.' "

Counselor Oscar A. Dilk then prevented Fort from calling George Benson immediately to the stand, as had been his intention. "May I inquire if it is the defense's intention to suggest that we substitute the Old Testament injunction of 'an eye for an eye' for due process of law as provided by the Constitution of these United States?"

Judge McGowan reprimanded Dilk. "This is not the time, Counselor, for cutting didos."

"Exactly my point, Judge."

"Mr. Dilk, consider yourself warned. Further remarks of that kind will be considered in contempt. Mr. Fort, have your witness sworn."

George Benson, though still in leg irons, had had his handcuffs removed. It was a real strain on that rambunctious man to try to talk without gesturing — and gesturing with his chains rattling was a real strain on the listener. Mr. Fort had arranged for their removal.

Duly sworn, Mr. Benson was asked by Mr. Fort if he, too, had been warned in his childhood to "remember the Fergusons."

"No," said Mr. Benson. "What the younguns in the Benson family were told was, 'Remember Grandpa.'"

"Did you, when so admonished. 'Remember Grandpa,' Mr. Benson?"

"Nobody had to remind me. I saw it happen to Grandpa."

"What was it you saw?"

"When I was seven years old . . . ."

"What year would that be, Mr. Benson?"

"I am forty-seven years old. Seven from forty-seven leaves forty. Forty from 1824 makes it 1784. The year was 1784. The Benson family was then living in Virginia near the banks of a creek called Little Muddy. At the end of October of that year, the time called Indian summer for reasons I don't need to explain to anyone here, including our visitors, my grandfather, a man near seventy, was down at that crick. He was getting a load of dauby mud to use in caulking our log cabin before winter started.

"Pa was working nearby, bringing in a load of pumpkins, gun with him, of course. I was playing in the cattails by the edge of the crick. I remember they were just beginning to fray out. They was well over my head, so I heard what was happening before I could see it.

"First I heard Pa's gun fire, then I heard him yell to Granpa, 'Injuns. Run for the house.' "

"Didn't he call to you?"

"He didn't know I was there. And Grandpa was deef and didn't hear anything 'til the second shot. Pa got that off just as an arrow winged him. But he made it to the house. Grandpa didn't have a chance. He started to run. First they put more arrows in him than a porcupine has quills. They scalped him while he was still alive. They cut off his privates while he was still alive. Then he died."

"And you saw all this?"

"I seen it all. I peeked out from between the sedges and seen it. I can still see it."

"But they didn't see you?"

"I wouldn't be here if they had."

"How did you get back to the house?"

"After sundown, when all the Indians

had left, Pa came down and found me. He thought the Indians had stolen me."

"And you spent most of the day there with the body of your murdered grandfather?"

"I wasn't right with it. I scrunched down lower and lower in the water while the redskins were prowling around. I kept hoping Grandpa might come to. But I was afraid to show myself and go to him."

"Did you remember this when you were at the sugar camp?"

"I remember it all the time."

Mr. Fort then turned his witness over to the prosecution for cross-examination. Senator Noble had but few questions to ask.

"Mr. Benson, had your grandfather ever killed any Indians?"

"Of course he had. He had lived on the frontier all of his life. A man don't live there without killing Indians."

"Whose land was he living on?"

"His own."

"Who owned it before he did?"

"Nobody."

"Didn't Indians own it?"

"Indians don't own land. They roam around over it. Hunting and killing."

"And getting killed."

Mr. Fort here objected. "The means by which the citizen of the United States got a foothold on this continent has no bearing on this case. Mr. Benson is to some degree responsible for the westward march of civilization in this country. But if we turn our attention to that subject we'll be here 'til the Fourth of July. And can then celebrate appropriately what we owe to men like George Benson's grandfather — who died in order to secure for us this beautiful country.

"Unless it is our intention to be here until the Fourth of July, we had better give our attention to the facts just related by George Benson. As a child he saw his beloved grandfather not only killed, but also hideously mutilated by a band of wandering savages while he, the grandfather, was peacefully employed in securing the family cabin against the winter cold. The question to be decided is this: Is that child, now grown to manhood, to be punished for remembering that bloody deed and for acting to redress, at last and in some measure, the fate, all undeserved, visited upon that brave old patriarch a half-century ago?''

After Fort had spoken, Mr. Patrick Conroy, as was proper for the most important lawyer for the defense, made the final plea for Benson. Mr. Conroy, always a strong and effective speaker, made a powerful speech. He introduced no new evidence of the kind Fort had, but he did remind the jury of the belief long standing on the frontier, that to kill an Indian was to strike a blow for the safety and well-being of the killer and his neighbors. Judge McGowan gave the jury an able charge. They were out no more than twenty minutes before they returned with a verdict of manslaughter. This verdict, after a recess for deliberation, was followed by a sentence from Judge McGowan: ''Two years in prison at hard labor.''

Mr. Conroy immediately upon the sentencing sprang to his feet and said, ''If the court please, we let the judgment go on the verdict and are ready for the case of Benson for killing the Indian boy in camp."

Judge McGowan, though the state also was ready for a continuation of the trial of Benson, adjourned the court for the day. It was growing late, the hearings had been emotionally exhausting, and McGowan had every reason to call for a halt. He instructed the court to reconvene Tuesday afternoon at two o'clock.

End of extracts from a letter by Charles Fort to Enoch Leverett.

On Tuesday, though it was noontime, nobody seemed of a mind to eat. The open space around the courthouse had for an hour been filled with many of those who had listened to or had heard about Monday's proceedings, too restless now to light and stop talking. The buzz was like that of a swarm of bees that can't decide where to settle. Was what had happened right? And, right or wrong, what would be the outcome for them?

The Indians, impassive in the courtroom, were still impassive as they stood together, too warmly dressed in their finery for the unseasonably warm April weather. They were motionless, their faces calm, their gestures restrained, but they were speaking to each other. What were they saying? Many in that crowd understood more than one Indian lingo, Delaware especially, but Miami and Seneca, too. These Indians, lookouts and listening posts for their tribesmen to the north (travel expenses paid by the government of the United States), were not now speaking to be heard. What they said was a matter of Indian gutturals, too low and throaty to be disentangled. Their thoughts were for each other.

The courthouse crowd had had no Indian training; their voices rose and fell. They cut the air with their gestures. They still felt stunned by yesterday's proceedings — battered, elated, depressed, scared. Where were they heading?

The Cape boy's testimony and breakdown! God in Heaven, how much more of that could they stand? The jury's verdict of manslaughter? How did they come to that? What was manslaughter, anyway, they asked themselves. Shooting at a deer, the hunter got careless and let go at any movement in the underbrush. A man was killed. Deadening trees, distance misjudged, and your pardner was brained by your axe. *That* was manslaughter, wasn't it?

Many who thought it wrong to have a trial at all believed that if a trial were held, such a sentence was wrong. Indians weren't witless. White men who killed white women were hanged. Indians knew that. A trial was a mockery where a man who killed a peaceful Indian woman was given two years in jail.

When the Indians swept down from the north, they would have two wrongs to right: killing Indian women and taking Indian men for fools.

Norry Culligan, who had just strolled along, all casual-seeming, tried, without being conspicuous about it, to stay as near Charlie Fort as possible. Charlie, with the other defense lawyers, was talking over yesterday's proceedings, and she didn't expect a word from him. A nod, perhaps. She would like to tell him that she knew that he had saved George Benson's life by what he did in court.

Thomas Gunn, jury foreman a woolly-headed giant, hair sheep-curly and sheep-colored, came up to Charlie.

"Mr. Fort," he said, "you got time for a question?"

"I'll take time," Charlie said.

"Manslaughter," said Gunn, "is unpremeditated killing, ain't it? Kind of accidental?"

"That's the way it's defined."

"Didn't Benson have killing in mind when he went to the Indian camp?"

"I didn't make that decision, Mr. Gunn. You jurymen did that."

"You want to know why we did, Mr. Fort? Way back there when that boy lay in the sedges and saw his grandfather hacked up by the redskins, something went into him and took hold of him and was his master. So what he did was manslaughter. No more murder than when a bull tosses a man. It was his nature speaking; nothing he had to plan. That's the way I seen it, after you put Benson on the stand. And it was the way I persuaded the other jurymen to vote."

Charlie hadn't himself thought of the killing in just such terms — though it had been his intention to remind the jury that they lived in a time and a place where the past still stained the present.

His plea had been made in court and had been successful. He didn't intend to enlarge upon it here. And before he could even thank Gunn, Sarah Benson, with children at her heels, not tall, but buxom enough to envelop Tom Gunn from knees to shoulders, threw her arms around the jury foreman. If a man's character is to be decided by the appearance of his wife, Benson was not a bad man; Sarah would certainly never see forty again, but to judge by her rosy unlined face she had enjoyed the last twenty of those years.

She was crying now, cheeks like plum blossoms in the rain. "Oh, Mr. Gunn," she said, "Tom Gunn. I can't reward you, but God will, for saving my husband's life. Me and my children will forever be in your debt. For the rest of your natural life you will be second in our hearts only to George Benson himself. Want for nothing.

Me and the children will be at your beck and call. Oh, God bless you for your noble heart."

Charlie, afraid that Sarah would next remember the part he had played in defending her husband, and knowing that Benson's troubles were not yet over, turned to his landlady, who was still close to him.

"Norry," he said, "I'm surprised you could bring yourself to come here after what we had to listen to yesterday."

"I closed my ears to the killings and listened to you plead," Norry said. "I fixed a pickup dinner for you and Hannah, if you want to invite her to the house." Norry didn't expect a miracle, but she didn't close the door on them, either. If Charlie wanted to say, "I'd like to talk over the trial with a woman of more experience than Hannah," she wasn't going to argue. That wasn't the reply she expected and it wasn't the one she got.

"I haven't seen Hannah," Charlie said.

Norry pointed. In a crowd of women, Hannah couldn't be missed. Surrounded by men, she loomed less spectacularly.

She was with men now — her father, Colonel Johnston, Judge McGowan, Jonathan Armitage, the prosecutor, a couple of the jurors.

"You sure you fixed the dinner for me and Hannah?"

"Unless you've found yourself another girl, Charlie."

"I'm susceptible, Norry, but I ain't fickle."

Charlie was of two minds about joining the crowd around Hannah. As it turned out, he didn't have to. Hannah, responding to his wave, came to him.

"Norry has fixed us a bite to eat at her place. Will you come with me there?"

Norry was heading quickly away from Charlie. Hannah watched her resolute departure. "Why is that woman so good to us?" she asked.

"She's an old lady without any children left at home," Charlie said. "We take their place."

Hannah looked at Charlie. It was easier for her to see in Charlie what Norry saw, easier than for Charlie to understand the feelings of a woman old enough to be the mother he'd never had.

"She's in love with you," Hannah said.

"My God, Hannah," said Charlie, "I've got enough troubles in this trial without you working your imagination overtime on Norry. She's a *grandmother;* didn't you know that?"

"She don't think of you as a grandson. Likely she had a young husband, just your spit and image. She looks at you and remembers him — and forgets all the time in between."

"I look at her and remember you. And the difference. Come on, let's eat."

Norry had put food on the table and covered it with a white fringed cloth to keep off flies. Custard pie, cream and brown like a Jersey cow; deviled eggs; pickled beets. Food pretty to look at, but look at was all they could do. They couldn't take the time to fill their mouths with pretty pink beets or deviled eggs or pie the color of a Jersey cow, though that was their intention. They sat down, picked up napkins, then rose, threw their napkins away, and clasped each other.

"I have to be in court in an hour,"

Charlie said.

"I know," said Hannah.

Their kiss was intended as a farewell. "Good-bye for a while. We part to meet again." It was not a farewell; it was an invitation, urgent but unacceptable. Hannah lost track of boundaries. Which was her mouth? Which was Charlie's? She did not know. It was a farewell kiss, but it opened a wound deep and asking in her body. Kissing Charlie good-bye hurt as no farewell bow could.

They gave the pie and the eggs to Scooter.

"He'll get so fat Norry will notice."

Scooter would not touch pickled beets. "I'll eat the beets." Charlie said, "It will be a long hard afternoon, and I better have something to run on."

After he ate the beets, Charlie's mouth was so red they had to kiss the stains away.

There were ten minutes left.

"Charlie," said Hannah, "we mustn't make love any more."

"Because it is wrong?"

"It *is* wrong," Hannah said, "but wrong

wouldn't stop me. Besides, afterward, I don't feel like I've done wrong. If I stole or lied, my conscience would hurt afterward. But afterward, now . . ." Hannah paused, thinking.

"Afterward — how do you feel, Hannah?"

"I feel blessed," Hannah said, startling herself with the holy word.

"So why must we stop?"

"You know why, Charlie."

"Yes, I know why."

"I've talked to Ora about it. She told me some things. I'm not ignorant."

"We're going to be married, you know, Hannah."

"I don't want to *have* to be married."

"You and I have to be married. You know that, Hannah. There'd be no sense in not. As soon as this trial is over."

"Then we mustn't any more — until the trial is over."

"No, we mustn't, Hannah. You're right."

Charlie held Hannah in his arms. No kissing now. She might have been ten years old or his mother. "But you must help me, Hannah.''

''I will help you, Charlie. I will. I always will. You know that.''

16

Judge McGowan was in his tall fan-backed chair a quarter of an hour before the afternoon session started. He leaned his head against the supporting curve of black walnut, a curve shiny from the hair oil of many heads that had rested there in the years since it had first been made. He closed his eyes and kept them closed. If people thought he was sleeping, they might let him alone. There was nothing to be gained but more pain in his midsection from listening to the talk of those who thought the entire trial was a big mistake, and the way it was being run a bigger one. As to the trial itself, a judge didn't override his jury. In England, two hundred years ago, it could be done. The jury got its instructions from the judge. ''Bring in a verdict of guilty,'' it was told, and did so. But even in England jurors had taken the bit in their teeth and found for guilt or innocence as their consciences dictated. And if their decisions left the judge thunderstruck, so be it. There were worse sights than a thunderstruck judge.

How a jury arrived at the decision that shooting a woman point-blank was manslaughter was beyond him. But with that verdict, he had no choice in his sentencing. Men are not hanged for manslaughter.

The courtroom was filling up. With his eyes closed he could tell that. He could shut out understanding of what was being said, but the increased volume of voices gave him the feeling of a sea moving nearer and nearer.

What made him open his eyes was not the sound of anyone's voice or of any sound whatever, but a feeling of warmth near him. He felt like he'd put on another jacket, or as if a cloud that had hid the sun from shining on him had moved on. What was next to him when he opened his eyes was the bulk of Black Antler, three inches away, hot with feeling, trembling with conviction, and with more than the usual mount of Indian lard on his bones to radiate all this.

"Judge," said Black Antler, "you did right not to condemn Benson to die."

McGowan opened his eyes wider and moved deeper into his chair to avoid the heat of Black Antler's body — and the enigma of his thinking. An Indian with a hatchet would surprise him — Johnston had his Indians under better control than that — but less so than Black Antler congratulating him on the light sentence he had given Benson.

"With the verdict what it was, I didn't have much choice in my sentence."

"No one should be killed for killing. It is not the Indian way. It is not the way of Handsome Lake and the Old Long House faith."

"What do you do with your killers?"

"Except in war, we are not killers."

"Sometimes, surely?"

"Sometimes. That man is made an outcast. He will not be spoken to or fed. He is cast out."

"Doesn't he die?"

"If the Great Spirit wills. We do

not kill him."

"Are you telling me you think these men up for trial for murder should not be found guilty?"

"Found guilty. Not killed."

"Set them free, they'll do the same thing over again."

"I did not say 'set free.' I said 'not killed.' "

"Put them in prison for the rest of their lives? They'd rather be strung up."

"I think so. But to kill for killing is not our way."

McGowan nodded toward the line that had once again formed at the back of the room. "It is their way."

"With your people, not our own. They have been at war with your people. They want them killed because that is war."

"What if they knew you were here asking me to spare them?"

"They think I am crazy."

"You know what my people would say? That you're crazy like a fox. That you'd persuade us not to hang the killers so that the tribes up north can claim to Johnston and Calhoun, 'They did not keep their word. They did not have a fair trial.' Then they would kill every settler in the Fall Creek valley. You know that, don't you?''

''I know that.''

''Then why do you tell me that these men, even if found guilty of murder, shouldn't be hanged?''

''I tell you what I think is right. I tell you because I think that right is what you want to do.''

''The boy you were teaching was killed. You heard how he was killed.''

''We cannot bring Folded Leaf to life. What he was learning might not die.''

Judge McGowan stared at Black Antler. Beyond him, around him, the courtroom was now filled with people, who were silent, watching.

''My God, Black Antler, you don't help me much. I can't sentence according to Seneca Faithkeepers. Or according to what strikes me or you as right or wrong. I judge according to law. I sentence according to law. I have sworn before God to do so. And before God I will do so.''

McGowan rose. He towered, a tall gaunt man, over the Seneca. He struck the table in front of him with his closed fist.

There is one Indian who's going to think twice before he talks back to McGowan again was the thought in the courtroom.

It was a true thought. Black Antler, who was not one of the observers brought down from the north by the government, took a seat by himself in the courtroom. The people he knew best had been killed. Neither whites nor reds trusted him. Both believed in killing. Even to the whites, an Indian's plan for sparing a white appeared a plot. Black Antler believed in the words of Handsome Lake, "Do not punish killing with more killing"; he felt the presence of Folded Leaf, now able to communicate directly with Handsome Lake, reassuring and commending. He sat at ease. He had done what he could.

Judge McGowan gaveled the courtroom, already on edge and more stirred up than ever by his seeming dismissal of Black Antler, into silence.

George Benson, given a new lease on life by the light sentence he had received yesterday, was brought to the prisoners' box. Not only had his chalk color brightened; he appeared to have gained weight during the recess. He was no longer the sagging sallow man who had listened to Ben Cape's account of the death of Folded Leaf. He managed his leg irons like gaiters — no effort at all, an adornment, if anything. His blue eyes were once again saucy and bellicose. Once again he was the hero — the man who had saved the whites, defied the Indians, and was cunning enough to control the court. George Benson, above the law and born to command.

If the court hadn't known for a fact that Benson had spent the night and morning in the straw of the Pendleton jail, eating boiled beans and sowbelly, they would have been convinced that he was fresh from a tavern and one pony too many of corn whiskey. What was bubbling inside George Benson was something stronger than corn — hope, raw, bubbling, uplifting.

After Armitage, for the prosecution, had summarized the case against Benson, Fort put Benson on the stand. He had no intention of spoiling the effect Benson's account of the death of his grandfather at the hands of Indians had had on the jury the previous afternoon. He wanted *that* to stay in the jurors' minds, not Benson's admission that he had killed a stripling. He kept his questions brief.

"Mr. Benson, you have been accused of killing the Indian boy named Folded Leaf. Did you do so?"

"I did." He had admitted it a half-dozen times elsewhere, and, faced as he was with what he thought a sensible jury, there was not much point in lying.

"Wasn't the death of the squaw sufficient revenge for the death of your grandfather?"

"I didn't kill Folded Leaf for revenge."

"What was your motive, then?"

"The boy was crawling toward me. I killed him to protect myself."

"Was he threatening you with a gun or knife?"

"Have you ever fought Indians, Mr. Fort?"

"I never have."

"If an Indian has designs on your life,

he don't go brandishing his weapons about.''

''The boy didn't have a gun, did he?''

''No gun. But he could've had a knife. Seeing what I've seen in the past, I wasn't taking no chances.''

''So you killed Folded Leaf in self-defense?''

''I did. And if you'd been there, you'd of done the same.''

Judge McGowan didn't permit talk like that in his court. ''Your defense attorney is not being tried for any crime, Mr. Benson. Confine yourself to answering his questions, not to speculating as to what he might or might not have done.''

''Yes, your honor,'' said Benson, who was even more eager than his lawyer to preserve the good will the court had displayed toward him yesterday. ''I killed the boy because he was threatening me.''

Charlie, doubting that Benson would do himself any more good on the stand, said, ''The defense rests.''

Dilk then took over the cross-examination of Benson.

Judge McGowan, who had seen every

Indiana lawyer, and many from other states, perform before him, felt sorry for Benson. Dilk was no natural orator like Fort; no birds would fall charmed from the trees when he talked. But he would take that jury over the logical jumps of the killing so smoothly it would end up with "murder" in its mouth without knowing how the word got there.

Dilk made no reference to the verdict returned by the jury for the killing of a squaw — except to praise the jurors for their attention to detail and devotion to duty. They blossomed under his commendation.

There was not a jot of difference in law between the two killings — and McGowan knew it and knew that Dilk knew it. What Benson and the jurors knew was hard to say. Benson got healthier-looking by the moment. McGowan tried not to see him. He wanted to pass a note to Benson reading, "Keep in mind that Dilk is here to prosecute you, not defend you."

The direction in which Dilk was moving was at once apparent to McGowan. He was carefully, guardedly, leading the jurors to believe that no matter what the law said (and those jurors didn't know what the law said anyway), there was a world of difference between shooting a squaw and bashing out the brains of a small boy. Dilk was so guiding the jury that it could in good conscience, and all as legal in their minds as a Philadelphia lawyer full of scrapple and scuppernong, call one killing "manslaughter" and the other "murder."

Benson faced the questioning unsuspecting, pleased with himself, the jury — and even with Dilk, who was laying the trap Benson would spring.

"Did you kill Folded Leaf, the Indian boy?"

"I did," said Benson.

Then Dilk produced something from a kind of carpetbag he had.

"Do you recognize this garment, Mr. Benson?"

The garment he held up was a calico blouse, of a kind that could be bought in Pendleton. These blouses were much fancied by Indians because of their bright colors. This one had been red, but it was now so stiffened and discolored by something that had been spilled upon it that little of the original red was visible.

Benson looked, but did not speak.

Dilk repeated his question.

"No," said Benson. But his face did not say no.

"Do you recognize what kind of a garment this is?"

"A shirt."

"For a grown-up or a child?"

"A child, it looks like."

"What age would you say?"

"Ten or twelve."

"Would you be able to identify the shirt if you could see the color?"

"Well, I can't see the color."

"Do you know why you can't?"

"The shirt's dirty."

"Do you know what that 'dirt' is?"

Benson sat in silence.

"Well, I'll tell you, Mr. Benson, and the jury, what that dirt is. You may then find that your memory has been refreshed when you hear."

Dilk held the blouse, first facing the jury, then the accused.

"The rusty brown stains are blood. Great gouts and spurts of blood fell, probably from the head, onto this garment — especially about the front, shoulders, and back. If you'll notice here, Mr. Benson and gentlemen of the jury, where the color is more gray than rust and the blouse is stiffened almost as if it had been starched, that discoloration was not caused by blood. That gray matter is human gray matter, a boy's brains spilled out of his shattered skull onto his pretty red store-boughten blouse. Now, Mr. Benson, that what you called 'dirt' has been explained to you, do you recognize Folded Leaf's red shirt as it looked before you smashed his skull against a tree butt?"

Benson got to his feet. He was a sick-looking man again. "You know why I killed that boy. Counselor Fort told you. He explained it all. My grandfather . . . This boy would grow up and do the same thing."

Dilk, without replying, took from his carpetbag a second garment, a pair of buckskin pantaloons as bloodstained as the blouse. He held the pantaloons from the waistband for all to see. One leg was intact; the other had been sheared off at thigh height, so that what was left of it hung in a few tatters of bloodstained buckskin.

"A boy with a leg like this was going to be a threat to whites?"

"He was crawling toward Ben Cape right then . . . you heard me say so."

"I heard Ben Cape say he was trying to get some help."

"I killed him out of pity. Yes, I did. He was suffering. it's just like the counselor said. I did it to put him out of his misery. I knowed he was suffering. I took the quickest way. . . ."

Judge McGowan stopped his ravings. "Sit down, Mr. Benson. Speak only to answer questions."

Benson sat and Dilk then addressed himself to the jury.

"Gentlemen of the jury, I see I need not tell you that the case you had to consider yesterday and the one you have to consider today are very different. In the first, you found the prisoner guilty of manslaughter for using his rifle on a grown squaw. In the second, a boy, who went where his parents went, with no choice of his own, was taken by his heels and had his brains knocked out against a tree.''

Dilk held up the shirt. He demonstrated where the material had been stiffened by the spilling of brain matter. He held up the pantaloons, touching the shattered leg as tenderly as if it were the small boy's shattered limb.

''Most of you have now, or have had, children this size in your house. Look at his shirt! Look at these pants, leg missing! That boy would never have walked again. Poor helpless child. Taken by his heels like a rabbit and brained. If the one case was manslaughter — and I have not argued against that verdict — is this not murder? If the one was the act of an evil man, was this not the act of a brutal murderer?''

Judge McGowan had given the jury a clear charge before it had retired for its verdict on the murder of the squaw. He saw no need of repeating it.

417

He said only, "The charge is as before."

The jury, soft-footed in their moccasins, went into their little room behind the benches where they sat. Dilk left the shirt and pantaloons on the table before him. The courtroom was silent. Benson's bull neck had bent. His head hung on a curve that even his neck's heaviness seemed incapable of supporting. People had given up looking at the Indians. There was no telling from their appearance how matters stood with them.

The skin across Judge McGowan's cheekbones was tight. One eyelid twitched. He rolled a pencil between forefinger and thumb.

The jury, after an absence of not many minutes, returned, silent as before. They were men who knew how to manage their bodies: no stumbling, shuffling, seating, and reseating.

"Have you reached a verdict?" asked Judge McGowan.

Thomas Gunn, the big Scot with sheep-textured hair, rose.

"We have."

"What is the verdict, Mr. Foreman?"

Gunn replied in a level voice, "Guilty of murder in the first degree."

The prisoner was remanded, and the court adjourned.

17

The court had adjourned late, near suppertime. After that verdict, the strength appeared to have gone out of the onlookers' legs. Many still sat as if felled by a blow. What kind of a sentence could McGowan give after a verdict like that? The shirt and pants of the dead boy were spread out on the table. A few people filed by for a look and blanched at the sight. The boy had died a terrible death; no two ways about it.

The Cape family was strong enough to stand on its feet and start toward the Baldwin home. Hannah knew she should go with them; she was expected at her cousins', depended upon to help with the cooking and clearing up. She knew that she should be feeling sorrow for George Benson, his wife and six children. If

Colonel Johnston had his way, if murder in the first degree of an Indian carried the same punishment as the murder of a white, George Benson was already dead, his wife a widow and his children fatherless. Hannah was sorry, but at the moment she honestly was grieving more for Charlie. Charlie had done nothing more than lose a case — his life wasn't at stake — but she loved Charlie. This she knew was wrong, but you hurt where your heart was. And now she couldn't even find Charlie.

She lingered in the courthouse yard. She struck up conversations with first one person, then another, so that her own family, turning their heads to look for her, would think her detained out of courtesy and friendliness.

When they were out of sight, she gave up make-believe friendliness and searched in earnest for Charlie. He was still in the courtroom, backed into a corner with McGowan and Giddings and Noble. Charlie saw her over the heads of companions and left them to join her.

"Let's walk in the woods," Hannah

said, though she knew as well as he did why couples around Pendleton walked in the woods. "Where else can we be alone?" she asked. "To talk."

"I don't know," Charlie answered.

He didn't know that he felt like any more talk. He'd had his fill. Dilk's words still rang in his ears. The verdict clanged in his head like a fire bell. Murder. Murder.

"It's the beginning of the end," he said.

"The end of what?"

"The trials. Bemis's already confessed. God knows what that Wood boy will say, once they put him on the stand. Old man Wood boasted to everybody long ago about the part he played in the massacre."

"I know a place to rest," Hannah said, ignoring the trial. There were dark shadows under Charlie's eyes. His cheeks looked hollow.

This was a time when she should think of Charlie, not of herself. Standing up hadn't done any good anyway. Besides, she and Charlie had come to an agreement: no more love-making until they were married. Love-making itself wasn't wrong, but the baby that Ora said was sure to come if you didn't want it would be a shame to her parents — and to herself. A girl who couldn't wait! She was a girl who *could* wait, wait a thousand years, rather than have a poor infant born to be called a wood's colt. She would comfort Charlie, let him talk to her about the trial and what he thought he might do for poor Johnny Wood. She would tell him how Reba had belittled Johnny, practically pushed him into the killing. Then, before they went home, there might be time to talk about the wedding. What she would wear. Would her father marry them? Would they have a honeymoon on one of the river boats plying between Madison and Cincinnati?

"I know where there is a leaf cave," she told Charlie.

"What's a leaf cave?"

"Come on and see."

She and her Baldwin cousins had discovered the leaf cave. Fox grapes, climbing a sycamore tree at the edge of a branch, had reached the top limbs, then spilled downward, making a green umbrella above tree roots clear to the water's edge.

"It's a little leaf house," she said. "It belongs to me and the Baldwins. Look," she said, "we marked off the rooms with pebbles."

"Which room is mine?"

"Every one is yours. Lie down. Rest."

"Are you going to stand up and watch me?"

"No. You lie down and rest, and I'll sit beside you. Forget the trial for a while."

He felt like lying down. The land sloped gently toward the branch in the right way for resting. Hannah, with some idea of being a nurse to a man who had suffered a setback, dampened his handkerchief in the branch and wiped his face. After that she kissed his closed eyes, ran her tongue along his eyelashes, made him a mustache out of her braid, undid his collar so that she could feel his Adam's apple, ran her tongue along the grooves of his ear like a worm in the tunnels of a half-eaten apple, and finally picked up his head and rocked it against her breasts like a nursing baby.

He forgot there ever had been a trial and didn't care who was hanged. Rocked like a baby, he responded like a baby, and Hannah yelled, "You promised, you promised."

"I promised not to do anything to make us have a baby. I'm not."

"You will be in a minute."

She was right. He had her bodice half unbuttoned.

"*You* promised to help me," Charlie said. "Then you come in here and lie down with me and hold me and kiss me. What help is that?"

"It is not making a baby. It is helping you to forget the trial. It is helping you to forget Dilk and Benson."

"Dilk and Benson?" he asked. "Who are they?"

Hannah would not waste any breath answering foolish questions like that. He unbuttoned and she buttoned. This was becoming less love-making and more wrestling. And Hannah was more eel than otter. He had sometimes wondered how he'd make out as a rapist. Hannah sure wasn't the girl to practice on.

"I love you, Hannah," he said, trying to recall to her the purpose of these embraces.

He, not Hannah, relaxed when he said that. She turned him onto his back, sat on top of him, and looked him in the eye.

"I hate you, Charlie Fort. You are not a man of your word. You are not strong in body or soul. I never want to see you again."

Having said this, Hannah leaped to her feet and ran, hair streaming, bodice half unbuttoned, out of the house of leaves. Charlie's first impulse was to follow her. He jumped to his feet, then thought better of it. In the first place, he might not be able to catch up with her. And if he did, on the outskirts of Pendleton, what would people think? They'd think that what had not happened had. They'd have the name without the game.

He went back into the leaf house and thought, If this branch were big enough, I'd just jump in. He could afford the thought. It wasn't. He started walking home, home being Norry Culligan's house.

Hannah, always a brisk hand with broom and dishrag, outdid herself that evening at the Baldwins'. Her father watched her with sympathy. He was downhearted himself and wished there was some wood-chopping or tree-felling he could do to sweat away some of his misery. Keep out of the way was about the best he could do — and that didn't do much to relieve his feelings.

Pendleton wasn't a town big enough or fastidious enough to prohibit pig-keeping. Enos Baldwin, Lizzie's brother, who owned Pendleton's one general store, had a big family, set a good table, and there was always plenty of slop for the hogs. The wash-up that evening was big. Caleb carried the bucket of slop, while Hannah carried the table scraps, to the pen out behind the privy where Spot and Pinky lived.

A pig admiring the sunset may not be the prettiest sight in the world but a pig with his snout in the gruel of dishwater and discarded cabbage leaves, eating with sounds of a hand pump working on a well that's about to go dry, ought not to move anyone to tears. Nevertheless, Hannah was crying.

Caleb said, "There ain't been no sentence set yet."

Hannah wasn't crying about George Benson or his orphans-to-be or his widow. She was crying about Charlie, sad, tired, repulsed, reviled. Told he was weak in body and soul. His defense of Benson had gone to pieces. She saw him now stretched out on his attic bed recalling, as she was, every painful word that had been spoken that afternoon.

She said, "I'm never going to give any pig I'm going to eat a name. I think if it's going to be meat, you should treat it like meat from the beginning. Not give it a human name, then go out one day, knock it on the head, and fry it. I will never do that as long as I live."

She threw her apron over her face and sobbed. Caleb doubted that his manly daughter was crying her heart out over pork that had been named. He doubted that her feeling for Benson was strong enough to cause this outburst.

"There was no way in the world," he

said, "Charlie Fort could have got a decision for Benson in the face of the evidence Dilk showed the jury."

Hannah continued to sob.

"He got jurors to bend the law in the squaw's case. He's a good lawyer, but a jury's got to judge by the law. Not by smooth talk."

Hannah used the apron to dry her eyes, then uncovered her face.

"That's what I told him he was, Papa. Just a smooth talker."

"When did you do all this?"

"This evening — just after the trial was over."

"That was piling the punishment on pretty high."

"I know it. I'm sorry for it now. But he said some things that made me mad."

"That temper of yours is going to get you in real trouble someday."

"I'm in real trouble now."

"What kind of trouble do you call real, Hannah?"

"Charlie hates me, I think."

"Well, you go tell him you're sorry for what you said, and he'll stop hating you, I expect."

"Tell him right now?"

"It's no more than first dark — and less than a five-minute run to Mrs. Culligan's. You'll feel better, and he will, too, like as not, if you say, 'Charlie, my tongue ran away with me.' Never let the sun set on your wrath. Well, it's too late for that. Sun's down already. But my advice to you, Hannay, is to sashay over there, say you're sorry, then run back home with a clear conscience."

Hannah took off her apron, threw it to her father, and started off at a headlong run.

Her father watched her go — both with appreciation for her clean run, knees not clacking together in the hen run of most women, and with appreciation of his own understanding of the heart problems of the young. Most fathers would have lost long ago the memory of the wound a few ill-chosen words can have on a young heart. Most fathers would not have had enough understanding and trust to send their daughters after dark to carry a message of contrition to a courter.

Courting, he surmised, was what young Fort had in mind with Hannah. He wasn't blind to Hannah's faults. Her height and her quick tongue were enough to scare off most boys. But Fort had a tongue of his own and inches to spare.

Caleb went into the Baldwin hubbub feeling that in spite of his heaviness about Benson, some things in the world were still hopeful and headed toward happiness.

The run went out of Hannah when she saw the glimmer of light in Mrs. Culligan's house. It was one thing to know that she'd like to tell Charlie she was sorry, say, "Charlie, you are not weak in body and soul. I love you with all my heart. Don't shame us by making us have a baby so that people will say we had to get married. But if that's what you must do, I love you anyway." It was another thing to walk bald-faced up to Mrs. Culligan's door, knock, and ask to see Mr. Fort, please. She knew what the outcome of that would be insofar as Norry Culligan was concerned. "What chance has the poor boy?" Mrs. Culligan would tell the neighbors. "The big girl knocking on his door bold as brass, at bedtime. If I hadn't been there, I reckon she'd of gone right up the stairs to find him. In bed or out."

But her father had been right. She wouldn't be able to close her eyes once that night until she had said, "Forgive me, Charlie." Why did she think she was so much more tenderhearted than Charlie? He was likely suffering as much as she was. More, perhaps. He was the one who had been given those cruel names. What if he had called her such names? Ugly — or mean?

Her run had slowed to a walk. Her walk was one step at a time, but she continued in the direction of the glimmer. She climbed the steps of Mrs. Culligan's little front porch noiselessly, so that, if at the last minute her courage failed, she could turn and run home and no one need be the wiser.

She hadn't the power in her arm for a real knock. Just touch the boards as if, in the dream in which she was walking, all she had to do was touch the wood with her fingers and the door would fly open and

Charlie would take her in his arms.

It wasn't a dream, or if it was, no one else was in it. There was no answer to her whisper of a knock, or to the second knock, which was a murmur. Silently she went along the small porch to the window of what, besides the kitchen, was the one downstairs room. The glimmer of light she had seen came from a candle set on the night table at the foot of the stairs to light Charlie to the attic. At first, in the gloom of its flicker, she saw nothing but the dim outlines of furniture. Then, as if they were in a picture filled in little by little by a hand determined that she miss nothing, she saw the two white bodies on Norry Culligan's bed, a bed built against the wall across from the window. The white bodies at first were no more than outlines. They were short and long, round and slab-sided, hairy and hairless, dark and fair, asleep and awake. They were male and female. They were Charlie Fort and Norry Culligan. When Hannah saw this, the entire bed, with the bodies on it, seemed to move to the very edge of the window, so that she looked down and saw, in spite of wavery candlelight, every detail of the faces and bodies of Charlie Fort and Norry Culligan. Charlie was asleep, lying with no leg or arm extended in affection toward Norry Culligan, and the sight comforted her some. Oh, God, in our extremity what banquets we make of crumbs! If Norry Culligan in the light of the day was an old lady, in candlelight she didn't show it. Short, plump, and white as a squab. She was on one elbow, her back to the window, watching Charlie as he slept.

Hannah crept away from the window, down the porch, past Scooter, who expected her to give him something to eat. There was no run left in her. She crippled home like a string-haltered horse. She hadn't known that anyone could feel so sick without being on his deathbed. Ben, coming home after Folded Leaf's death? *She* couldn't vomit up the ball of stone that rested midway between her chest and stomach. *She* couldn't shed the tears her heart was floating in.

Charlie hadn't meant a word of what he said. Love her? Marry her? That was the kind of talk he used to get a girl down on her back with her clothes off, kissing and cooing and clasping. He had probably asked Norry Culligan to marry him, too. And at her age he wouldn't have to worry about babies.

In the midst of these thoughts, another, even more troubling, came to her: I brought it on myself.

If I had loved him this afternoon when he wanted me to, this would never have happened. Then an even bleaker thought came to her. Perhaps it would have happened anyway. Perhaps it had been happening all along. Just because Charlie is the one man in the world for me doesn't mean that I am the one woman in the world for Charlie.

She longed for some remedy for her pain. If there were nettles or a bramble patch, she'd like to walk through it, roll in it. She'd like something to tear her skin in so many places and so deep that the pain on the outside would make her forget the pain on the inside.

Her father was waiting for her under the beech tree at the end of the lane that led to the Baldwins'.

"I was getting uneasy about you," he said. "A midnight visit wasn't what I had in mind."

"I didn't even go in."

"Wasn't anyone home?"

"They both were. Charlie was in bed."

"So you didn't get to deliver your message?"

"Mrs. Culligan delivered it."

"Well, are you forgiven?"

"No. It's all over."

"Cheer up, Hannay. Quarrel in the evening; kiss in the morning. That's the tune lovers play."

"No. I'll never speak to Charlie Fort again."

Caleb knew better than to try to reason with the lovesick. Reason to the lovesick was like fire to the feverish. It sent them clean out of their minds.

"I'm going to bed," he told his daughter. "Poor Johnny Wood is going on the stand tomorrow. Armitage'll make mincemeat of him, I don't doubt. His troubles outweigh yours a thousandfold."

"Ben had to tell what he did, didn't he?"

"Yes. But Ben hadn't done anything."

"He told what Johnny did."

"Did *you* want him to lie?"

"Yes. To save Johnny."

"I don't think the good Lord gave Ben the power to lie."

"He gave it to me," Hannah said. "I got my share of lying power and Ben's added to it. I would have lied to save Johnny."

"You go on to bed now, Hannah, You're overwrought. No use staying up worrying about might've-beens."

"No use," Hannah agreed. "No use in the world."

18

The courthouse was filled an hour before the trial was to begin next morning. The prisoner to be tried that day, Johnny Wood, had not yet been brought over from the jail. Judge McGowan was not yet in his place. The word was around that the judge alternated these days between praying and drinking glasses of water spiked with baking soda. No one envied him his job. The jury, with eleven other jurors to back up each individual juror in his decision, was not in a place so stony lonesome as the judge. It is easier to say "We all did it" than "I did it."

The lawyers, dragging in from a night of playing seven-up (some said worse), or working up their cases, or writing letters home, were as early as the spectators.

The defense attorneys were having a conference. Charlie Fort had arrived first, hoping to see and talk to Hannah. He saw her, all right, talking to, or being talked to by, O. A. Dilk. When he caught her eye, and his eyes were instructed to say, "I love you with all my heart, Hannah," she looked at him with a stare as vacant as if he were a passing coon hound.

He was glad for the attention he had to give to the problem that faced the defense. Looking at Hannah, he might cry.

Noah Beazley said, "Is there any point getting that Cape boy up here and having him repeat once again what we already heard?"

"No use for us," Charlie said, "but the prosecution may insist on it."

"Maybe not," Beazley argued. "Charlie, you know Dilk better than the rest of us. Why don't you ask him if he'll agree to a stipulation, if we do, that the Cape boy's testimony be made a part of the court record and that we spare the boy — and ourselves — another repetition of that bloody story? Dilk ought to be willing — looks like he's trying to stand in well with the boy's sister."

"Dilk's not the big gun for the prosecution," Isaac Vickers reminded them. "Armitage and Noble are."

"Little guns can signal big guns. Dilk will try harder in this one instance to see it our way, and to get others to see it our way. If he won't, what've we lost?" Beazley said.

"Say they agree to the stipulation," Charlie said, "what's our next move?"

"Put the accused on the stand. He's got a right to defend himself, however you look at it. One boy, obviously worked up, says young Wood shot an Indian woman, first in one tit, then in the other. That don't make real-good sense. It sounds more like what a fourteen-year-old boy would like to see."

"His stepmother bragged at church that the boy had given as good an account of himself as any man at the massacre," Fort said.

"Watch yourself, Charlie," Vickers said, " 'Massacre' is the prosecution's word, not ours. And that Mrs. Wood is kind of teetery on her own rocker, if you ask me."

"Now, now, Isaac," Beazley said. "When you and Charlie are around, all the ladies get kind of teetery on their rockers. That don't undermine their *judicial* judgment."

Charlie wanted to get away from that subject.

"I can see some point in our putting young Wood on the stand. He's the unlikeliest-looking murderer I ever saw, and probably the unlikeliest the jury ever saw. The jury's going to have a hard time finding that sweet-faced boy guilty of murder in any degree. Let alone first. Let alone murder, the way Ben Cape says he committed it. I doubt the Wood boy's that much of a marksman, anyway. My God! First one tit and then the other. He ought to be in a circus if he can shoot like that.''

''Yeh, he sure is wasted out here shooting Indians if he can do that,'' agreed Vickers.

''All right,'' said Beazley, who was older than the others. ''I can see it's a subject you boys like to dwell on. But are we of the same mind about putting young Wood on the stand?''

''Yes,'' said Vickers, ''there's everything to gain and nothing to lose. Charlie, you talk to Dilk.''

Charlie hoped to talk to Hannah as well as to Dilk, but Hannah, as he approched, turned her back and walked away. Dilk, as Beazley had suggested, was eager to spare the Cape boy any further torment on the witness stand. In addition, he did not see that much could be gained for the prosecution by hearing the story repeated once again.

''I think I can promise you, Charlie, that

the prosecution will agree to the stipulation. You put the Wood boy on the stand now and then we'll cross-examine. But don't say I didn't warn you. I'd never let a witness like that testify if I was representing him."

"Why not? What worse can be said than what we've already heard?"

"Something worse can always be said," Dilk replied.

The prosecution agreed, as Dilk thought they would, to the stipulation. Ben Cape's testimony as to what he had seen Johnny Wood do at the sugar camp was read into the record and Johnny was put on the stand as a defense witness. Noah Beazley, solid and fatherly, took over for the defense.

The courtroom audience believed the evidence that had been brought in by Ben Cape to be patently true. They didn't think that Ben had the spark to make up a story to save his own life, let alone the gumption or inclination to fabricate a story to endanger someone else's life.

Dilk, who had been responsible for the

guilty verdict brought in yesterday afternoon, had this morning off. He was making good use of it, sitting on a front-row bench with Hannah by his side.

Beazley put Johnny on the stand. The boy put down a book he had been reading. Could a young man guilty of murder be that nonchalant? The door, because the weather was still June in April, was wide open. Two white butterflies flew in, then flew out. Give him a beard and long hair and Johnny, with his open hazel eyes and dark damask-rose complexion, could be the picture of the young Jesus seen helping in the father's carpentry shop. Even Armitage wouldn't dare be too cross-grained with such a witness, and certainly Beazley wasn't. He was firm but gentle with the boy, and the boy responded, neither nervous nor truculent. He went into the questioning as if all he had to do was to make his whole story known to be understood and excused.

Beazley: "Did you accompany your father and your uncle to the Indian sugar camp?"

Johnny: "Yes, sir."

Beazley: "Did you have a gun?"

Johnny: "Yes, sir."

Beazley: "What was the purpose of the gun?"

Johnny: "I was going squirrel-hunting."

Beazley: "Did your father and George Benson have guns?"

Johnny: "Yes, sir."

Beazley: "Were they going squirrel-hunting, too?"

Johnny: "No, sir. They were hunting Mr. Clasby's horses. They thought the Indians might have stolen them."

Beazley: "Did they take their guns so they could kill the Indians?"

Johnny: "They always took their guns when they left home."

Beazley: "To kill Indians?"

Johnny: "No, sir. To protect themselves."

Beazley: "But you took yours to kill squirrels?"

Johnny: "Yes, sir. You can ask Ben Cape if I didn't. I stopped in there to ask him to go with me."

Beazley: "We've already asked Ben that question, and he says you asked him

443

to go squirrel-hunting."

Johnny: "Yes, sir, that's the truth. That's what I asked him."

Beazley: "But Ben says that you gave up your squirrel hunt and joined your father and uncle in an Indian hunt."

Johnny: "No, sir. I never did that."

Beazley: "Well, what do you call it then? You shot and killed an Indian woman."

Johnny: "No, sir. I never shot and killed any Indian woman."

Beazley: "You're under oath, you know, now. If you don't tell the truth now, it's not just a lie. It's perjury. Perjury is punishable by law."

Johnny: "I know that. I'm telling the truth."

Hannah tried not to stare at either Charlie or Johnny. She had failed one and the other had paid her back in kind. Or maybe neither one had really loved her. Johnny had certainly never said so. Charlie had said so time after time, but with Charlie it was perhaps a habit. By looking steadily at Johnny, though, she could avoid catching Charlie's eye. If she did that, she might catch fire the way they said dry leaves could be kindled by a magnifying glass.

Johnny didn't look at her. He looked into space, waiting for Mr. Armitage's questions.

Jonathan Armitage, as if he himself understood that any too rough handling of this soft-spoken stripling would prejudice his case with the jury, shed all of his prosecutors' tactics. He spoke like an uncle to a nephew, one who'd been absent for a time and was now anxious for the latest news.

Armitage: "I'm Jonathan Armitage, Johnny. I'd like to talk to you some more about what happened at the sugar camp. You were there, I believe?"

Johnny: "Yes, I was there."

Armitage: "You saw some killing take place there?"

Johnny: "Yes, I did."

Armitage: "Would you mind telling us the names of those who were killed there?"

Johnny: "The Indians, you mean?"

Armitage: "Yes, the Indians."

Johnny: "I never did know the names of all of them. I knew Ben's friend, Folded Leaf. And the old woman, Talking Crow. And Folded Leaf's sister, Moon Ring. The men were Red Cloud and Tall Tree. But they weren't killed at the camp."

Armitage: "How many Indians were killed in all?"

Johnny: "All together, you mean?"

Armitage: "That's what I mean."

Johnny: "Eight."

Armitage: "In his testimony before the grand jury, Johnny, the Reverend Cape said that there were nine dead bodies at the sugar camp. Do you think the Reverend Cape was lying? Or maybe he can't count?"

Johnny: "Oh, no. Mr. Cape would never lie. And of course he can count."

Armitage: "Then how do you account for the difference between your figures and his?"

Johnny: "You asked how many Indians were shot. There were eight Indians and one white woman."

Armitage: "Who shot the white woman?"

Johnny: "I did."

Armitage: "Why?"

Johnny: "I shot her because she was doing what was wrong, and she was trying to get me to do what was wrong. When a woman does that, I know I have to put up a fight. I have to protect myself, or I know I'll join her in wrongdoing. I know my weakness. I know wrongdoing when I see it because I've done it."

Armitage: "What wrong were you afraid of doing?"

Johnny: "That girl . . ."

Armitage: "Wide Eyes? The Indian girl?"

Johnny: "I don't know her name. But she was white. She said she was white. She showed me she was white. She was no Indian."

Armitage: "How did she show you she was white?"

Johnny: "First she said it. 'I am white.' Then she showed me. She tore open her dress and did what a woman shouldn't do. Showed me."

Armitage: "Showed you what, Johnny?"

Johnny: "You know what. Pointed them at me. Pointed those two things a woman has at me. The way a man points a gun. I seen a woman do it once before and I know what she has in mind when she points her tits at you. I won't let it happen again."

Armitage: "What happened the first time, Johnny?"

There was a muffled outcry from the middle of the courtroom, and Reba Wood, standing, addressed the judge.

"Judge McGowan, Lawyer Armitage has no right to hound my boy. He's my stepson, and his father isn't here to protect him, so I will. Armitage, you stop your prying into what has nothing to do with this case. The boy ain't on trial for anything but the shooting at the sugar camp, and nothing else, so don't you forget it. He ain't no more responsible here for his past life than you are. And I don't reckon you're about to spill all that, are you?"

The people in the front half of the courtroom turned around to stare at Reba. Even the Indians, accustomed as they were to their own squaws taking part in all of their councils except those to plan wars, were startled. They broke their rigid line to face each other and talk.

Judge McGowan, who wanted some decorum in his courtroom, especially with Indians present, was able to gavel all except Reba into silence.

"I demand a fair trial for my boy," she shouted. "He ain't being tried for whatever he thinks he did in the past, is he?"

"Madam," said McGowan, "your boy, as you call him, will have a fair trial. But you, Madam, will not be able to listen if I hear one more word out of you. Is that understood?"

"Yes, sir," said Reba, who hadn't heard a commanding voice from a man since the death of her first husband and who liked the sound. "Yes, sir," she said, and sat.

Then Judge McGowan spoke to Armitage. "Counselor, instruct your witness that there is no need for him to go into what he thinks is right or wrong for a woman to do. And tell him that this is no time for him to tell us his past history."

Armitage: "Johnny, you heard what the judge had to say?"

Johnny: "I did."

Armitage: "Very well. Did you or did you not kill Wide Eyes?"

Johnny: "She died after I shot her. But I wasn't shooting to kill her. I shot her to stop her from doing what she was doing. I was just trying to stop her. She said, 'I love the Lord Jesus Christ and I am as white as you are.' Then she pulled out first one, then the other, and pointed them at me. I shot one and that didn't stop her. So I shot the other. If you love the Lord Jesus Christ, you shouldn't do that. I know someone like that, and all she wanted was fuck."

Judge McGowan pounded the court to silence. Then he said, "Sheriff Brady, remove the prisoner from the courtroom." Johnny Wood went with Brady as if happy to get out of the limelight and back to his book.

Reba Wood followed. McGowan was inclined to tell her what she had told Armitage: "Don't hound that boy any more." But there was no precedent for a judge to instruct a stepmother about her conduct with her stepson.

McGowan, when the two were out of the room, gave his charge to the jury.

"You have heard a clear-cut confession of murder. The young man believed he was killing a white woman, though as a matter of fact he was shooting a woman who was at the very least half Miami. She was in no way threatening or endangering the young man's life. He believed she was doing something wrong. The law does not empower us to shoot those whose ways are different from ours, or whose conduct we condemn. The law does not give us the right to act upon our hindsight and excuse killing by the conclusion that the killer, if brought up in a different manner, might not have killed. Brought up in a different manner, I might not be on this bench or you in that jury box. The law does not ask us to be God Almighty and to judge how we came to be what we are — or why we do what we do.

"The law is very clear on one point. If this was a premeditated killing — not in self-defense, not accidental — the

451

defendant is guilty of murder in the first degree. That is all you have to decide.''

The jury, given their charge, was not out long, and even without McGowan's help they would not have been long in coming to a decision. It was not a case, as were Benson's and Bemis's, of shooting an Indian. A matter like that took some thinking about. By his own confession the Wood boy had shot a white woman because he didn't like the looks of what she was doing. For that reason alone. The boy was guilty of murder. And it had to be remembered that this was a young man who might murder again, the very first time he saw a white woman do something he believed wrong.

Brady brought the prisoner back into the courtroom to hear the verdict. Tom Gunn delivered it: ''Guilty of murder in the first degree.''

If this meant anything to Johnny Wood, his face didn't show it. The words might have come from the page of a book he was reading. Those in the courtroom had no fault to find with the verdict. If the woman had not been an Indian and had done what Johnny Wood said she did, the case would of course be more clear-cut. But there was no license even to shoot loose white women, and a man who thought he had that license was, for the sake of other white women, better punished early than late.

No one knew what the Indians, with the exception of Black Antler, thought of the decision. Black Antler was against what he called "murder for murder," a belief he had picked up from Handsome Lake, and he let everyone, red and white alike, know what he felt. Because he was a Faithkeeper, the Indians let him talk. Because he was an Indian who opposed the hanging of white men for killing Indians, the whites believed him to be either crazy or a devious Indian plotter of some kind.

One other Indian, a Miami chief, the most resplendently dressed Indian at the trials, did make his convictions known. He was named Lone Fawn. The whole of the Pendleton - Fall Creek community could not have produced the amount of finery Lone Fawn wore at any one time: doeskin leggings bordered with white fur, a cape festooned with foxtails, a bonnet of horsehairs, necklaces of shells. In the unseasonably warm weather, he was undoubtedly too warm under these layers of skins, furs, and shells. The Miamis were a people willing to sacrifice comfort for admiration.

Lone Fawn, like his tribe's woman Wide Eyes, had more than a dash of white blood, and spoke English better than many of the woodsies.

Lone Fawn approved wholeheartedly of the death sentence for those who had murdered the Indians at the sugar camp. But what he particularly liked was the method of the punishment. Indians had never used hanging, which, from what he had heard of it, was a manner of killing, slow, dignified, and ceremonial. All took place at a height where the hanging could be well viewed — and the punishment, he understood, went on often for as long as ten minutes. Though slow, there was none of the hacking and slicing, the removal of ears, fingers, and privates that he personally thought lacked dignity. The hanging death, as it should be, was obviously not painless; there was a considerable amount of convulsive twitching and jerking to entertain the onlookers.

These whole affairs, he had been told, were conducted with admirable gravity and decorum. It was not exactly a religious occasion, like the whites' celebration of the birth and death of their God Jesus, but their priests were present and there were prayers by these priests and by the man to be strangled, if he felt like praying.

The condemned man was blindfolded before he was hung — for what purpose Lone Fawn did not understand. It was considered, he thought, a kindness. He himself would prefer in such a predicament to be permitted to look at the world for as long as he was able. In any case, those who gathered for these events, and they were very popular with whites, were not blindfolded. And what with prayers, last-minute speeches, and the adjustment of nooses, trap doors, and the like, the hanging of a single man sometimes took over an hour.

The cessation of his movements did not mean that the strangled man was dead. Lone Fawn had heard of more than one man hanged, adjudged dead, cut down, and then restored to life in a twinkling by a few gasps of fresh air. The authorities were then put to the trouble of rehanging the once-hanged man. To avoid this embarassment and duplication of effort, a doctor nowadays, he had been told, listened to the heart of the hanged man before he was cut down to determine if he was in fact dead, or was only, as the whites said, playing possum — alive, but appearing dead.

Lone Fawn, like the other Indians at the trial, had been invited to attend the hangings if they took place. It was an event he did not intend to miss. Justice would be done; but, beyond this, Lone Fawn had a natural bent toward the solemn, ceremonious, and fatal.

19

Charlie Fort, at the end of the day following the Woods' trials, sat at his attic table trying to put together something readable, and appropriate, for the *Western Spy*. Readable he could certainly manage; appropriate was a horse of a different color.

He was determined to keep out of his report, even though he knew that his father would see that it met his eye alone, everything about his breakup with Hannah. He was too sore-hearted to put that misery into writing. Writing, he *might* manage. But afterward, how could he read those bleak words except as an inscription on a tombstone, "Hannah Cape, the girl I loved and was courting, has given me the mitten and is now being squired in Pendleton by that rising young lawyer and politician O. A. Dilk."

Hannah, heart of my heart.

He tried to prevent himself from rehearsing his last meeting with Hannah in an effort to create a new scene in which everything he had done would be erased and he and Hannah would walk away from that leaf house hand in hand, an engaged couple with the date for their wedding set. That was what he had planned. And actually, what had he done that was so terrible? Unbutton a few buttons and kiss what the buttoning had covered. What had that fondling girl expected? Oh, God, whatever it was, he wished he had done it. Or had not done it. In college he had read the story of that man Prometheus, condemned to have his liver forever eaten, but never consumed, by a bird of prey. He knew what that man felt. When Hannah turned her back on him to talk with Dilk, he felt beaks tearing at his entrails.

The pain had never ceased except for that night when Norry, nurse and mother and mistress, had made him forget and sleep.

Norry kept clear of him now. Food on the table, bed made, water in the jug, but she herself always gone on neighborly acts. Gone, anyway.

If Norry was embarrassed or shamefaced, he wasn't. He wished

Hannah were one-hundredth as kind and understanding. If Norry would get over being so skittish, he'd like to talk to her. Ask her advice about Hannah. How could a girl turn about as fast as Hannah had? Love him to death one minute, then give him a stony stare, while smiling at that cast-iron prosecutor Dilk the next.

He could talk to Norry — and it would help him — if he could ever find her at home. But he couldn't, or wouldn't, write his father: "Girl thrown me over; case gone to hell."

He had managed to get onto paper, in what he believed was publishable form, an account of Johnny Wood's trial and the jury's verdict. He had toned down Reba Wood's outburst because he didn't believe his father would print a story like that.

What was left to report was sad and short.

Extracts from a letter by Charles Fort to Enoch Leverett:

John Wood, Sr., after he learned of his son's testimony and of the jury's verdict, refused the services of the defense lawyers and pleaded guilty.

His speech, addressed to Judge McGowan, was very moving. He said that he was as guilty as his son of killing a squaw; and that if his son had been found guilty of first-degree murder for this act, he should also be found guilty. He said that he was an old man, that his son was the only tie that he had to life; that his present wife hated him; that he had been able to survive thus far in life in part because he had always fought Indians; and that he would consider his death now, if the judge so decreed, as the often expected termination of many of those fights. What he had never expected was that his death in such a fight would come from the hands of white men, not red men. He had never expected his countrymen to come to such a pass, and now that they had, he would prefer to be dead. In any case, said he, the jury, after its morning's verdict, was bound to find him guilty of murder in the first degree. His son had killed one Indian squaw. He had killed one squaw and two Indian children. He was therefore three times as guilty as his son.

The old man was impressive. He had his Bible with him and held it in his hand as he talked. He looked like an Old Testament character himself, tall, thin, gray, his face severe and, as we judge faces, righteous. His lawyers could not have done better for him than he did for himself.

I was glad I was not on that jury, though Wood Sr. was right. The jury could not, after its morning's verdict, find for other than first-degree murder. It could not, under the law, do otherwise anyway; but the law, and I write as a defense attorney for these men, has never in the past taken the same view of a white killing an Indian as of a white killing a white. These four men, five if Clasby can be located, are standing at the point of a turnabout in history. And if they are all found guilty and all sentenced to death, they will be punished for what men here-to-before have been praised for.

Wood Sr. refused to permit his lawyers to say anything in his defense. The prosecution, after young Wood's confession, chose to stand mute.

Judge McGowan's charge to the jury was short. He told them that they were to pay no heed to Mr. Wood's desire to share his son's fate; Mr. Wood's wishes should play no part in their decision. That should be based solely on the question: Did John Wood, Sr., commit murder? And in what degree?

The jury was out about five minutes. Perhaps less. Tom Gunn, the foreman, a big round-headed Scot, seemed too dry-mouthed to pronounce the verdict. Up to this point, the jury's decisions had likely not been too difficult to reach. Bemis confessed. Benson was guilty of needless brutality. Wood Jr. was a young killer capable of killing again. But this God-fearing old man, this Indian fighter from away back, whose life was embittered, his wife up to God-knows-what devilishness, and his son guilty of murder as a result — finding him guilty of murder must have seemed to them more of a blow than any man should be asked to deliver to another.

Gunn got the words out. "Guilty of murder in the first degree." He croaked a little as he said them. Then he sat down without looking up.

Sheriff Brady led Wood, crying and kissing his Bible, from the courtroom.

Judge McGowan rose, appeared on the point of speaking, but did not. He picked up his gavel, but did not use it. He stood turning it over and over in his hand. People did not usually leave the court until McGowan announced that court was adjourned. They were right to stay. It was not yet adjourned.

"Four men," said Judge McGowan, "have now been found guilty of murder in the first degree. On Monday at ten in the morning those men will appear before me for sentencing. Until that time the court stands adjourned."

Judge McGowan then brought his gavel down with so much force his real desire appeared to be to smash courthouse, lawyers, witnesses, jurymen, onlookers, the whole sorry lot.

End of extracts from a letter by Charles Fort to Enoch Leverett.

Charlie put down his pen and tried to reread what he had written. It read like slop to him. His feelings had seeped into it. A newspaper writer should report happenings; not his own feelings or his conjectures about the feelings of others.

He picked up his pen, wrote at the bottom of the page, "I am overwhelmed by grief." Then he tore up all he had written and threw it in the bushel basket Norry had provided him for just such purposes.

He intended to make another start on his *Spy* article but didn't have the heart. He put his head on his desk and cried. Four men who had depended upon him for defense were likely going to die. Hannah was no doubt at this very minute with the man who had played a big part in convicting them. Charlie could see her kissing Dilk's eyelids, caressing his Adam's apple.

"Oh, God, why did I ever leave Cincinnati?"

20

Caleb was determined that before the Fall Creek town meeting started, and that was what it had as well be called, there should be a regular hour-long meeting for worship. It was Sunday. If ever men stood in need of prayer, these were the men. Soon Judge McGowan would pass sentence on four residents of this community. These four men needed prayers; and Judge McGowan needed prayer perhaps more than any of them. Caleb himself wanted, on his knees, his face hidden from sight, to learn insofar as possible what God's will for him was.

People had already begun to assemble in the yard. What they talked about while they waited for services was not his concern. But once they came into his home, it was going to be church for one full hour, and God have mercy on them all.

Oscar Dilk had made the ride over to the Capes' for two reasons, one personal, one professional. He would have ridden over for either reason alone. He wanted to see Hannah. Once this trial was over, he didn't know when he would see her again. Certainly no lawyer in his right mind would think of settling down in Pendleton, where legal problems were confined to lost shoats and failure to make promised payments on wagons bought back in Philadelphia. He would move on and, he had no doubt, up; and his feeling was that Hannah would be the woman who should go with him.

She would need a little "gentling," as these westerners called breaking fractious horses. Slow down her movements, put a little more dignity in her speech. But the girl was naturally a lady, had no vulgarity in speech or act, and was a practicing Christian. She was, without being the greatest beauty, the most strikingly beautiful woman he had ever seen. No matter where he went, or how high, eyes would not stray from them if that tall woman was by his side.

Oscar Dilk's mind told him these things, but without thinking of the future, or laying plans for it, the wooing of Hannah Cape appealed to him. He looked forward to it. It was his first reason for being here today.

The second was also important. It was in the air that Judge McGowan's sentence on the next day would be for death. Here, along this creek, was where the four men lived who were now in jail. If there was to be any attempt at a jailbreak before that sentence could be carried out, it would start here. Dilk was killing two birds with one stone, actually three. Smell out the settlement's likely response to a death sentence; make what he had in mind for Hannah clear to her; and, to cap it all, show the community that he remembered the Sabbath day to keep it holy. He always had, but it was a fact and there was no point hiding it.

Hannah was already dressed for church when he arrived an hour before church time.

"Are your shoes too fancy for a little walk, Hannah?" he asked.

Hannah had one pair of shoes to her name, and they were designed for walking. What else were shoes for? She was able to refrain from asking this question.

"No, Mr. Dilk. Walking won't hurt them."

"Don't call me 'Mr. Dilk.' My name's Oscar. I don't like it but it's better than Mr. Dilk."

"Did anyone ever call you 'Ossie'?"

Dilk was delighted. "No one ever did. Would you like to?"

Hannah hadn't the heart to disappoint the good man. "Yes, Ossie."

Dilk led Hannah down toward the bridge that crossed the branch between the Capes' house and the Bemises'. Hannah leaned against the railing of the bridge.

"If you make a wish over running water, you get your wish, Hannah; did you know that?"

Hannah, remembering when she had stood at this bridge with Jud Clasby, didn't hear the question.

When the question was repeated, she thought, What I should wish is that some man like Dilk would fall in love with me and marry me and save me from falling in love with men like Jud Clasby and Charlie Fort.

"Yes, I know that."

"Have you got a wish?"

"I just wished it."

"Can you tell me?"

"No, of course not. If you tell anyone, it won't come true."

Dilk clasped one of Hannah's hands between both of his. It was a big hand, but thin and flexible. He put it solemnly on the left side of the good broadcloth of his jacket.

"Can you feel that, Hannah?"

"Yes," said Hannah.

"What is it, Hannah?"

"It is your heart."

"Do you know what it says, Hannah?"

"No."

"It says, 'Ossie loves Hannah.' "

For a second, Hannah, feeling that thud under broadcloth, hearing that dark heavy-faced man call himself Ossie, feared she would laugh.

That is your trouble, Hannah, she told herself. You laugh at good men and let mashers and murderers have their way with you. She made another wish over running water. "Make me a better girl, God."

"Does Hannah say she loves Ossie?"

The wish took hold sooner than she had expected.

"I will when I know you better."

That was exactly the kind of answer Dilk wanted. He didn't care for forward girls, girls with their hearts on their sleeves, girls who leaped before they looked. Hannah wasn't going to say "love" like "good morning" or "pass the salt." When she knew him better, she would say it.

The dinner bell, which served on Sundays at the Capes' as church bell, rang. Dilk thought about kissing Hannah, but a reserved, thoughtful girl like Hannah wouldn't care for a man who started fondling her before the vows were said — and with church bells still echoing.

The text upon which he preached his Sunday sermons usually came to Caleb Cape like the air to his lungs, without thought. The texts flooded into his mind, a provision of God for his need and requiring no struggle on his part.

Before this sermon, he struggled. What words of God would bring most comfort to the families of prisoners who would hear on the next day the sentences of Judge McGowan? Which might be "Life imprisonment." Or "Twenty years at hard labor." Or "Hang by the neck until dead."

"My God, my God," Caleb prayed, "help me."

There would be present not only those fearing that the sentencing would be harsh, but also those who feared that without death sentences all of them would die at the hands of the northern tribes.

Black Antler would be there. He had Caleb's permission to preach, after church services were over, his own kind of sermon to as many as would listen to him.

If Caleb had possessed his soul in quiet and trusted God's providence more and his own wisdom less, a text would no doubt have come to him. As it was, he had searched his Bible Saturday night 'til his eyes were red in the candlelight and a half-dozen moths lay wing-scorched in a sacrificial circle on the table. When he had given up, stopped relying on his own quick wits and good sense to light upon something suitable, God spoke to him in the night. Nothing except the Twenty-third Psalm would be able to speak to the condition of all who would be present next morning.

Summer in April was gone. April, too, for that matter. It was now May, which had arrived with a cloudy sky and a raw wind. "A blackberry winter shaping up," they said, that season when freezing weather matches the snow of blackberry blossoms, or snow itself falls with skim-milk whiteness onto the creamy blossoms of the berry vines.

"It's a lazy wind this morning," said Lidy Stout to Sarah Benson. "Goes right through you instead of around you."

The change in weather was a godsend. What else could you talk about with a woman whose husband was lying ironed, in jail, awaiting sentencing the next day?

Sarah Benson had cried until she had nothing but swollen slits behind which eyes had to be guessed. All six Benson children had been crying, the two-year-old imitating big brothers and sisters.

Blackberry winter had already hit Reba Wood. She was as stern as an icicle. No tears glistened on her tight cheeks.

Ora Bemis, big with child, had not chanced bearing her baby in church, or of falling in crossing running water.

In Pendleton, the lawyers lodged, the prisoners lay, the judge pondered, the crowds awaited the next day's sentences like a race-track crowd for the money-running.

Here the deed had been done — men of this church had killed their traditional enemies; inside this church a dying woman had used her last breath to stain a killer with her blood. Here sat the families of men who would at 10:00 A.M. on the morrow hear a judgment of life or death, freedom or imprisonment.

The room was crowded, every bench filled, and children either sat on their parents' laps or squatted between their feet. The change in temperature made the crowding bearable, even a blessing. It was a comfort to be wedged between objects soft and warm.

Only Black Antler had to generate his own heat. There was no one willing to cuddle up to that big bleak Seneca. He stood alone, leaning against the wall, his austere dress as far from that of the Miami Lone Fawn as a gray Quaker's from a furbelowed fop's. No headdress, plain moccasins, bare legs, breech-clout and apron, and a doeskin jacket. Bare legs were not considered conventional for churchgoing, but after one look at Black Antler's face, heavy with thought and some kind of savage compassion, the lack of clothing on his nether parts was forgotten.

Caleb, warmed by his own love and concern, stood before them. The verses that had filled his heart rose to his mouth and filled the room. He had searched for them, true, but perhaps they had been sent. They had come to him like a gift. He poured them forth like a gift. "Yea, though I walk through the valley of the shadow of death, I will fear no evil: for thou art with me; thy rod and thy staff they comfort me.''

The words filled his mouth like a draught of cool water. The words a man speaks are always more comforting than the words he hears. The ''I love you'' he hears may weigh like a burden. The ''I love you'' he speaks lightens the burden he has been carrying and gives at least a part of it to another to share. Caleb knew that. He labored to put the taste of the words he spoke on the tongue of every man present.

''Surely goodness and mercy shall follow me all the days of my life.''

Caleb was never sure whether the words that were in his heart got spoken or whether they simply thundered in his veins so loudly he thought he heard them.

''We are met as Christians. We say, 'Thy will be done.' We have made laws we believe will bring the kingdom of Heaven nearer to earth. We must abide by them. We must pray for Judge McGowan as well as for the men who await his decision. We must remember that all things work for good for those who love the Lord.''

These, he believed, were the words his lips said. Inside, another set of words pounded to the beat of his heart. ''God, let this hour pass. It is more than we can endure. Let it pass. Let it pass.''

It did not pass.

This is more than we can endure. Kill for killing. Or refrain from that and be killed for not killing. His final prayer was tears, with a few broken words floating on that tide.

Hannah, seeing the state into which her father had fallen, rose, went to the front, and said, ''Let us sing.'' Many could not. The sides of their throats clung together like slices of meat hung in the sun to dry. Hannah sang. Oscar Dilk, with his lawyer's throat, sang. Lizzie sang. Their hymn was a psalm, ''Lift up your heads, oh ye gates.'' Caleb sat with his head in his hands. He was no true Christian. Why was the prospect of men going home to Jesus so horrifying? Well, it wasn't where they were going, but how they were being sent there, that was so horrifying.

He lifted his head when the singing stopped.

Black Antler, before the congregation could decide that the meeting was over, took the preacher's place in front of the fireplace. He did not have Lone Fawn's elegant English, learned from Englishmen themselves. But he had English, guttural but of a natural eloquence and gravity.

They were against him before he could say a word. They only waited for him to dig his own grave deeper with that tongue of his that had tasted (they believed) the liver and lights of white men. His heavy-boned, dark-eyed face hung above them like the mask of all the bogey men they had been taught to fear from childhood days: the Indians! The Indians! Dark, like the devil; slant-eyed, like men from the underside of the world. hair plucked to form a scalp lock — an act of bravado — for easier scalping. Half-naked, or hung about with animal finery. And such a one here in a Christian church while white men, because of kin of his, were threatened with hanging. And not content to be there, listening in silence, but rising to speak of forbearance, long suffering, forgiveness. In God's name, who was the Christian here? Such words in a heathen mouth were nasty as snakes in the cistern at home.

Black Antler talked of death — "The Being That Is Faceless." He argued against what he called "death for death," "murder for murder," "blood for blood."

Who was he to urge white men not to follow their own laws, not to hang their own culprits? He of a race who tortured its enemies, sliced them and ate them like dogs.

He explained it to them, the difference between war and nonwar. "In war we risk the fate our enemies risk. That is what war is. But when there is no war, when one man strikes down another in anger or madness — or drunkenness, for that is something you have taught us — we do not then strike down that man. We have not his excuse. We are not drunk or crazed or angry.

"Brothers, the man who kills should be locked up if he is dangerous. If he is not dangerous, shun him. Shame will then overcome him. It is easier to die than to be an outcast. But to kill the killer! How are you different from the man you punish? And without his excuse. That is not the way of the Faithkeepers!"

From the back of the room a voice called, "You were sent here by the northern tribes to talk us into freeing the men in jail. If we do that, you will have no excuse for not slaughtering us."

The cry was taken up all over the room. Caleb Cape had asked enough of them in the mere presence of a red man at a time like this; but asking them to listen to him, hear him urge them to become Faithkeepers, was more than they could stomach, Sunday or no Sunday, church or no church. Caleb or no Caleb. The man would have to go.

Shouts of "Out, out!" leaped from one to another, then grew to a chant.

Black Antler moved unhurriedly to the yard. He had no intention of staying inside, where, while he could be battered, his friend's home might be wrecked. Outside, he stood his ground. He did not try to defend himself; he held out his arms.

"I offer you myself. Here are my arms. My face. My hair. I will not run. You are drunk without drinking. Mad without reason. Strike. You will feel better. I will not be harmed."

"We'll see about that," yelled Lafe Brewster, who was holding an axe handle. He struck Black Antler two blows with a woodsman's muscle, pounding first on the right arm, then on the left. He stood back waiting for the arms to drop, the fingers to curl, the man to fall.

Nothing happened. Black Antler clenched and unclenched his fingers a few times, then, hands and arms spread as before, he again said, "Strike."

Brewster might have done so had Caleb not put himself in front of Black Antler.

"Who is the savage here, Lafe Brewster? Drop that axe handle."

Brewster dropped it.

"Black Antler is here because I asked him. He will eat with us. Those who want to join us are asked to. It is a solemn day. Tomorrow will be more so. Let us break bread together and pray for strength for tomorrow.''

Oscar Dilk and two families from down near Pendleton stayed. The others, getting onto their horses, into their rigs, or stepping it off on shank's mare, left the place at once.

"I should have known better," Caleb apologized to Black Antler. "Are you hurt?"

"No," said Black Antler. "I was with the Great Spirit. I'm not hurt."

Eleven whites and one Indian sat down to the dinner that had been prepared for half a hundred.

21

The weather next morning had worsened. No rain yet, but a cast-iron sky, and an icy wind out of the north like a warning from the tribes up there, waiting the news of this day's happenings.

The crowd had gathered early. Some few were jovial. They believed the game required of them by the government had been played. Judge McGowan would do what he had to do: give four men jail sentences that would soon be commuted for good behavior or by what other dodges lawyers had up their sleeves for taking care of their deserving clients.

Others were gloomy. "The government means business. It hasn't sent a former general and present senator down here as prosecutor to have them made light of by any token sentence, even of hard labor. Calhoun didn't send Johnston as far north as the Lakes on a pleasure jaunt. He made *promises* to the Indians up there. The government hasn't committed seven thousand dollars for any foolery. Monroe don't care about Fall Creek. He cares about raids, all the way from the Lakes to Chicago and Cincinnati. It's four lives against forty; against four hundred. Expect the worst. Hope for the worst."

"Hope for the worst today," some agreed, "if you want to see a tomorrow."

Judge McGowan arrived at nine o'clock and closed the courthouse door behind him.

"That man hasn't the face of one come to tie a wedding knot," it was observed. McGowan's face had been scanned to determine the sentence that he must already have in his mind. On the sheets of paper McGowan carried with him the words he would say, the sentences he would pronounce, were in fact already written. He put the sheets on the table and got onto his knees, with his face on his chair. The cold hard floor hurt his knees; the slippery walnut chair seat was not an easy headrest.

"God, God," he prayed, "help me."

"Why did McGowan come an hour early?" an outsider asked Caleb Cape.

"He came to pray," Caleb said.

"He a prayin' man?"

"What would you do if you had the life or death of four men in your hands?"

"Skedaddle."

The lawyers, defense in one group, prosecutors in another, knotted together, both groups long in the face. The defense believed they had lost. How else read four jury decisions of "murder in the first degree"?

The prosecution knew it had won. But what McGowan would do, they did not know. If he sentenced as he was expected to by the War Department, the Justice Department, and the Bureau of Indian Affairs, he was honor bound to judge the taking of life, be it white or red, in the same way. If he did that, four men would hear within the hour a sentence of death.

Charlie Fort, whose heart had received its own death sentence earlier, decided to appeal. Hannah, wrapped in a big doeskin cape, was thin as a taper, with the steady well-rounded flame of her red topknot lighting her. She was with her own family, separated, happily, for the time being from Oscar Dilk.

Charlie went to her, greeted her parents and Ben, then said, "Hannah, may I speak to you alone for a few minutes?"

Hannah did not have the redhead's usual blue or brown eyes.They were her black-haired father's gray eyes, and when Charlie spoke her name the whole of her life flowed up into them and looked out at him. Charlie drowned in them. He could not speak.

"I am waiting," Hannah said when they had left her parents.

"Hannah, we love each other. We were going to be married."

"We did love each other. We were going to be married," Hannah said.

"What did I do?"

"You know."

"I told you we wouldn't make love again 'til we were married. We didn't."

"No," said Hannah. "We didn't."

"Are you going to marry Dilk?"

"He hasn't asked me yet."

"He will. What will you say?"

"Yes."

"You don't love him."

"Not the way I did you. That's one reason I'm going to marry him. I can trust him."

"You can trust me."

Once again Hannah's eyes filled with the whole of herself. She lived in them. She was without protection of any kind.

"Charlie," she cried.

As she spoke, Oscar Dilk came to her side.

"Charlie trying to appeal his case, Hannah?"

"I'm not the winner today, Oscar, and I know it. In court or out."

"Your luck will change once you get back to Cincinnati, Charlie. Us Hoosiers got the advantage here on our own stamping ground."

"You planning on settling down here? Becoming a Hoosier?"

"That's my plan. But not this neck of the woods. I'm no farmer. But I plan to grow with the state. Hannah agrees with me. Don't you Hannah?"

"Yes, Ossie," said Hannah.

"Court's opening," Oscar said. "Come, Hannah, let's not straggle."

The door of the courtroom was opened by Fenton. Charlie watched the crowd pour in, Hannah and Oscar together at the forefront. He felt he had already heard the sentence.

Outside, it was raw, near to mizzling. Inside the courtroom the temperature was like that inside a body — warm, moist, bloody. The room was so packed, breathing was nearly like that of one body. There was not enough space to breathe in except when your neighbor breathed out. The Indians alone were given elbow room. Though their people had been the victims, they were looked on now, as always, as the enemy, the cause of all the trouble. No one wanted to touch them. The raw weather had at last justified all their rich gear. The crowd was near to blaming them for the change.

Colonel Johnston was standing, as were many. He had his back to Judge McGowan, and faced the crowd. Caleb Cape, standing also, was near enough Johnston to feel the strength of the man's character. It was strong as the sun in midsummer. Caleb was no weakling, but it would take God's help to face this man down if they ever found themselves on the opposite side of an issue. They were, Caleb believed, on the same side now: one law for all.

Johnston, an Indian's opposite in looks, corn-tassel-colored instead of cornstalk tall, had by some means acquired their training in stoicism. He was for them; but it was not this that gave him his standing with them. The Six Nations had known innumerable men from Washington who were for them, but always from the outside; white men whose duty it was to help the People. Johnston was *of* the People. Not by any formality of adoption — as many a white had been — but because by some means the Great Spirit had entered this white man's soul so that he looked out on the world with the eyes of a red man.

Caleb understood this. Johnston was of the People. Caleb couldn't see into Johnston any further than he could into Black Antler or Lone Fawn. But he did recognize the same metal when he was close to it.

The lawyers were at their tables: defense and prosecution separated. The jury, although dismissed, had returned. The courtroom was quiet. Judge McGowan silenced whatever rustlings and whisperings there were with a light tap of his gavel.

"Sheriff Brady," he said in a voice as dry as if his throat had been shingled with weathered boarding, "bring in the prisoners."

Luther Bemis was the first in. He had lost weight and color, but he was still Luther Bemis, his own man and walking a path he had chosen.

The two Woods were composed. Each, in a different way, appeared to be elsewhere. Wood Sr., within the privacy of his mind, had said farewell to Indiana and Reba and had returned to York state, there to relive the good life he remembered with his first wife. He was absent from the courtroom and the sentencing, although he seemed to know his whereabouts.

Johnny Wood, Caleb thought, didn't know where he was or have any good place he could return to. Bless Hannah, Caleb thought, for every cookie she had ever carried to that poor boy. I should have prayed for him more.

Benson was the last man into the courtroom, twenty pounds lighter, much of the red bleached out of his threatening rebellious face. If the sentence was not to his liking, he was the man, if the means were at hand, to shoot the judge.

Judge McGowan rose. He gazed for what seemed a long time at the prisoners. His eyes went from one face to another. To remind himself that these were men like himself? Or to search their faces for some sign that would alter his sentencing?

Caleb thought, The judge looks like he's been pulled through a knothole. He's no newcomer to the bench. He's sent men to the gallows before, but never a white man for killing an Indian. Johnston could do it — hang the men with his own hands, probably. Not McGowan.

After McGowan had searched the faces of the prisoners, he turned to the courtroom and began to speak. It was expected of him, but he spoke, it seemed, less to inform his listeners than to explain himself to himself.

"I have no wish unnecessarily to harrow your feelings," he began. "We are a civilized and Christian people. That is what we call ourselves — Christian, civilized. As such we have sent missionaries to the Indians so that they, too, might become Christian and civilized. There is no record of any hostile act by any Indian against a white before the Indians were mistreated by us. How did we mistreat them? You know that story as well as I do. But because whites did it to Indians, you tell yourselves it doesn't count. Did you ever think that it counted more because a Christian and civilized people did these deeds against a wandering forest people, without books, without schools, without churches?

"What did we do? We took away their land, first of all. Oh, yes, we paid for it sometimes. Not enough. But meanwhile we had given them a taste for whiskey, so we got most of the money back that way. We gave them our diseases, which they had never had and which killed them. We cut down their forests so that the game their lives had depended upon vanished.

"They fought back. They were not cowards. We outnumbered them. We pushed them farther and farther west. And even when two men, three women, and four children came to boil maple sap in what was their old home, to hunt in forests they had always called their own, we did not have the heart of decent men, let alone Christians, to say, 'We have more than enough. It was once yours alone. Rest. Take your ease. Share. Help yourselves.'

"No, instead of that, we fell upon them. We killed women and children. In ways more horrible than I will again describe to you. But in ways I ask you not to forget.

"How could any man murder Red Cloud, the descendant of chiefs whose name alone ought to have been his passport and protection from Maine to Georgia and from Mississippi to the Atlantic? The blood of a Red Cloud has for the second time gone up before Heaven crying aloud for vengeance. The blood of a friend of the white man rests upon your consciences and has imprinted a stain too deep to be washed out by anything but the blood of our Redeemer.

"Justice under the law requires certain punishment of murderers. But only repentance and the mercy of God can cleanse our own souls of the stain of these acts, which would not have been committed except that the murderers expected the approval of the people of this community. Four men alone will suffer under the law of the land. Everyone here must suffer under the law of Heaven for making it possible for those men to believe that it was no sin to kill an Indian.

"Luther Bemis."

Bemis, rigid, white, walked to the judge's bench.

"Luther Bemis, I hereby sentence you, for the murder of the Indian Red Cloud, to be hanged by the neck until dead."

Bemis, head high, but staggering a little, returned to his place.

"George Benson."

Benson moved not an inch. Brady, the one man in the room who could probably move him, stepped in his direction.

Judge McGowan shook his head. "Let him alone, Sam. He's near enough." This had a peculiar ring, half-funny, but all faces were too stiff with dread to even half smile. "I can sentence from here. George Benson, for the murder of the boy Folded Leaf and the woman Talking Crow, I sentence you to be hanged by the neck until dead."

John Wood, Sr., stepped forward without being summoned, eager, it appeared, to be relieved of his life.

McGowan's voice, trembling for the first time in pronouncing sentence, said, "John Wood, for the death of the Indian boy Hawk Diver and the girl Elder Blossom and the girl Long Toes, I sentence you to be hanged by the neck until dead."

Wood Sr. returned to his fellow prisoners almost jauntily. His troubles were over. Everything settled. Nothing more to worry about.

"John Wood, Jr."

"Yes, sir," said Johnny pleasantly.

"Step forward, please."

Johnny looked at his father inquiringly, his glance asking, apparently, "Which direction is forward?" Wood Sr. gave his son a gentle push forward.

"Yes, sir," said Johnny, looking up at Judge McGowan. "Did you want to speak to me, sir?"

McGowan leaned back momentarily in his parlor chair and closed his eyes. Caleb thought, Is he going to sentence him with his eyes shut?

Then the judge leaned forward with energy. "I must speak to you, John. You killed the Indian woman Wide Eyes. I . . ."

Johnny interrupted the judge. "She wasn't an Indian."

McGowan said, "You are not to speak, John, but to listen. For the killing of Wide Eyes, the Indian . . ."

"I told you what she did, Judge McGowan. She took them out and pointed them at me. A woman should be punished for that. A woman . . ."

On a gesture from McGowan, Brady took Johnny Wood by the arm.

"John Wood, if you are not silent of your own will, the sheriff will force you to be silent. For the murder of Wide Eyes, you are sentenced by this court to be hanged by the neck until dead."

Before this sentence was finished, a woman's scream drowned out the final word. Reba Wood, standing at the center of the courtroom, was trying to make her way through those standing and over those sitting. "Stop it. Stop it," she screamed. "You can't kill a boy for that."

"Take the woman outside, Sheriff," Judge McGowan said.

Johnny Wood, when Brady released him, went back to his father's side. "Take her out," he echoed. "She's a bad woman, too."

Caleb Cape received permission from the court to spend the nights before the impending execution in the jail with the prisoners. Judge McGowan, instead of setting the date some weeks in the future, put it only ten days in the future. A man suffered more, he said, in anticipation of that final fall than he did in the fall itself. Caleb could have found no rest at home away from these men of his church; particularly since one of them, Luther Bemis, would never, except for Caleb's word, have been in jail at all.

He did not know that his presence gave much comfort to anyone except John Wood, Sr., who brought up in the habit of Bible-reading and prayer, valued the nearness of his pastor in this hour of trial, though it was less of a trial to him than to the others. Dying without any sickness? What more could an old man ask? And after doing, in spite of the verdict of the court, what he'd been brought up to believe was right: rid the country of Indians. His conscience was clear.

Benson didn't set any store on Caleb's presence. He had ears for only one thing: the sound of a posse come to kill guards, batter down stockade and jail door, and set him free. Set them all free. Restore the state and the country to its old and rightful ways of thinking: rid the country of Indians. He had depended upon his sister, Reba, to stir up action for the rescue; but something had happened to Reba. He didn't understand what it was, but he waited for others to take up his cause.

Luther Bemis had not faltered in his steadfast belief that he had done the right thing in confessing. Right doing hadn't lifted his spirits, however. He thought constantly of Ora and the child, due now at any time.

Caleb gave him what consolation he could.

"Lizzie and Hannah are with her," he told Lute, "every minute. Lizzie had three children with no help from anyone but me. Hannah's as good as any man with an axe or a gun. Ben's going over every day to look after the stock. Ora's in good hands."

"They ain't my hands, though," Lute said. "They ain't my hands. Oh, God, Cale, they ain't my hands. My son will be born and I will never touch him."

"I had a son," Caleb said. "My first born. A redhead like Hannah. Her disposition more than Ben's."

"Where's he now?"

"Dead."

"How old?"

"Four. Lacking ten days."

"What was his name?"

"Named for me."

"We plan to . . . we planned to call our first for me. Not that I like Juniors much. Or Big Lutes and Little Lutes. But Ora wouldn't hear to anything else."

"You might have a girl."

"Ora don't think so from the way the baby kicks. And no more Oras for Ora.

She don't know where her mother got that outlandish name. If ours is a girl, it'll be Phoebe. Don't that sound pretty? It's my mother's name. Ora don't hold back a thing when it comes to giving to me. My name, my mother's name. She'd be right here in my place now if she could.''

''I believe that,'' Caleb said. ''I believe she would.''

''You wander around. You lay with women. Some one color, some another. Babies may come, but if they do you're far gone by that time. Then without your asking for it or expecting it, all that changes. A woman who ain't just a woman, but Ora, your own wife. Your own baby. Your own God who brought you together. Then, this. Is it punishment, Cale? Maybe I deserve it. But Ora don't. She's suffering. Does the baby deserve it? No father? God, God, Cale, help me. Why at this time? I've killed Indians before. Got nothing but thanks from all concerned for the job.''

''Except the Indian, I reckon,'' Caleb said.

''Well, Cale, you know as well as I do,

499

nobody expects a varmint to thank you for killing it. This is a turnabout. What I want to know is, why now? Why at a time just to hit me? And Ora? And the baby?''

Caleb could only groan.

''Don't tell me God moves in a mysterious way.''

''He does. But I won't tell you.''

''Shut up, you two,'' George Benson said. ''Sleep's the only thing left to us. The court's robbing us of our lives. You rob us of sleep.''

It was a cold night. There was no means of heating the jail. Making prisoners comfortable wasn't regarded as a duty of the court. And at this season, though it happened once every two or three years, no one expected such a drop in temperature. The jailhouse had been thrown together hurriedly. The straw on the floor had thinned out and not been renewed. The wind, seeping between floor boards not properly fitted, lifted the straw here and there in little eddies. Caleb wrapped his blanket as closely about him as he could. He left his boots on. Moccasins would have been more comfortable for sleeping, but boots were what he wore and what he kept on.

Luther Bemis, wrapped as closely as he in his blanket, was not sleeping. Caleb knew. Lute had his head propped on his folded arms. Thinking, reviewing, remembering, longing, perhaps dreading.

Caleb went as far into his own conscience, his own self-knowledge, his own godliness, or lack of godliness, as he could. "Greater love hath no man than this." Would he take Lute's place on the gallows if it would be permitted? He thought he could do that. He had already had many more years of good life than Lute. Lizzie, with Hannah and Ben, could make out better than Ora alone with a newborn baby. He thought he could do it. Then he wondered, Could you change places with him without anyone's knowing that you, Caleb Cape, minister of the gosel, had made that sacrifice? Could you take his sin on your shoulders? Become in the eyes of your neighbors the one who did the killing, and who died for the killing? No, he thought, I couldn't do that. Only one man was able to do that.

He put his hand out to Lute. No use saying, "I would suffer this for you if I could." What consolation was that to a man who knew it wasn't possible? "I would if I could, but I can't."

"Try to sleep, Lute."

"No use."

"Let go and sleep will come."

"I ain't afraid for one minute of the noose. Nobody who's been out in Indian country and fought Indians could be. I was prepared for far worse if caught out there. You know the things they do. I figured I could face them as good as any Indian. Lose my balls. A red-hot poker up my ass. Fingers chopped off one by one. You know the games they play as well as me. I faced *them*. A twitch at the end of a rope is a play-party game compared with them. But then there was no Ora. There was no son. It's *now* that's tearing my heart out. Now. Now. Oh, God, why now?"

"God knows," Caleb said. "God knows." He spoke in human despair, not preacher's conviction.

"Well, if He does, I wish to God

He'd tell me."

Caleb turned face down in the straw. He kept silent, he believed, but his shoulder went up and down with his crying.

Bemis reached out a hand to the man who had brought him to God. "I'll tough it out, Cale. I'll tough it out."

Book Three THE VERDICT

22

O. A. Dilk believed in constitutionals, that is, something good for O. A. Dilk's constitution. Lawyers' work required sharp brains, strong vocal chords, and an iron butt. Those Oscar knew he possessed. But he had no intention, while these lawyer's tools were kept in good condition, of letting legs and lungs rust from nonuse. He had been a plump boy and would be a stout man before he was thirty if he neglected his constitutionals. He didn't intend to neglect anything that he believed would advance him.

All the lawyers, with the exception of Noble, who had had to return to Washington, were staying on for the execution. Their presence would dignify the occasion. The defense would stay to show the men they had defended unsuccessfully where their hearts were;

the prosecution would stay to see that what they had argued for was duly carried out.

Colonel Johnston and the Indians were still in town. They would not leave until they were able to send word to the tribes that the government had finally kept its word, that the men responsible for the Indian massacre had all been hanged by the neck until dead.

Judge McGowan, with other courts on his circuit awaiting him, had left Pendleton. There were those who said that other dates or not, McGowan could not face the results of his sentencing. He could say the word that required the deed; but the deed itself he could not witness. Whatever the case, he was gone.

Except for the absence of Noble and McGowan, the town was, if anything, more crowded than when the trials had been in progress. Oscar, out at six for his before-breakfast constitutional, noted more horses and rigs than he had at any earlier time. The trials, whatever the results for the four men who would hang and their families, were a gold mine for everyone in Pendleton with a loft to rent or a meal to sell.

Those who couldn't find accommodations were in a hard row for stumps. The weather, instead of clearing and warming, continued overcast and cold. Temperatures every night were dipping into the low thirties — freezing or thereabouts. A good rain might warm things up; but a good rain in this kind of weather would become in short order a bad sleet.

Oscar, who despised slackness in dress, was turned out as nattily for his constitutional as he had been in court — except that outside in this kind of weather he wore a greatcoat. He had walked a mile into the woods, two thousand paces — he always numbered them — and was entering the outskirts of Pendleton when he first heard, then saw, a rider, a long-legged boy on a big roan approaching from upriver at a thundering pace. His immediate thought was: It's happened. They're going to storm the jail. Find Brady. Recruit the guards.

At the edge of the woods, Oscar,

running, intercepted the rider, who pulled up to avoid running him down.

"Hannah," he shouted, "what're you doing here? And in that getup?"

Hannah, on a lathered Oak, asked, "In what getup?" Her mind was not on her clothes.

"Trousers," said Oscar. "You're wearing trousers."

Hannah had on a pair of Ben's buckskins, a little tight in the bottom and short in the leg.

"It's raining at our place. I had to dress in a hurry."

"Surely you had time to put on a skirt? I thought you were a boy."

"Now you know better, don't you, Ossie?"

"I know better, but I don't know as I like it any better. My sweetheart riding astraddle, legs uncovered for anybody to see."

"Not unless they can see through buckskin. Ossie, something wonderful has happened. Help me to get into the jail."

"You can't get into the jail — with all those men. It wouldn't be decent. And not

507

in that outfit."

"I've got to see my father."

"I can get him to come out for you, I reckon. What's happened?"

"Luther Bemis has a new son. I was up all night with Ora. I promised her I'd get the news to Lute as soon as possible."

"You could stop over at Mrs. Culligan's and borrow a skirt of her."

"No. I won't do that. I don't want her skirt. If you won't help me the way I am, I'll ask a guard to get Pa."

Hannah left Oscar standing in his tracks, gazing after her as she kicked Oak into a gallop. He liked spirit in a girl, but britches were a mite too spirited for his taste.

Matt Holmby, the guard on duty, was perfectly willing to fetch Caleb Cape out of the jail to talk to his daughter. If he saw anything unbecoming in a woman in trousers astride a horse, he didn't say so.

By the time Caleb reached her, Hannah had dismounted and thrown the reins over Oak's neck — who was trained to be ground-tied.

Caleb came running, white in the face and out of breath.

"Something wrong at home?"

"No, no. Good news. Lute's baby was born last night. It's a boy, black-haired and big like Lute. I was there all night."

"How's Ora?"

"Fine. She wanted Lute to have the news as soon as possible."

"Lute ought to hear this firsthand."

"Ossie said they wouldn't let me in the jail."

"Ossie?"

"Mr. Dilk."

"So it's Ossie, now? Well, he's probably right. But they ought to let Lute out of the jail into the runway. He can't climb the stockade without help. You could talk to him there, without going in with the men."

Holmby wouldn't assume the say-so for letting Lute outside of the jail for as much as one minute without getting Sheriff Brady's permission. Who knew but that hidden in the woods behind Hannah were fifty more horsemen ready to bust into the jail the minute a door was opened?

Sam Brady in his Sunday pants, but carrying a rifle, was back at once with the guard.

"I tell you what we'll do, Reverend. Your daughter can talk with Bemis outside the jail but inside the stockade walls. You and I will wait outside here for them to finish. I think you know me well enough to know I ain't carrying this gun for show.

"Matt, you take Hannah inside the stockade. Bring Bemis out, and lock the jail door behind you. You join us out here. Hannah, I ain't ever shot a woman yet, but if I see you climbing over that wall, with or without Bemis, I'll shoot."

"Luther Bemis came to the jail of his own free will," Hannah reminded Brady.

"He didn't know what he was getting into when he did. Now that he does, he may have changed his mind about staying."

"How much time do I have?"

"Twenty-thirty minutes. You got to remember, the more you tell Bemis the harder you make it for him. Just give him the news and get out."

Hannah followed Holmby inside the stockade and waited there for him to bring Bemis out. Neither she nor Lute spoke until the stockade door slammed on them.

"Ora?"

"Fine. You've got a baby boy."

Luther Bemis clasped Hannah in his arms. Hannah was startled but knew what he was doing. He felt more than words could say. She was the only person to whom he could let the longing in his arms speak. He held her very closely, rubbed his bearded face against hers. He did not kiss. She was Ora and Luther Bemis, Jr., rolled into one. Kissing, as she had learned, could reach down into something that had no part in what Lute felt now. She was his wife, his son, his mother. She was life, and he was about to lose life. She was glad that Ossie, who might not understand such things, couldn't see. Her face, when Lute stood away from her, was as wet as if the rains had finally come. There had been no sound from Lute, and she hadn't known he was crying.

"Oh, thank God, Hannah. Thank you for

coming. Tell me everything. Did she have a hard time? What's the boy look like?"

Hannah was able, getting hold of her own shyness, to put her arms around Lute's neck and kiss him on the cheek.

"First of all, she said to tell you she loved you. She kissed me and said for me to kiss you and say it was from her."

Bemis put his hand to his cheek, holding the kiss close, it appeared. "Ory, Ory."

"The baby started coming about candlelighting time last night."

"She's so little. Did it go hard with her?"

"In the beginning. But she's pure grit. She said she'd have this baby and have it in one piece and have the job done in time for me to get the news to you this morning. And she did."

"And she's fine?"

"She said to tell you she could shingle a roof today if she had to."

"That Ory! What's the baby look like?"

It was big, red, wrinkled, and had a great thatch of black hair. Hannah tried to make this general babyishness sound a little more like Luther Bemis; and Lute when a baby and Lute Jr. *had* probably looked alike.

"He's got your hair, Lute. A big mop of black hair. He's a big baby. Ten pounds and not fat. Ora said to tell you he had your appetite."

"Ory, Ory."

"She's all right. Mama's with her and won't leave her 'til she's up and around."

From outside came the sheriff's voice. "That's about long enough, Hannah. Wind it up. Matt's coming in to take Mr. Bemis back in."

Bemis took Hannah's hands in his. "Tell Ory," he said, "that she's carried my life and that she is my life. And that because of her I'm glad I was born — even to come to this end. I won't send her any kiss by you, because that would be so scanty a part of what I owe her. Tell her that. Tell her that what I've got for her is too much for a seventeen-year-old to carry: which is Luther Bemis, body and soul. Tell her we'll meet again in the hereafter. I know it. Tell her to pray for me."

The guard waited politely, a little to one side.

"And God bless you, Hannah, for bringing me the word.

"All right, Matt. Lock me up. I've had my say."

Oscar Dilk was waiting with her father and Brady when Hannah came outside the stockade.

"You go on over to your Aunt Rebecca's," Caleb told her. "I'm going to talk with Lute for a while, then I'll be over. Everything all right at home?"

"Ben's taking care of things. Mama and I've been with Ora."

"That was the right thing to do. Tell Rebecca I'll be over to have dinner with her. You better get some sleep now."

Oscar said, "I'll walk you over to the Baldwins' and take care of your horse. He's been ridden hard. He needs a rubdown. Your aunt can fix you up with some proper clothes, I expect."

"Who can care about clothes at a time like this? Men going to die. A man never going to see his son. I wouldn't care if I was naked."

"Now, Hannah, you're overwrought.

You know as well as I do, you do care. And you've got to care more and more. One reason I've been so proud of you is that you've always been so neat about your person."

"Neat about my person?" Hannah repeated. She knew what the phrase meant — tidy — but it was nothing she'd ever expected to be praised for by a young man. No girl had ever been loved, had she, for being neat about her person? But then Ossie, though he had seemed to link their futures together in his talk, had not yet spoken of love. Maybe love, like nakedness, was a little too barefaced a subject for Ossie to mention offhand. Well, she respected him for it. Ossie was a serious dependable lawyer, not a man to consider love and nakedness subjects to bandy about like the weather and the crops any time the notion struck him.

"Neat about your person," Oscar repeated firmly. "Fastidious about your dress, I might say, for a backwoods girl. And where we're going, that'll be important."

Hannah wanted to say, "Where *are* we

going?" But she had an innate shyness about prying into the thoughts that lay beneath another's words. If Ossie had wanted to say, "When we are married," he could have. All declarations and explanations that have to be asked for were worthless. She knew that. In love, everything has to be a gift. Asking for is a payment; and giving then becomes merchandise for which payment has been received. She was too proud to ask; but too obstinate to forgo her belief that Ossie was the one man who could save her from being a girl she couldn't respect; and from running headlong back to a two-timer.

She put her arm through Ossie's.

"This early in the morning," said Ossie, "people seeing us together might get the wrong idea."

Hannah, withdrawing her arm, couldn't hold down that edged tongue of hers. She wasn't asking for anything sweet now, so it was all right to put a question.

"What kind of wrong idea, Ossie?"

"Ideas young girls like you don't know anything about, Hannah. Why don't you ask me where we are headed?''

''Where, Ossie?''

''Up.''

''Far up?''

''I don't see any limit but the sky.''

''Will we be angels, Ossie?'' Hannah asked. That wasn't her razor-sharp tongue; that was her limber pink twig for tickling.

''Not for a long time yet, I hope, dear,'' Ossie said, and gave her arm a little squeeze, people or no people, pants or no pants.

23

Lute knew what he had to do, and he knew that he couldn't do it without help. All of the day and all of the night after Hannah's visit his mind was aflame with plans. On the afternoon of the second day he asked Caleb to come to his corner of the room to talk. The room had been divided by choice into corners, serving as individual living areas. The Woods in one corner, Benson in one, Lute and Caleb in the third. The fourth corner was equipped with wash bench, bowl, pitcher, and water bucket. And a bucket chamberpot. The chamberpot was emptied four times a day, not quite often enough. The straw over in that corner stank some, but everybody had a chamberpot in his bed chamber at home and was accustomed to using it accurately without benefit of light.

Lute's corner was at the end of the same wall as the wash bench and chamberpot. He got less of the privy smell than Benson and the Woods. Caleb leaned against the wall, and Lute paced in front of him.

"Cale, I've got to see that baby."

"There's talk of letting everyone's folks in here the night before."

"Ory might not be able to make the trip . . . and, able or not, I don't want my son to pay his first visit to his father in prison."

His last, too, Caleb thought, but said nothing.

"I am going to see that boy if I have to burn this place down to get out."

"I don't know what you'll burn it with," Caleb said.

"You got any better plan?" Lute asked.

"I've been thinking about it."

"I'd come right back. You know that."

"I'd have to bank on it, anyway."

"It wouldnt be any harder coming back than it was coming in."

"It would be harder." Caleb felt he had to make Lute know the new bond he'd have to tear. "There's the baby to leave now, as well as Ora. And the sentence to face. You didn't have either of them when you confessed."

"I knew the baby was coming. And what the sentence might be. I ain't changed my mind about thinking what I did was right."

"I don't know that what I've got in mind is right, or will work," Caleb said, "but this is it. They don't let you and the ironed men out for air together. The men with leg irons can't get over the stockade. You can get over but not without help. They'll let me out with you."

It took Lute a little while to take this in.

"You mean you'd help me?"

"I'll help you. Now I'm not helping you to escape. You keep that in mind. I'm helping you to have one look at your son — then you hotfoot right back here. A day for the trip, a day for the visit, a day to return."

"If I never showed up, they wouldn't hang you."

"I know that. If that was all there was to it, there'd be nothing to worry about."

Lute was silent, letting the meaning of this sink in. "You mean that, don't you, Cale?"

"I mean it, for me. What you decide to do's your own business."

"I'll be back."

"We got to get you out first."

"There's no use trying to make it in daylight. I'd be caught before I was out of town."

"Brady ain't going to swallow any story about you wanting to exercise by moonlight, either."

"You're right. Brady ain't ever had a hanging before and he's going to see that this one's done right — the equal of anything they do over in Ohio. Matt

Holmby told me he's building a gallows tall enough and stout enough to hang a horse from.''

"The taller and stouter, the better for you.''

"I know that. I don't hone for any sycamore limb with a skittish horse kicked out from under me.''

"It can't be done in daylight.''

"The hanging?''

"The escape.''

"How, then?''

"I got another idea. Best not tell you. Just put you on edge. Get you so fidgety you'd be a dead giveaway.''

"That part'll come later, Cale.''

Caleb ignored this. "Every night Matt comes in here. He locks the stockade door, but leaves the jail door open. If I can get us outside, you climb from my shoulders over the stockade and start running. You know the way home better'n any man here.''

"How can you get us outside?''

"It may work and it may not. If it works, you'll see how.''

Johnny Wood seemed to do all of his living at night. In the daytime he was gone away, far away, not in the jail, scarcely in life itself. Not unhappy, it appeared, or fearful. At night he dreamed, talked to himself, screamed.

The night after Caleb's talk with Bemis, Johnny had one of his screaming dreams. The minute it started, Caleb, disregarding contents, emptied water bucket and chamberpot pails, and ran with them to the jail door. There he clanged them together, crying, "Matt, Matt."

Holmby, roused by the screaming and banging, was inside the jailhouse in seconds.

"What's going on here?"

Caleb, at his side, said, "The boy is having a fit. Grab his tongue. He'll choke to death."

Holmby had rushed in without a lantern, and in the dark it was a little hard to find the boy, let alone his tongue. Holmby's handling awakened Johnny. The screaming stopped; tongue-swallowing was no longer a danger.

Caleb was at Holmby's side when

Johnny quieted down.

"You gave us all a good scare tonight, Johnny," Caleb said.

"You all right now, boy?" Holmby asked.

"It was just a bad dream. I'm all right as soon as I wake up."

Holmby said, "Everyone else ready to settle down now?"

No one but Benson answered. "Nobody's keeping us awake but you."

"Thanks for coming, Matt," Caleb said. "I could've done it myself, but the boy's your responsibility, not mine."

"All I had to do was wake him up."

"Tonight, that was all. Some other night might be different."

Caleb went to the jailhouse door with Holmby, like a courteous host.

"Ain't you getting tired of your stint in here, Reverend?"

"I am. But it's where I belong 'til it's over."

"Well, I'm glad I'm on the outside instead of the inside."

"At least I can sleep."

"I can, too. Don't think I stay awake

nights watching those walls. I check 'em every day for signs of burrowing. No other way to get out. They're hog-tight and horse-high.''

"Well, I won't be disturbing you the rest of the night. Never knew the boy to have such a fit of screaming before."

"What's ahead of him's enough to make him scream."

"I don't think it's come home to him what's ahead."

"What's he scream about?"

"Something he did in the past likely."

"The shooting?"

"I couldn't say as to that."

"Well. Good night, Reverend. Get inside. It's freezing cold."

"Good night, Matt. You maybe saved a life tonight."

Two hours later George Benson got up to use the chamberpot. It was not in place, and he went bellowing to Caleb's corner. "What did you do with the pisspot?"

Caleb, sitting up, said, "I'm afraid I left it outside when I went out to rouse up Matt."

"What d'you expect me to do now?"

"It can't smell much worse over in that corner than it does now — pot or no pot."

"I ain't used to pissing on the floor."

"We're all learning new tricks in here, George."

Benson leaned over Caleb menacingly, then straightened up.

"Where's Lute?"

Caleb said nothing.

"Where is he, Cale? He sleeps here beside you. He couldn't leave without you knowing it. Where'd he go? How did he go?"

"Have you looked over in the Woods' corner?" Caleb asked.

"What'd he be doing there?"

"Who knows?"

Benson, with a way-stop at the privy corner, went to the Woods. John Wood, Sr., who was a little deaf, didn't hear him. Johnny, sleeping lightly after his nightmare, did.

"What's wrong now?" Johnny asked. "I ain't screaming again, am I?"

"No, you ain't, Johnny, but I am. I'm

about to scream my head off. Luther Bemis's gone.''

"How could he go?''

"I don't know. But I aim to find out.''

Benson had no buckets to bang, but his lungs were stronger than Caleb's.

At the door to the jail he bellowed, "Matt, Matt. Man loose. Come running, Matt. Man loose.''

Matt came running, locking stockade *and* jailhouse door behind him this time, and with a lighted lantern in his hand.

"What's wrong now?''

"Luther Bemis's gone.''

"That can't be. He was here during the ruckus just a while back.''

"Well, he ain't here now. Look for yourself.''

Holmby looked. He kicked up the loose straw, he shook Bemis's blanket.

"He's gone,'' he finally agreed.

"What you plan to do about it?''

"First of all, get Brady. What's done is up to him.''

Brady was there in ten minutes, nightshirt tucked into his pants and a big bearskin coat on top of his nightshirt. The

526

night was bitter cold, a wind like a knife had come up, and there were occasional splatters of sleet. Brady had a lantern and he, too, had a look around.

"You sure Bemis was here, Matt, when you come in here the first time?"

"I seen him," Holmby said. "He was right there on his pallet beside the preacher."

"Well, he wasn't *beside* the preacher, because the preacher, according to you, was at the door pounding and yelling when you came in."

"His pallet is beside Cape's."

"I don't know how you could see him without any light. You said yourself you could hardly find the boy, who was yelling."

"I seen him," Holmby insisted.

"Well, you couldn't be pulling the boy's tongue out and watching Bemis at the same time."

"I never even got hold of the boy's tongue."

Brady snorted. "Hunting the boy's tongue, then."

"You saying that while I was busy,

Bemis got up and run?"

"He got up and done something. He's gone, ain't he? Did you lock the jail door when you came in?"

"I locked the stockade door. Even if he run outside, that's as far as he'd get."

"It's as far as he'd get without help."

"Who'd help him? The two Woods was right under my nose."

Benson said, "I'm trying to help you find him. I wasn't trying to help him get away."

"Caleb Cape?" Brady asked Holmby.

"He was right by my side hunting with me for that tongue."

"Somebody helped Bemis over that stockade. He's gone, and nobody but a cat could get over without help."

Caleb stepped into the circle of lantern light.

"Sheriff, I boosted Bemis up so's he could make the climb."

Holmby said, "Reverend, you're out of your mind. You was right beside me."

"Matt, while you were hunting around in the dark, I was outside with Bemis."

"Cale," Brady said, "you know what

you've done, don't you? Helped a condemned prisoner escape. That's punishable under law. That's obstructing justice."

"I know that," Caleb said. "I knew it when I did it."

"That ain't the half of it, Cale, in this case. We let one condemned man escape here and every buck in the Six Nations will claim a right to lift the hair of every white man between here and the Lakes. When you helped Bemis, you wasn't just helping one man make a getaway. You were risking the lives of hundreds of innocent men, women, and children. You know that, don't you? What in God's name got into you, Cale?"

"The man'll be back. He come to jail of his own free will. He'll come back the same way. I helped him so's he could have one look at his newborn son. I couldn't do less for a dying man. Nobody could. He gave me his word he'd be back."

"I reckon God knew what He was doing when He put preachers in the world, Cale. But even He didn't figure on their lacking common sense. Bemis won't be back,

Cale. Not once he gets a look at his wife and child. Then you're not only going to have a jail sentence on your hands. You're going to have a lot of scalpings on your conscience.''

''If Lute don't come back, hang me. That ought to satisfy the Indians. Four men sentenced. Four men hanged. That's keeping our word.''

''You mean that, don't you?''

''I mean it. I've preached it all my life. I'd better not be a turncoat when it comes to practicing it.''

''It's a good thing you feel that way. I'm going to set men to tracking Bemis right now. Bring him back, or not bring him back, you broke the law. But if they don't catch Bemis or if he don't come of his own free will, I wouldn't like to be standing in your shoes. Not before God. Or this community. Not if the tribes start rising.''

Caleb had told Luther Bemis that he didn't have wings. For the first two or three miles, Lute thought he did. Or thought he didn't need wings. Could float

530

like a cloud, blow like the wind, move like a spray of sleet. He didn't know what the weather was like. Didn't care. He knew he was outside, not hemmed in by walls, by stale straw and the stink of five unwashed men. He knew he was running home, running home to Ora and their baby.

He remembered the night he gave the baby to Ora. They had waited a longer time than they had expected for a baby to come. That night he said, "I gave you a boy tonight, Ory; I know I did."

"How can you tell?" asked Ora, green as grass in such matters.

"A man can tell. He came big and black-haired like his pa. Like to tore me asunder. You wait and see. You won't come round again. Now, I went through what I did without a whimper. When your time comes, you remember how I bore up under the ordeal. Not a whimper. You do likewise."

"You weren't dead silent," Ora reminded him.

"I didn't say be dead silent. I said whimper. I didn't whimper."

"You groaned some."

"You can groan, if you do it low."

"I'll be so glad to have him I'll cry for joy."

"How'd you like twins?"

"They don't run in my family."

"Maybe nobody in your family ever did it twice."

"Is that how you get twins?"

"How'd you think? Think they just chopped one baby in half to get two?"

"I never thought about it — single or double."

"You think about it now. You want twins?"

"Yes, I do. A boy and a girl."

"I can't promise that. Can't even *promise* two. But I know the way to go about it."

"Once in a while I've heard tell of triplets."

"I wouldn't want to burden a woman of mine with three. Two at a time's plenty. No use being hoggish."

They had had one only, but he had been right. She never came round again. And he was right about a boy, big and black-haired, as Hannah told him. He wondered if Ory remembered on the night the baby was coming their talk on the night they got him. And if she had been quiet, no whimpering, just a groan or two, in the way he'd told her would be all right.

My Ory, my Ory. A man with a good woman oughtn't to get mixed up with God. There ain't room for both in a man's life. A man with a bad woman like as not needed God. But one good woman was all the holiness a man could handle. God and a good woman got in each other's way for a man who wanted to please both.

He'd have to slack up. He'd run three or four miles without being winded. But twenty miles at that pace was more than he could do. He knew the way, all right, but by eye, not by soles of his feet. There wasn't a peep of light, not from an opened owl's eye, let alone a star or a moon. In dark like this you could run in circles. He'd fallen a half-dozen times already, still so buoyant with joy he bounced up like rubber. But a bad fall like that last, over the dropped limb of a storm-tossed sycamore, and he could rot here, a pile of bones.

He might have guided himself by the sound of the creek, but the wind through the trees drowned out the sound of water, and wind points no arrows toward home. When he slowed down the cold hit him. He was hot from running, sweaty; but he was also soaked through by the sleety rain. He hadn't given a thought when he burst out of that jail to the kind of weather he'd be traveling through, and it wouldn't have done much good if he had. You didn't enter jail with a wardrobe designed for jail-breaking in the middle of a blackberry winter. He had on the moccasins he always wore, linsey-woolsey pants, and a deerskin jacket over a calico shirt. He'd had just enough sense to grab up the jacket as he went out the door; but the jacket didn't do anything for him below the hipbones. The sweat and the sleet was freezing round his butt and balls. He couldn't get a midget on a night like this, let alone twins. Let alone Ory's dream of possible triplets.

Running at the pace he'd been going was out of the question. It was out of the question also, unless he wanted to end up an icicle frozen in the shape of a man, to go at anything *but* a fair pace.

He had traveled on foot through forests all his life; but never on nights like this. On nights like this he holed up inside a shelter of some kind, with an easy fire to fight freezing.

He hadn't a thing to guide him but the slope of the land. It was uphill all the way home, and when the going slanted downward he got uneasy.

There was a trace running between Pendleton and the settlement on the creek. He had started on the trace, missed it, and, instead of backtracking to find it, had believed, in the first joy of his escape, that he could make faster time in the cutoff through the woods. In daylight, in decent weather, he could have. But he had better have stuck to the trace. The trace knew the way home and he didn't, not now, not with his feet. Half the effort that should have gone into moving ahead was spent in climbing up and over fallen trees, into and out of branches that wet him to the knees. By God's grace, he never fell flat in one of those heavy running little streams, but insofar as wetness went, lying down in a little creek or standing upright in a sleet storm were one and the same. He was wet through. The wind pierced his clothes with what felt like the spikes of a red-hot currycomb. He was dog-tired, but in this kind of weather there was no stopping to catch his second wind. The inside of his nose ached with the burn of the icy wind, and with each breath he had to burn it again.

By pure luck he stumbled onto the trace once more and swore never to leave it. The trace wasn't too different from the uncleared woods; streams crossed it, boulders abounded, but except for an occasional stump never cut down to road level, there were no trees, fallen or upright.

He had run in circles and, for a minute or two on the trace, he thought he might be traveling in the wrong direction and end up where he started, back in Pendleton. The idea was so terrible it cheered him up. Run all night and find yourself at morning light right where you'd started from — in jail.

There was no sign of morning light, and wouldn't be even when morning came if this storm didn't let up. He didn't know at what time he had started or how long he had been running. He had overestimated his strength, paid heed to heart instead of his legs. He was still stronghearted, but it was his legs he'd have to run on.

He was counting strides now. Running numbers seemed easier than covering miles. He slowed down. Not because he had to, he told himself, but because there'd be little point in reaching home too played out to talk; too bleary-eyed to see his son. Lie there in worse shape than the new mother. No sense in breaking jail for that.

He had taken a commonsensical pace, slow enough to keep him moving, fast enough to keep him from freezing. He had covered perhaps another mile when he heard horsemen behind him. They couldn't see him, but being run down by a horseman who couldn't see you wouldn't lessen the pain. There was only one explanation of horsemen out on a night like this and riding fast on this road: they were hunting him.

He got off the trace and back into the woods as quickly and quietly as he could. Snatches of conversation reached him as the posse passed. They thought he, had picked up a horse somewhere. He wished he had. The idea had never occurred to him in the swiftness of the chance to leave. Riding horseback seemed a second-rate way to travel from jail to love. He wanted to run. Caleb had a horse over at the Baldwins' — and, for that matter, he might have stolen one. He was due to hang anyway. 'Bout as well be hung for a sheep as a lamb.

He stumbled to his knees against a fallen tree, at the opening of a hollow tree, it proved, and was almost startled into an outcry when a nest of young raccoons ran against him to escape from the log. He explored the opening with his hand. Big enough for him to crawl into. He didn't fancy the idea of crawling headfirst into the jaws of some mama possum or coon; but no mother, he thought, would linger behind with her young ones scattering as those had.

He didn't know how cold and wet he was until he got into the dryness of that great fallen beech, still warmed by the animal heat of the varmints he had dislodged. He had known he was cold; he hadn't known that his whole body was caught up in continuous small shiverings. His flesh moved in ripples, bone deep, like those a brisk wind stirs up on the skin of a pond. He knew what that uncontrollable shivering meant: his body was in danger of freezing. Inside the log, where the chips and leavings of the animals' nesting (the sweet-sour sickening smell, without doubt of skunk) made him a mattress, the shaking let up and finally stopped. He was like a run-down clock: the ticking unnoticeable until the silence sets in. He was more aware of the ease and comfort of his muscles, which no longer twitched, and of his teeth, which no longer chattered, than he had been of all the shaking and chattering while it went on.

The log was large enough for him to roll over in but not long enough to cover his feet. Some of the warmth that was returning to his body would surely be carried down to his unprotected feet — perhaps was already doing so. They were giving him no discomfort. He thought he heard more horsemen go by up on the trace. Inside his log he couldn't tell whether daylight was coming or not. If it was still sleeting, his feet had accustomed themselves to that, and no longer reported the state of the weather to him.

If it was nearing sunup, there was no use exposing himself to another band of searchers. He had as well snuggle down amidst the leaves for a little rest and a few winks of sleep before he finished his run.

The men Sam Brady had dispatched in the search party were back at Pendleton by noon — without Bemis — and with no word of him. It was still storming, well below freezing, and the men were gray with cold and weariness.

Brady met them outside the jail with others of the town who had learned of the escape. Three or four jurymen, Tom Gunn with them, had made the ride. The jury had taken an unpopular stand with many of the community. Letting prisoners escape would seem to some a confession of mistake. But Gunn and others had meant that verdict and didn't intend any escapees to say likewise to their neighbors.

Brady was dour. "No luck?"

"We didn't see hair nor hide of him."

"I don't understand how a half-dozen men on horseback couldn't run down a man on foot."

Jim Mullins, no juryman, nothing at stake for himself or any decision he had made, faced up to Brady angrily.

"Sam, you don't know what you're talking about. We were out in a blinding storm and couldn't've seen a buffalo if it didn't bump into us. Our eyes were froze together half the time — and when they was open all we could see was sleet. What chance did we have to find a man on foot dodging around between trees?'"

"Did you go to his house?"

"We did. His wife had a new baby, but we didn't spare her from looking under and in her bed. He wasn't there and hadn't been there.''

''The Capes'?''

''Searched there, too.''

''Look,'' said Gunn, ''what guarantee we got that home was where he was heading?''

''Cale Cape says so,'' said Brady.

''Cale Cape helped him get away, didn't he?''

''He did. He admits it.''

''Where's the first place Bemis and Cale would figure we'd hunt? Home and the road to home. Bemis's been a wandering man all his life. Might suit his fancy as well as his need to take off in the opposite direction from home right now. If he wanted to take up with his wife again later, he could, sometime when we wasn't riding his tail.''

Brady said, ''Cale Cape told me he was heading home. It goes against my grain to think a preacher would lie to me.''

''Don't it go against your grain to have a preacher help a condemned man break jail?''

''It does, it does,'' Brady answered.

''Well, us freezing here ain't going to

find Bemis or save the preacher from his backsliding, if that's what he's done," said Gunn.

"You're right, Tom. There's been enough dying — past and to come — without anybody coming down with lung fever. Get on home. Get your feet in a bucket of hot water and get some quinine and whiskey in your system. You done what you could. I'm going to talk to Cape now."

Brady went directly to Caleb, who was stretched out on his pallet.

"You hear that?"

"Now, Sam, you know good and well sound don't carry through two log walls. I didn't hear anything. And if you want me to know, you'll have to tell me."

Caleb got to his feet. He was as tall as Brady but forty pounds lighter, better built for preaching than strong-arming. But the two men could look each other in the eye, steady blue to steady gray.

"What's the bad news, Sam?"

"You said you couldn't hear."

"I can still see. I can read your face. The news is bad."

"Bad for you, anyway."

"How about Bemis?"

"Gone. No trace of him."

"He was heading home."

"That what he told you? Or what you're telling us?"

"Both."

"He ain't home. Ain't been there. Not to your place, either."

"He could've broken a leg on the way."

"Yeh, or been frozen to death, the weather being what it was last night. Or maybe he never went that direction at all. Headed south and has given us all the slip. I'm giving you the benefit of the doubt. Taking your word that you believed he would go home when he said so."

"I still believe it."

"It won't make any difference, as far as you're concerned, which way he headed. You helped him escape. There's a prison sentence for that. And a lynching, like as not, if the word leaks out that you're the one who broke the government's word to the Indians."

"I've told you I'm ready to hang in Bemis's place. Four men killed and four men hung. If I know Indians, it'll tickle their fancy that one of the men ain't a killer. Indians have got a great funny bone, if people only knew it.''

''You likely won't last long enough to tickle the funny bones of many Indians if this gets out. Don't you know there'd of been more of an outcry against McGowan's sentence except people around here agree with Johnston? Better four men than forty or four hundred.''

''I make four.''

''For God's sake, how do you figure on making the official roll call at hanging time? You plan on just mounting that platform, singing the doxology, then saying, 'Me, too, please'?''

''I'll leave the working out of the program to you, Sam?''

''I ain't ever hanged anybody before. I got enough to worry about with the ones McGowan's handed me without taking on volunteers. You know that.''

''Let 'em break in and lynch me then.''

''In the first place, that won't satisfy the Indians. That'd just be a little horseplay amongst whites. In the second place, I'm running this jail and I'm going to run it right. Or as right as I can. I've had one escape, and there's not going to be another, let alone a lynching, as long as I'm here. I have a gun. I ain't worrying about doing what I was elected to do here in this jail. Keep the prisoners in, and hang those sentenced to hang. If you can get yourself sentenced to hang, I'll hang you. If not, you're going to have to tough it out as a preacher who got the wool pulled over his eyes by one of his backsliding church members. I'm not going to be a poor sheriff just to salve your conscience as a preacher."

"I hadn't thought about it in that light."

"Didn't you give any thought to your family? While you're off getting lynched, what're they doing?

"My family's grown up enough to look after itself. Bemis's family's just started."

"Your boy, and girl, too, ain't passed the point of needing a little guidance."

"They've got Lizzie to look to."

Brady shook his head. "I've always heard preachers' wives were in a hard row for stumps. I believe it. Up to now you were in here through my goodheartedness. You're here as a prisoner now. The grand jury will meet to indict you for helping a condemned man to escape.''

''That's no more than fair.''

''I ain't concerned with fair. It's legal, and that's my lookout.''

The minute Brady left, Benson clanked over to Caleb. ''So you did let Bemis loose?''

''Yes.''

''*You* broke the law, too?''

''Yes.''

''You played favorites.''

''There was no way of getting you ironed men over that wall. You know that.''

''You got a weakness for rascals.''

''Maybe. If so, I've got my fill of them here.''

Benson knocked him down. A real jawbreaker on an ordinary jaw. Caleb got up and stood, arms down, facing Benson. He had an impulse to say, ''Too bad you don't have a log to bust my head open with," but he swallowed it.

"Bemis had never seen his child."

"You think seeing them makes it easier to part with them?"

Caleb shook his head. "I don't reckon it does."

"If Luther Bemis makes his getaway, and the Indians kill my wife and children, I'll hold you responsible for their murder."

Caleb wanted to say, "Look, who started this?" But he kept that thought to himself. "You heard me tell Brady I was willing to hang in Bemis's place."

"I heard Brady say he couldn't accommodate you. Your intentions may be good, Cale — but I've heard you say more than once what the road to hell was paved with."

"Bemis said he'd be back. I think he meant it."

"Maybe he did when he talked to you. Then he breathed fresh air and hit for freedom. Or maybe he's dead now. Either way, I hope they string you up. Your son testified against me. I wouldn't be here at all except for that. Then you help Bemis to escape — with no thought for me or Sarah or our six children. You got Bemis so wrought up he confesses. Without you and your family, nothing would've been made of our clearing out a little nest of red men. I can tell you, when that posse gets here, they ain't going to wait for the courts to deal with a man who turned on his own kind.''

''There ain't no posse coming, George. In five days you're going to have to face your Maker.''

''If I do, you're going with me.''

''You heard me say I was willing.''

''Willing to take Bemis's place. What good'll that do me?''

''I'll pray for both of us, George.''

''Start praying,'' said Benson, and knocked Caleb down again. This time Caleb stayed down.

Luther Bemis knew exactly where he was when he woke up — and knew that he had slept longer than he had intended. He didn't know at what time he had crawled into the log; and he couldn't tell from inside it what the time was now. It was no longer night; he could tell that. He could tell also that it was still storming. Such light as did seep past the barrier of his feet and the blockage of his body had no sunshine in it. The warmth he had felt when he first crawled into the log had left his body. He was no longer shivering, but he was cold and stiff. He had better get out, taking his chance on searchers being in the neighborhood, before he was permanently log-shaped and immobile.

He could still squirm. He had to travel the length of the log like a snake, using the muscles of butt and back to propel him — together with what help he could get from elbows and head. His feet did not give him much leverage.

He lay still for a few minutes after he was clear of the log, scanning the sky, listening for searchers. The gray sky sagged close to the earth. It was day, all right, but where the sun was he had no notion. The day had the feel of midmorning. Had he slept four or five hours? Five or six? He recognized no landmarks. The sleet, which had slacked off, had been replaced by a ground fog, rolled up from off the warmer creek. He could hear no sounds — no travelers, no wind. The drip of water from trees, ice melting, fog condensing, nothing else.

He sat up carefully. He expected aches and creaks; perhaps a numbness that would have to wear off before he could sit at all. He had to move slowly, but he felt no pain. His back hadn't turned to wood during his entombment. Encouraged, he put his hand to the ground, preparing for the same slow rise to his feet. He was half up, had one foot under him, when he collapsed. He did not have a foot. Lying on the ground, he lifted his other foot, then let it drop. Nothing. From the ankle down, his feet were clods, clumps of unfeeling flesh as incapable of supporting him as a cowpat.

Frozen. Not frost-nipped, but frozen to the bone. He knew exactly what had happened to him and what would happen next. Without care, and maybe with it, his toes would drop off. And before they dropped, there'd be pain and rotting flesh and the stink of a dead animal.

And meanwhile he couldn't walk. No

pain yet. But no more chance of walking than if he had two buckets for feet.

He sat there, filled with a kind of sardonic humor. Life hangs upon hinges of chance. He met Caleb Cape and got converted. Converted, he had to confess his sin. Confession put him in jail. Caleb Cape got him out of jail. And here he sat in worse case than bedded down on the straw and with death ahead at the end of a quick clean jerk. Not putrefying here alone in the drizzle and freeze of a blackberry winter.

He didn't try standing again. His legs ended someplace above the ankle, and he was in deep enough trouble without breaking some bones with a forward topple.

He had no way of judging how far he'd traveled toward home — not a landmark to be seen in the smother of ground fog. He was not in pain now, but would be as soon as blood in his calves, blocked off from its regular flow, began to pound in his veins.

He could crawl. He didn't have the pants for it, and he couldn't figure out any way to make leather kneepads out of his deerskin jacket for his knees. Knives weren't permitted in the jail, and deerskin put together with gut thread by Ora wouldn't part with anything but a knife. But he *would* crawl. He wasn't going to die here festering while there was still a chance of getting home and seeing that baby.

Animals on all fours can make good time. A bear, for all of his weight, was about as brisk as a squirrel. But man had lost the knack. Lute started out. Crawling over a log instead of jumping it, crossing a branch, the water to his chin, making knees and hands do feet's accustomed work wore him out, wore out the knees of his pants, tore the flesh off his kneecaps. They were raw and bleeding. When they got down to bone he wouldn't be able to travel at all. If he could tear the sleeves out of his jacket and use them, folded, as kneepads, he might, putting one pad at a time before him, still be able to cover ground. He took the jacket off, but, short of chewing all night, there was no way of getting the sleeves out. He tried using the entire jacket as a carpet to cushion the way for him. To do this he had to get off the jacket with a sidewise roll before each forward movement. Doing that might save his knees; it also slowed him down so much his frozen feet would have dropped off long before he reached home. The veins in his calves were throbbing more painfully. His feet were, happily, still unfeeling.

He sat on his jacket too bone-weary to make the effort to get it up and put it across his shoulders. The ground fog had thinned out; the temperature had dropped. A small icy wind had sprung up and went through shirt and skin clear to his heart. He could now make out where the sun was: halfway down the afternoon sky. It would be dark, or at least twilight, here in the woods in a couple of hours. If tonight was as cold as last night, and with no log to protect him, he'd have lost more than his feet by morning. Cold enough to freeze the balls off a brass monkey, he thought, and I'm flesh and blood and no monkey. He wasn't a man to die sitting down. But how could he die any better a mile or two farther and his knee bones scraped clean of flesh. They were as red already as a dish of pickled beets.

What had he done wrong? Turned to God? Had a drink? Confessed? Broke jail? Got a son? Come back to civilization? "Come back to civilization" held about the whole of what was wrong, he reckoned. Out where he'd been, west of the Mississippi, there were no jails, sons were got by chance, killings didn't have to be confessed, and God hadn't staked out a claim yet. Would he give up Ora and their son got by plan, and the warmth in the emptiness of his heart that Caleb's conversion had brought him, to be back west again? Two feet to stand on? Two knees of flesh instead of bloody bone? No death sentence ahead?

By God, he wouldn't. He'd die crawling. He got the jacket out from under him, threw it ahead of him, and crawled onto it.

24

Charlie Fort and Norry Culligan sat in Norry's kitchen drinking tea. They were melancholy. They, or at least Charlie, had passed completely beyond embarrassment, self-consciousness, shame. Something had happened a long time ago; someone had been kind to him when he was desperately unhappy. Some bond attached him to this woman. He would be hard put to give it a name; a bond of loving-kindness, perhaps.

Norry had another name for what she felt for Charlie: just plain yearning love. She couldn't kill the girl hidden deep inside her matronly frame. That girl wanted to lie once again in Charlie's arms and smell once again the Florida Water with which Charlie splashed his face after he shaved. She knew what she wanted, but she was a hardheaded Irishwoman (Ahearn before her marriage) and she had no intention of throwing away what she had in pursuit of what she knew she could never get. Charlie held her hand sometimes, patted it gently in the way he would a kitten that had strayed near. She was at least as smart as a well-trained kitten; she didn't try to climb up his arm or wrap herself around his neck. She tried not to purr.

They were both blue, down in the mouth this afternoon. Bleak freezing weather outside, which had showed signs of fairing off around noon, then had turned arctic again within the hour. Fairest sunshine wouldn't have cheered them, though it would have made them more hopeful about Luther Bemis's fate.

"My God, Norry," Charlie said, glad Norry was a Papist and as used to God in the conversation as any Harvard man, "what would you do if you had only a few more days to live?"

"Do just what I'm doing," Norry said.

Charlie took hold of her hand and held it tight. That was a nice thing for her to say, but he couldn't return the compliment.

"What in God's name got into Cale Cape, do you think, to help Bemis break jail?"

"Nothing got into him. It's always been there. Milk of human kindness."

"Milk of human kindness!" Charlie

repeated. "That's not the axle grease that keeps legal wheels turning. He's going to get a jail sentence, if nothing else."

"Is that the law?"

"It's the law. And unless I can do a better job defending him than I did defending the four men that are going to hang, jail's where he'll go."

"There's no way you could've saved those men. What they done was the opposite of what Cale done."

"What Cale did's just as illegal, if not as bad."

"You got it all arranged to be his lawyer?"

"He said I could."

"You charging him?"

"No."

"I didn't reckon you would be. You think you'll get to see Hannah more, defending him."

"It entered my head."

"It's an ill wind," Norry said. "What's she see in that Dilk, anyway? He thinks he's finer than frog hair. Hannah ain't going to be any more than a crutch to him, helping him climb the steps to the statehouse.''

''Maybe Hannah'd like to climb some statehouse steps.''

Norry took her hand out of Charlie's, folded her arms, and looked at the young man with blue eyes still life-filled. ''Don't run the girl down just because she gave you the mitten. And if you want to climb statehouse stairs, you can. No need of a crutch, either. I'd like to tell that girl a thing or two.''

''There's a thing or two you'd better be quiet about, Norry,'' Charlie said. He'd gotten that easy with Norry.

''I'm no fool,'' Norry said. ''Except now and then I do lose my head.''

They were both able to laugh. Charlie hated to leave the warm kitchen and Norry's talk for the cold attic and the facts he'd have to send the *Western Spy*. Between losing the case, losing Hannah, and his misery at the thought of the hangings he'd have to witness, he'd about dried up as a source of news for his father. But there was no way as defeated lawyer and unsuccessful lover he could excuse himself from getting this latest news off to his father. The report of the unheard-of sentencing had gone off the day it was handed down. Since then he had indulged himself in senseless lacerations: Where did I make my mistake with Hannah? With the trial? He'd relived every remembered word and act. Was it that act? That word? What had condemned him? Another word, another act, would Hannah be in his arms? Four men, jailed perhaps, but with their lives still ahead of them if he had said the right word? Made the right move? Occasionally he would come upon a forgotten word, an unremembered act, and think, There! There! I lost all there. He couldn't be sure; and even if he was right in his conjecture, the mischief was done: the girl lost, the men as good as dead.

The best he could do now was not to forget the past, but stop reliving it. If he wasn't careful, he would soon add another ache to his miseries: How did I fail my father?

Pen in hand, he set about remedying that. And in the act of trying to tell his father and the *Spy* readers what was going on in Pendleton, some of the tightness at the base of his throat loosened; the stone in his chest lightened a little.

Extracts from a letter by Charles Fort to Enoch Leverett:

During the night, Matt Holmby, guard at the Pendleton jail, was summoned by the Reverend Caleb Cape, who has been staying in the jail with the condemned men. Holmby was told that Wood Jr. was having a fit. He *was* screaming. What he was having, it now appears, was a nightmare.

While Holmby was seeing to young Wood, Cape helped Luther Bemis, the only unironed prisoner in the jail, to climb over the stockade wall. Bemis's escape was not noticed until two hours later, by George Benson, who called Holmby, who then roused the sheriff.

Cape confessed to Sheriff Sam Brady that he was the one who had boosted Bemis over the wall. Bemis, Cape claimed, was only making a trip to his home to see his newborn son, and would be back. If he did not return, Cape declared, he was perfectly willing to be hanged in Bemis's place.

Hanging Cape, who had had no part in the massacre, would not satisfy the Indians, Brady told him. Cape could and would be tried for helping a prisoner to escape and would undoubtedly be jailed. But he, Brady, could not on Cape's say-so take him out and hang him. Bemis was the guilty man, the man McGowan had sentenced to hang, and the man the Indians wanted to hang.

The sheriff immediately dispatched a half-dozen men on horseback to ride along the trace leading from Pendleton to Bemis's home. There was no absolute assurance, of course, that Bemis would stick to the trace; or even that he would head home rather than southwest toward his old hangouts with his partner, Clasby, also wanted for the killings — and still missing.

The searchers left some time after midnight. The weather, which was blustery and cold with some sleet at that time, got worse toward morning; the thermometer dropped as low as twenty degrees just before sunup.

The search party found no signs of Bemis either on the trace or in the woods. They searched his home and that of the preacher and were convinced that Bemis had not been there. It is of course possible that he died of exposure during the night. Or, as Brady believes, never headed home at all.

In any case, the riders returned to Pendleton at noon today with their report.

Caleb Cape is being held in jail until a grand jury can be summoned to indict him. Brady is so outraged by Cape's act that he'd be perfectly willing to hang him himself if somebody would give him the legal authority to do so.

Brady was less outraged, however, than the Indians. Lone Fawn, a Miami chief, and Bent Arrow, a Seneca brave, representing the Indians who have gathered here to see that the executions take place per government promises, went to Brady and accused him of doing what has been done before in such cases involving the murder of Indians: giving the criminals a stiff sentence, then seeing to it that they have a chance to escape.

Sam Brady, whatever he may have thought of the sentences, is a good backwoods sheriff, who considers it his job to carry out the sentences handed down, not to help prisoners evade them. He was fully as mad at the Indians' accusations as they were at Bemis's escape.

His language was too strong for public print. But what he told them, in effect, was to head for the woods if they thought they could do a better job of finding Bemis than his men had done. The two Indians left at once, and the feeling here is that Brady will shed no tears if they scalp Bemis. Brady has been so determined to carry out this execution, his first, properly that he finds it hard to forgive the two men, Bemis and Cape, who have spoiled his record.

Brady has had, or is having, erected the most impressive gallows ever heard of hereabouts — let alone seen. Platform of oak timbers, twelve feet above the ground. The hanging beam, a walnut timber a foot through, attached to a support of the same wood rising about eight feet above the platform. Brady has been scoffed at for the size of this structure, for the use of black walnut; for rope and hangman, both imported from Cincinnati. It is a little odd for the most solidly built structure in town to be the gallows tree. But, though Brady's motive is more likely vanity than any regard for the expeditious dispatch of his prisoners, the prisoners can be thankful that when they go through the trap door in that platform, nothing except their necks is going to break. Nobody's going to have to be hanged twice, as has happened before, when beams or ropes break.

Brady has chosen, probably with Colonel Johnston's advice, a very picturesque site for this melancholy drama.

The gallows has been erected on the north bank of Fall Creek, just above the falls. The gallows stands on a smooth, rolling piece of greensward, spacious enough to accommodate the more than a thousand spectators who are expected to flood into Pendleton on the day of the execution.

Rising above the meadow is a low but extensive ridge, which will provide balcony seats for those who want a clear view of the event without being caught in the press of the sight-seers who will clog the meadow.

Colonel Johnston, the Indian agent, expects to offer his Indian observers, Senecas, for the most part, a place on the ridge so that they can clearly see that the government's word has been kept and can carry a report of the fact back to their tribes. He no doubt also believes that it would be a wise thing to keep the Indians and the whites from being elbow to elbow at a time of so much emotion.

Many here have believed the settlers would never take McGowan's death sentences lying down. But so far, they have. Only one man, as far as is known, still expects or hopes for an uprising that will save him; that is George Benson, one of the condemned men. The defense was able to persuade the jury to find Benson guilty of no more than manslaughter in the shooting of the squaw. The defense was unable to do anything for him, however, when the manner of his killing the Indian boy was made known to the jurors. Hope of an uprising is all the comfort Benson now has — and he clings to it. That is, unless the Governor of Indiana, James Brown Ray, should take it into his grandstand-loving head to issue pardons. He has done the like before. But it is thought here that he is not likely to lock horns with Calhoun in the War Department, Johnston in the Indian Bureau, and undoubtedly, backing up both, President Monroe himself.

Thus matters now stand, with the execution date only four days distant: Clasby vanished, Bemis escaped; the preacher in jail with the three remaining condemned men; the Indians not returned from their search for Bemis; the gallows waiting.

End of extracts from a letter by Charles Fort to Enoch Leverett.

Charlie put down his pen. He had done his duty. The *Western Spy* was now as up to date as he was on the state and whereabouts of the four condemned men and on the preparations for their hanging.

He went over to the room's one small window. Day was ending. There was no sun to disappear; no glimmer of rose or red embers through the western trees. Day's gray was darkening. Day's cold was deepening. He steamed up the window pane, breathing on it. Smoke from chimneys curled like feathers against the darker air. He could see the outline of the jail. No chimney there, no smoke, no heat. The Indians who had gone after Bemis had stripped themselves of their finery for the hunt, but Indians didn't die of cold. They had lived in the open long enough to know how to survive bad weather. Had they believed the story Bemis told Cape, that he was heading home? He didn't know.

He didn't care. He had to face it. A gallows built. A preacher in jail for wrongdoing. A baby with a father he'd never see. Six Benson orphans. A boy, young Wood, dying before he'd lived. And he still didn't care.

What he cared about was his own breaking heart. What he cared about was Hannah. Give him back Hannah; no, not just "give her back," but have her come running to him of her own free will, arms open, and he'd let the whole of Pendleton march up to that gallows and swing by their necks until dead. All except Norry. He wouldn't sacrifice her even to get Hannah back; at least he hoped he wouldn't. But the others? It was an odd thing that love given and returned had made him love everyone, red or white, man or woman, city or backwoods; made him love himself. This man with so much love in his heart. But love, once experienced, then withdrawn, had shrunk his heart. There was room now only for his own pain and indifference to the suffering of others.

He had sworn to himself to be done with going over and over the past; sworn to himself to be concerned instead with what he could do now. What *could* he do? Hannah wouldn't listen to a word he had to say. She was never alone, always with Dilk or her family. Should he beat up Dilk? He wasn't at all sure he would be able to do it. And would Hannah be any more sympathetic if he tried? Would it soften her heart to see him with two black eyes and a broken nose, given him by her Ossie? If he thought it would, he would be off in a trice for the breaking and blackening. But might it have the opposite effect? Convince her she had picked the right man — the winner.

In the cold room Charlie's face burned. He hoped he wasn't coming down with the grippe, although thoughts about lung fever might take his mind off his heartbreak. He leaned his face against the window glass. It might have been ice. He could hear the rising wind in the spruce trees and floor joints creaking as the cold deepened.

He was glad for the reading of his college days. He was suffering what he knew had been suffered before. Those who had suffered had given him words better than his own for what they — and he — felt.

"Western wind, when wilt thou blow?
The small rain down can rain, —
Christ, if my love were in my arms
And I in my bed again!"

Western wind, western wind. This wind was out of the north. For as long as it blew from that direction the small rain never could rain down. Cold weather, death, and raids were what this wind promised — and never his love in his arms again.

Western wind, western wind, when wilt thou blow?

If I cry, Charlie thought, my face will freeze right here to the glass.

25

The sky was coming still nearer to the earth. The bitter cold of nightfall was at hand. There was light enough to have crawled on, but Luther Bemis had given up crawling an hour back. His knees were worn down to raw nubbins of bloody bones. The throb in his feet had passed beyond pain and had become a sickness that filled his whole body. He knew what was happening. His feet were dying, and the poison of their death was being passed through the veins of his entire body.

In the early days of his hunting in Indian country he had steeled himself to the chance of Indian capture and torture. Prisoners were staked out, feet roasting in a slow fire. He had seen it done. If it happened to him, he was determined to take it like an Indian. He had heard braves sing and joke while the flesh of their feet sizzled and smoked like venison on a spit. In a way, what he was going through now was, though not arranged by Indians, Indian punishment for an Indian killing. Slower, which was worse; and without an audience who would encourage him to suffer it like a man, which was also worse.

He was now sorry that when he heard the horsemen last night he hadn't run out and hallooed to them. If he had done that, he would be resting on cozy straw now with two sound feet — not a pain in his body. But he could never have done that. There was the chance that he might see Ora and their baby and he had to take that chance. This was going to be a harder way to die than with a broken neck at the end of a rope. But Ora would know why he had chosen it.

The pain, or the poison from his dying feet, or the blood he had lost from his knees, or the lack of food, caused him to faint — not to the point of unconsciousness, but to the point of leaving his body behind. He could see his body stretched out with his jacket under his buttocks, his knees bloody, his feet bare (they had swollen so that his moccasins, he thought, caused him more pain), his closed eyes (he could see under the lids) sunk deep into his head. This man is dying, he thought. And thought, also, He is better off here than inside his body. Though he was absent from his body, above it, he was a sick spirit and would like to puke. He floated, but the floating was pretty much like seasickness. He could see, but what he saw didn't stand still — feet went in and out like a pig's bladder being blown up; blood gushed and clotted from his knees; trees, though there was next to no air moving, were limber as buggy whips.

Now to the movement of what was there, but which was, he knew, stationary, was added figures he knew were imaginary: two Indians. This was, he supposed, the result of his thinking that his frozen feet were Indian punishment for his Indian killing. The sight of the two men made him glad. It would be easier to endure the pain if he had witnesses to his hardihood.

One of the Indians spoke in English. He knew it was English, but he replied in Delaware because that was the language he was accustomed to using to Eastern Indians. The Indian said, to the body stretched out on the ground, "This would have been your last night."

"I have more nights."

The Indian replied in Delaware. "One only, except that we found you."

To his companion, a younger man, the Indian spoke in Seneca, a language Lute could follow when he was well. Now he could not understand. The young man moved away, trotting.

The Indian who remained said, "He will bring ice. There is some at the edge of the stream. I will bind it to your feet with sycamore leaves. You will have less pain."

"Who are you?" Lute asked.

"Lone Fawn."

Lute came down closer to the Indians — and to the pain in his body.

"Miami?"

"Yes."

"At the trial?"

"Yes."

"Wide Eyes?"

"My niece."

Lute was moving in and out of his sick body. "It should not have happened."

"It should not."

Lone Fawn took jerky from his pouch and offered it to Lute. "Eat."

"I cannot eat."

"Hold it in your mouth. The juice will do you good."

"The good is all past."

Lone Fawn pressed the jerky to his lips,

and Lute opened them and let the meat rest inside his mouth.

"I am going to die. Why take the trouble to save me?"

"I want to see you hang."

Lute began to chew the meat. "You deserve to see that."

Lone Fawn took off his fur-lined cape and put it around Lute's shoulders. "A rabbit can die here of cold, and without shame. It is shameful to hang. It is a shameful way to die. Killed by your own people. I want my people to see that."

"I am willing."

The younger Indian returned with foam-ice held in a cup of leaves. Lone Fawn filled each moccasin with the ice and leaves, then shoved Lute's feet into the moccasins. If the Indians hadn't been there, he would have screamed. A shoe of red-hot steel couldn't have hurt more. He was determined from childhood to be an Indian's equal in endurance. Lone Fawn watched him closely.

"The moccasin is too small," he gasped.

"Your feet will feel better soon."

"You are very kind, Lone Fawn."

"I have a reason."

"I will never be able to climb the stairs to the gallows."

"Perhaps not. In that case I will be glad to carry you."

"What's your plan for getting me back to the jail?"

"A travois. Where the trace is smooth, we will pull it. Where it is rough, we will carry it."

"Where's the travois?"

"Watch. We will make it."

They made it before his eyes. Two poles. Lone Fawn's jacket and Bent Arrow's extended between the poles by means of their sleeves. The two Indians were left in shirt sleeves. Lute was lifted onto the travois; it was not long enough to hold him comfortably, but comfort was something he had long since forgotten. Lone Fawn spread his cape across Lute's body and tucked it under him at shoulders and hips carefully as a mother with a babe.

"Good night, Mother," Lute said.

Lone Fawn did not smile. "I have told

you why I am keeping you alive."

"Perhaps we will all die."

"In time."

Day was gone. Indians were owl-eyed, and needed to be to travel in this starless night.

The cold was perhaps less bitter than it had been the night before, but it was still a blanket of iron. Lone Fawn had been right; Lute's feet pained him less than they had earlier. The cold was no help to his knees; the broken flesh strained to pull itself together, to protect the exposed bones. Give up, give up, he ordered it. The pull of the flesh toward a meeting was as painful as the parting had been.

He had lost weight, had gone, he supposed, from around two hundred to perhaps a hundred and seventy-five. Yet he was no featherweight. The Indians handled him as if he were. Lone Fawn was perhaps fifty. Bent Arrow, twenty. They carried him, moving out of the rough part of the woods where they had found him, moving fast even in the darkness. The cold, if they kept up at this rate, would never reach them. Their gait, even in the darkness and over broken ground, was smooth. They were treating him as captives were treated by the tribes before the tortures started: fed well, wounds cared for, addressed courteously. The captors wanted a strong and brave man to die, for after his death they would eat him. Lute would not be eaten. They would not take his strength and courage into themselves that way. But when the white men hanged him, his spirit would come to them.

When they reached the trace and began to pull, rather than to carry, the travois, the passage was less smooth. The ice around his feet had melted. He could feel the throb of his shattered knee bones in his groin. He kept his mouth clamped shut. No one would eat him, but he would like to be thought worthy of eating. A strange ambition to have at the end of his life, but better than none: be brave enough to provide food for other brave men.

The trace had become a jumble of rocks and roots, of partially cleared tree land. The Indians prepared to carry him again.

Lone Fawn put more jerky in his mouth.

"You might have escaped if you had headed in the other direction."

"I know that Clasby went that way, and escaped."

"Clasby is still running. Yes."

"I didn't want to run. I wanted to see my son. Then I would come back."

"Why come back?"

"I had done wrong. I was willing to be punished."

"Willing to die?"

"Yes."

"The Great Spirit tell you to do this?"

"Yes."

"The Great Spirit of the red man tells him to live. How old is your son?"

"One week."

"You kill at the wrong time."

"I was drunk."

"You are as bad as the red man."

"Worse."

"Would you like to see your woman and boy?"

"Look at my feet and knees."

"We will bring her to you."

"How?"

"On horse. Or travois if she is not well."

"She is well and strong. When?"

"The last night."

"They won't let you do that."

"They will let us. You will see."

Lute, when they picked up the travois, felt in the combination of its sway and his sickness that he was out of his mind and dreaming. Dreaming that Indians had rescued him, were carrying him, feeding him, and promising him that he should be reunited with Ora and their son. It was the kind of dream dying men had, he supposed, to make their last hours bearable.

Luther Bemis was away from the prison a night, a day, and a second night. Lone Fawn and Bent Arrow returned him on the morning of the third day before the execution. Bemis's knees were healing, but he would never again have the use of his feet. The Indian treatment of sycamore leaves and ice had kept the pain down but they could not restore life to dead flesh.

Susan Danforth, who had some medicine — two-thirds of a bottle left over from the time when her husband had died of a growth — gave the bottle to Norry, who knew, through Charlie, of Bemis's pain. Charlie gave the bottle to Brady.

"This is nothing but a painkiller, Fort. Opium, more than likely," Brady said.

"Well, you weren't planning on keeping him here for a permanent cure, were you, Sam?"

"I'm not responsible for his getting froze."

"You can ease his pain, though. McGowan didn't say anything about torture before the hanging, did he?"

"Didn't say anything about starting him to craving opium the way he used to crave whiskey, either."

"It can't last long if it does start."

Brady gave the bottle to Caleb. "Give Bemis a spoonful of this when he gets noisy. It's something Ike Danforth had for pain before he died."

The spoonful Caleb gave Lute at noon that day kept him asleep or unconscious until nightfall. When he came awake, he couldn't remember where he was, or figure out the time of day. He wasn't hurting — but he could remember the pain he had suffered.

"Ory," he said, "I'm better. What time is it?"

Caleb, who was sitting on the straw beside Lute's pallet, said, "It's Cale, Lute. Ora ain't here."

"Where am I?"

"Pendleton jailhouse."

"How did I get here? I was on my way home."

"You were. Your feet froze."

"I dreamed two Indians picked me up and carried me."

"It wasn't a dream. They did."

"Why? They got no reason to love me."

"They don't love you. They want to see you hang."

"Hang?" It all came back to Lute. "That's what I'm here for, ain't it?"

"That's why."

"I wanted to see Ory and the baby. Made the damn-fool mistake of crawling into a short log — or I would've made it. I was well on the way."

"You're going to see Ora and the baby."

"How? I sure can't climb that wall again. Got no feet."

"The Indians are going to bring her and the baby here."

"What Indians?"

"The two who brought you here — Lone Fawn and Bent Arrow."

"Why are they going to do that?"

"Don't ask me to explain Indians to you. You know them better'n I do. They liked the way you talked on the way back, for one thing."

"I was out of my head most of the time."

"They liked what you said. They've heard plenty of white talk. Men wanting to sell them whiskey and grab their land."

"How they going to get Ory in here? She sure can't climb that wall."

"Brady will let her in."

"Why'll he do that?"

"The Indians did him a good turn. Brought you back here so he could have a hanging according to Hoyle. And he don't cotton to the idea that any savage has got a kinder heart than Sam Brady."

"And there's one other reason, I reckon, for Brady's letting them have their way."

"What's that?"

"I didn't know what I was saying all of the time, but most of the time I knew what I was hearing. There's more Indians in striking distance of Pendleton than you might think. And Brady likely ain't had the wool pulled over his eyes about it, either. If a couple of Indians want me to see my wife and baby, it'll be easier for him to say yes to them than to have a showdown with a couple of hundred. Oh, God, Cale, you think I'm really going to see them?"

"Don't take the Lord's name in vain, Lute. Praise Him."

"I am praising Him. I'm singing. Glory Hallelujah. Praise God in the highest. That's my song of glory. Cale, you think I could have one more spoonful of that medicine? I'm beginning to feel the pain again."

"It's nothing but dope."

"Going to be hung for a murderer. 'Bout as well swing as a dope fiend, too."

"You ain't got long enough left, Lute, to

get to be a dope fiend. My idea's to space this medicine out to last you. Specially through the time Ora's here."

"That's right. I don't want to be bawling while she's here. And the baby. Hell of a way for a baby to see his father for the first time. Bawling and screaming. What if Ory won't come with the Indians? It's nothing she'd ever do in ordinary times. Nothing I'd let her do. That Lone Fawn ain't spent his entire life trapping beavers, I'll tell you that. He may be red, but he's a ladies' man if ever I saw one."

"That's white talk. Indians don't treat women that way. You know that. Spoils their medicine for war."

"For war, yes. They ain't fighting a war now."

"Until they get you hanged, in their own minds they are. They stay away from women at such times."

"Ory don't know it. She'll lock the door and shoot one of them through it."

"If I could send Hannah with them, she'd warn Ora."

"Well, Cale, don't let any grass grow under your feet. Get the word over to the

Baldwins and to Hannah.''

''I can't get the word to Hannah. I'm as much a prisoner here now as you are.''

''What'd you do, Cale?''

''Helped a condemned man escape.''

''Me?''

''You see anyone else missing?''

''They going to put you in prison for that?''

''They already have.''

''I wouldn't have done it . . . if I'd . . . Well, I reckon I would. For how long?''

''I don't know. But don't shed any tears. For quite a spell I figured you weren't coming back at all. Thought I might end my days here.''

''My God, Cale, I'd never run out on you. You know that.''

Cale, squatting beside Lute, who was stretched out on his pallet, took his hand.

''I'd save you this if I could, Lute.''

''I believe you would.''

''At least I've now figured out how to get word to Hannah. Fort's my lawyer.''

''You got a lawyer now, Cale?''

''Fort volunteered. I got a right to see my lawyer. Fort'll come over and he'll take the word to Hannah. Hannah'll take the word to Ora."

"Hannah may be afraid of the Indians herself."

"The shoe'll more likely be on the other foot."

Lute laughed. He'd supposed he'd never laugh again. How a man in his straits could laugh, he didn't know. But he had. He had a wife and a son and a friend. And he'd done the right thing finally, and he didn't doubt the Lord would honor him for it. There were a lot of men laughing with less.

Caleb stared at Bemis.

"I ain't losing my mind, Cale. I'm just thanking the Lord."

Caleb said, "I'll give you a broken dose of this medicine now, a small broken dose. You have another sleep, then I'll feed you whatever Hannah can scare up over at the Baldwins'."

There's no use planning in this world, Charlie thought on his way to the Baldwins', no use chewing your fingernails over "Should you" or

588

"Shouldn't you." While he was sitting in his attic room, or holding Norry's pitying hand trying to figure out whether his chances would be harmed or helped by seeing Hannah again, chance decided what he had been unable to decide. Gave him no choice. He had to see Hannah. He couldn't possibly tell her father, "I can't take your message to Hannah. She's got a new beau." Here were Indians willing to bring Bemis's wife and son to see him if he'd risk the embarrassment of breaking in on Hannah and Dilk in the midst of a little courting. You may have lost your heart, Charlie, he told himself, but you haven't lost your mind, have you? Put in the balance against what it means to Bemis to see his wife and baby before he dies, what's it matter what you or Hannah or Dilk feels?

The night was still cold and bleak, but the wind was shifting from north to northwest. The sky, which had been a solid sooty gray, was breaking open in places, so that an occasional star could be glimpsed. If the wind continued to shift, the blackberry winter might soon be

589

replaced by a cold rainy spring, long overdue.

In weather like this, Dilk and Hannah couldn't be holding hands in the hammock or taking a moonlight stroll. The best a courting couple could expect on a night like this was to share the fire with the old folks and younguns, and drink the mulled cider, if any was provided. This idea gave Charlie pleasure. Hannah would remember him, while Dilk told the Baldwins about the cases he'd won and the campaigns he expected to wage in the future.

When the Baldwin door opened, the scene was as he had imagined it: the old folks in the inglenook and the younguns, including Dilk and Hannah, in a semicircle facing the fire.

After paying his respects to the Baldwins, Charlie said, "I have an urgent message for Hannah from her father."

"I hope Cale hasn't come down with typhoid, cooped up there on half-rations and drinking cistern water," said Rebecca Baldwin.

"Cale's health is holding up fine."

"Well, what is it, Charlie?" Dilk asked, as if he were empowered to speak for Hannah.

"Hannah's father asked me to talk to her alone. It's a private matter. If Hannah'll put on a shawl and step outside with me, I'll tell her what he wants her to know."

"Charlie, you may not know it, but Hannah and I have an agreement — what concerns one of us concerns the other. I'll just step outside with the two of you."

"Is this true, Hannah?"

"Yes, it is true. What one of us does, the other is going to know about. We agreed on that."

"Hannah, your father said for me to tell you this and no one else. But since Oscar's a lawyer and since you and Oscar have this agreement, he'd be willing for him to hear it, too, I reckon."

Hannah put on a shawl. Dilk, showing his hardihood, went outside in his shirt sleeves.

"The long and short of it, Hannah, is this. A couple of Indians, Lone Fawn and Bent Arrow, will bring Luther Bemis's wife and baby here so that Lute can see them before he dies. And Brady agrees to the visit. But Ora isn't going to ride off with two Indians without some assurance that what they say is true, that they'll bring her here to see Lute."

"And Cape wants Hannah to ride with these two savages to take this message to Ora?" Dilk asked.

"That's what he wants. That's the word I was asked to deliver."

"Cale Cape is crazy."

"Don't you say that about my father, Ossie."

"I apologize, Hannah. My language was too strong. What I meant was your father's too trusting. Send you off with those two red men to tell Ora Bemis to come with them? How's he know what their intentions are toward you?"

"He trusts them, Ossie, just as you said."

"Well, trust apart, how's it *look*? One girl riding off with two men. It don't *look* good, whatever their intentions may be."

"What do *looks* matter, Ossie? What matters is that Lute gets a chance to see his wife. I don't care about looks. God doesn't care about looks, either.''

''Well, I care. I'm going to be judged by looks. What I do, and what you do, no matter how good our intentions are, will be judged by how they look. No, Hannah. You can't go. I set my foot down.''

''I am going.''

Hannah put an end to the argument.

''Tell Father I'll go with the Indians. Tell him to let me know when. Ora'll have the baby and will need a woman with her coming here.''

''Hannah, I forbid you.''

''You tell Father, Charlie. I'm going inside now, Ossie. My mind's made up.''

Dilk stamped after Hannah inside the Baldwin house. Charlie was perfectly willing to argue for as long as Hannah was party to the argument. Without her, there was no point freezing on the Baldwins' front porch.

26

The two Indians, with Ora, Ora's baby, and Hannah, rode into Pendleton in the late afternoon of the day before the date set for the hanging.

Sam Brady was outside the jail stockade awaiting them, with the additional guards he had ordered for the night. Brady didn't fear a rescue posse as much as George Benson hoped for one, but he didn't plan to be taken by surprise, either. He and the guards were all well armed.

The sight of Brady's musket filled both Ora and Hannah with the fear that the sheriff wasn't going to let Lute see his wife and baby.

Lone Fawn, before either woman could speak, addressed the sheriff in his elegant English, learned beyond the northern lakes from the British. Lone Fawn had made a pause at the Indians' camp outside town to don some of his finery. Diplomatic dickering was not harmed in his opinion by a little fine dressing. Beside him, Sam Brady looked like a farmer going squirrel-hunting, and both men knew it. Lone Fawn spoke slowly, using simple words, reversing the usual practice of Indian-white conversation. Brady felt his dander rising at this, as Lone Fawn knew it would. But what could the poor sheriff do? He already had a jail filled with whites condemned for shooting Indians. He surely wasn't going to add himself to their number.

"Mr. Brady," said Lone Fawn, "I have here with me the wife and newborn child of one of your prisoners. We have come by easy stages so as not to tire mother and child. The trip was made in the hope that you would permit the father to step inside the stockade corridor for a few minutes so that he can see his wife and infant son."

Lone Fawn's tone was that of a civilized man speaking to a savage from whom not much could be expected in the way of humanitarianism.

Brady understood the tone. "Not a single prisoner of mine is coming outside that jailhouse. The last time that happened, your husband, Mrs. Bemis, made his getaway. I don't figure on letting that happen twice."

"It couldn't very well happen twice, Sheriff," said Lone Fawn. "Bemis no longer has feet to walk on."

"I hadn't finished, Lone Fawn, if you'll be kind enough to let me get a word in edgewise. I'm not letting any prisoners out. But there's no law says I can't let prisoners' wives in. Or if there is one, I don't know about it, which is just the same. Mrs. Benson is already in there, and has my permission to spend the night with her husband. Mrs. Wood could have been here but her husband didn't want her. You, Mrs. Bemis, can be with your husband tonight — if you want to."

Ora, at that word, jumped from her saddle, ran to the sheriff, and threw her arms about his neck.

"God will reward you, Mr. Brady."

Brady said, "After what I've gone through the last few weeks, I deserve some reward."

The Indians, responsible for this reunion, were left unregarded on the outskirts of the rejoicing. Hannah, the baby in her arms, reined Oak close to them.

"Lone Fawn," she said, "I thank you and Bent Arrow. I will never forget. In time to come, if I can help you, remember that."

Lone Fawn said, "Thank you, Miss Cape. Tell your people this. Tell them that Indians are gentlefolk when they meet whites who are gentlefolk. Farewell."

"Before I leave the baby for his father to see, I'm going to take him to the Baldwins to wash and feed. They will give you some supper."

"We will ride there with you, but we will eat at our own camp."

It was the hour before suppertime, cold and gusty. It was the first evening in a week when the clouds had been thin enough for a sundown to be seen. Through the trees in the west, chinks of rusty light, stains of yellow and saffron were visible. On earth the season was spring, in the sky the colors were of fall and the dying year. The light was the color that seeps through a window made of dried and scraped bladder skin — light as murky and yellow as the liquid the bladder once held.

The single street was crowded with people; they were like sight-seers come to a fair. Hannah was glad that the baby she held in her arms could not know that these were travelers, many from long distances, come to see his father hang. The town had no sidewalks. Hannah had to rein Oak carefully to avoid those on foot.

Lone Fawn, quick to understand the feelings of another, said, "It is the same with us. When there is to be torture, death, and a feast, families will travel for many miles to be present."

"Why?" asked Hannah.

"Death is something all must face. They come to learn how to die. They come to rejoice in bravery. They do the man an honor by their presence. They do not watch a dog die. Or a snake."

"I don't want people coming to watch me die."

Lone Fawn smiled. "You will live to be an old lady covered by blankets. You will close your eyes and not open them. What will there be to watch?"

"Maybe I will do something bad and

be hanged."

"No," said Lone Fawn. "That will not be your way."

The three riders, four, counting the baby — the big half-naked Seneca, and Lone Fawn, outfitted like the Miami chief he was, and the long-legged redhead on the muscled stud horse with a baby in her arms — were not unnoticed in the crowd. There were no other Indians on the road, although there would be plenty present at the hanging in the morning. But they were, on the advice of their chiefs and of Colonel Johnston, making themselves scarce until that time.

Hannah glared so much defiance at the press of people around them that many decided that she was a white, captured early and turned Indian herself, and there was no stronger breed of Indian to be found anywhere than these whites turned red.

One man, his face unsmiling, tipped his hat. Hannah was almost past him before she recognized Oscar Dilk.

"Ossie," she called, and reined Oak toward him. Dilk shook his head and stepped back into the crowd.

"You must say good-bye to the red men before your white man will be friends again," said Lone Fawn.

Caleb Cape did not expect sleep on this last night. He had no inclination toward sleep but he would not have permitted himself to close his eyes if he had. He supposed there were a good many nights of sleep still ahead for him. A few missed here and there meant nothing. But for these four men, this would be the last. He intended to be awake, to pray, to talk, to quote remembered Bible verses if they were wanted. Brady had bent over backward letting the two women spend the night with their husbands. He hadn't bent far enough to permit candles or lamps. Brady was determined to have four men to hang in the morning. Whether their wives spent the night with them or not wouldn't change that. But a candle turned over in this straw and he wouldn't have men, wives, or jail. Nor me, Caleb thought, which probably wouldn't worry Brady any.

The thing Caleb wished was that the roof was off the jail so that the men could, on this last night, see stars. There might be only a few, but Hannah had said when she brought the baby that there had been a sunset that night — a kind of a sunset, anyway, a smoldering in the western sky. And if the clouds had parted enough for that, they might have parted enough now for a few stars to show. On this last night, he'd want a look at sky and earth himself. That had been his real home, not logs and sawed timber.

But on his last night he might be in different case from any of these men. What did Luther Bemis care about the state of the sky or the shape of stars? When Ora had carried that new baby to him, kneeling to put him in his arms, Lute had made a sound the like of which Caleb had never heard before. Maybe God had made a sound like that when he first saw Adam. Lute sat up so he could rock the baby and nuzzle his face against his. Then Ora bent down so their three faces touched.

Caleb had doled out the medicine to

meet Lute's needs; enough to cut down the sharpest pangs, but yet leave him still sufficiently awake to know who he was and who was with him. If he forgot where he was, no harm in that. There was nothing Caleb could do to offset the smell of the rotting flesh. Lute had got so he didn't notice it, and since it was Lute's flesh, Ora was glad to be near it, rotting or not.

The guard gave the squalling baby back to Hannah, who came for it in an hour.

"He's hungry," Ora apologized for her son.

"Don't you suckle it, Ory?"

"No."

"I always thought you would."

"I had a reason not to."

"You never told me."

"No. I will, though. You'll see I was right."

It was full dark when the baby was taken back to the Baldwins' by Hannah.

Caleb gave Bemis another broken dose. "If the pain gets bad, let me know."

"You don't figure there's enough in there to quiet down Benson, do you?"

"It would take the whole bottle to do the job."

Benson was screaming at the top of his lungs, bellowing like a bull with his head caught in the slats of the manger.

Part of the time he couldn't be understood — there were no words to understand; part of the time he could. What he was bellowing against was not the prospect of his death. He could face death. But in jail, condemned to die because his neighbors and friends wouldn't raise a hand to help him, that cut him to the quick. He cried out against them, not because he had to die, but because they had died in their souls. They had yielded to their enemies.

It made it worse, of course, that the turncoats were men he had helped, men who owed him neighboring debts, men who would watch him swing tomorrow. He beat the wall with his fists.

"I ain't crying for myself. I'm crying for my country. What's it coming to? God, God, God."

Benson banged his head against the log wall of the jail. Sarah tried to stop him, put her arms around him (too short and plump to encircle more than a quarter of his frame).

"No, George, don't take on."

Benson banged his head more. "Take on! What I'm taking on is a hangman's noose."

"Not now you ain't, George. We're here together. Get a little rest. Lay down and put your head in my lap, George, and sleep."

"My eyes are going to close forever soon enough. Until then I'm going to keep them wide open. Don't talk sleep to me."

Between the head-pounding, the bellows, and Sarah's entreaties, nothing more could be made out in the way of words.

Ora came to Caleb, who was leaning against the door where he could catch a whiff of the fresh cold air that blew into the room.

"Cale, I did a wrong thing, but it might help George."

"I don't think you could do anything very wrong, Ora."

"I didn't know there'd be any medicine

604

for Lute's feet. I knew he'd be in pain, so I brought this.''

She held up a pint bottle of whiskey.

''How'd you get it in?''

''Hanging on a cord under my skirt. There's one more. They didn't search me. I know it was wrong.''

''Ora, there's such a mix-up of wrong and right in this jailhouse tonight, I don't know as God Himself could sort things out. And a snort of whiskey to quiet George and give us all some rest wouldn't go against His grain, I'm certain. But it'll go against George's grain if he thinks we're trying to shut him up. Of that I'm certain.''

''I could tell him I brought one for Lute and one for him. It would be a lie, though. George never entered my mind.''

''A lie like that'll weigh as much here tonight as a flyspeck in a bushel of apples. You maybe didn't know it, but God maybe sent that bottle by you just for George. I'm not certain in my own mind what God thinks of hanging. But I'm sure as can be He don't want George dying all night long, dreading tomorrow. To say nothing of

605

what he's doing to poor Sarah and the rest of us. You take the bottle to him.''

"What'll I tell him?"

"Just what you said to me. He knows Lute used to like a drink. George thinks he's forsaken by all. A remembrance from you would touch his heart."

"What if it drives him roaring crazy?"

"He can't roar much more than he's been doing. It's more likely to quiet him down."

It did that. George greeted Ora like the only friend who had kept him in mind, downed the whole bottle, and took Sarah's suggestion to rest his head in her lap and snooze.

Ora talked with Sarah for a minute, then returned to Caleb.

"Cale, the time I was mad at you for saving Lute? I'm not mad any more. Lute's at peace with himself. He never would've been if he'd done what I wanted — run. He'd of hated himself, and me, too, likely, before too long had passed. Your words didn't save me, Cale, nor your prayers. I thought they did. Now I know better. Nothing but Lute's example's done that. I know that now, and he does, too."

"Ora," said Caleb, "don't make me cry or you'll have to give me a sip from your other bottle. Preachers just preach. They more'n likely love the sound of their own voices. But it takes men like Lute, who live out the words they've heard spoken, to bring the light home to others. You've had a couple of years with Lute. That's better'n a lifetime with some men who don't know there's anything to be found between bed and board — except money-making."

"Don't think I don't know that, Cale. I'm not shedding any tears for me."

Caleb took the spoon and half-empty medicine bottle from his pocket.

"Ora, you dole this out as you think Lute needs it. If it's too little, he'll let you know. So I'd start out on the scarce side to begin with, if I was you."

"What're you going to do?"

"Me and John Wood are going to say Bible verses to each other. Have a kind of Bible-verse hoedown. See who knows the most. We'll soft-pedal it, though, so you and Lute can get some sleep."

"With so little time left, I don't think we'll waste it on sleep."

Before going over to the Woods' corner, Caleb stood again at the crack of the door, where the whiff of the outside world came to him. Maybe he, not condemned to hang, was giving more thought to dying than the men who were. And *he* was giving little enough — not because he didn't try, but because death was so shapeless. Where was the handle to grab death by? You could think about the ways in which it came. When he had believed his offer to take Bemis's place might be accepted, even required, he'd done some wondering and hoping about the skill of the man being brought over from Cincinnati. Would he get that knot in just the right place? Caleb thought he had as much grit in his craw as the next man, but strangling for ten or fifteen minutes at the end of a hemp rope, like a kitten strung up by boys, wasn't any departure he would have planned for himself.

He could think about the ways, but death itself? "Verily I say unto thee, to day shalt thou be with me in paradise.'' This He said to the malefactor. And, this time tomorrow, four malefactors would be in paradise with Jesus, for all believed in Him, though all, like the thief on the cross, had sinned.

The strangest thing about dying (even in his and Lizzie's wild grief at the death of their son, it had been true) was the way in which life went on while death settled down. Death spread its black wings, all right, but the dying themselves weren't carried away from earthly concerns 'til those black wings folded and death's searching eyes turned another direction. Little Caleb had been too young to know what death was; but he and Lizzie knew. And Lizzie, who would have laid down her own life to spare her boy, was still enough of this world to say to her husband when he brought the wrong spoon for the boy's medicine, ''Not that spoon, Caleb. It'll tarnish.''

How were malefactors, stained as they were, not just with earthly concerns about spoons, like Lizzie, but with wrongdoing blood-deep, going to feel at ease in paradise? Or the angels with them? And here now, the time left, no longer days but hours, and their concerns not much different from those a night before a barn-raising or cornhusking.

George drunk as a coot. John Wood conning Bible verses like a Sunday-school teacher making sure he knew the next day's lesson. Johnny roaming around in his mind. Picking up chips out of the past. Over on their pallets (he had given Ora his), the Bemises murmuring like any young couple reunited after separation. He with his nose to the crack, not fated to die in the morning, savored the earth to the bottom of his lungs. He wished he belonged to some church that had thought out long ago words and acts suitable for men's last hours on earth. Words the dying believed in; words that would make a bridge for them between jail tonight and paradise tomorrow. He felt the need of more than he, with nothing but his memory of the Scriptures and his heartache, could provide. God help me.

As the murmur from the Bemises became more audible, he leaned his ear to the crack to hear the wind's cold nighttime talk, a talk that knew nothing of death — or everything; he wasn't sure which.

"You let me know when the pain's too great," Ora said. "There's no sense you bearing it just to show me you can. I know you can. I know you can do anything."

"Except stay away from the damned whiskey bottle."

"That's past."

"It's a good thing I never before had a sip from Cale's medicine. Whiskey can't hold a candle to it. You might give me a quarter-spoonful more. I can feel the throb again."

Ora measured the medicine by feel, her finger in the bowl of the spoon.

"Did you like our baby, Lute?"

"Like him? I never seen another his equal. Did you?"

"No, I never did."

"Well, what do you expect? Ory, one thing you got to promise me. Don't you stay a widow. You was meant to be a mother."

"I am a mother. I was meant to be an old maid, built squatty and with a harelip. And I would've been an old maid if you hadn't come along."

"You ain't got an old-maid bone in your body, Ory."

"Only bones I did have 'til you taught me different was old-maid bones. No, I'll never marry again. I don't want to and it wouldn't be fair to any other man. You'd be in my mind all the time, and the next one would know it. And know I thought he was a poor little mullein stalk beside you."

"Poor little mullein stalk's all I am now."

Ora put her hand on him.

"No, you ain't, not even now."

"I was 'til you touched me."

"Lute, I've got to tell you something. Might be best not to. I don't know. Might put a burden on you, and God knows, I don't want to do that. You know how easy the baby come."

"Hannah told me. But it wasn't the same as hearing it from you."

"He didn't cause me one speck of

612

trouble. He just popped out like a pea out of a pod. One minute I was in the family way. The next minute we had our family. Or its beginning. Oh, I wish you could've been there. You'd have laughed to see him. It was like he was tired of being inside so long. He hopped right out, and no bawling, either. Or from me, either, because he didn't cause me an iota of pain.''

''That's the way I told him to do it when I got him. You remember that night?''

''I'll never forget.''

''But why don't you nurse him? Don't you have any milk? I always figured I'd like to see you nursing our baby.''

''I had milk. Lizzie made suction pumps out of teacups to take the milk away from me. She fed it to him on a sugar-tit.''

''That seems a roundabout way to go at it. You got tits to suit a baby's needs better than anything made of muslin or cheesecloth.''

''I did it on purpose.''

''You weren't mad at the poor little tyke, was you?''

''I loved him.''

"Mad at me."

"You getting out of your head, Lute? You need some more medicine?"

"A quarter of a spoonful, maybe. Scant quarter."

After he had his medicine, Lute said, "Where'd your hand go?"

"No place."

"Thought maybe you'd lost it. I missed it. Well, you still being pumped with teacups?"

"No. I dried up. That's what I wanted to do."

"Why, Ory?"

"You know why."

"I got an idea, but I want to hear you say it."

"I wanted you to give me another baby. A nursing mother can't get in a family way. You know that — except now and then. I know a woman back home who had a baby nine months and two days after she had twins, and she was running over with milk."

"How'd you figure, nursing or not nursing, there'd be any way for me to give you a baby — me locked up in a jailhouse, and you twenty miles away?"

"I trusted in the Lord."

"Well," said Lute, "keep right on trusting. You didn't figure on getting here to the jailhouse yourself, did you?"

"No. But I thought you'd get home somehow, willy-nilly."

"The lord don't really put His heart into helping jailbreaks, Ory. You know that."

"I knew I'd see you."

"If I'd had sense enough to stay out of that log and made it home, we'd never have stopped until we was west of the Missouri."

"We can't be sure we'd of got there."

"No, we can't. And Cale offered to be hanged in my place. He don't know I know — but Benson told me. And they might've done it. Nobody knows what to think nowadays."

"We do. We're thinking the right things."

"We are. Praise the Lord. If we'd run, the three of us might be dead by now. The Indians haven't given up on Clasby."

"I hope they catch him."

"Women like to go to church more than

men but it's harder for them to be Christians. It just don't seem to come natural to them."

"I'm a Christian now, Lute. I'll bring our children up to be Christian."

"Children?"

"Our little boy and our little girl."

"You even know the denominations?"

"You called the turn last time."

"Calling the turn and taking the trick are two different matters."

"Lute, we haven't said one word about love."

"When we live it, we don't have to say it."

"We could say it, anyway."

"I can tell you the truth. You're the woman I tramped ten thousand miles and waited ten years to find. You're my Ory. I love you. You're the mother of my children."

"You said children."

"That's what I said. Give me a quarter-spoonful. A little dose."

She measured the medicine with great care.

"Ory, you're going to have to be the man."

"There's no way I know to be that," Ora said.

Lute laughed. "That's the second time I've laughed when I'd of sworn there wasn't one laugh left in me. Ory, I'm man enough for both of us from the knees on up. But I ain't got no feet. And I ain't got no knees to speak of. I'm going to have to lay right here on this pallet — and if you and the medicine work together like they're doing now, I'm going to give you a little girl. I ain't got the force for another boy, but I think I could just about make us an eight-pound girl. You understand what you got to do, Ory?"

"I understand. First I got to get my drawers off. What'll the preacher think of that?"

"In the first place, he can't see you. In the second place, he don't expect you to sleep with your clothes on. Take off everything but your shimmy."

"I'll take it off, too."

"You'll be cold."

"Not tonight, Lute."

"You never been up there on top before."

"I'll keep you warm."

"My God, my God," said Lute. "Oh, my blessed sweet Saviour."

Before he got to Bible verses, old John Wood wanted to do some remembering, and Caleb listened. He didn't plan to spend the night preaching. Those that preaching hadn't already reached weren't going to be reached by it tonight. If anyone wanted prayers or Bible verses, he had them — and it eased his own heart to say them. But his heart's needs didn't figure anywhere near the top of the list tonight. On the top of the list were the four who were going to die.

"You think things hit you all of a sudden," Wood said. "But they don't. Now this here sentencing is a sudden thing in the eyes of the rest of the world. White men being strung up for killing their natural enemies. I reckon I'll go down in history like George Washington. I ain't the first President, but I've got a chance to be the first man to have his neck in a noose for killing an Indian.

"It'll seem sudden to the rest of the

country. Not to me. I been heading for that noose for some time. I can see it now. I started that direction when I bought that land in York state the developers had cheated the Indians out of. Land that wasn't good to anybody *but* an Indian. Useless except for trapping and hunting, and we was farmers. Why did we buy it? Because we could get it for next to nothing. We didn't give a passing thought to the Indians we drove out. Some of them like as not died just as sure as the ones at the sugar camp. I was asking for the noose then, but I didn't see the warning. Or didn't heed it.

"Next I headed west. I'd lost about all I had when I bought into that venture, anyway. Why west? More easy money. Free land, nothing to do but clear it and kill Indians. Well, I lost my wife on that trip. That's the price I paid for free land. And I married Reba. That was more of the price.

"Marrying Reba was another step toward the noose. Though I sure didn't see it at the time. She was just more free land, I reckon, and at seventy-two I wasn't the man to handle acreage like that.

"I ain't blaming Reba, I'm blaming myself. Though she ain't blameless, God knows that. I went out with brother George to kill Indians as much as to show her I was still as much a man in some lines as anyone else. And she done what she done with John Jr. as much to show me she was still as much a woman in some lines as anyone else. I've trod a misery path right straight toward the gallows from the minute I bought that tainted land in York state. It's no quick ending, the way people think.

"For myself, what's to come tomorrow will be a relief. I'll jump off that platform like a bird and spread my wings heavenward. I believe in the Lord Jesus and I believe that He forgives those that believe on Him.

"Whether He can forgive me for what I done to John Jr.'s going to test Him some. For me it's pure godsend, and I thank Him for it. I seen too many old men die wheezing and sweating and puking blood to mind this quick little jerk tomorrow.

And I been asking for it for a long time. I been praying, 'Noose, come get me.' I didn't know I was doing it, but I was. I sure was."

Caleb thought "Noose, come get me" was carrying praying a little far. "Ask and it shall be given" didn't include that.

"Cale, you know what Scripture's been going through my head?"

"No, John."

"Nothing you'd think. Not Job. Not Cain and Abel. Not Jesus on the Cross. Nothing with blood in it or sin in it, or death. What in the Bible's like that?"

"The whole life of Jesus," said Caleb.

"No, no. You're forgetting His death. You're forgetting the swine and the blasted fig tree. His birth! His birth! That's what I've been remembering. All that rejoicing. That's what I'll do tomorrow. Be born again. Rejoice."

Johnny, who had been lying on his pallet, listening, but not joining in the conversation, sat up.

"I am going to die tomorrow."

Caleb did not know any honest way of denying this. "Those who believe on Him

621

have everlasting life, Johnny."

"I don't want everlasting life. I've had enough of it. Tomorrow I'm going to go to sleep. I been looking forward to it. What I'd like is one good game of jackstraws before then. This is just the place for it. Ten thousand straws here but not enough light to see to play by."

"The verses I've been thinking of," said Wood Sr., trying, Caleb knew, to turn the talk to something less painful to him than his son's wanderings, "are those of the birth."

"Not the resurrection?"

"No, the birth."

Old Wood began, "My soul doth magnify the Lord, and my spirit hath rejoiced in God my Saviour. And his mercy is on them that fear him for generation to generation."

And on old Wood went, until he reached, "The day spring on high hath visited us to give light to them that sit in darkness and in the shadow of death to guide our feet into the ways of peace," and then young Johnny joined him.

When they finished, Caleb said,

"Johnny, I had no idea you remembered all that."

"I remember everything I read."

"Now," said Wood, "I'm going to lay down and get a little sleep. I've said my say and repeated the Good Words and I think I'll sleep."

Caleb told the two Woods good night and returned to the door crack, where the smell of the earth came to him.

Johnny Wood, when he judged the night was half through, came to him.

"There's a prayer my mother taught me, my real mother, not this woman living at our house. Say it with me. It'll make you feel better."

"Maybe I don't know it."

"Everybody knows it."

What Johnny said was true.

"Now I lay me down to sleep.
I pray the Lord my soul to keep.
If I should die before I wake,
I pray the Lord my soul to take."

"I'm going to sleep now," Johnny said. "You do the same. You've said your prayers. There's nothing more you can do."

Johnny was right. There was nothing more he could do — but he didn't leave the door crack until a knife blade of gray morning came into it. With the light came Matt Holmby.

"The women are to be out in half an hour," he said. "Rouse them up. There'll be a good breakfast for the men. We leave here at eight."

"The hanging isn't until ten."

"Brady don't plan on there being any hitches. We'll leave early."

"How're we going?"

"Wagon bed. Men still in irons. There won't be any last-minute rescues if Brady can help it."

"What's the weather like?"

"Cold, but not freezing. Might be a sprinkle or two later."

"Did the man from Cincinnati get here?"

"He came yesterday. Everything's in order. He spent the night at Brady's."

"I hope he slept well."

"It's business with him. It's how he makes his living."

"I hope he's good."

"He says he is. 'Only two mishaps in more than a hundred hangings.' "

"What's he call a mishap?"

"Rope broke once and they had to chase the man. He was a fast runner."

"That'd put wings on any man's feet."

"They run him down on horseback finally. Didn't take much hanging to finish him off after that."

"What was the second mishap?"

"Hung the wrong man. The hanging went all right, but they got the wrong cell."

"Didn't the man tell them?"

"Sure. But they all think some mistake's been made."

"Will they let me go with the men?"

"You can go. Say a prayer with each man. But after that you have to come back here 'til the grand jury meets."

"I was prepared for that."

Ora didn't need any waking up. She was wide awake and fully dressed. Lute looked drowsy.

"I gave him enough to let him have a real sleep toward morning. There's enough left to see him through the ride out there. He don't want any at the last minute."

When Caleb went to wake the Bensons, Ora said, "Lute, I won't do it if you set your foot down. But if you were dying of lockjaw and your body was bent hoop-shaped, I'd be by your side. If you had the pox and your face festering with sores, I'd be by your side. Why can't I now? I'd like the last thing for you to see to be the look of love in my eyes. And that's the last thing I want to see from you.

"I'm going to bring the baby. He won't know what's going on. Afterward I want to tell him he seen how brave his father died. The other'll be there, too."

"You pretty sure about that, Ory?"

"Sure as sure. You called the turn for the boy. I can for the girl. She's lodged there. I felt her. She's there. I've got her named."

"I'd like to know, if it ain't a secret."

"Laura. That's as near to Luther as I can get for a girl. You're going on ahead of us, but the three of us will be coming on to join you."

"You come then, all of you, if your heart's set on it."

"You just look in my eyes when the time comes, Lute. I'll fix myself where you can. All you'll see is the love, then a little wait and we'll all be with you. That's the sum of it."

Caleb gave Sarah Benson Matt's message. George was awake and grumbling, thoughts of what ten o'clock would bring chased clean out of his mind by whiskey miseries.

"I need some hair of the dog."

"I can get it for you," Caleb said.

"You been packing a bottle all these years and us not knowing it, Cale?"

"Lute didn't touch the bottle Ory brought him."

"Fetch it," George said. "Fetch it."

John Wood, Sr., was awake, neat as a man living in straw could make himself, Bible in hand.

"It's the birthday of my life, Cale. It's what I was born for. Going home to Jesus."

Johnny was sleeping soundly.

"It's completely slipped his mind what day it is," his father said. "I don't see the point trying to remind him."

"There's no point," Caleb said.

When Holmby came for the women, Caleb stood at the door to bid them farewell. He could not prevent the tears from running down his cheeks. Both women were dry-eyed, spines straight. Ora took his hand.

"You're a good man, Cale."

"I'm a jailbird now myself."

"If you get a long sentence, I'll come over with Lizzie to visit you."

"God bless you, Ora."

"You going out with the men?"

"I got leave from Brady to stay with them 'til the last."

"I'll be there, too. When you married us you said, ' 'til death do you part,' and that's the way it'll be."

Caleb couldn't speak for the tears in his throat.

27

Judge Amos McGowan was at the jailhouse at fifteen of eight.

"Cale," he said, "you know I'll have to convene a grand jury for your part in Bemis's escape."

"I know that," Caleb said. "I helped a prisoner escape. I figured that would happen. I'm prepared."

"Well, no use being overprepared. Many a grand jury's been convened without indicting."

"I'm prepared for an indictment. I wasn't acting blind."

"An indictment's not a conviction. You know that."

"There's a chance, though."

"The indictment's unlikely. The conviction's unlikely. They could happen, true enough. It's true, too, that a judge hearing the case could suspend the sentence. Circumstances sometimes warrant that."

It took a minute for Caleb to take in all that McGowan was sawing. Then he took the hand McGowan held out to him.

"You going out to the hanging?" he asked.

"I am. When I sentence a man to hang, I sentence myself to be present at the hanging. It tears me apart. I have to say to myself, 'Except for you, this wouldn't be happening.' When the time comes when I can't observe what I've ordered, I'll resign from my judgeship. A man has no right to impose upon another suffering he can't witness. What's too much for the law to see is too much for the law to require."

McGowan turned abruptly from Caleb. He'd said more than he intended.

He had ridden up from the south, where there had been a real spring; he had passed serviceberry blooming on the crest of the hills and redbud come to life on sleeping hillsides. Dogwood showed up like stars against the green of new-leafed trees. Papaws were blooming, a blossom with no more color than a bacon rind. There were thrushes singing in the hazel bushes, and crab-apple blossoms were thick with insects.

Spring was always later up north; but he hadn't been given to understand how much damage the blackberry winter up here had done. Spring *had* come on; the seasons could be delayed by weather, not done away with. But the earth had a blasted look, not dressed with any fall colors or burnished with glare ice and icicles, the way winter was. Browned where it should be green, streaked here and there with ragged bloom where it should have been a bower. McGowan made himself a part of the crowd waiting to see the men come out of the prison to be loaded onto the wagon that was to take them to the gallows. He didn't care for those onlookers, jostling and joking, with more excitement but no more pity than if they were on their way to see a two-headed calf or six-legged dog. He made himself a part of these people to escape being seen by the condemned men. *He* had to see them. They had enough anguish this morning without being tormented with facing the man they believed was responsible for what lay before them. For himself, he believed he could take any kind of abuse: be spat upon, cursed. He wouldn't wish those acts to be among his last, so he tried to spare the four condemned men the sight of his face.

The weather was clearing but still raw and cold; a little ketchy, showers before midday or he missed his guess. The wind went through his greatcoat as though it were mosquito netting. His filly stamped her feet; what she wanted was a good blood-warming run.

Either Colonel Johnston or the sheriff or both had brought in state militia — around twenty, it appeared — to see that the proceedings were orderly. They weren't afraid of trouble with the Indians; so long as the proceedings *were* orderly, the Indians would be content.

The militia was there to lock horns, if necessary, with those who had a different opinion: those who believed that Indian-killing was on a par with ridding the country of wolves and copperheads. There was no telling what spark might light such tinder — the sight of the gallows itself might be enough to do it; to cause this rabble, a thousand strong anyway, to sweep up from the meadows where they were to watch, to the ridge where the Indians were to be stationed, there to speak what was in their hearts: No white man shall die for an Indian. What followed after that massacre would be an Indian war raging over the whole of the old Northwest Territory — with Indians who could run, winning, and settlers who couldn't, losing.

Judge McGowan was speculating on these possibilities when he was roused by a voice.

"I didn't expect to see you here this morning, Judge."

"Fort! I supposed you would have gone back to the civilized comforts of Cincinnati long before this."

"One thing and another has held me. For one thing, if I had had Dilk's power over the jury, these men wouldn't be riding out to the gallows this morning. So I feel some responsibility for them. I feel

I belong with them."

"It's the same with me," McGowan said. "A good deal more so, if anything. You lost to Dilk. I didn't lose to anybody. My choice was my own."

"It was the law's choice," Charlie said.

"It took a man's tongue to speak the law's words. I spoke the words. I intend to see what the law requires."

"Mind if I stick with you? I never been to a hanging before. I may need someone experienced to bring me round when the necks start breaking."

"I'm experienced," McGowan said grimly, "What was Brady's idea, getting things under way so early? It's no more than a half hour's ride out there."

"He don't want a slip 'twixt the cup and lip."

"Fort, sometimes you're too jokey for your own good."

"I know that, Judge. God knows I know it. But when things get really bad, what's left but joke?"

"You might try crying, Fort."

"I don't notice you're crying."

"I'm not joking, either. Why's Brady

starting so early?"

"A straight answer is, Brady's determined to have this go off without a hitch. You see the gallows he's had built?"

"No. I came directly into town from the south."

"It's an edifice, I tell you. There's not a church spire as tall or a barn as stout in the whole of Indiana."

"I'm glad to hear it."

"It's an awesome sight. A thing to kill men with. It's like looking at a two-ton musket ball."

"Better for all concerned than bird shot."

"Oh, it'll do the job, all right. No doubt about that. Brady's only worry is getting the men to it without being waylaid."

"He can stop worrying. If Brady don't hang them, this crowd'll lynch them. *There's* something to cry about. Or joke, if that's what you do when you feel bad. This crowd killed Indians as long as it was safe. Now that they're outnumbered, they'll hang their own neighbors to save their necks."

"You were the one who sentenced them."

"The law sentenced them."

"The law didn't take into consideration that no one had paid any attention to the law for a hundred years when it come to killing Indians."

"Attention will be paid from now on."

A flatbed wagon, pulled by a matched pair of black carriage horses, driven by Matt Holmby and with Sam Brady on the seat beside him, came through the crowd, which parted silently to let it pass.

"What's that for?"

"To take the men to the gallows."

"Pretty fancy. Matched blacks. Equals the French Revolution. Why don't Brady let them walk?"

"I told you. For one reason, he wants to be sure to get them there; for another, one of the men can't walk."

"They were all walking when I last saw them."

"Bemis can't walk now."

"The man who confessed?"

"He's the one. He escaped and got his feet frozen."

Holmby and Brady climbed down from the wagon seat. The militia lined up separating the two men from the crowd, which was pressing in closer. Holmby went inside the stockade, locking it after him. Brady stood, gun in hand, by the wagon. One of the militia men came to Brady. Neither McGowan nor Fort could overhear the conversation, which was short. Brady nodded his head, and the militiaman led Ora Bemis, her baby in her arms, to Brady. They did not talk, nor did Ora move from Brady's side when Holmby and Caleb Cape brought her husband, seated on a chair, out of the jail.

"My God, my God," said McGowan, "what have they done to the man?"

"Not a thing but let him escape. His feet ought to be amputated. But why cut a man's feet off one day and hang him the next?"

"I wouldn't have recognized him. Who's the baby?"

"His. It was born while he was here. That's why he was running away. To see it."

"Looks like he's had his punishment already."

"Tell the law that, Judge."

When Caleb and Holmby put Lute's chair on the ground, Brady nodded to Ora, and Ora went to her husband. No one could hear what either of them said, but they talked for two or three minutes. Then Ora kissed her husband and after that held their son down so that he could receive his father's kiss. They parted without tears and with a handclasp.

"When I go," said Judge McGowan, "I hope I have a woman like that by my side."

After Ora stepped past the militiaman and back into the crowd, Brady beckoned to Fort.

"We'll need your help to get this chair up onto the wagon, Charlie."

Just before the four of them, Caleb, Holmby, Brady, and Fort, put their backs into the hoist, Brady said to Bemis, "Lute, you can lead off. You're in pain, and I won't keep you waiting and watching."

"Thank you, Sheriff. Charlie, you did

your best for me. Don't fash yourself about the way things turned out."

"You got your medicine, Lute?" Caleb asked.

"I don't intend to go to glory doped up with painkiller."

"Better that way than shivering like a dog shitting bones."

Lute laughed. "Three times now."

"What's that?" asked Caleb.

"Just pleased, Cale, the way you can bring the word of God to a man in his time of need."

"You're near enough God now, Lute, you ain't in much need of a go-between."

Bemis had lost weight, but a straight lift, with care not to let the chair tilt and lose the passenger, gave Charlie a catch in his back.

"Lawyers sit and talk too much," he said to Caleb, hoping to make some opening for talk about Hannah.

"City lawyers," said Caleb.

"How's Hannah?" asked Charlie, lawyers not being his real interest.

"Fine, last time I seen her. She'll be out at the hanging. She grieves for young

Johnny Wood. She and Johnny were kind of sweethearts when they were younguns.''

''Hannah and Dilk plighted their troth yet?''

''Plighted their troth? If you mean set a date for marrying, no. And I doubt they ever will.''

''Dilk acts like a man in love.''

''If you want the last word, ask Dilk. Or Hannah. But if you're asking me, the person Dilk's in love with is Dilk.''

''I'm glad to hear it.''

''Not if they marry. That's nothing, if you care for Hannah, to be glad about. Now if you'll excuse me, I've got to get on the wagon with the men.''

Charlie rejoined McGowan. ''Bemis's a brave man,'' the judge said. ''I've been through this before. Been the cause of it, you might say. I've seen men with no more control than babies.''

The crowd, full of talk about Bemis and the state he was in — how were they ever going to hang a man who couldn't stand up — quieted as Brady and Holmby brought the two Woods through the stockade doors.

John Wood, straight as an arrow, Bible in hand, white beard and white hair neatly combed, was everyone's idea of a God-fearing patriarch. When a man like Wood was headed for the gallows something had gone amiss with the country. The crowd's murmur was wordless, nearer a groan or a sob than talk. It was angry, like bees swarming, undecided where to light, maybe not going to light. From his cradle to now, the old man had heard talk of moving west. Presidents had talked about it. Jefferson had sent Lewis and Clark to open the way. Newspapers had printed that story. Preachers spoke of the West as if it was the Promised Land. But there was no way to go west and live without killing Indians. Now the old man, for doing what everybody knew had to be done, was going to be shipped on a wagon out to an empty field and there, in front of gloating Indians, hanged by his poor old neck until dead.

"The crowd's not happy," said Charlie.

"It's not so unhappy it's ready to risk its scalp to save John Wood's neck."

Johnny Wood didn't make the crowd any happier. He had a book, too. Not a Bible, but some storybook, and he read as he walked, not seeing where to go, but guided by Holmby. He wasn't reading like a man so distraught he was trying to hide from himself facts he couldn't face, but like a reader so caught up in what's happening in his book, he stumbles upstairs to bed not knowing or caring where he's going.

At the wagon, Holmby spoke to him. Johnny smiled sweetly, handed Holmby the book, climbed over the wagon wheel onto the bed of the wagon. There Holmby handed him back his book.

"What's that the Wood boy's taking with him?"

"One of his novels, I reckon."

"Brady ought not to have allowed that. Makes the boy look half crazy."

"Nobody around here's ever thought much else."

"Being a bookworm's not crazy."

"Here in the backwoods it's looked on as next to."

Before he reopened his book, Johnny saw someone in the crowd he knew. He stood, waved, called, "Good-bye, good-bye."

Charle turned to see who was receiving Johnny's farewell. There was Hannah, hat off in spite of the cold, threatening weather, waving, crying, and calling, "Good-bye, Johnny. Good-bye."

There was no angry buzz from the crowd now; sick at their stomachs was more likely what they felt, Charlie thought. Bad enough for the old man to end this way, but to have his son go with him, smiling and waving and reading stories! God would have some explaining to do when old John Wood reached Heaven.

Benson, hands tied behind his back, leg irons on, Holmby at one side, Brady at the other, came out of the stockade bucking and curvetting like a colt who has for the first time felt the touch of leather. For a minute the crowd forgot what was to come, caught up in the excitement of what was happening. How a man so bound, ironed, and held down could still manage to plunge and lunge was beyond imagining.

" 'Bout as well try to wrap up chain lightning," said McGowan, "for use in the parlor lamp."

"How're they going to hang him?" Charlie asked.

"Once they get the noose round his neck and cut off a little of his air, he'll calm down fast."

"They've got to figure out a way to get him on the wagon before they can do that."

"Brady can handle him," McGowan said, "if Benson forces him."

Benson forced him. The arm the sheriff held was turned backward in an armlock that made Benson go limp.

"What happened, Judge?"

"Benson got hurt. And if I know Brady, he'll get hurt more if he don't quiet down."

Benson stayed quieted down, and they loaded him, with two of Brady's men, deputized for the occasion, on each side of him.

"Where's the deputies' guns?"

"Who's afraid of a gun when he's on his way to keep a date with a noose? They don't plan to shoot Benson, just to get him there in one piece and hangable. The militia's got enough guns to see to that.''

''I'll ride out with you, if that's all right with you, Judge.''

''I'm not riding.''

''How'd you plan to get there?''

''I'm walking. I've got a high-strung mare, and it wouldn't sit well with me to go prancing out to a hanging on a mettlesome animal. It's only a mile and a half, and walking weather.''

''Might come on to rain.''

''Let it. I hope I don't have to close my eyes to sunshine and fair skies.''

''I'll walk with you. Maybe take my mmind off my troubles.''

''*Your* troubles. Don't let any of the men on that wagon hear you say that. You'll lose cases a lot more sorrowful than this before you're finished, Charlie.''

''I doubt it, Judge.''

Holmby kept the two mares down to a walk. This was not hard to do. They were pulling an unaccustomed load. Sam Brady, musket on his arm, rode beside the wagon. The militia was ahead, behind, and on both sides.

Behind the wagon rode or grudged a hundred or more persons. A few friends and relatives. Many more, those making a day of it, who planned to begin at the beginning and stay to the bitter end.

"I'm glad I walked," Charlie told Judge McGowan. "I would've frozen to death on horseback."

The thermometer wasn't that low. It was the rawness and the wind that went to the bone. Overhead there was just enough blue now and then to make the quick clouding up more hateful. The evergreens turned black in the dark periods. The maples, sycamores, beeches, oaks, walnuts still carried a touch of the pink and saffron of their first unfolding.

The road they followed was no road but an old logging track down to where there had once been a stand of ash, the settler's most valued tree. The men on the wagon, except Bemis on his chair and Holmby on the seat, were on the floor. All were lurching about. One of the deputies had left Benson to keep Bemis from being thrown from his chair.

When they came through the woods to where the stand of ash had been cut, the gibbet was visible.

Judge McGowan stopped in his tracks, rested his face in his hands for a minute, then lifted it for another look.

"You were right, Charlie. I never seen the like. I never did."

"Wonder what trees think, being put to that use?"

"Don't say things like that to anybody else, Charlie."

"You're the only one, Judge. And you can't bring witness against me."

"Look at those coffins. Four of them!"

"Isn't that usual? They don't sack the men up like potatoes, do they?"

"Coffins are usual, of course. But I never saw them lined up before like so many horse troughs."

The wagon proceeded at a steady pace, but the crowd accompanying it pulled up at the sight that lay ahead. There was a sound, no longer an angry buzzing, no murmur of spoken words. The sound was of a hundred people sucking in their breath at one time.

It was so big. It seemed unfair to kill a man with anything so much bigger than he was. What chance did a man have against a machine like that? It belittled human beings. Yet it was designed by human beings, by men who built houses and corncribs and pigpens. Buildings were to shelter and protect. A gallows was a wooden cannibal, timber reversing its role as man's helper. It was raw timber, but it shone black against the stormy sky.

From the crossbeam, heavy as the ridgepole in a hay barn, hung the rope. At the end of the rope was the noose, shaped like the head of a water moccasin. When the wind gusted, the noose lifted a little. It was ready to strike.

"My God, Judge, that's death itself."

"It is. It's meant to be. So were those muskets the four men carried into the sugar camp. Only, those poor peaceable women and children had no warning. I know you defended these men, Charlie. You got to know them. Don't forget that those men asked for this machine."

"No, Judge, they didn't ask for it."

"They knew the law."

"The law had kept its eyes shut for a hundred and fifty years."

"They knew a man gambles when he tries to hoodwink a sleeper — even when the sleeper is the law."

"If they didn't," Charlie agreed, "they know it now."

The wagon had not paused when the gallows came in sight. The men on the wagon bed were faced away from what they were approaching, and, though the crowd must have told them what had come in sight, no man turned his head to have a look.

Charlie and Judge McGowan stood to one side to let their fellow sight-seers pass on. The meadow surrounding the gallows was filled with people.

"How many do you think?" Charlie asked.

"Five or six hundred."

"Is it always like this?"

"Always."

"Why?"

"More than one reason, likely. This is something we're all headed for."

"Hanging?"

"Death. Might pick up some information here that would stand you in good stead when your time comes."

"No," said Charlie. "These aren't learners. These are people come to a play. A terrible, terrible play. The dead really die. The widows' tears are real. The orphans are orphans for life."

"It does look more like a crowd come to a show or a picnic," agreed McGowan, "than a death watch."

Small fires had been lighted to offset the numbing wind and to heat water for tea.

"But," McGowan added, "look up there on the ridge. That's no picnic crowd."

The ridge above the meadow was a long one. At its top, like rimrocks, stood a double line of Indians, straight, not lounging, quiet, not talking. They had come to see what none of them had ever seen before: white men punishing white men for the killing of red men.

"Indians don't think much of hanging," McGowan said.

"Not even of whites?"

"They don't think much of us for thinking up hanging. You know what they call hanging, Counselor? 'Weighting.' They don't hang anyone. They got no word for it. They say we 'weigh' our men to death. They don't like it. They think it's nasty. Torture tests a man. He gets to be a man to the very last. He's got something to fight against. Our men are dead from the minute their head goes into the noose."

"I'll take the noose any day."

"You been raised white — or you wouldn't."

"Eastern white, too. Indians are history to us. I never saw so many red men before in my life. I thought Colonel Johnston was empowered to bring a few chiefs and sub-chiefs here. Not this mob."

"Johnston was given the money to pay the expenses for some Indian leaders so that they could see for themselves that we were keeping our word. He wasn't given the authority to tell anybody, red or white, to stay away."

"They all Senecas? They make us look like a poorhouse crowd out for an airing."

"I can't tell who's who from here. But it's a mixture. Senecas, Miamis, Mohawks, for sure. Hurons, likely; Chippewas, maybe. Mostly Iroquois."

"Iroquois?"

"Harvard don't have much to do yet with the New World, I reckon."

"No courses in Iroquois when I was there, anyway."

The wagon had come to a stop at the foot of the gallows when Charlie and the judge reached the meadow.

On the gallows platform, built high because Brady was a big builder, but a boon to men who preferred broken necks to strangulation, the Cincinnati hangman was already stationed, black peaked hood, with its cat-slit eyeholes, covering his face.

The sun came out momentarily, no warmth to it, but bright. Oh, God, Charlie prayed in his heart, don't mock them with sunshine. Let their last sight be of bleakness. The sky clouded up again.

"Is Brady going to leave them all on the wagon, then march them up to the platform one by one?" Charlie asked.

"Not unless he's a bigger fool than I think he is. All some hothead would need to do would be to shove Holmby off that seat, slap the reins across the backs of those carriage horses, and Brady'd've built a gallows and imported a hangman for nothing."

"Nobody could get away with that, could they?"

"Not without a lot of shooting first."

Brady was no fool. All the men were walked up the steps to the gallows platform — with the exception of Bemis, who was carried up on his chair. Then the wagon was driven away. Charlie thought he saw Luther Bemis look after the matched blacks as much as to say, "I had a good team for the last ride."

Near the platform, almost at its edge, he saw Ora Bemis and her baby, Lizzie Cape at her side, Hannah at her mother's elbow, and Oscar A. Dilk at Hannah's elbow.

"If you don't mind, Judge," Charlie said, "I think I'll move back a little."

Judge McGowan said, "That suits me to a T. I'll go with you. I think it's my duty to be present at a hanging when I condemn a man. But I don't go so far as to think I have to be close enough to hear the chunk of his vertabrae as his neck breaks."

"Can you hear that?" Charlie asked, his own throat not working very well as he whispered the words.

"If you stay this close, you can."

There were plenty who did want to hear that sound, and the two men had no trouble moving back a half-dozen steps, through mothers holding children, children eating fried cakes, men with blood showing brighter than usual in the skin over their cheekbones.

"I wish it would rain," Charlie said. "I wish we'd have a three-day downpour."

"Some cleansing is needed," Judge McGowan agreed.

28

The condemned men knew the order of what was to come. Bemis, old Wood, Benson, young Wood. A prayer for each by Caleb Cape if it was wanted. Parting words from each, if anyone had anything to say.

The hangman spoke to Bemis. "We'll set your chair on the trap. When the latch is pulled you'll go through just as smooth as a man standing."

"No," said Bemis. "I don't go to my death on any chair."

"You can't stand."

"How long does it take you to pull that latch?"

"One second."

"I can stand for one second."

"Man, you got no feet. All you got's two running sores. Look at the wrappings. Smell them."

Caleb spoke to the hangman. "What've you got to lose? If he can't stand, he'll drop anyway. If he can, he's happy, and you've done your duty."

Bemis was white with pain and swaying a little. "Cale, you say the Lord's Prayer. That's what I want to hear. Ory and the baby are right down front. I've seen them. They've seen me. I'll set while you're praying. Then the minute you finish, pull the chair back. I'll stand, the trap will open, and I'll go to my death on my feet, the way a man ought to."

The hangman turned his slit-eyes toward Caleb, and Caleb knew what he was pondering: a man being hanged for murder oughtn't be too particular about the way he went. On the other hand, who had more right than a dying man for a last request?

Lute said, "Put the chair on the trap, the noose on my neck, and pray. When you finish, I'll stand. You'll see. Don't you men have any faith in God?"

The question was addressed to the hangman. Lute knew about Caleb's faith.

The hangman said, "Yes."

"Test it," said Lute. "You're not in what's thought of as a very nice line of business. Better show God your faith."

"It's no skin off my nose if you get tangled up with that chair and we have to hang you twice," the hangman said.

"That's what I been telling you," Lute said. "Fix the noose and chair. Pray, Cale. Ory and me decided those would be the last words we wanted to hear together on earth."

The chair was moved forward. The noose's clublike knot was placed just back of Lute's ear.

Caleb's voice was strong and steady as any Sunday in his sitting room at home. "Our Father which art in heaven, Hallowed be thy name." It had the ring of old times to Lute.

Lute looked down, as Ora had told him to do, into her eyes, and it was the way she had said it would be: lost in love everlasting. The Lord's Prayer came on, Caleb steady as a pump bolt. "Forgive us our trespassing." As Lute looked, Ora held up the baby and said, strong enough to be a part of the praying, "Laura," and people thought what she said was "Lord." Was that only last night? Lute had had his last laugh, but he smiled, remembering Ory aghast at being told she'd have to be the man. They had told themselves they would say the last words, "For thine is the kingdom, and the power, and the glory, for ever. Amen," together. Their voices mingled with Caleb's.

At "Amen," the chair left him, and Lute did more than stand. He went — up toward God, or out toward Ora — in a kind of swoop before he fell that made the crowd gasp.

"How could he do that? Nothing to stand on and nothing to stand with?"

Ora answered whoever spoke. "He was a good man going home to God."

The sound the judge had said could be heard was heard. Lute, after the fall, hung perfectly still, a young man dead before thirty. Below the platform, in sight of all, the doctor listened for a heartbeat. When he heard none, the militiamen loosened Luther Bemis, born in Ohio, died in Indiana, from the rope and placed him in one of the coffins.

Only then did Ora, crying, run to press her face against his. Lizzie, carrying the Bemis baby, went with her.

Hannah, with Oscar Dilk by her side, stayed where she was.

"Justice," said Oscar, "is a terrible but necessary thing."

Nobody wanted old John Wood to be hanged. It was like striking your grandfather. It went against the grain of every bit of training any one of them had ever had. Gray hair, Bible in hand, face worn with years of hard work. Kill this old man? Do him bodily harm? What he needed was a rocker by the fireside and a dish of something warm and comforting.

They took his Bible away from him.

"I'm not going to fight the rope," he told the hangman. "I'm ready to go. You don't need to tie my arms behind my back. Let me go with my Bible in my hand. It's been my comfort and guide for seventy-two years. Don't take it away from me in my hour of need."

The hangman, Bible in hand, said, "You don't have any idea what you'll do with your hands once you feel that rope round your neck. I know. You think you're prepared to go peacefully. Nobody can prepare in his head. Your hands will decide in spite of you to fight for life."

Caleb had an idea. "John, put the Bible over your heart. That's where it belongs anyway. The belt to your britches will hold it in place. You think God cares where you carry it?"

"No, Cale. God don't care."

"If you've got it next your heart, are you willing to let your hands be tied?"

"Soon as he gives me back my Bible, I'm willing."

Caleb took the Bible from the hangman and placed it inside Wood's shirt. The hangman tied the old man's hands.

"You want something from the Bible, John? Or a prayer?"

"I'm going to die, Cale, saying the same words you said that night in jail."

Hands tied, noose adjusted, John Wood, Sr., stepped onto the trap door. When the latch was pulled, there was just enough weight to the old man to tauten the rope, but that was enough to kill him. He hung as light as a leaf, moving a little in the cold wind. Only one man was needed to carry him to the coffin. He lay stretched out there like a half-grown boy, his Bible a visible lump on his chest.

"Poor Johnny," said Hannah. "Having to watch his father die."

"Have you forgotten what 'poor Johnny' did?" Oscar asked.

"No, nor why," Hannah answered, shorter than she had intended.

The minute John Wood was stretched out in his coffin George Benson went to the hangman.

"Put the rope on me," he said. His hands had been tied behind his back in the jailhouse fracas. "Let's get it over with."

"There's time for prayer, George."

"You pray right on, Cale, you God-damned hypocrite. You're the one who's standing in need of prayer. Pray your lungs out for yourself. I wouldn't be here except for that whey-faced blubber of a boy of yours. Oh, yes, you couldn't keep him off the witness stand, lying and lying about me. Where's he today? Why didn't you bring him here so's he could see what his lying did for a man. You shitepoke preacher. Turn the other cheek, you preached. Well, not *your* cheek, or your family's cheek: turn your neighbor's cheek, that's what you preached."

Benson raised his voice 'til it carried to everyone in the meadow, over the smoke of the little fires and the crawling babies and the hot-eyed red-checked backwoodsmen.

"Friends and neighbors: I called you that once. I was at your beck and call when you needed me, my team, my time, me and my wife. No man ever asked George Benson for help and got a no. I helped raise your barns, shuck your corn, deaden your trees.

"I saw my own grandfather cut down by the redskins. I fought my way through them to come west. I was fighting for you at the sugar camp.

"Did the government ever help us? We was on our own. Whose side is the government on today? The redskins'. Look there."

Benson nodded toward the coffins. "Two good white men killed by the Indian lovers. Dead as doornails to please men taking their ease in Washington: Calhoun and Monroe. Dead to please an Indian agent whose pocket is lined with pay-offs from both sides. Anybody ever hear of a poor Indian agent?"

The hangman stepped forward to put an end to this harangue. This was no farewell speech.

"You've had your say, Benson."

"I'm just started."

"I've got to be in Cincinnati tomorrow."

Benson shouted to the crowd. "The hangman's got a date in Cincinnati tomorrow. He wants to hurry this up."

The crowd responded to that. "Let him wait. A condemned man's got a right to make a speech. Go on, George."

Benson went on. "Here's our chance. A thousand of us here. A hundred of them up there on the ridge. It'd all be over in ten minutes. You going to let that good old man and that young Indian fighter die without lifting your hands? Let's show those men sitting behind their desks in Washington how we handle things out here in the West.'

There was not the stir of a whisper from the crowd. Not a movement. Even the wind appeared to die down. The smoke from the fires went straight up, silent pillars.

Benson heard the silence. He listened for a half-minute, a whole minute.

Then he shouted, "You bastards. You sons of bitches. You Indian lovers. If ever I called you friends and neighbors, I take it back. You dirty yellow bastards. You're lower than the red men. They fight for their own. All you want to do is save your own necks. 'Love thy neighbor as thyself.' That's what you been preaching all your life, Cale Cape. Let it sink in how much anybody's listened to you. Failed, failed. You've all failed. Cale Cape! You don't practice what you preach. May God have mercy on your soul.

"Now, hangman, I've had my say. Spring your trap. You been in such a hurry."

Before the trap dropped for him, George Benson, whose hands had appeared to be tied behind him, brought them up in front of him untied. He made a lunge for the rope, and before the hangman, stout and slow, got to him, Benson's feet were already off the floor of the platform.

The crowd screamed. In the match between Benson and the gallows, Benson was the underdog. In the contest between life and death, he was life. Even the Indians on the ridge broke their silence as he and the hangman grappled. Benson was bear-sized, but, with his life at stake, agile as a squirrel. The Indians wanted this man killed — they had no intention of permitting the man who had massacred their women and children to escape. If the whites couldn't manage the affair, they would kill him themselves with pleasure. The white man's "weighing" of his criminals, though it did the job, as the deaths of Bemis and Wood had proved, was not much of a spectacle for observers, or much of a test of the manhood of the condemned men. Who would eat the heart of such a man? Who knew whether there was courage in it? As well eat pig or dog.

"Hannah put her hands over her face. "God help him, God help him," she prayed.

"Hannah, you don't know what you're saying," Oscar rebuked her.

"I don't want to see people die."

"Why did you come here?"

"To say good-bye to Johnny."

"You going to pray for him to escape, too? A man legally tried and condemned to hang?"

"I don't know. I don't know. I didn't know it was so terrible."

"Take your hands down, now. It doesn't look right for the promised wife of one of the prosecuting lawyers to be sobbing because a man he won a verdict against is going to be hanged."

"I'm not sobbing. I'm praying."

"Take your hands down."

"I can't pray with my hands down."

"I didn't say anything about not praying. I was talking about the looks of the thing: a prosecutor's wife taking on over the legal execution of men her husband worked hard to convict. Now take your hands down."

She took them down. "I'm not your wife."

George Benson's moment of freedom was a moment only. His feet had no more than left the platform than the combined weight of Brady and the hangman broke his grasp on the rope. Brady had his hands retied in an instant, and Benson then was sent through the trap door by the hangman, his life three minutes longer than Brady had planned it.

One of the four condemned to be hanged still remained alive: young Johnny Wood. Below him in their coffins lay Luther Bemis, and Johnny's father and uncle. If what he had witnessed upset him, his face didn't show it.

"Why do they keep him waiting, Ossie?"

"There's a rumor the governor may be bringing a pardon."

"If he is, it's cruel to keep Johnny waiting."

"The governor has other things to do than to save murderers from the law."

A half hour went by. No governor. An hour. No governor.

"Look at Johnny. They're torturing him. He's not tough like Benson and Bemis."

"He was tough enough back in February."

"He can't stand it. He's suffered enough, just watching, without all this waiting."

When an hour had gone by, the hangman picked up the black hood, which the other men had refused, and approached Johnny.

"Looks like the governor's not coming," said Oscar.

At that word, Hannah, moving quickly, left Oscar, scooped the remains of a little bonfire into an empty iron kettle, overlaid the coals with a handful of twigs that had been gathered for the making, and, with this pot of fire blazing in one hand, ran up the steps to the top of the platform. She was gone before Oscar could forbid her.

On the platform, the twig bonfire leaping above the pot's brim, she faced the Indians on the ridge. "Spare the boy," she screamed, "spare the boy!"

She held her hand unflinching in the flame, trusting in the Indians' respect for bravery.

"Spare the boy," she pleaded. "Spare the boy." She held the pot higher, so that all on the ridge could see what she was doing. Some on the ridge understood English, she knew. But even if they did not, even if they couldn't hear her, Hannah hoped all would understand her request.

Charlie Fort understood. He gave the

judge a shove, tripped up a militiaman who got in the way, and would have knocked down Dilk, except that Dilk, appalled by Hannah's wild act, had melted away into the crowd, determined not to be associated with anything so outlandish.

Charlie snatched the kettle from Hannah, handling it as carelessly as a bouquet of flowers, and threw it down the opening where three men had lost their lives. After what had just happened there, no one would be standing in that space.

"Lard, lard," he shouted as he took Hannah in his arms. "Bring me some lard."

Neither he nor Hannah saw the Indians on the ridge make their sign "we are satisfied."

Nor did the governor, the Honorable James Brown Ray, who, without much regard for the safety of the crowd, came riding in at a hard gallop, his horse much lathered. The impression he gave — he had done this once before — was that of a man sparing neither himself nor his mount to come at breakneck speed to save an endangered human life. The crowd loved their governor. Judge McGowan said under this breath a word he would not permit in the courtroom.

Dismounting, Governor Ray ran up the steps to the gallows, as if a man's neck were already in the noose and nothing except the speed of James Brown Ray could save him. He stopped in front of Johnny.

"Young man, do you know who now stands before you?"

Johnny could not take his eyes off the coffins below.

"Look at me, boy. Do you know who I am?"

"No," mumbled Johnny, taking one swift upward look.

"Well, sir, it is time you should know. There are now, sir, but two persons in the universe who can save you from the noose. One is the great God of Heaven; the other is James Brown Ray, governor of the sovereign state of Indiana, who now stands before you. Here is your pardon. I have ridden long and hard to bring it to you. Now, my son, go and sin no more."

The governor handed Johnny his pardon. Johnny let the rolled parchment slip from his hand.

"What is my sin, sir?"

The governor turned to the sheriff. "Brady, what's wrong with this young man?"

Johnny asked the sheriff, "How can I sin no more if nobody'll tell me what my sin is?"

Sam Brady said, "Governor, we've all been through a lot this morning. This boy's father and uncle are lying there below you. Johnny had a long wait, not knowing what was to come next. He's not in his right mind at the minute."

Johnny said, "I know the difference between right and wrong. I resisted, didn't I, Sheriff?"

"Bore him for the simples," the governor said, speaking the language of these backwoodsmen. Then he descended the steps, mounted his horse, and rode slowly through the crowd, taking the salutes of the electorate.

29

By early afternoon the meadow was almost deserted. The wagon, bearing the three coffins, had left soon after the departure of the governor. Brady drove, alone. Guards were no longer necessary.

Charred remains of fires dotted the meadow. The sun, bright but still not warm, had come out. Families had started for their homes. With that gallows above them and what they had seen there so recently still in their minds, the meadow had lost its appeal as a place for picnicking.

Lizzie gathered Ora, her baby, and Johnny Wood for the ride back to Pendleton.

Hannah and Oscar Dilk had ridden over to the meadow with her; but Dilk had disappeared, and no one, least of all Hannah, knew whether he had walked back or ridden with others. Charlie Fort would take his place with her on the return ride.

Caleb had Brady's permission to walk back. "I need some time alone to think and pray, Sam. I'll be back in the jailhouse about as soon as you are."

Brady, mounted on the seat of the wagon-turned-hearse, said nothing.

"I helped another man escape," Caleb said. "I won't do it for myself."

"I believe you Cale, After a day like this, a man's got to believe something. A prayer for me wouldn't do no harm. I don't want ever again to be in charge of a hanging."

Caleb told Lizzie what was in his mind. "There's still some Indians up on the ridge. I think Black Antler's there. I'm going up to talk to him. I've promised Brady to go straight back to the jailhouse afterward."

"We'll be all right, Caleb. Charlie's going with us."

"How about Johnny?"

"He's walking in his sleep. He does whatever we tell him."

Hannah and Charlie, before they climbed in the wagon, drew Caleb a little apart from the others.

"Hannah," Caleb asked, "how's your hand?"

Hannah held it up. It was inside a pillow sham filled with pure leaf lard.

"It still throbs."

"Hannah, what with one thing and another, I haven't had a chance to tell you that was a brave act. Charlie, you could use a little lard yourself."

"I haven't had time to think about *my* hand yet. Mr. Cape, Hannah and I've got a favor to ask you. When Hannah's hand's healed enough to put a wedding ring on her finger, will you marry us?"

"Marry you? Hannah, I thought you and Oscar Dilk were keeping company?"

"We were keeping company," said Hannah, "but we don't love each other."

"Not much point getting married, then," agreed Caleb. "And you two do?"

"We do," answered Charlie, as if already in the midst of a marriage service. "We love each other. We had a misunderstanding, but we understand each other now."

"This true, Hannah?"

"Yes, Papa. I love Charlie and will

never marry anyone else.''

''That being the case, I guess it's lucky Charlie wants you.''

''Papa! You talk that way and he'll change his mind.''

Caleb reached out to take Charlie's hand, remembered the burns, and didn't.

''You're a lucky man, Fort. She's the apple of my eye. Tell your mother, Hannah, I'll be up on the ridge for a short spell. I'll more than likely overtake you on the way back.''

On their way to the wagon, walking with their stride that fitted, Charlie said, ''Hannah, before you make up your mind once and for all about marriage, there's something I've got to tell you.''

''I'll listen,'' Hannah said, ''if you're sure it's something you want to talk about.''

''I don't want to talk about it. But you've got to know about it.''

''Even if I already know about it?''

''You couldn't.''

''I do.''

''How could you?''

''I saw.''

"My God, my God. Oh, Hannah, I did that to you?"

"What you did to me was to prove to me I was going to marry you, Charlie, no matter what."

"I'll have to tell your father."

"You've already told him all he needs to know. That we're going to be married."

From the wagon Lizzie called to her daughter, "Hannah, you and Charlie can spoon right here in the wagon and not keep the rest of us waiting."

Caleb wanted to have a word with the Indians. But more than that, though he was scarcely aware of it, he wanted to climb out of this valley of death. He wanted to climb above it.

The afternoon had warmed up. The sun, acting like a human who hadn't wanted to witness the morning's horrors, had finally come clean out from behind the overcast. All had now gone; only Brady's big death machine loomed and the thin smoke of a half-dozen fires still smoldered.

Above, a few Indians lingered, Caleb didn't know why, unless, quite naturally, to rejoice in the justice that had finally been done: the murder of an Indian accepted by whites as being wrong as the murder of a white.

As he neared the top of the ridge, winded after his days of inactivity in the jail, he recognized three of the dozen Indians above him. Lone Fawn, the powerful Miami; Bent Arrow, the Seneca who had helped bring Bemis back to the jail and to his death. A little apart from his tribesmen stood Black Antler, not talking with the others.

Caleb was greeted courteously. He returned the greetings, then addressed himself to Black Antler.

"Black Antler," he said, "I am sorry I didn't give you a chance to speak longer that Sunday at my house. I know that you and followers of Handsome Lake preach against what happened here this morning. Perhaps I should have given you more time."

Then he turned to all, speaking in Delaware so that none would miss his meaning.

"What you saw this morning was ugly.

It was right. This will be remembered as a great day both for the red man and the white man. On this day for the first time white men punished their own kind for killing Indians. This day, three white men gave their lives so that the killing between whites and reds would be finished. It *is* finished. Now we will live peacefully together. Handsome Lake's prophecy will come true. We will long remember this day and celebrate it."

Caleb shook hands with all, except Black Antler, who kept his arms folded. To him, Caleb raised his arm in the Indian salute of farewell. Black Antler responded in kind. Caleb started down the slope, but slowly, loath to pass the spot where the price of the new peace had been paid.

Black Antler spoke to the Indians who remained. "Leave me."

"This is the appointed place," they replied. "He will be here soon. We will leave then, Black Antler, after we have heard his message."

Two messengers, not one, arrived. Plains Indians — Osages, well mounted on horses which bore the marks of hard riding.

"We have him trapped on an island at the junction of the Illinois and the Mississippi. He cannot escape unless he becomes a fish or an otter. He will be caught before you can arrive — but they will not begin the feasting until you get there. It was your kin Clasby killed. Your men have been with us. It is your right before ours to partake of the feast."

Caleb, halfway down the slope, heard the laughter. They have much to rejoice about today, he thought.

Black Antler waited silently until both Caleb Cape and the Indians were out of sight — Cape into the woods on the far side of the meadow; the red men heading westward on the far side of the ridge. He could still see the slow swing of the killing rope. He could still hear the jubilation of the red men in anticipation of the pleasures to come.

He was able to shut both from his mind. For the first time since Folded Leaf's death, tears covered his face. The memory of those two, Handsome Lake, the prophet and seer, and Folded Leaf, the boy who might have outdistanced the master, became one.

Black Antler was bereft, but not alone. The spirits of both, the boy and the old prophet, lived and spoke to him; he replied and he was heard by them. He spoke the words he had first heard from Handsome Lake and had later taught to Folded Leaf.

What remained? The bodies of men vanished; but their words and wisdom lived on. Their spirits did not die. The sun and the earth remained. The trees, plants, and animals to which the earth gave life did not die. Sun and earth had mothered and fathered him. The animals, as much as Folded Leaf and Handsome Lake, were his brothers. The willow, the birch, the elder, comforted and protected him. He was sad, but not alone.

He knelt and scooped up a handful of the already sun-warmed earth. He kneaded with it the leaves at hand, aspen and maple and dogwood. He held his two fists clenched on earth, then turned earth's bounty sunward in the old Indian gesture of worship. Black Antler's hands, reaching upward, blotted out the rope. The smell of the crushed leaves was sweet. The sun was warm. He said the two names. "Handsome Lake. Folded Leaf."

The earth his hands held, the names his spirit honored: what else did a man have?

VALEDICTORY

In 1824, in the state of Indiana, four white men were formally charged with first-degree murder for the premeditated killing of nine Indians — two braves, three squaws, and four children. These white men were indicted, tried by jury, found guilty, and sentenced to die. A fifth white man, the ringleader of the murderers, would undoubtedly have been tried and convicted, too; he fled the scene before he could be apprehended. Three of the condemned men were hanged. The fourth, a youth, was saved from the gallows by a last-minute reprieve.

This is historical fact. So far as I can discover, this was the first time in the history of the United States that white men were tried, convicted, and executed for the slaughter of Indians. Before then, and for many long years thereafter, the killing of Indians remained a persistent accompaniment to the westward thrust of this nation. Across these pages of American history, the bloody stain persists.

So complex and prolonged a clash of cultures should not be oversimplified. Some understanding may come from the knowledge of the hazards that beset the early settlers: the Midwestern winters against which they had insufficient protection, the loneliness, and the fierce retaliation of a proud people that resisted invasion of their land and destruction of their way of life.

It was almost twenty years ago, while reading among historical records of Indiana, that I came across a reference to what was called "The Massacre at Fall Creek." Curiosity led me to explore further, but the path was not a clear one. The courthouse in Pendleton, where the trials were held, had long ago burned down; official records were destroyed in the flames.

There still exist some scanty accounts of the trials and executions, but these few and often contradictory eyewitness versions were written and published years after the event by public figures. It is not surprising, under the license of time and self-regard, that factual objectivity dwindled.

Over the years I remained haunted by the tragic events of the Massacre and the dread dilemmas they must have thrust upon whites and Indians alike; the more so perhaps because I had an Indian grandmother.

Most of the characters in this novel have no historic counterparts. They are my own invention. Even where the record has suggested some detail on the identity of participants, the resemblance between the novel's characters and actual persons is slight. In consequence, with only five exceptions, I have given all characters names of my own devising. The five historic personalities, who naturally appear under their real names, are: James Monroe and John C. Calhoun, respectively, the President of the United States and his Secretary of War; James Brown Ray, the governor of Indiana (who did appear melodramatically on a sweated horse to stay one execution);

Colonel John Johnston, Indian agent for what was then known as the Northwest Territory; and James Noble, lawyer for the prosecution, former army general and, in 1824, a United States senator.

The nine murdered Indians, the judges and the sheriff, the jurors, various court officials, and members of the defense and prosecution staffs have been fashioned upon such meager leads as the records provide. In only a few instances is substantial detail given. I am of course grateful to those few witnesses whose recollections prevented this event from being completely forgotten.

Readers may wonder about the authenticity of two Indians — Handsome Lake and Black Antler. Black Antler, the Faithkeeper, is fictive; he represents an almost unknown aspect of a Seneca religious philosophy that originated about the turn of the nineteenth century in the teachings of Handsome Lake. Black Antler, a disciple of Handsome Lake, embodies the idea of total nonviolence and the natural communion among all living things that Handsome Lake taught. As such he stands in stark contrast to both the whites and the Indians, and to the conflict that raged between them. Black Antler lives only between the covers of this book.

Handsome Lake, the prophet, visionary, and philosophical lawgiver to the Faithkeepers, is entirely real, and he set forth religious ethics not far removed from the compassionate concepts of Jesus. Handsome Lake never appears as a person in this novel — he could not, having died in 1815. (It is a matter of interest, albeit coincidental, that the religion of Handsome Lake endures into the present and has a devoted following of more than five thousand members among the Iroquois of the United States and Canada.)

So much for the evidence of history. The Massacre, real as it was, had no significant impact upon the increasingly violent and tortured relationship that followed between the whites and the Indians. My intention was not to reveal historic facts in a fictional setting, but to

open questions of more abiding truths.
And that is quite a different matter.

Jessamyn West